REYN

VOLUME 2

FUTURE PAST

WRITTEN BY KEL SYMONS
ART BY NATE STOCKMAN
COLORS BY PAUL LITTLE
LETTERING AND DESIGN BY PAT BROSSEAU
LOGO DESIGNER TIM DANIEL

FOLLOW US ON TWITTER: @KELSYMONS @STOCKMANNATE @DROOG811
LIKE US ON WWW.FACEBOOK.COM/REYNWARDENOFFATE
EMAIL QUESTIONS AND COMMENTS TO REYNCOMIC@GMAIL.COM
OR WRITE TO: REYN C/O KEL SYMONS
P.O. BOX 481301 LOS ANGELES, CA 90048
SEND A SASE AND WE'LL SEND YOU BACK A REYN STICKER

IMAGE COMICS, INC.
Robert Kirkman – Chief Operating Officer
Erik Larsen – Chief Financial Officer
Todd McFarlane – President
Marc Silvestri – Chief Executive Officer
Jim Valentino – Vice-President

Eric Stephenson – Publisher
Corey Murphy – Director of Sales
Jeff Boison – Director of Publishing Planning & Book Trade Sales
Jeremy Sullivan – Director of Digital Sales
Kat Salazar – Director of PR & Marketing
Emily Miller – Director of Operations
Branwyn Bigglestone – Senior Accounts Manager
Sarah Mello – Accounts Manager
Drew Gill – Art Director
Jonathan Chan – Production Manager
Meredith Wallace – Print Manager
Briah Skelly – Publicity Assistant
Randy Okamura – Marketing Production Designer
David Brothers – Branding Manager
Ally Power – Content Manager
Addison Duke – Production Artist
Vincent Kukua – Production Artist
Sasha Head – Production Artist
Tricia Ramos – Production Artist
Jeff Stang – Direct Market Sales Representative
Emilio Bautista – Digital Sales Associate
Chloe Ramos-Peterson – Administrative Assistant
IMAGECOMICS.COM

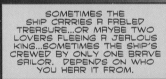

MY FATHER TOLD ME A STORY ONCE, ABOUT A GREAT SHIP ON AN ENDLESS SEA.

ALL CHILDREN IN OUR TRIBE HAVE HEARD SOME VERSION OF THIS STORY.

SOMETIMES THE SHIP CARRIES A FABLED TREASURE...OR MAYBE TWO LOVERS FLEEING A JEALOUS KING...SOMETIMES THE SHIP'S CREWED BY ONLY ONE BRAVE SAILOR. DEPENDS ON WHO YOU HEAR IT FROM.

BUT IN ALL THE VERSIONS, THE CAPTAIN CAN NEVER FIND A PORT, FORCED TO SAIL ACROSS EMPTY, BLACK WAVES FOREVER.

IT'S ALWAYS BEEN A TALE WITHOUT AN ENDING, ITS AUTHOR LONG PASSED.

PASSED DOWN OVER TIME, VERSES BECAME LOST. RE-INTERPRETED. RE-TOLD. THEN RE-TOLD AGAIN.

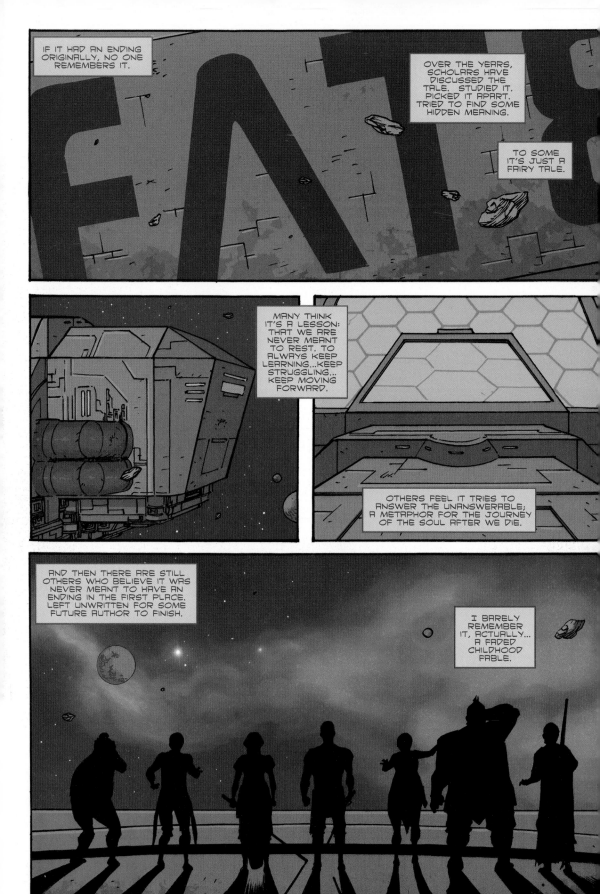

IF IT HAD AN ENDING ORIGINALLY, NO ONE REMEMBERS IT.

OVER THE YEARS, SCHOLARS HAVE DISCUSSED THE TALE. STUDIED IT. PICKED IT APART. TRIED TO FIND SOME HIDDEN MEANING.

TO SOME IT'S JUST A FAIRY TALE.

MANY THINK IT'S A LESSON: THAT WE ARE NEVER MEANT TO REST. TO ALWAYS KEEP LEARNING...KEEP STRUGGLING... KEEP MOVING FORWARD.

OTHERS FEEL IT TRIES TO ANSWER THE UNANSWERABLE; A METAPHOR FOR THE JOURNEY OF THE SOUL AFTER WE DIE.

AND THEN THERE ARE STILL OTHERS WHO BELIEVE IT WAS NEVER MEANT TO HAVE AN ENDING IN THE FIRST PLACE. LEFT UNWRITTEN FOR SOME FUTURE AUTHOR TO FINISH.

I BARELY REMEMBER IT, ACTUALLY... A FADED CHILDHOOD FABLE.

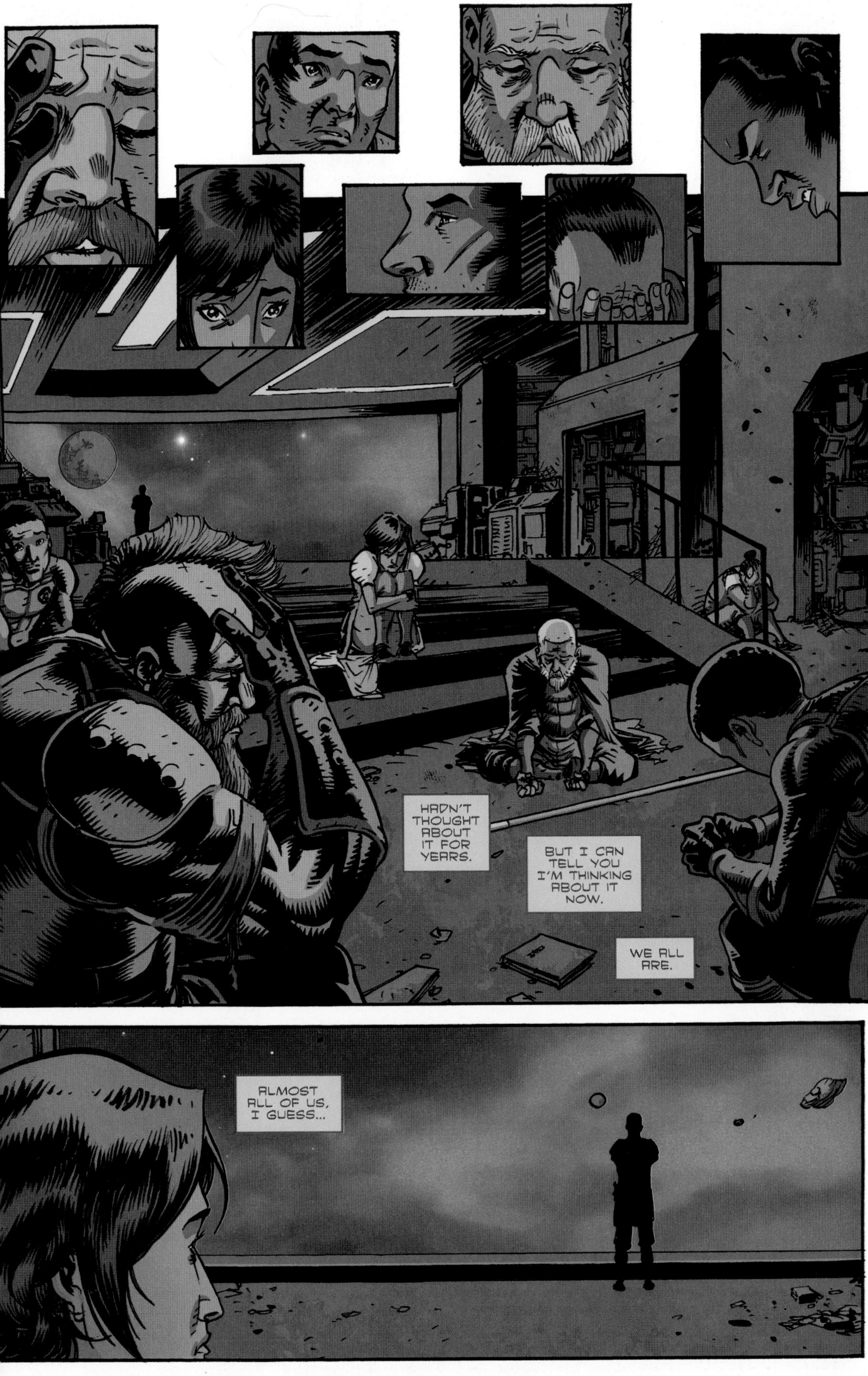
HADN'T THOUGHT ABOUT IT FOR YEARS.
BUT I CAN TELL YOU I'M THINKING ABOUT IT NOW.
WE ALL ARE.
ALMOST ALL OF US, I GUESS...

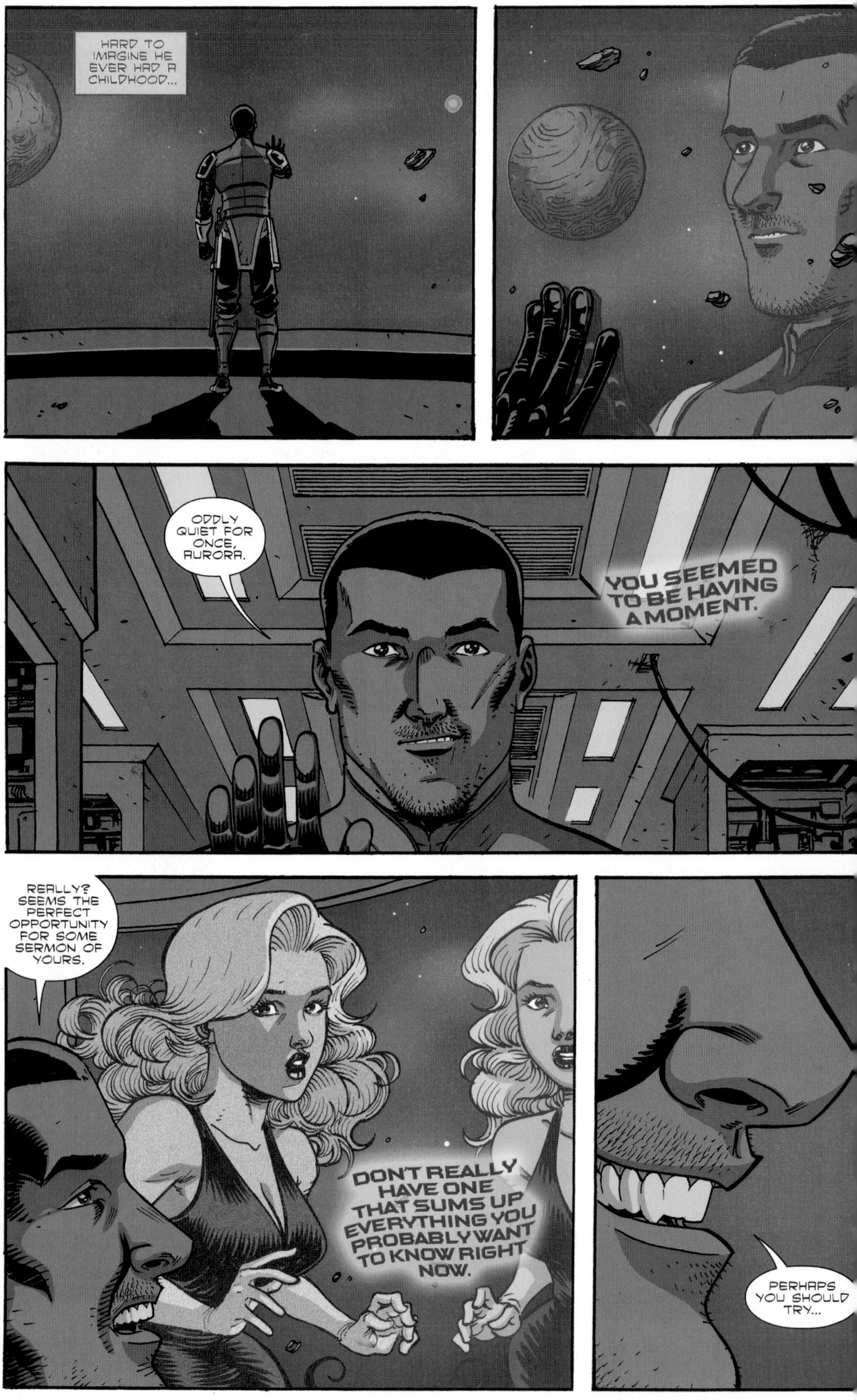
HARD TO IMAGINE HE EVER HAD A CHILDHOOD...
ODDLY QUIET FOR ONCE, AURORA.
YOU SEEMED TO BE HAVING A MOMENT.
REALLY? SEEMS THE PERFECT OPPORTUNITY FOR SOME SERMON OF YOURS.
DON'T REALLY HAVE ONE THAT SUMS UP EVERYTHING YOU PROBABLY WANT TO KNOW RIGHT NOW.
PERHAPS YOU SHOULD TRY...

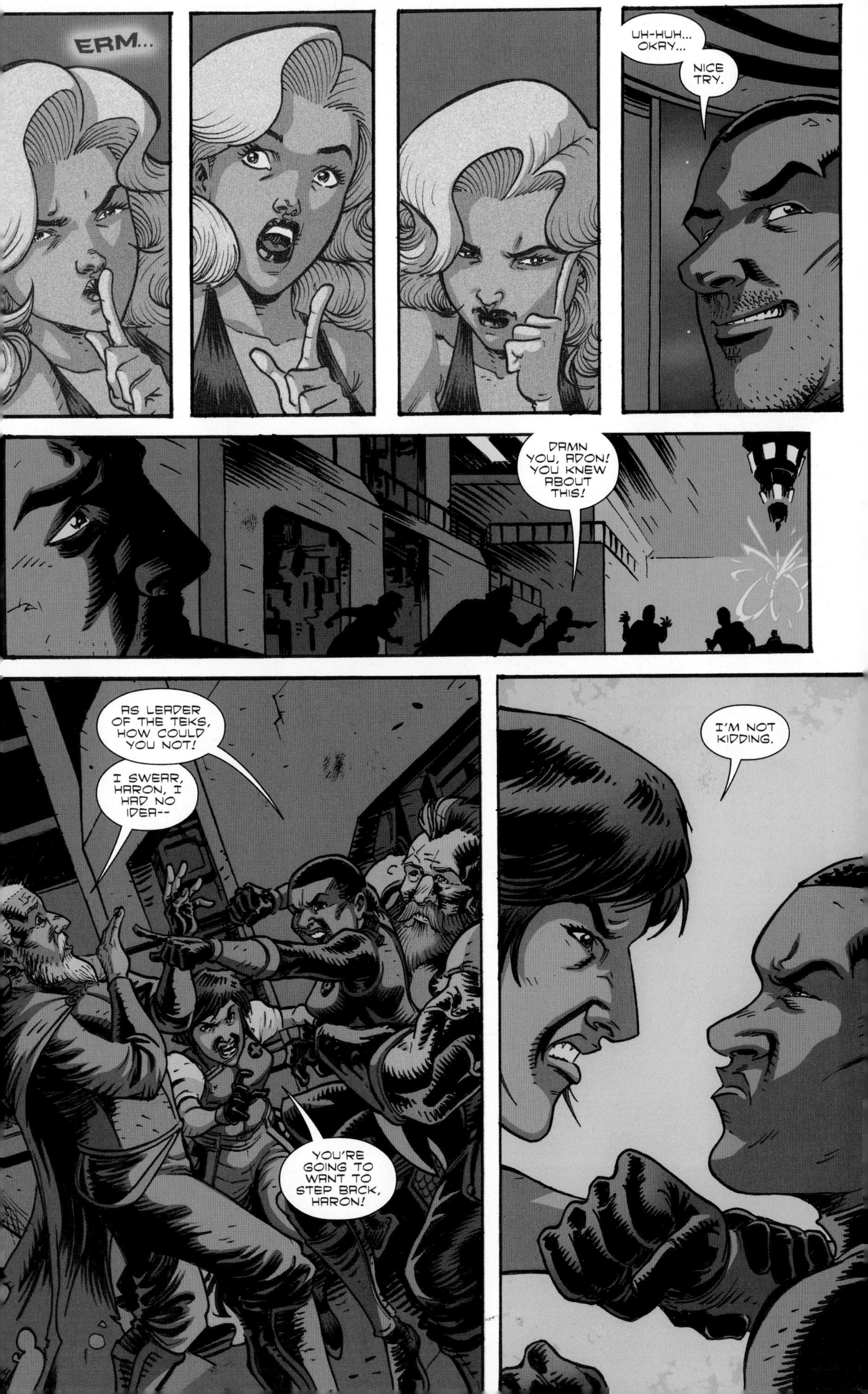
ERM...
UH-HUH... OKAY...
NICE TRY.
DAMN YOU, ADON! YOU KNEW ABOUT THIS!
AS LEADER OF THE TEKS, HOW COULD YOU NOT!
I SWEAR, HARON, I HAD NO IDEA--
YOU'RE GOING TO WANT TO STEP BACK, HARON!
I'M NOT KIDDING.

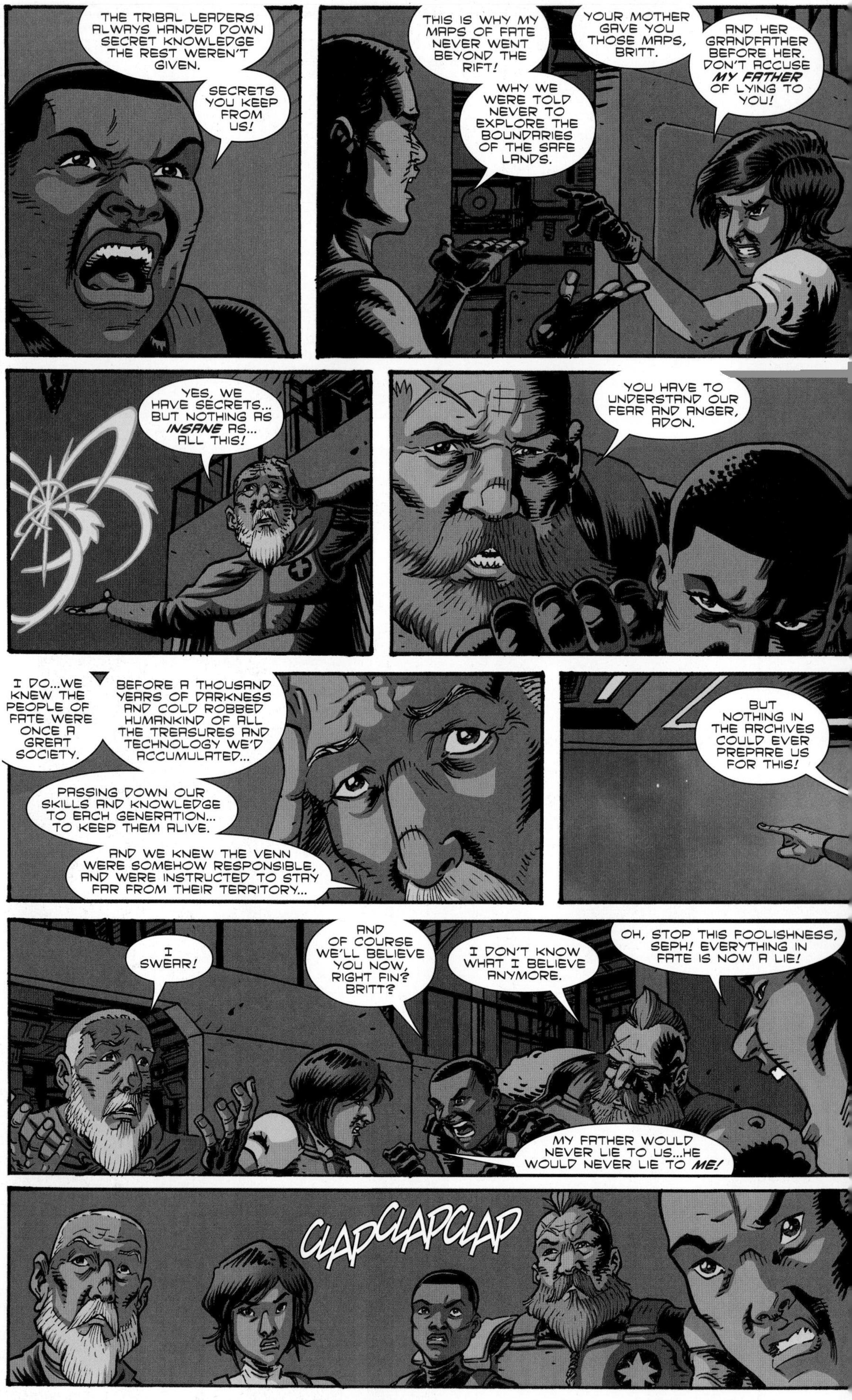
THE TRIBAL LEADERS ALWAYS HANDED DOWN SECRET KNOWLEDGE THE REST WEREN'T GIVEN.
SECRETS YOU KEEP FROM US!
THIS IS WHY MY MAPS OF FATE NEVER WENT BEYOND THE RIFT!
WHY WE WERE TOLD NEVER TO EXPLORE THE BOUNDARIES OF THE SAFE LANDS.
YOUR MOTHER GAVE YOU THOSE MAPS, BRITT.
AND HER GRANDFATHER BEFORE HER. DON'T ACCUSE MY FATHER OF LYING TO YOU!
YES, WE HAVE SECRETS... BUT NOTHING AS INSANE AS... ALL THIS!
YOU HAVE TO UNDERSTAND OUR FEAR AND ANGER, ADON.
I DO...WE KNEW THE PEOPLE OF FATE WERE ONCE A GREAT SOCIETY.
BEFORE A THOUSAND YEARS OF DARKNESS AND COLD ROBBED HUMANKIND OF ALL THE TREASURES AND TECHNOLOGY WE'D ACCUMULATED...
PASSING DOWN OUR SKILLS AND KNOWLEDGE TO EACH GENERATION... TO KEEP THEM ALIVE.
AND WE KNEW THE VENN WERE SOMEHOW RESPONSIBLE, AND WERE INSTRUCTED TO STAY FAR FROM THEIR TERRITORY...
BUT NOTHING IN THE ARCHIVES COULD EVER PREPARE US FOR THIS!
I SWEAR!
AND OF COURSE WE'LL BELIEVE YOU NOW, RIGHT FIN? BRITT?
I DON'T KNOW WHAT I BELIEVE ANYMORE.
OH, STOP THIS FOOLISHNESS, SEPH! EVERYTHING IN FATE IS NOW A LIE!
MY FATHER WOULD NEVER LIE TO US...HE WOULD NEVER LIE TO ME!
CLAPCLAPCLAP

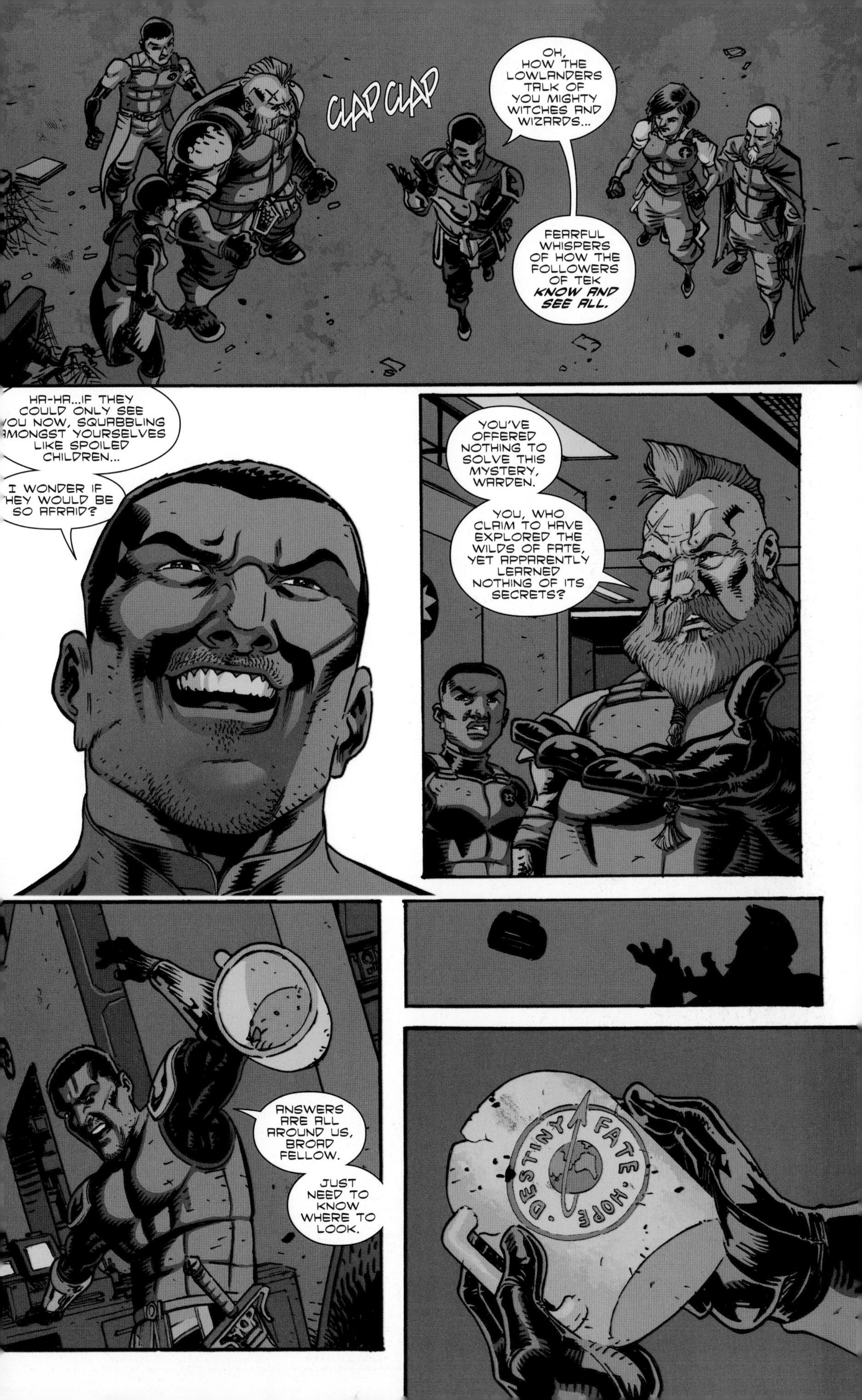
CLAP CLAP
OH, HOW THE LOWLANDERS TALK OF YOU MIGHTY WITCHES AND WIZARDS...
FEARFUL WHISPERS OF HOW THE FOLLOWERS OF TEK ***KNOW AND SEE ALL.***
HA-HA...IF THEY COULD ONLY SEE OU NOW, SQUABBLING MONGST YOURSELVES LIKE SPOILED CHILDREN...
I WONDER IF HEY WOULD BE SO AFRAID?
YOU'VE OFFERED NOTHING TO SOLVE THIS MYSTERY, WARDEN.
YOU, WHO CLAIM TO HAVE EXPLORED THE WILDS OF FATE, YET APPARENTLY LEARNED NOTHING OF ITS SECRETS?
ANSWERS ARE ALL AROUND US, BROAD FELLOW.
JUST NEED TO KNOW WHERE TO LOOK.
DESTINY · FATE · HOPE

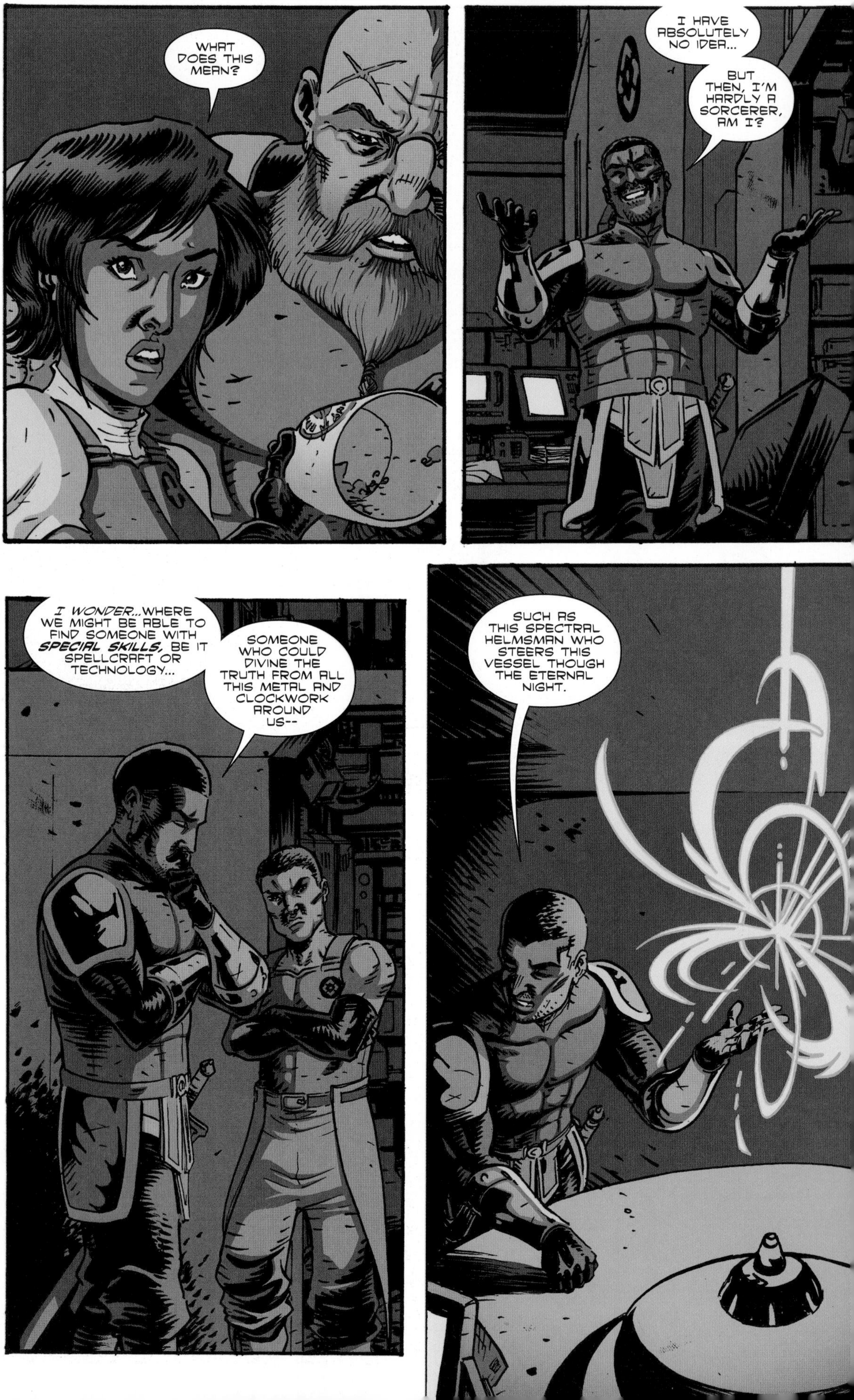
WHAT DOES THIS MEAN?
I HAVE ABSOLUTELY NO IDEA...
BUT THEN, I'M HARDLY A SORCERER, AM I?
I WONDER...WHERE WE MIGHT BE ABLE TO FIND SOMEONE WITH SPECIAL SKILLS, BE IT SPELLCRAFT OR TECHNOLOGY...
SOMEONE WHO COULD DIVINE THE TRUTH FROM ALL THIS METAL AND CLOCKWORK AROUND US--
SUCH AS THIS SPECTRAL HELMSMAN WHO STEERS THIS VESSEL THOUGH THE ETERNAL NIGHT.

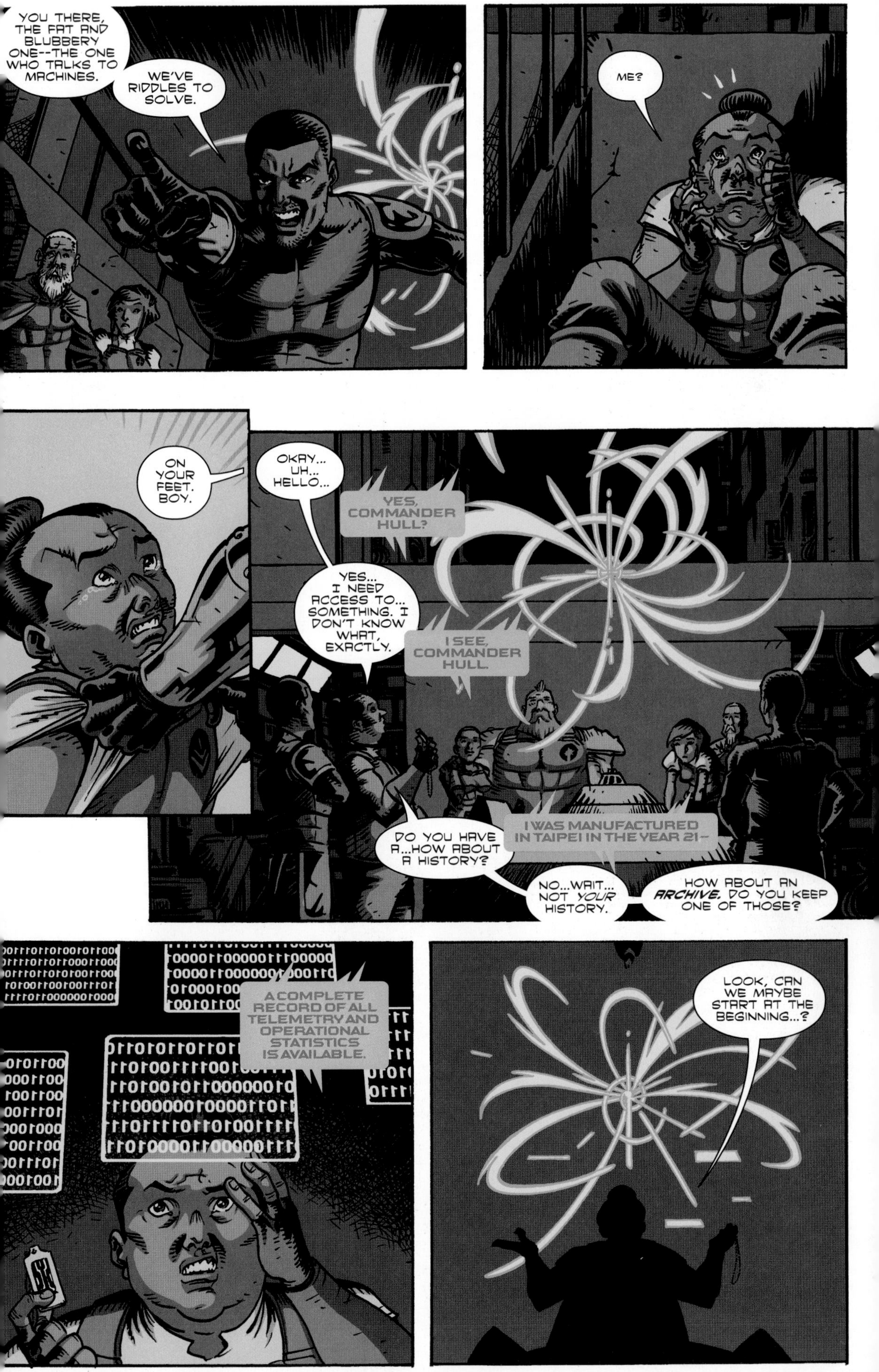
YOU THERE, THE FAT AND BLUBBERY ONE--THE ONE WHO TALKS TO MACHINES.
WE'VE RIDDLES TO SOLVE.
ME?
ON YOUR FEET. BOY.
OKAY... UH... HELLO...
YES, COMMANDER HULL?
YES... I NEED ACCESS TO... SOMETHING. I DON'T KNOW WHAT, EXACTLY.
I SEE, COMMANDER HULL.
DO YOU HAVE A...HOW ABOUT A HISTORY?
I WAS MANUFACTURED IN TAIPEI IN THE YEAR 21--
NO...WAIT... NOT YOUR HISTORY.
HOW ABOUT AN ARCHIVE. DO YOU KEEP ONE OF THOSE?
A COMPLETE RECORD OF ALL TELEMETRY AND OPERATIONAL STATISTICS IS AVAILABLE.
LOOK, CAN WE MAYBE START AT THE BEGINNING...?

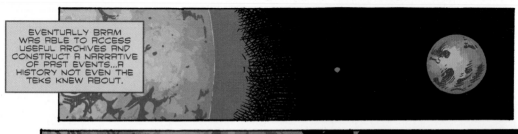

EVENTUALLY BRAM WAS ABLE TO ACCESS USEFUL ARCHIVES AND CONSTRUCT A NARRATIVE OF PAST EVENTS...A HISTORY NOT EVEN THE TEKS KNEW ABOUT.

OUR PEOPLE-- THE ANCESTORS OF FATE--COME FROM FAR BACK ALONG THE TIMELINE...WHEN WE LIVED ON A WORLD WHOSE SUN WAS DYING...

MAYBE NOT *DYING*... PERHAPS *EXPANDING* IS MORE ACCURATE... TRANSFORMING INTO A NEW CELESTIAL PHENOMENON.

AS THIS PHENOMENON GREW, IT BEGAN FEEDING ON THE MATTER CLOSEST TO IT...OTHER BODIES KNOWN AS PLANETS...

AS IT CONTINUED TO *CONSUME* AND *EXPAND*...

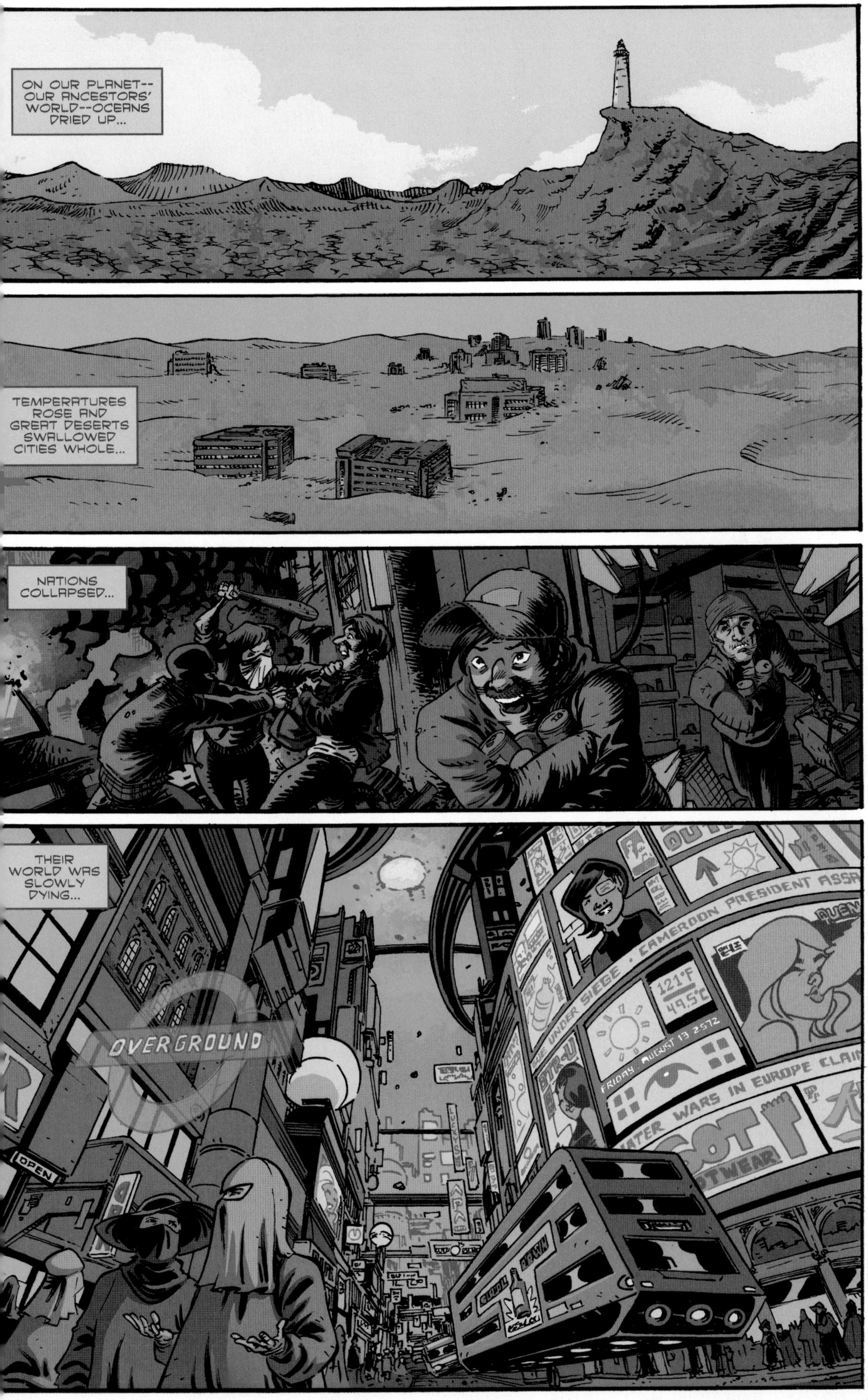
ON OUR PLANET--OUR ANCESTORS' WORLD--OCEANS DRIED UP...
TEMPERATURES ROSE AND GREAT DESERTS SWALLOWED CITIES WHOLE...
NATIONS COLLAPSED...
THEIR WORLD WAS SLOWLY DYING...
OVERGROUND
OPEN
CAMEROON PRESIDENT
UNDER SIEGE
121°F
49.5°C
FRIDAY, AUGUST 13 2572
WATER WARS IN EUROPE

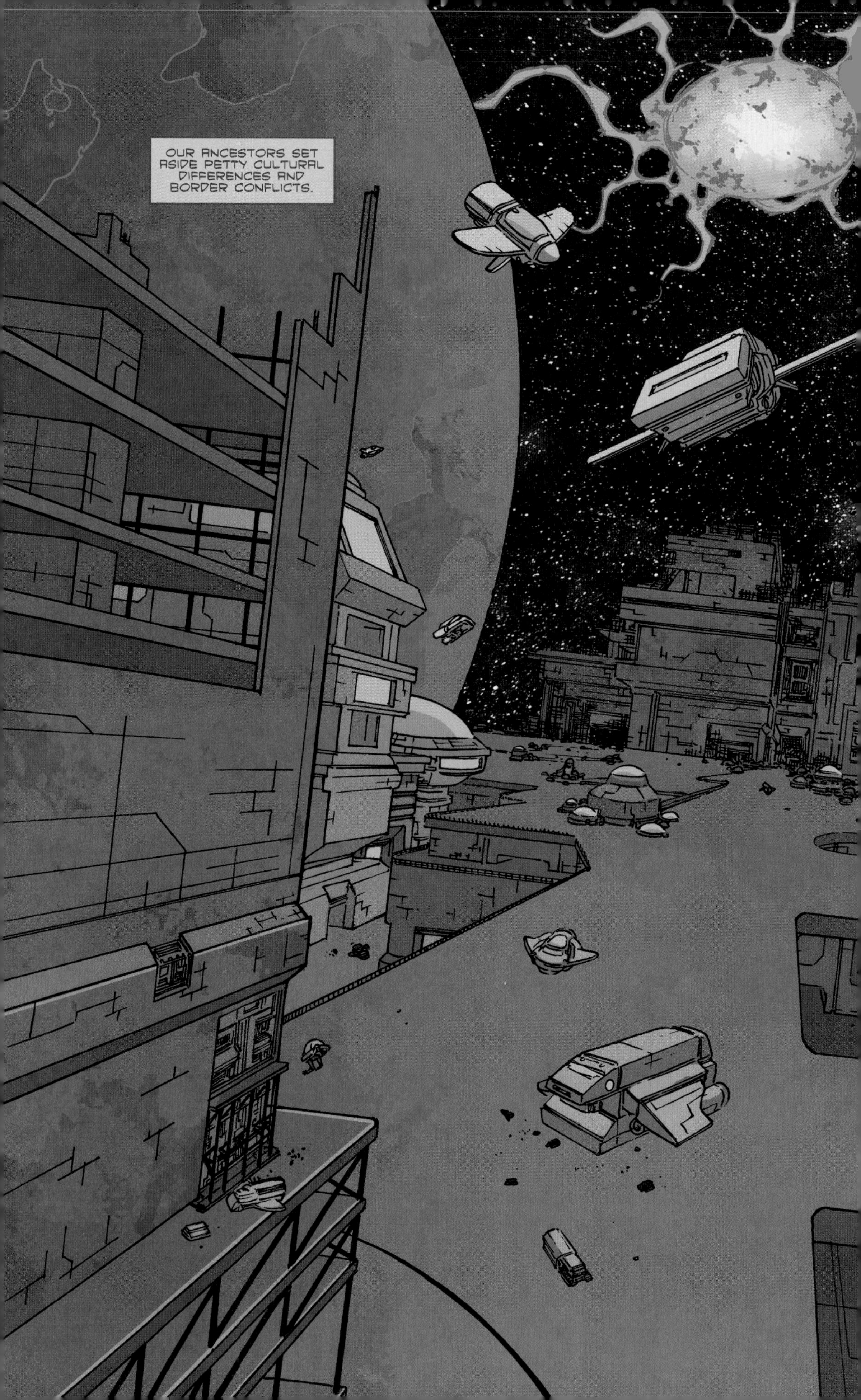
OUR ANCESTORS SET ASIDE PETTY CULTURAL DIFFERENCES AND BORDER CONFLICTS.

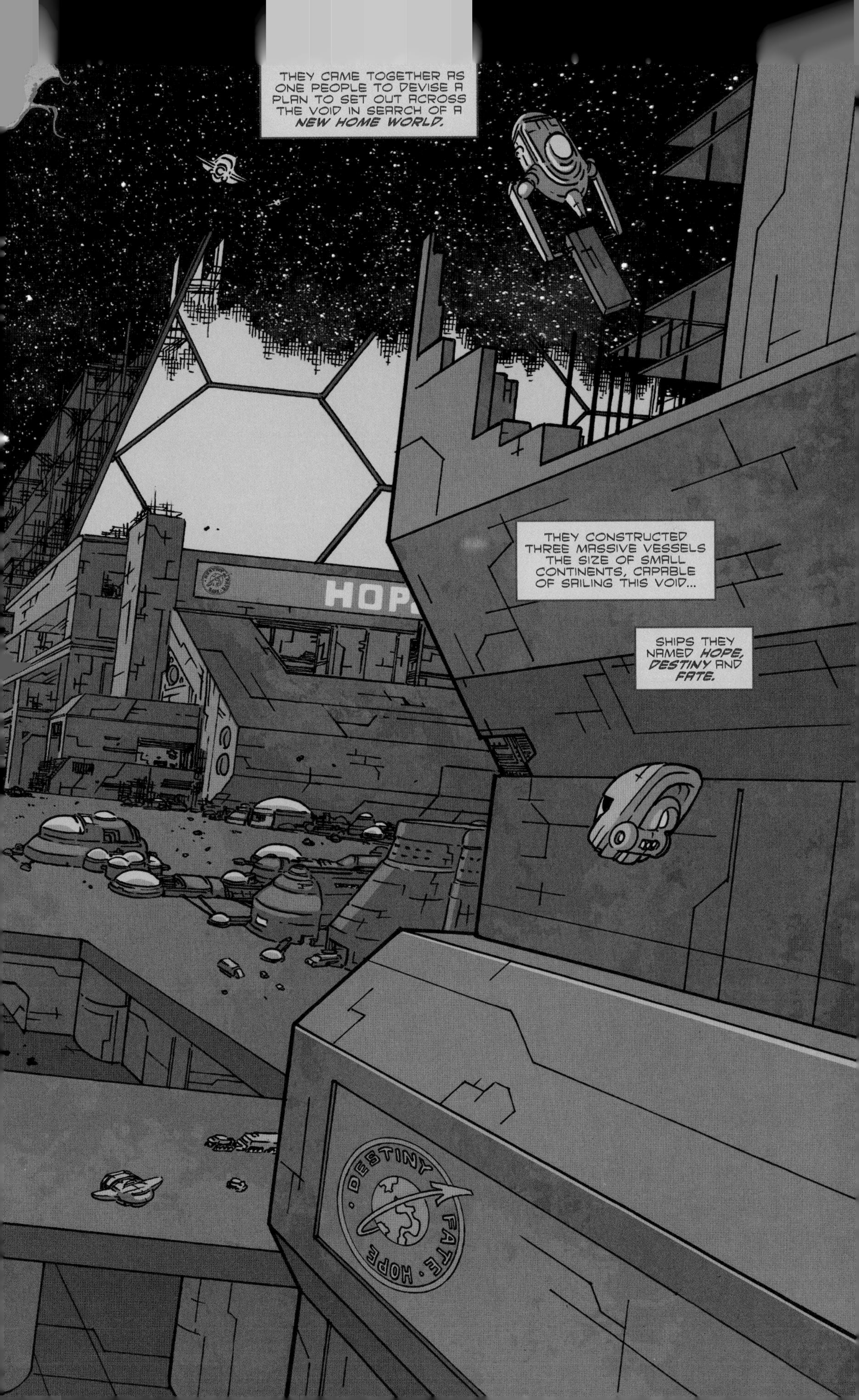
THEY CAME TOGETHER AS ONE PEOPLE TO DEVISE A PLAN TO SET OUT ACROSS THE VOID IN SEARCH OF A *NEW HOME WORLD.*
HOP
THEY CONSTRUCTED THREE MASSIVE VESSELS THE SIZE OF SMALL CONTINENTS, CAPABLE OF SAILING THIS VOID...
SHIPS THEY NAMED *HOPE, DESTINY* AND *FATE.*
DESTINY
FATE
HOPE

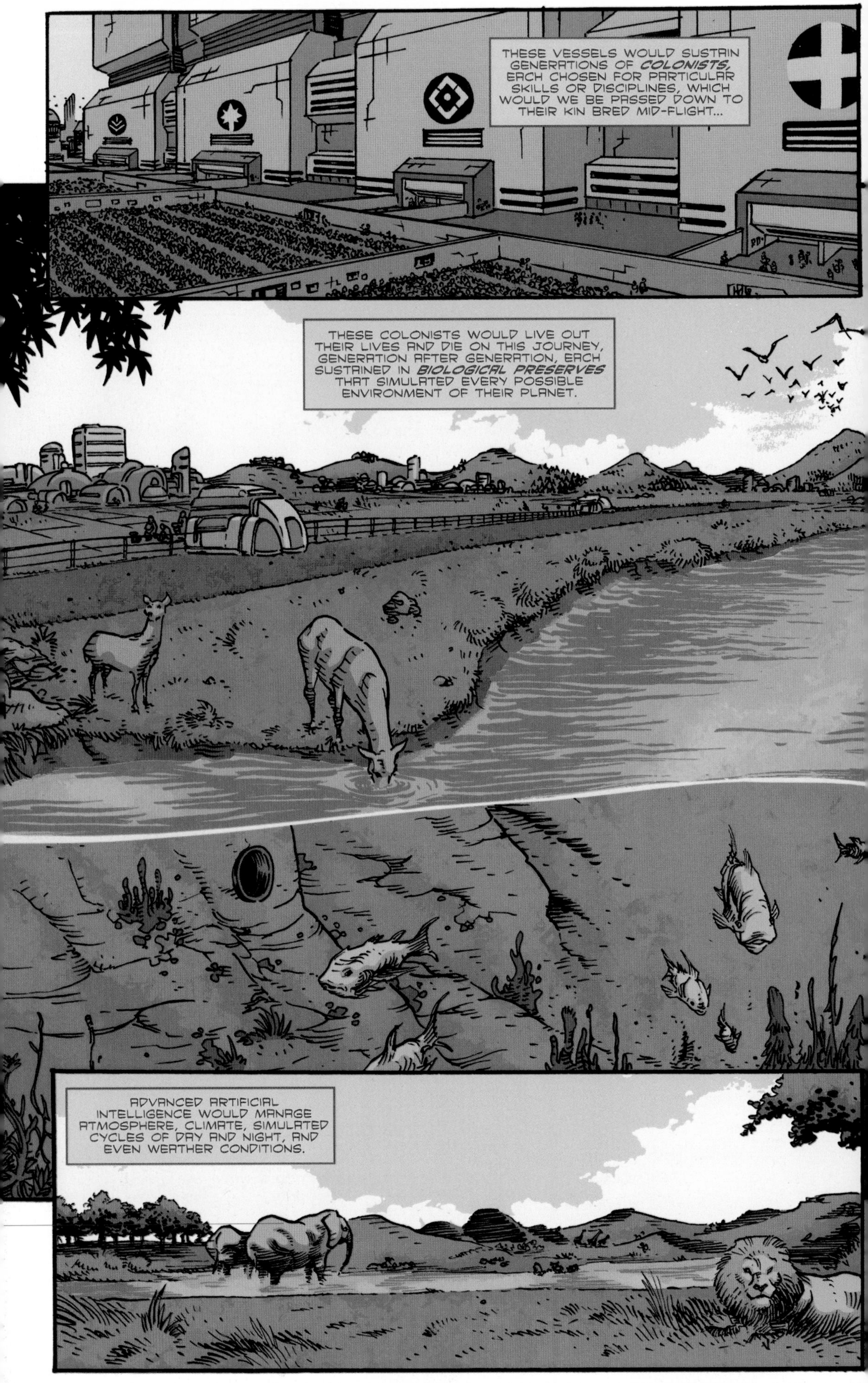
THESE VESSELS WOULD SUSTAIN GENERATIONS OF COLONISTS, EACH CHOSEN FOR PARTICULAR SKILLS OR DISCIPLINES, WHICH WOULD WE BE PASSED DOWN TO THEIR KIN BRED MID-FLIGHT...
THESE COLONISTS WOULD LIVE OUT THEIR LIVES AND DIE ON THIS JOURNEY, GENERATION AFTER GENERATION, EACH SUSTAINED IN BIOLOGICAL PRESERVES THAT SIMULATED EVERY POSSIBLE ENVIRONMENT OF THEIR PLANET.
ADVANCED ARTIFICIAL INTELLIGENCE WOULD MANAGE ATMOSPHERE, CLIMATE, SIMULATED CYCLES OF DAY AND NIGHT, AND EVEN WEATHER CONDITIONS.

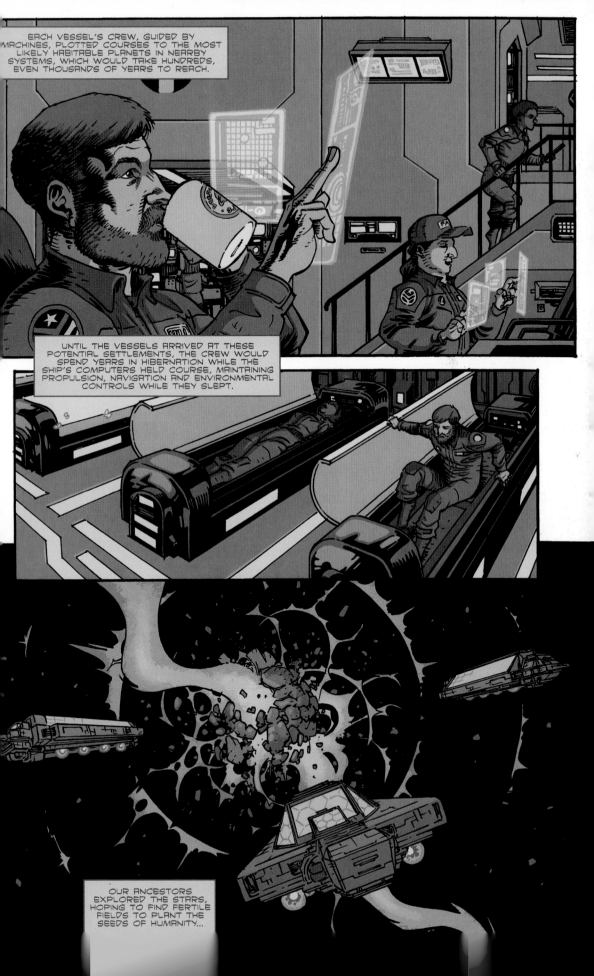

EACH VESSEL'S CREW, GUIDED BY MACHINES, PLOTTED COURSES TO THE MOST LIKELY HABITABLE PLANETS IN NEARBY SYSTEMS, WHICH WOULD TAKE HUNDREDS, EVEN THOUSANDS OF YEARS TO REACH.

UNTIL THE VESSELS ARRIVED AT THESE POTENTIAL SETTLEMENTS, THE CREW WOULD SPEND YEARS IN HIBERNATION WHILE THE SHIP'S COMPUTERS HELD COURSE, MAINTAINING PROPULSION, NAVIGATION AND ENVIRONMENTAL CONTROLS WHILE THEY SLEPT.

OUR ANCESTORS EXPLORED THE STARS, HOPING TO FIND FERTILE FIELDS TO PLANT THE SEEDS OF HUMANITY...

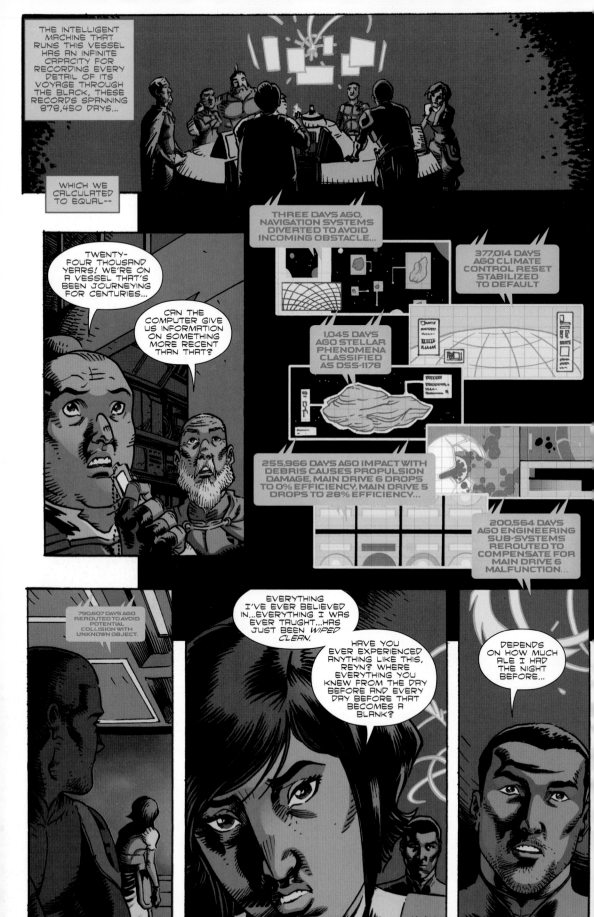

THE INTELLIGENT MACHINE THAT RUNS THIS VESSEL HAS AN INFINITE CAPACITY FOR RECORDING EVERY DETAIL OF ITS VOYAGE THROUGH THE BLACK. THESE RECORDS SPANNING 878,450 DAYS...

WHICH WE CALCULATED TO EQUAL--

THREE DAYS AGO, NAVIGATION SYSTEMS DIVERTED TO AVOID INCOMING OBSTACLE...

377,014 DAYS AGO CLIMATE CONTROL RESET STABILIZED TO DEFAULT

TWENTY-FOUR THOUSAND YEARS! WE'RE ON A VESSEL THAT'S BEEN JOURNEYING FOR CENTURIES...

CAN THE COMPUTER GIVE US INFORMATION ON SOMETHING MORE RECENT THAN THAT?

1,045 DAYS AGO STELLAR PHENOMENA CLASSIFIED AS DSS-1178

255,966 DAYS AGO IMPACT WITH DEBRIS CAUSES PROPULSION DAMAGE, MAIN DRIVE 6 DROPS TO 0% EFFICIENCY, MAIN DRIVE 5 DROPS TO 28% EFFICIENCY...

200,564 DAYS AGO ENGINEERING SUB-SYSTEMS REROUTED TO COMPENSATE FOR MAIN DRIVE 6 MALFUNCTION...

790,607 DAYS AGO REROUTED TO AVOID POTENTIAL COLLISION WITH UNKNOWN OBJECT.

EVERYTHING I'VE EVER BELIEVED IN...EVERYTHING I WAS EVER TAUGHT...HAS JUST BEEN *WIPED CLEAN.*

HAVE YOU EVER EXPERIENCED ANYTHING LIKE THIS, REYN? WHERE EVERYTHING YOU KNEW FROM THE DAY BEFORE AND EVERY DAY BEFORE THAT BECOMES A BLANK?

DEPENDS ON HOW MUCH ALE I HAD THE NIGHT BEFORE...

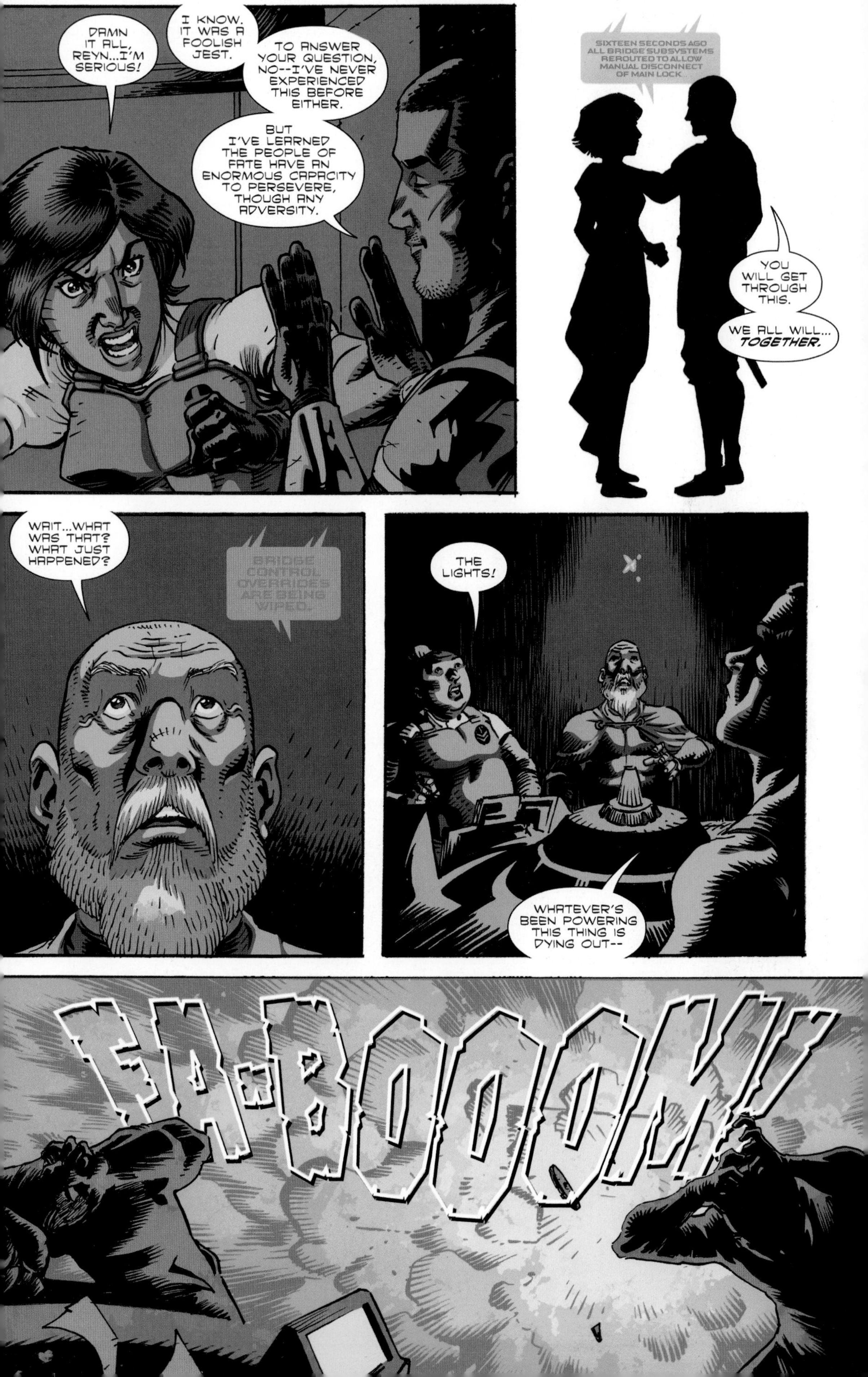
DAMN IT ALL, REYN...I'M SERIOUS!
I KNOW. IT WAS A FOOLISH JEST.
TO ANSWER YOUR QUESTION, NO--I'VE NEVER EXPERIENCED THIS BEFORE EITHER.
BUT I'VE LEARNED THE PEOPLE OF FATE HAVE AN ENORMOUS CAPACITY TO PERSEVERE, THOUGH ANY ADVERSITY.
SIXTEEN SECONDS AGO ALL BRIDGE SUBSYSTEMS REROUTED TO ALLOW MANUAL DISCONNECT OF MAIN LOCK...
YOU WILL GET THROUGH THIS.
WE ALL WILL... *TOGETHER.*
WAIT...WHAT WAS THAT? WHAT JUST HAPPENED?
BRIDGE CONTROL OVERRIDES ARE BEING WIPED.
THE LIGHTS!
WHATEVER'S BEEN POWERING THIS THING IS DYING OUT--
KA-BOOOM

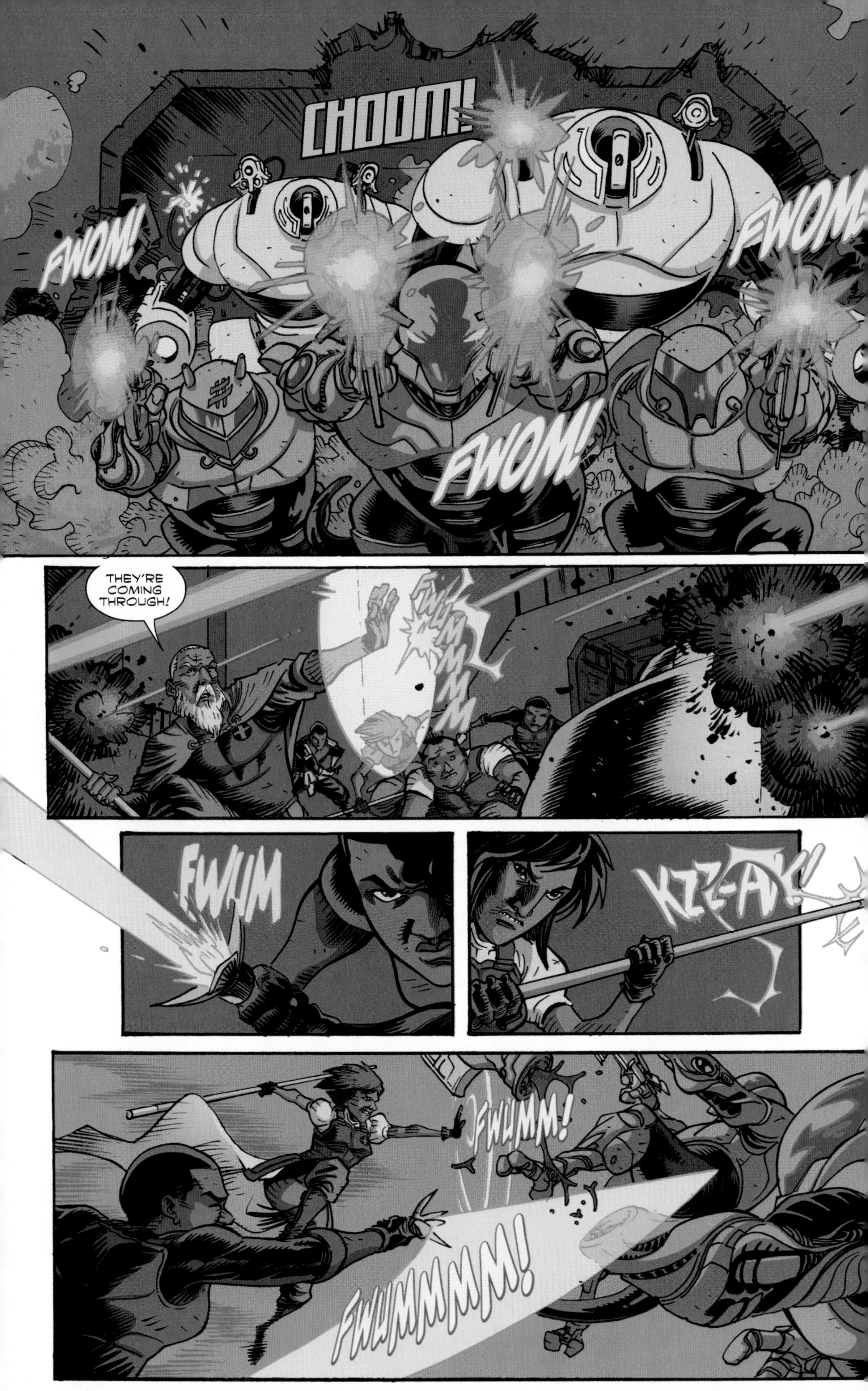
CHOOM!
FWOM!
FWOM!
FWOM!
THEY'RE COMING THROUGH!
FWUMMMMM
FWUM
FWUMM!
FWUMMMMM!

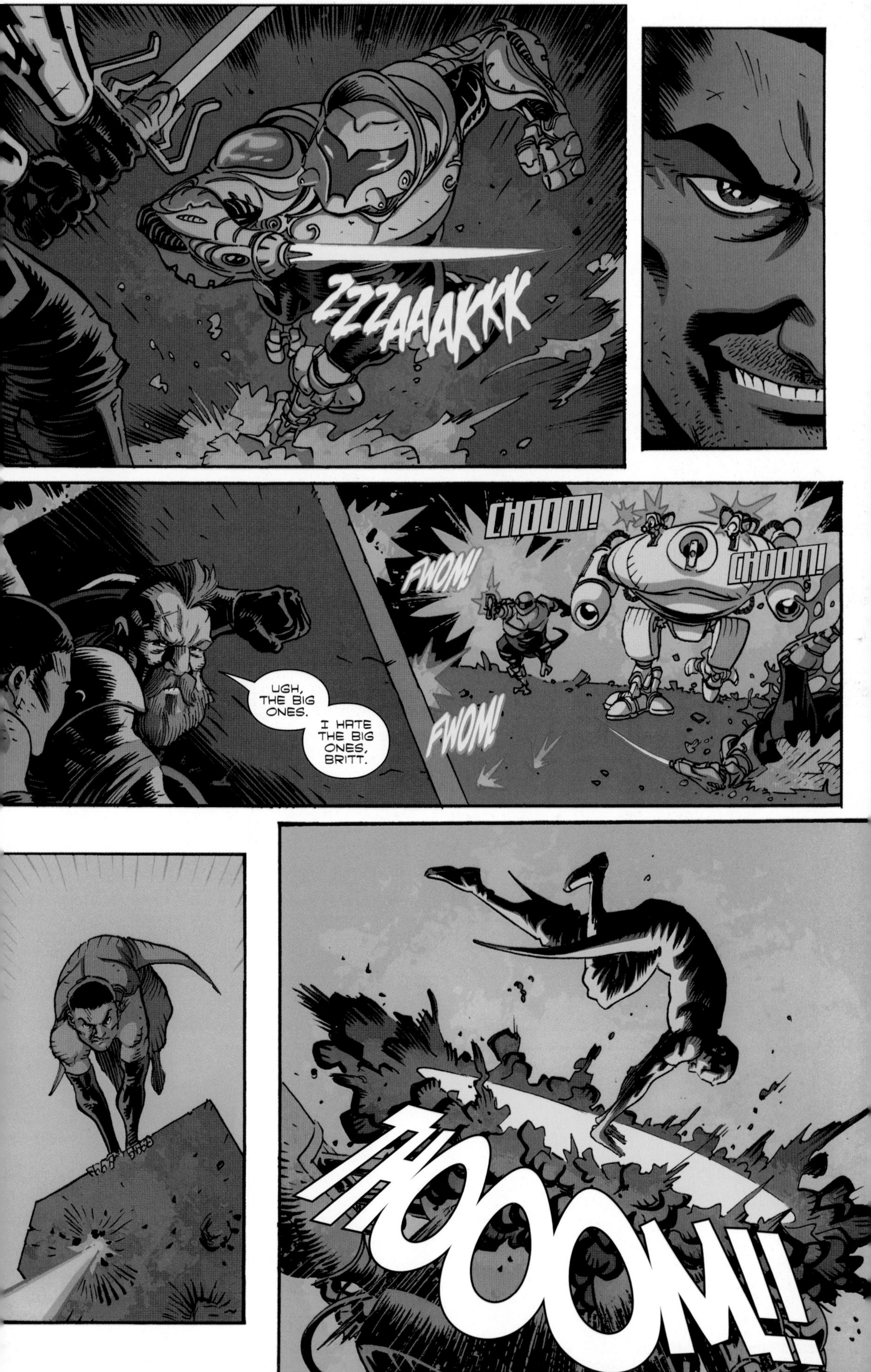
ZZZAAAKKK
UGH, THE BIG ONES.
I HATE THE BIG ONES, BRITT.
CHOOM!
FWOM!
CHOOM!
FWOM!
THOOOM!!

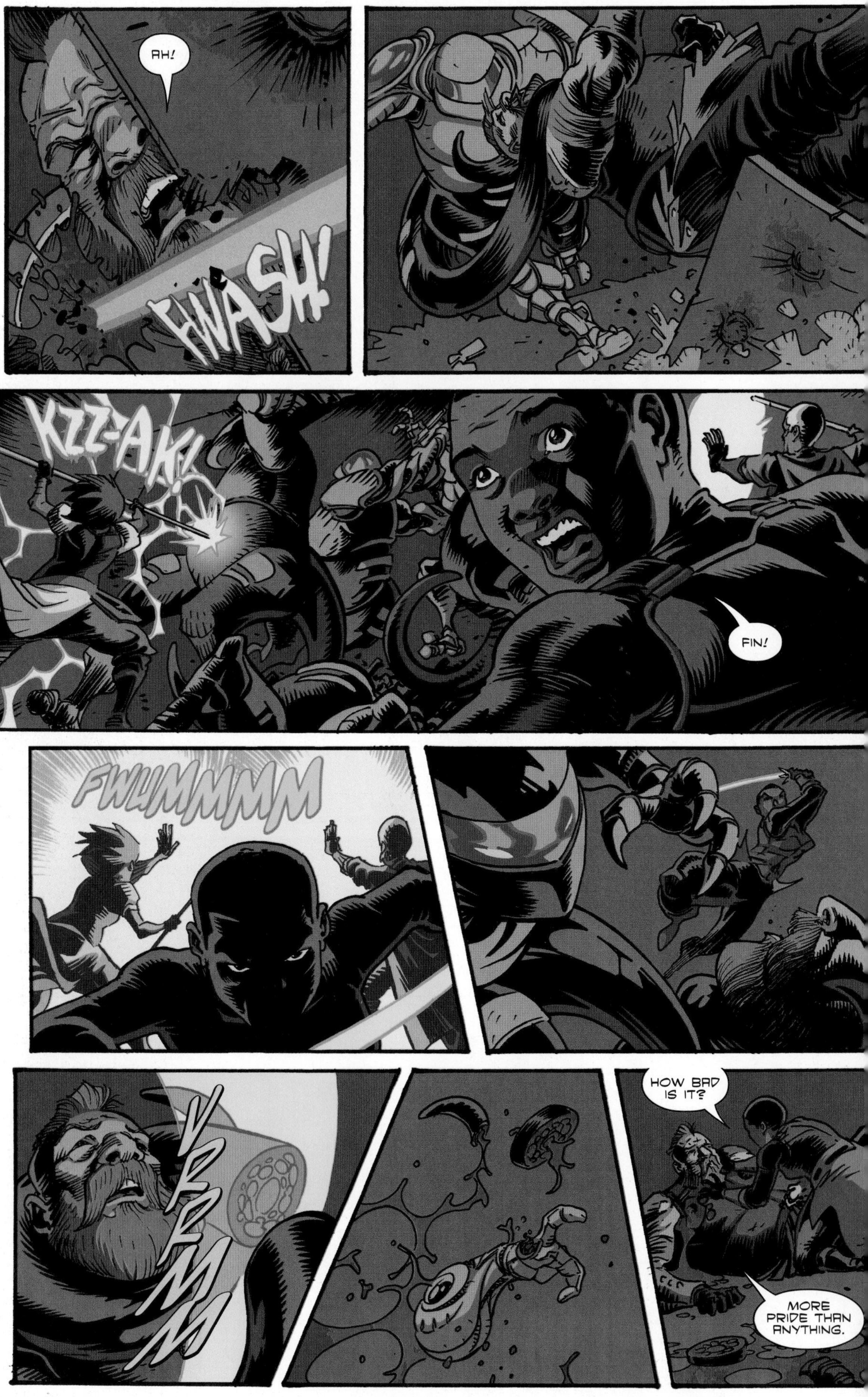
AH!
FWASH!
KZZ-AK!
FIN!
FWUMMMM
HOW BAD IS IT?
MORE PRIDE THAN ANYTHING.

BRAM! CAN YOU FIND A WAY TO KEEP THEM OUT?
THOP!
FWUMMMMM!
COMPUTER, I NEED TO CLOSE THIS--
ZT-- SECURING... BLAST...DOOR... KKT

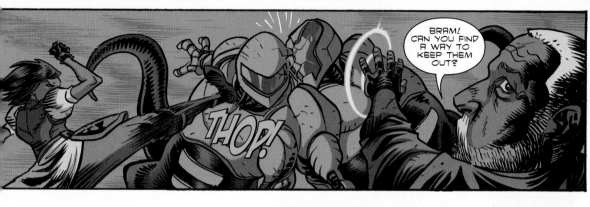

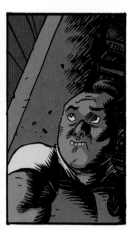

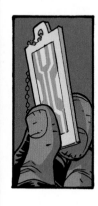

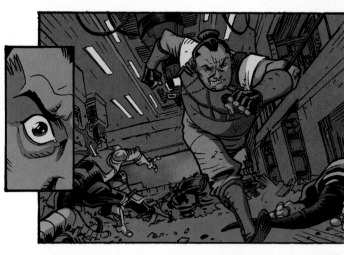

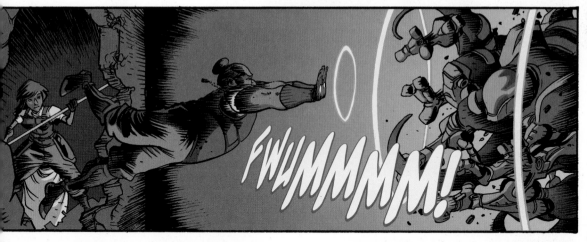

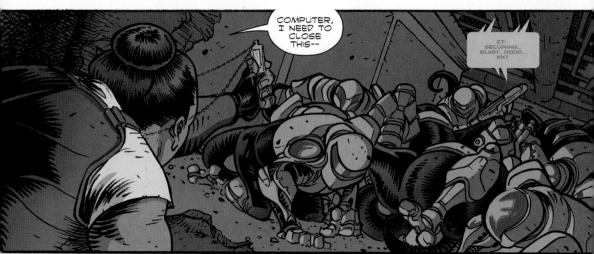

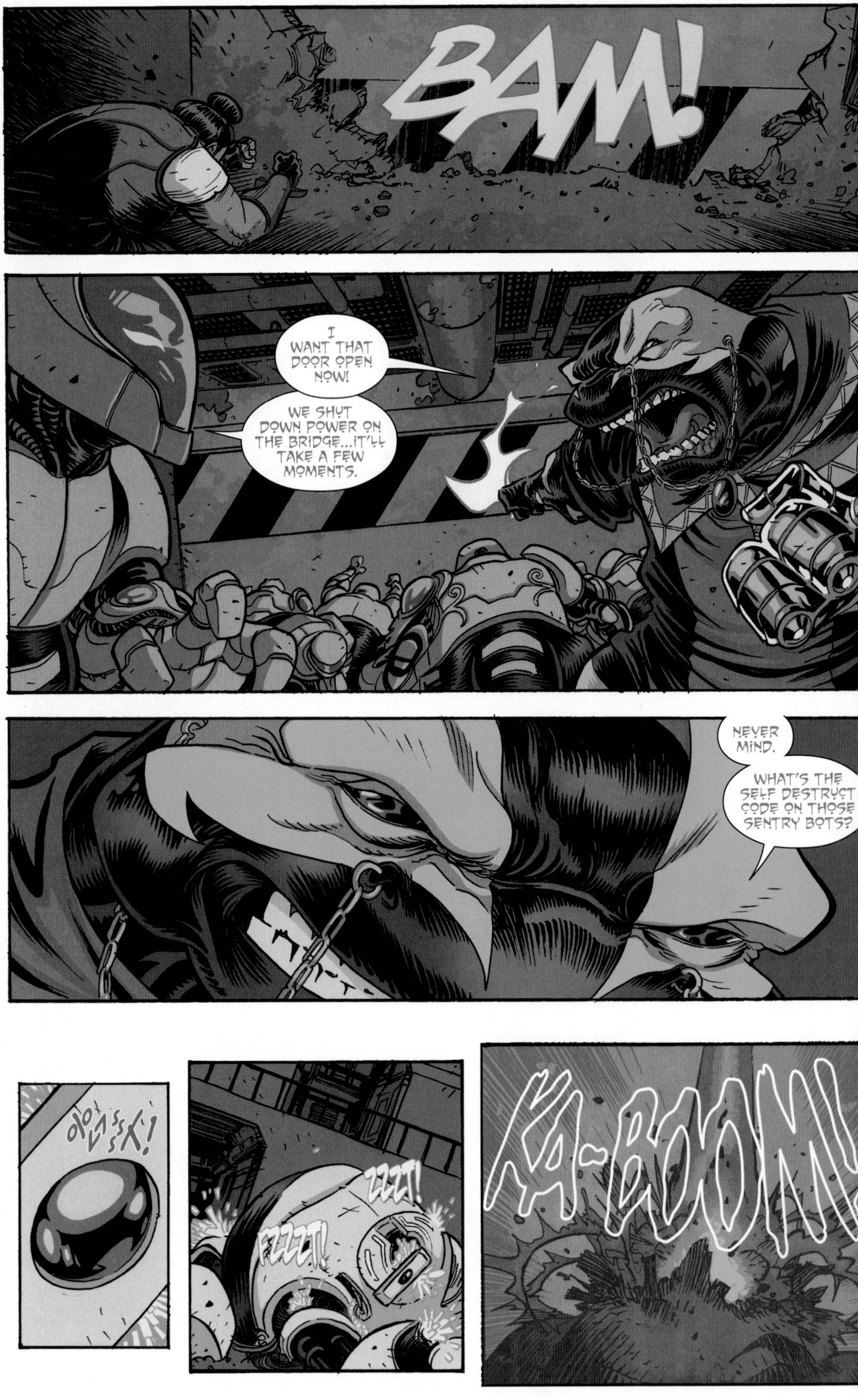
BAM!
I WANT THAT DOOR OPEN NOW!
WE SHUT DOWN POWER ON THE BRIDGE...IT'LL TAKE A FEW MOMENTS.
NEVER MIND.
WHAT'S THE SELF DESTRUCT CODE ON THOSE SENTRY BOTS?
ZZZT!
FZZZT!
KA-BOOM!

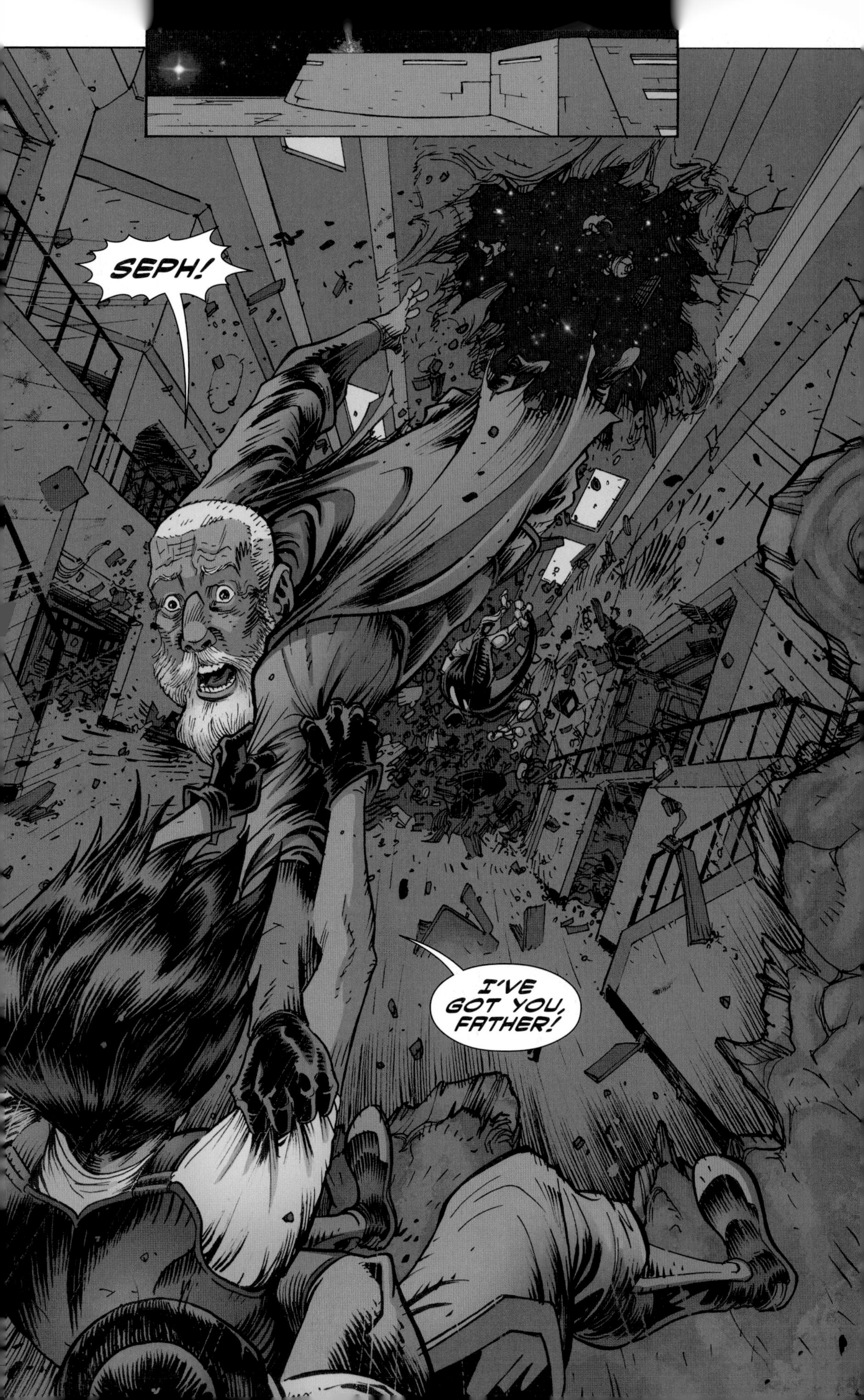
SEPH!
I'VE GOT YOU, FATHER!

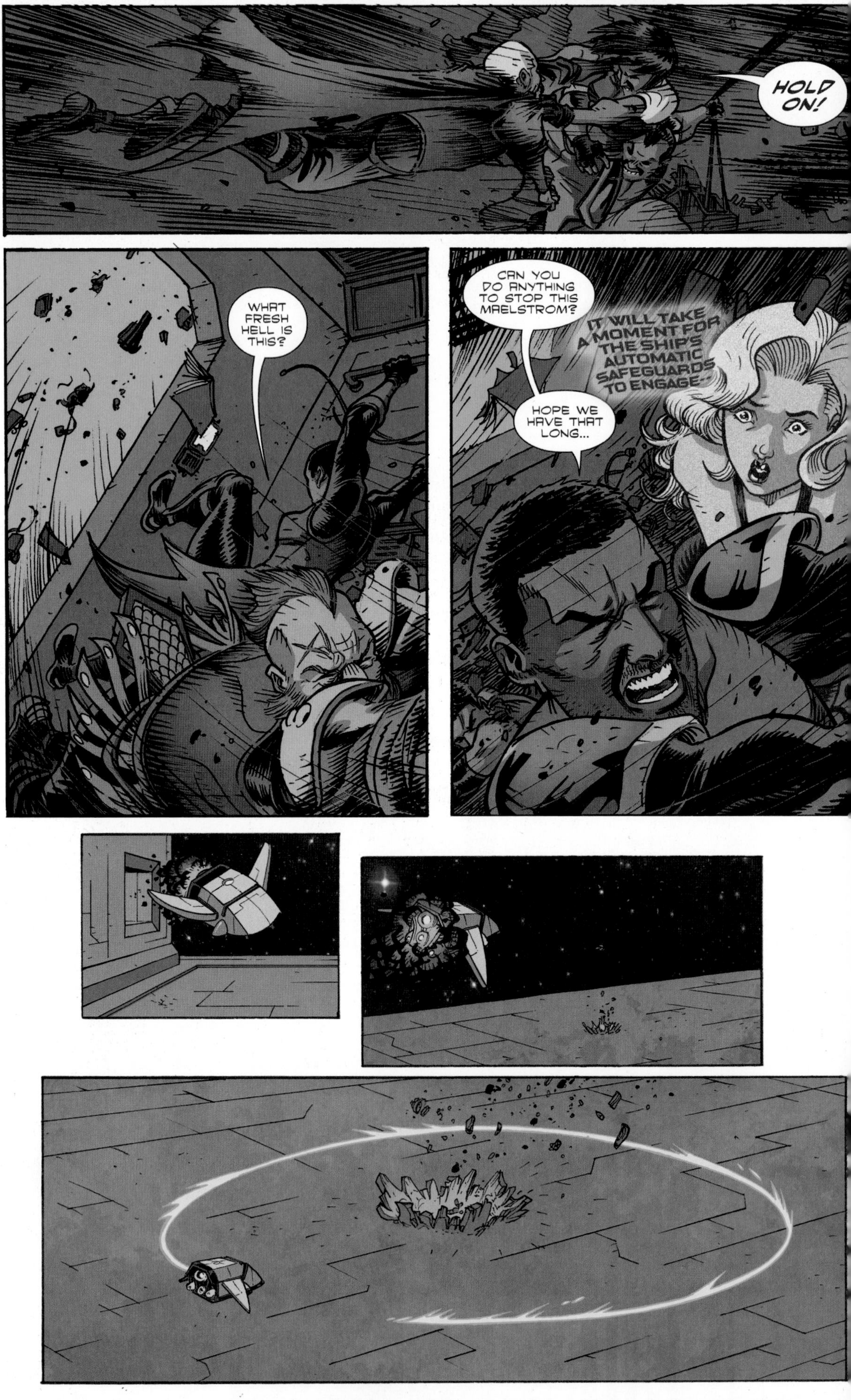
HOLD ON!
WHAT FRESH HELL IS THIS?
CAN YOU DO ANYTHING TO STOP THIS MAELSTROM?
IT WILL TAKE A MOMENT FOR THE SHIP'S AUTOMATIC SAFEGUARDS TO ENGAGE--
HOPE WE HAVE THAT LONG...

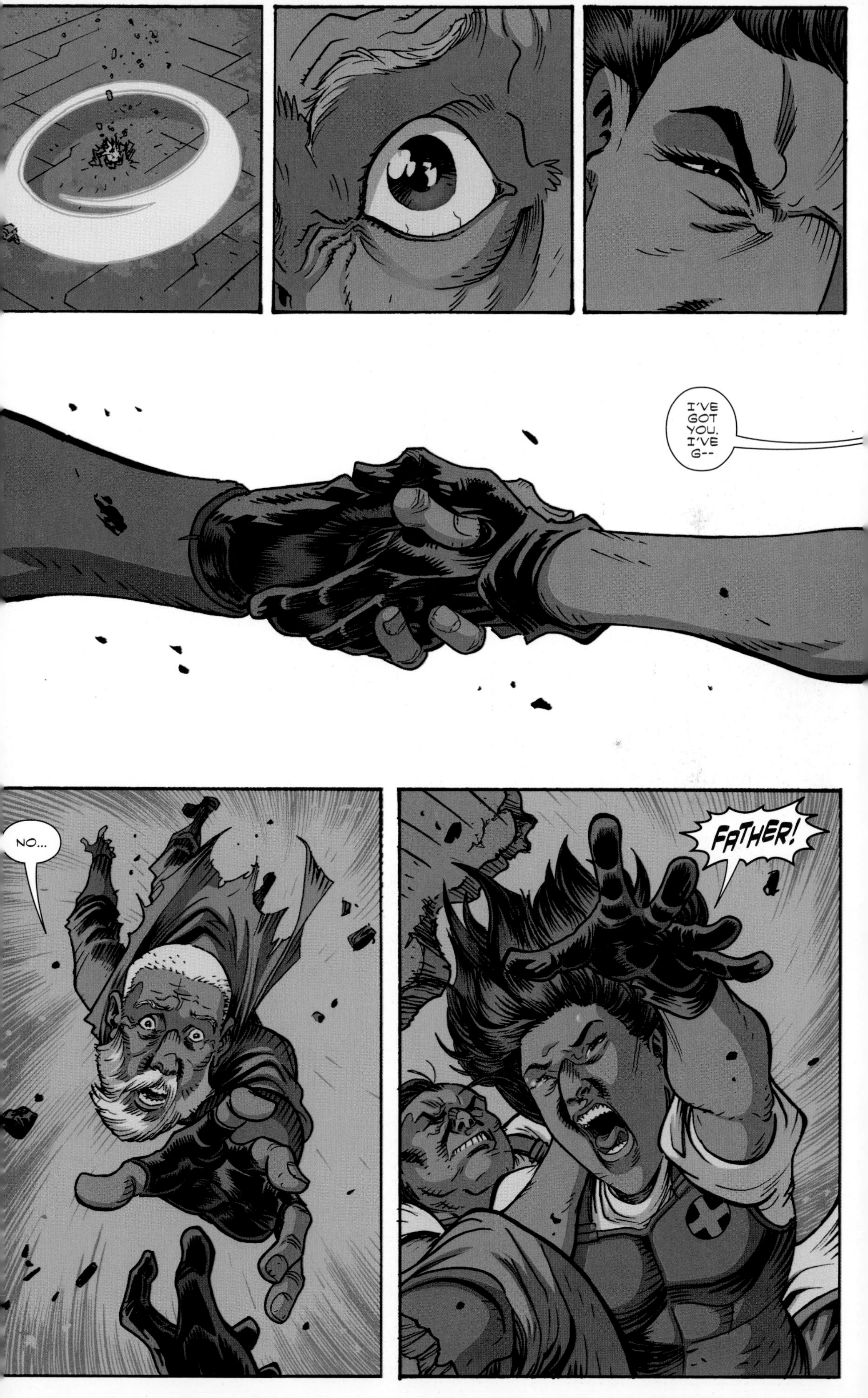
I'VE GOT YOU. I'VE G--
NO...
FATHER!

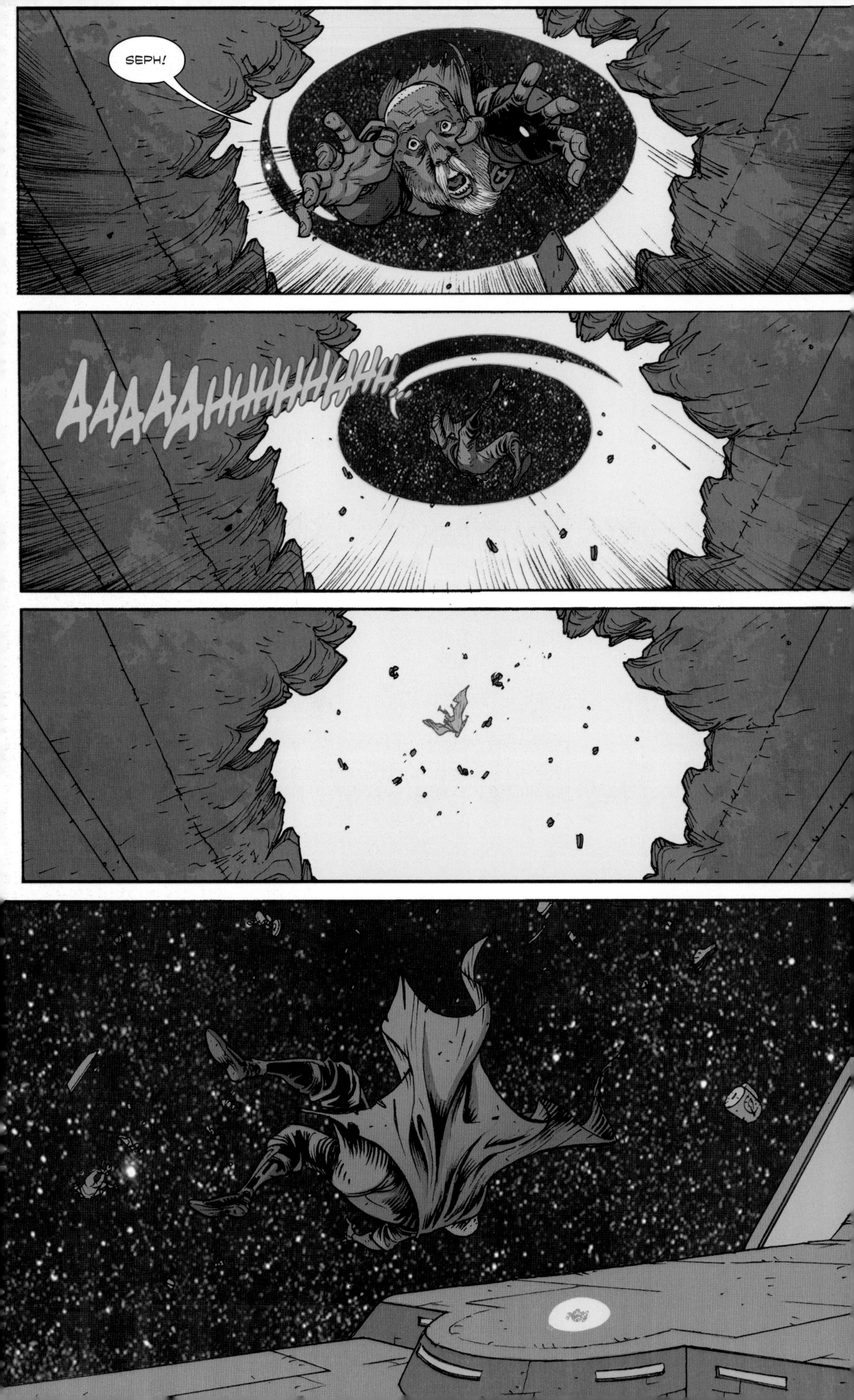
SEPH!
AAAAAHHHHHHHHH...

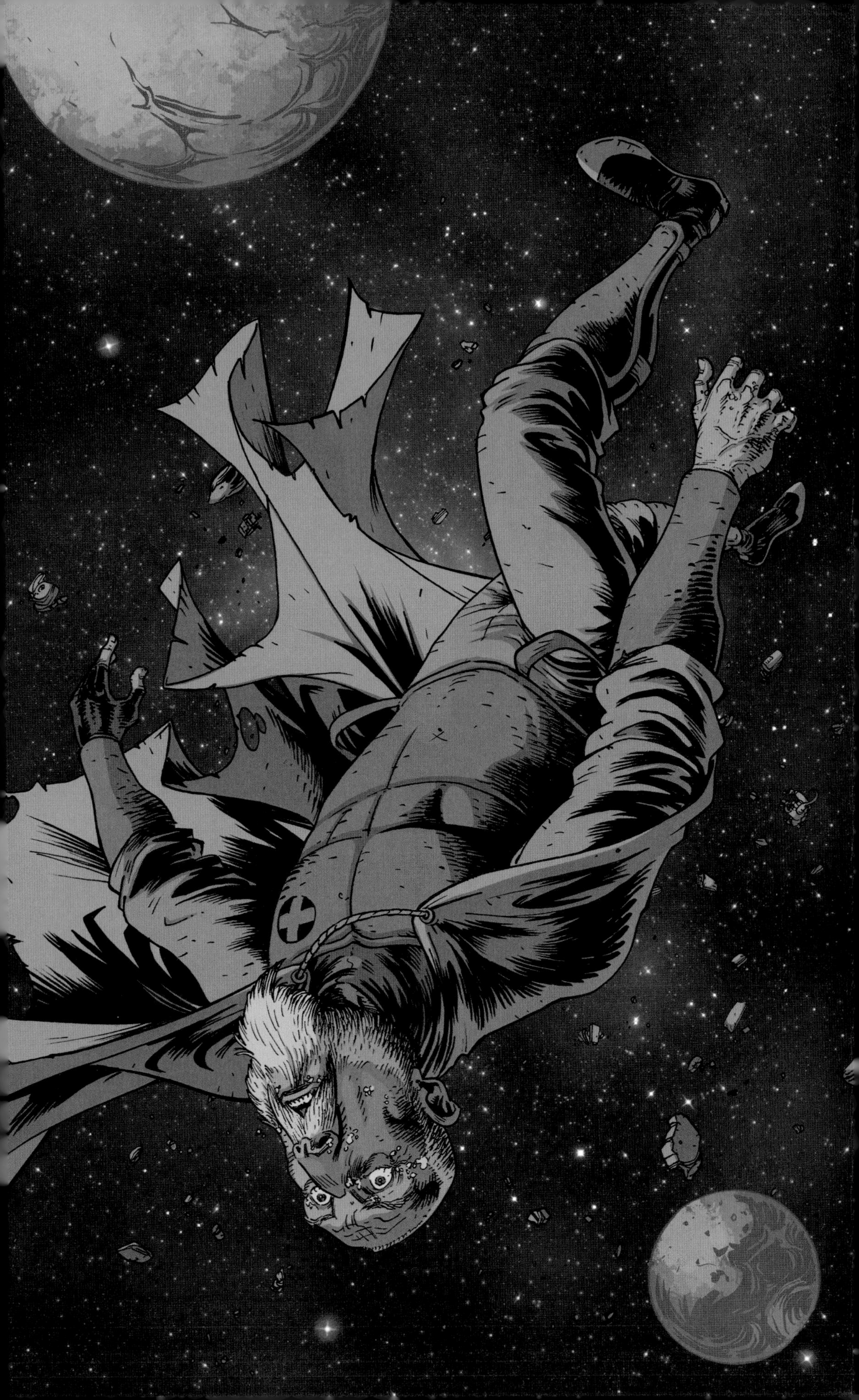

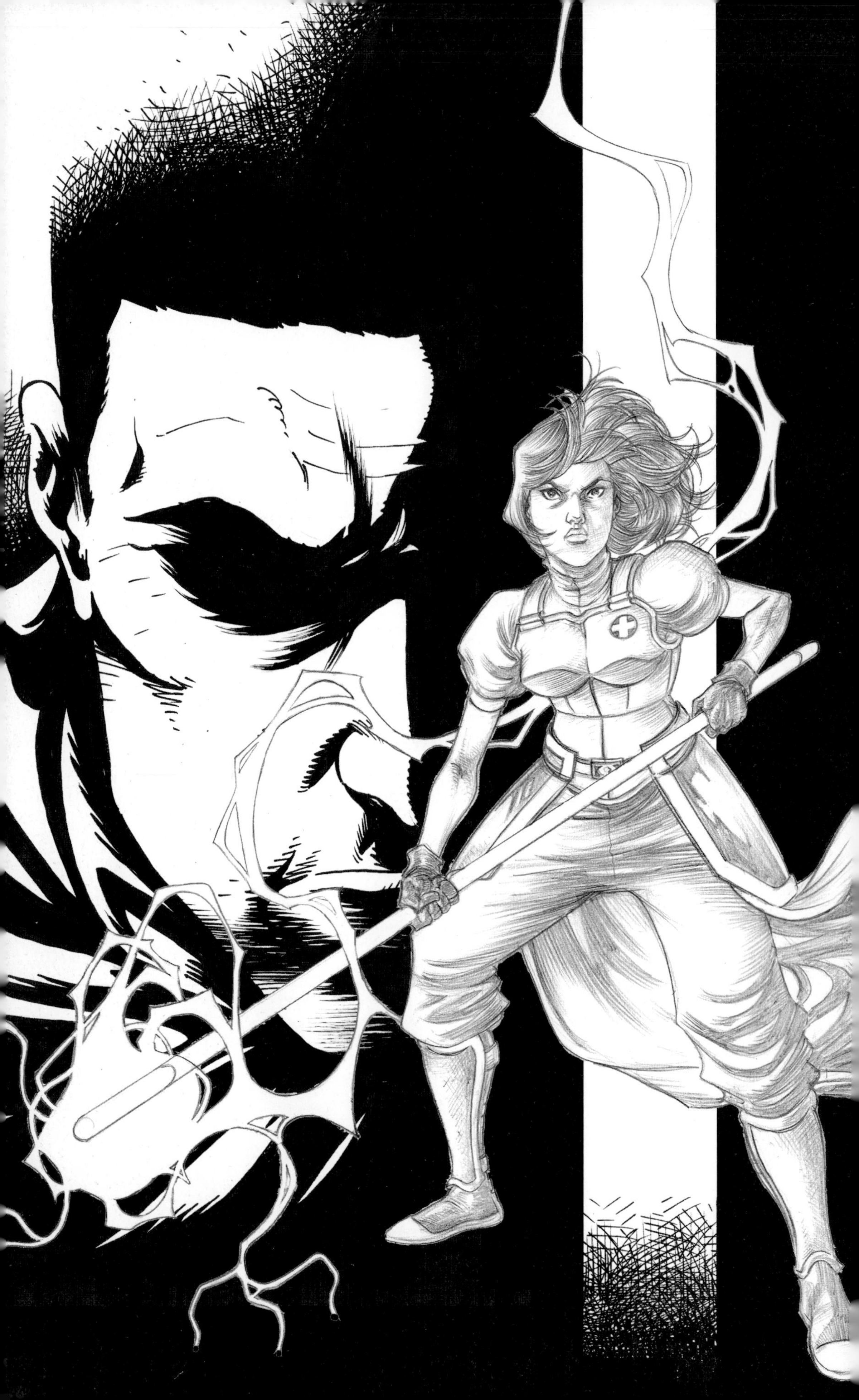

Chapter Seven

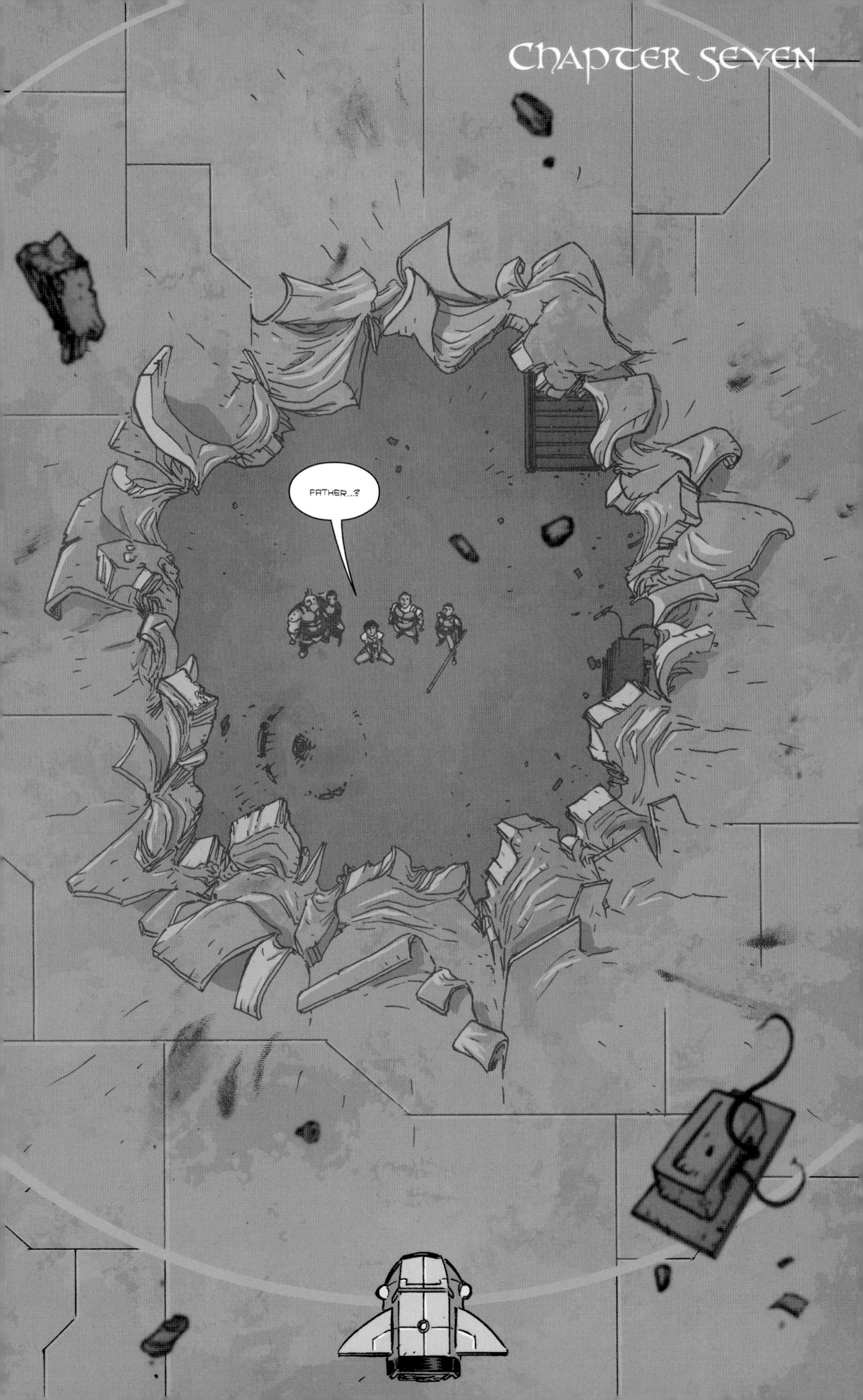
FATHER...?

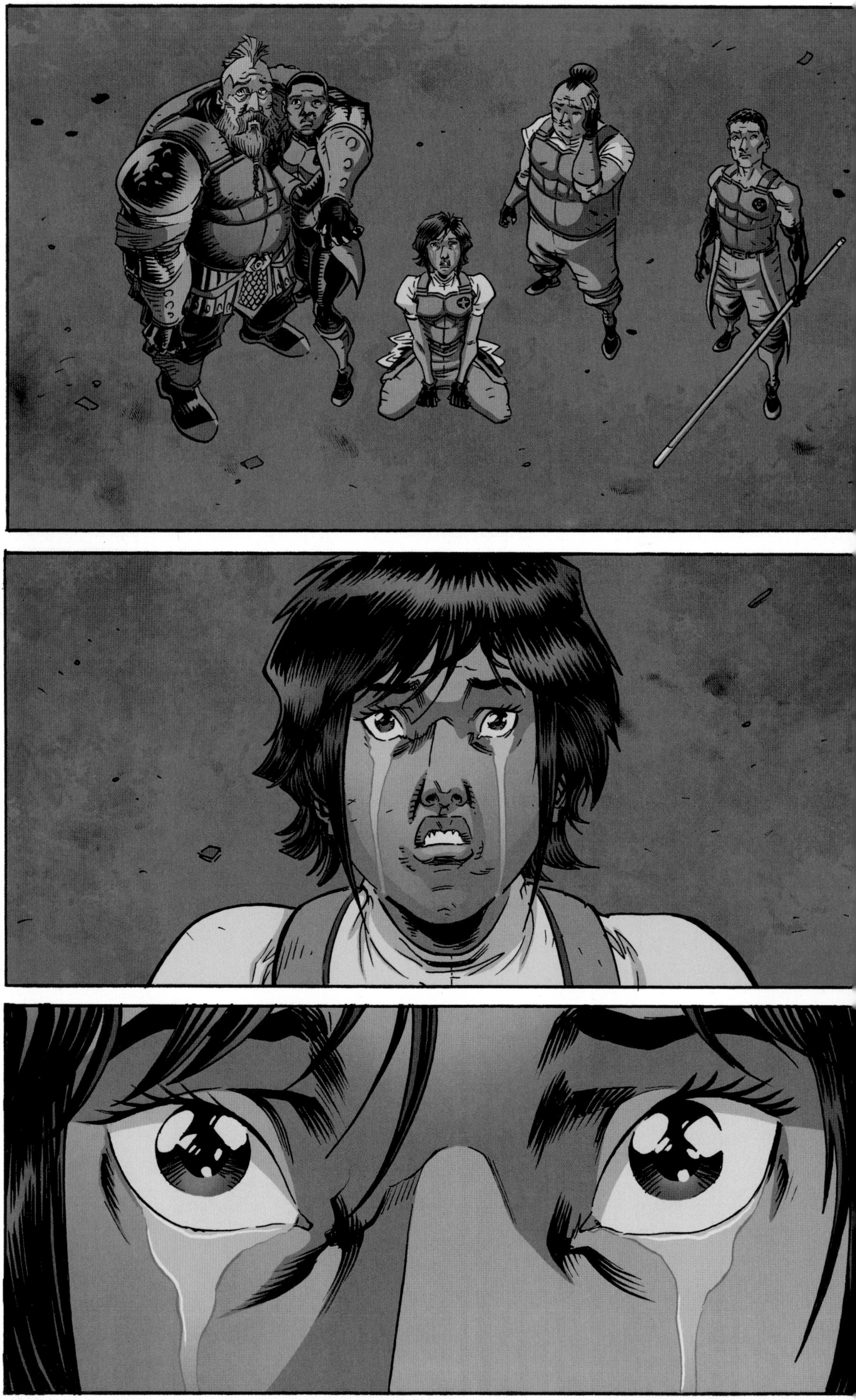

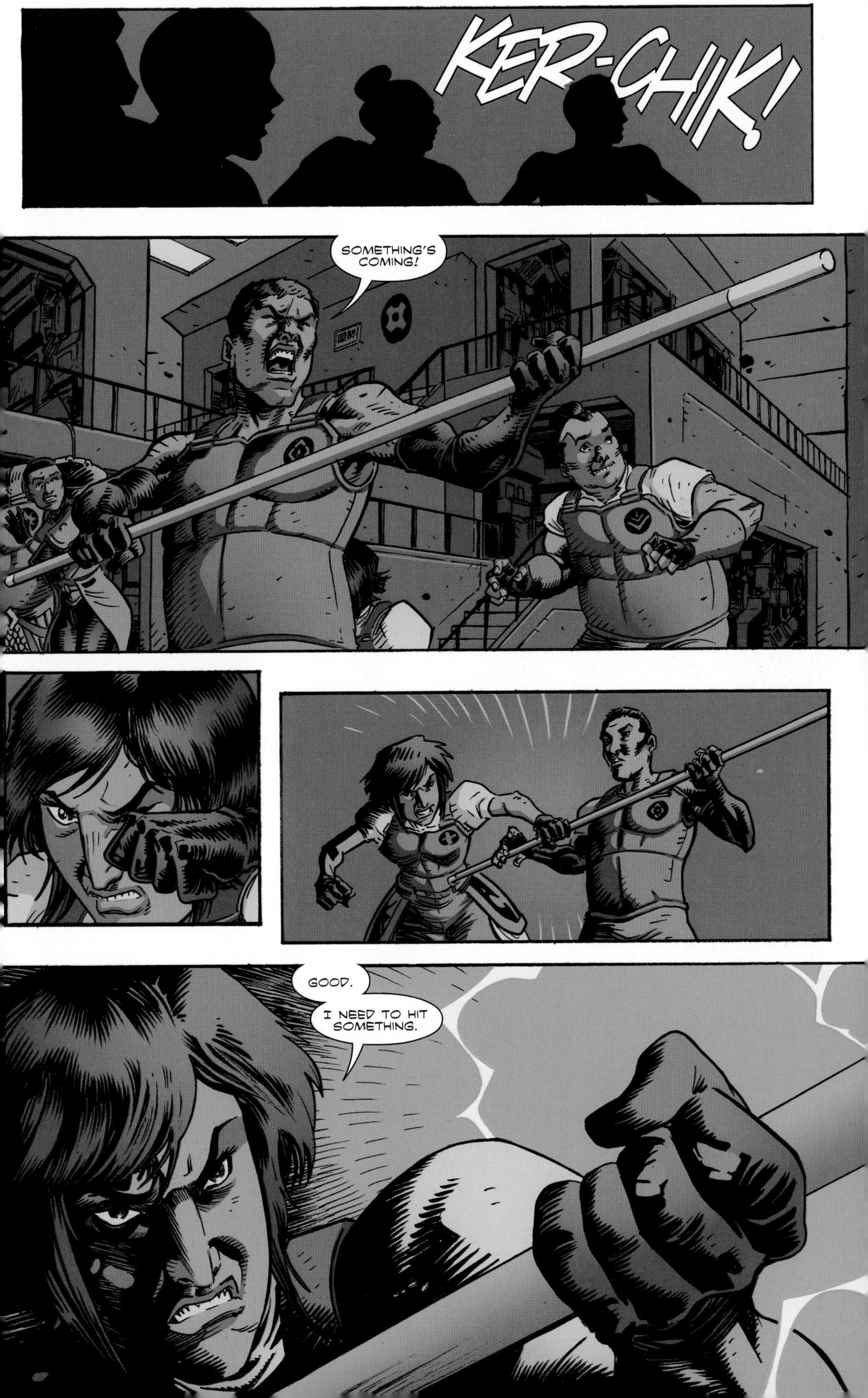
KER-CHIK!
SOMETHING'S COMING!
GOOD.
I NEED TO HIT SOMETHING.

WHRRR
MAINTENANCE
पतवार मरम्मत सिस्टम 船体修复系统
SHUK
OH, I DON'T LIKE THIS...
CHUK
MAINTENANCE
POP
SPLAT!
POP POP
SPLAT!
THERE ARE HUNDREDS OF THEM!

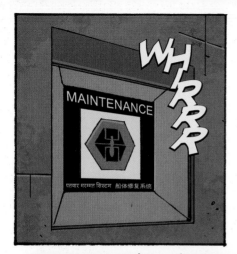

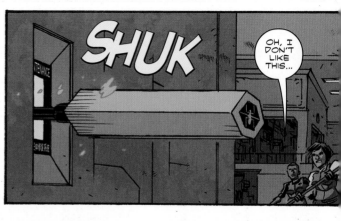

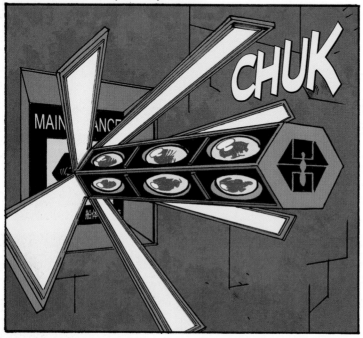

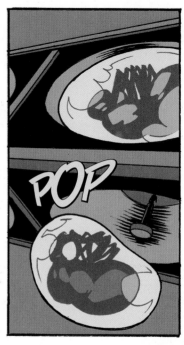

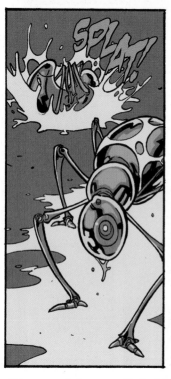

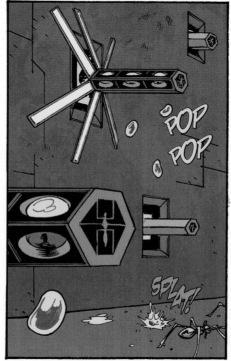

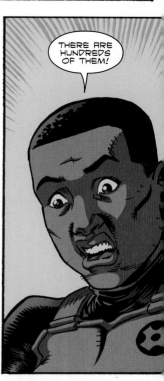

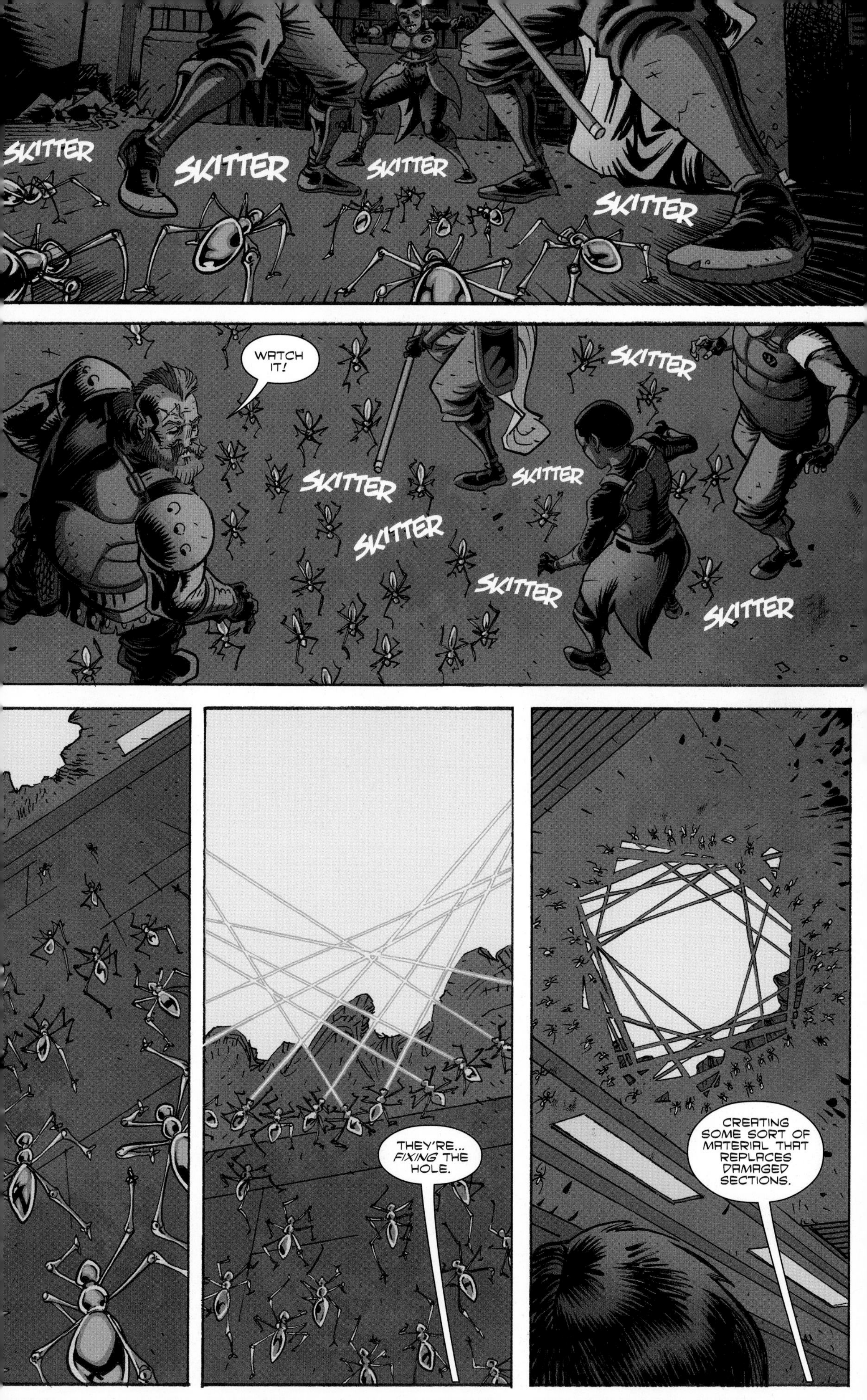

SKITTER
SKITTER
SKITTER
SKITTER
WATCH IT!
SKITTER
SKITTER
SKITTER
SKITTER
SKITTER
SKITTER
THEY'RE... *FIXING* THE HOLE.
CREATING SOME SORT OF MATERIAL THAT REPLACES DAMAGED SECTIONS.

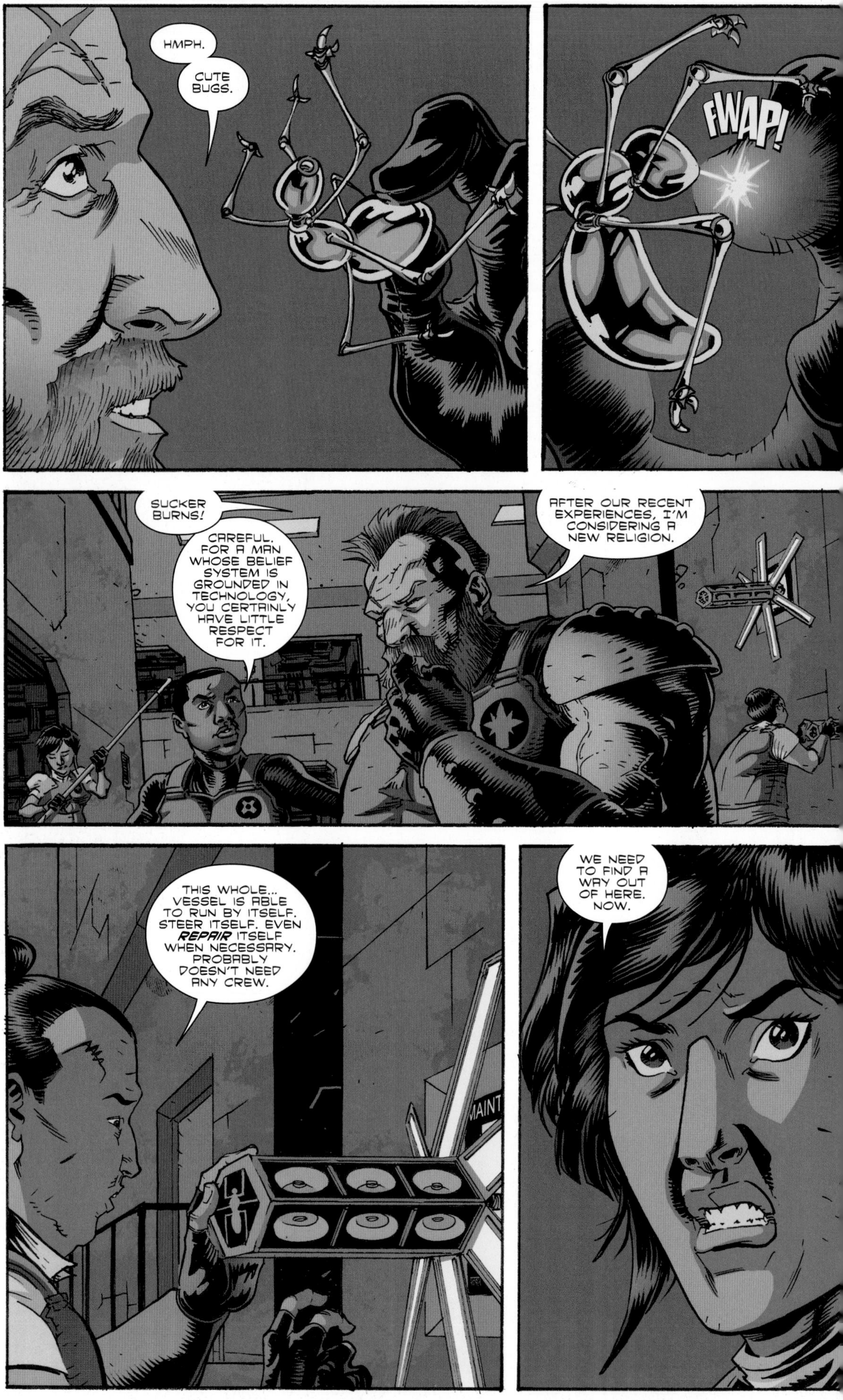
HMPH.
CUTE BUGS.
FWAP!
SUCKER BURNS!
CAREFUL. FOR A MAN WHOSE BELIEF SYSTEM IS GROUNDED IN TECHNOLOGY, YOU CERTAINLY HAVE LITTLE RESPECT FOR IT.
AFTER OUR RECENT EXPERIENCES, I'M CONSIDERING A NEW RELIGION.
THIS WHOLE... VESSEL IS ABLE TO RUN BY ITSELF. STEER ITSELF. EVEN *REPAIR* ITSELF WHEN NECESSARY. PROBABLY DOESN'T NEED ANY CREW.
WE NEED TO FIND A WAY OUT OF HERE. NOW.

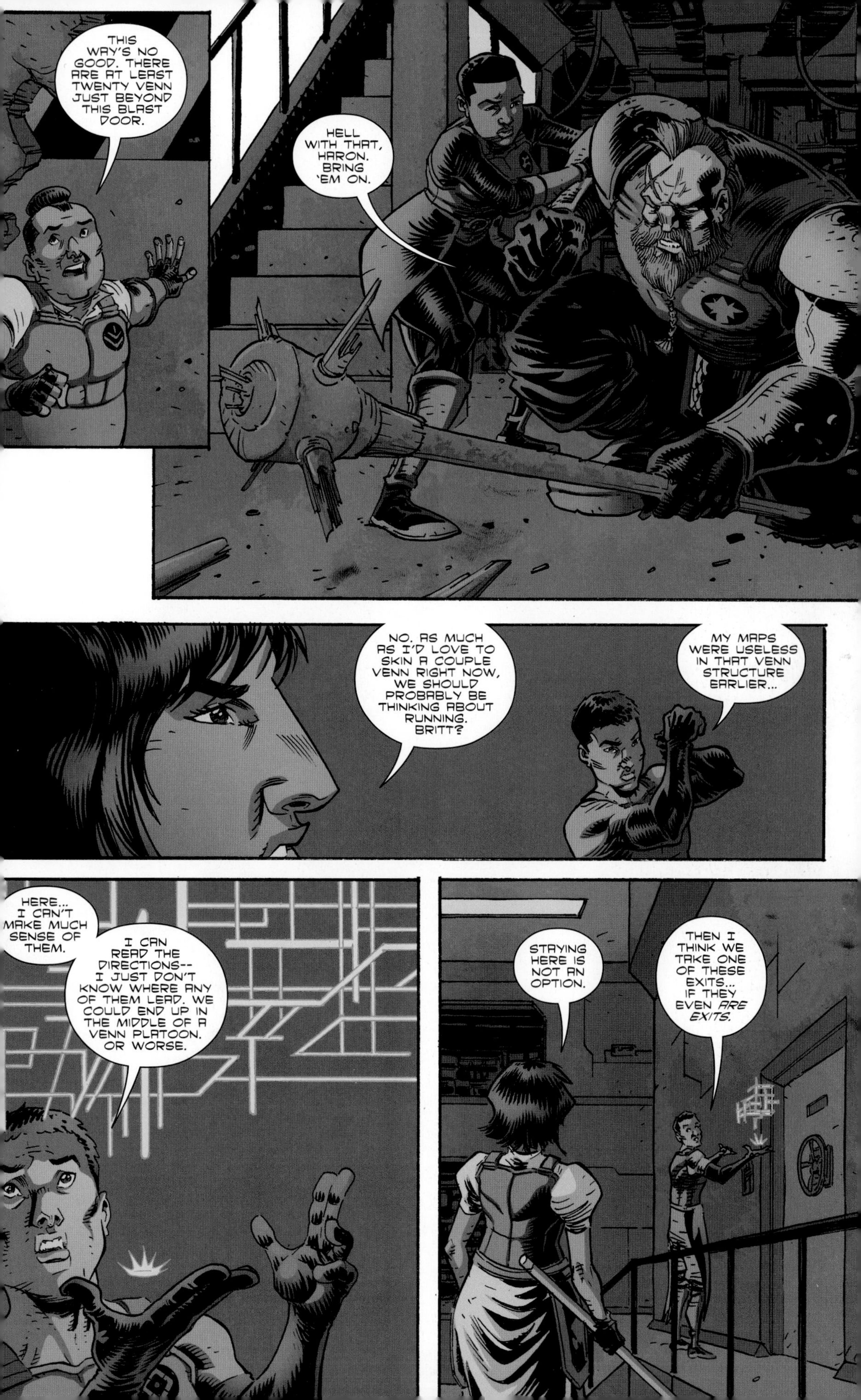
THIS WAY'S NO GOOD. THERE ARE AT LEAST TWENTY VENN JUST BEYOND THIS BLAST DOOR.
HELL WITH THAT, HARON. BRING 'EM ON.
NO. AS MUCH AS I'D LOVE TO SKIN A COUPLE VENN RIGHT NOW, WE SHOULD PROBABLY BE THINKING ABOUT RUNNING. BRITT?
MY MAPS WERE USELESS IN THAT VENN STRUCTURE EARLIER...
HERE... I CAN'T MAKE MUCH SENSE OF THEM.
I CAN READ THE DIRECTIONS-- I JUST DON'T KNOW WHERE ANY OF THEM LEAD. WE COULD END UP IN THE MIDDLE OF A VENN PLATOON. OR WORSE.
STAYING HERE IS NOT AN OPTION.
THEN I THINK WE TAKE ONE OF THESE EXITS... IF THEY EVEN *ARE* EXITS.

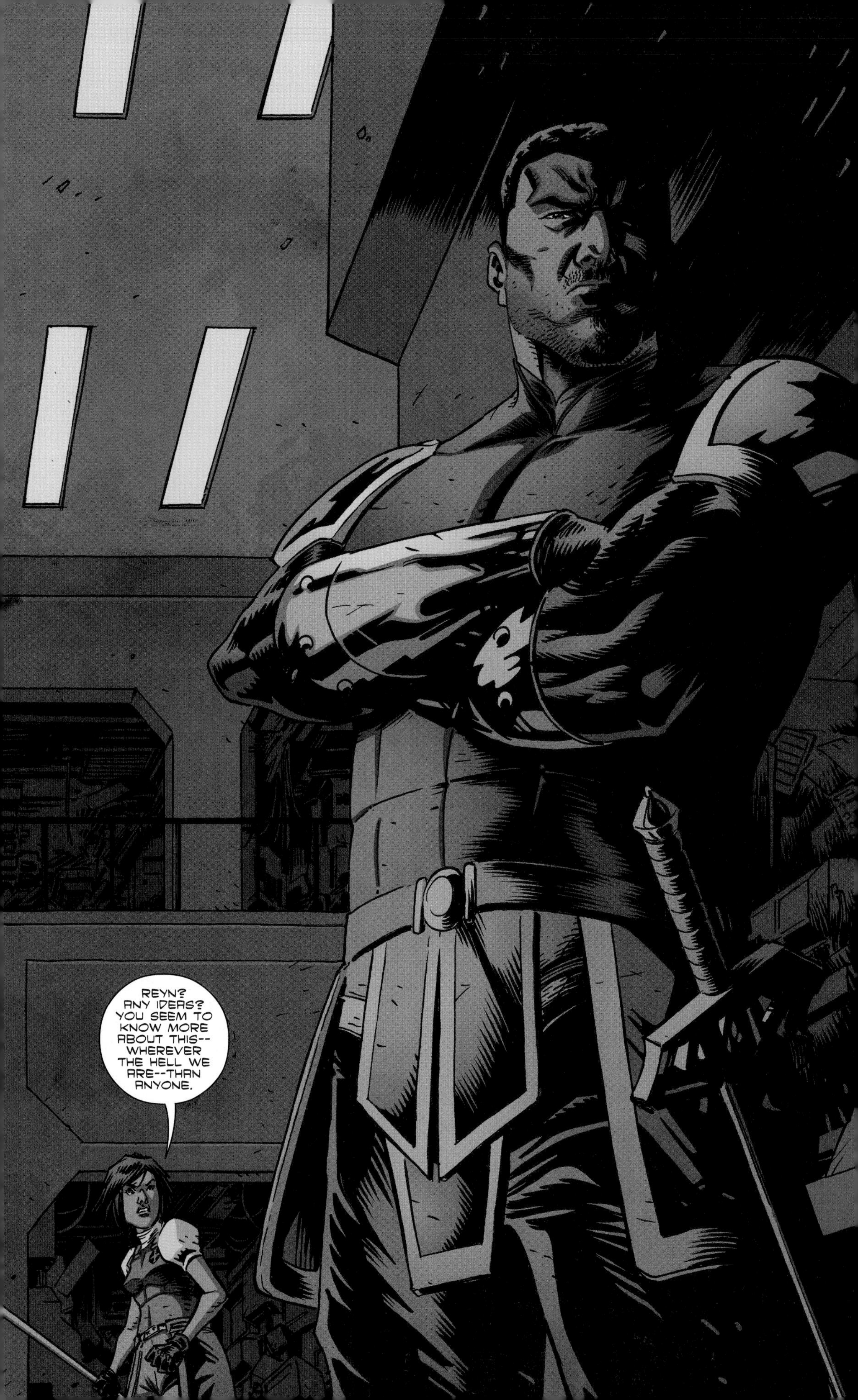
REYN? ANY IDEAS? YOU SEEM TO KNOW MORE ABOUT THIS-- WHEREVER THE HELL WE ARE--THAN ANYONE.

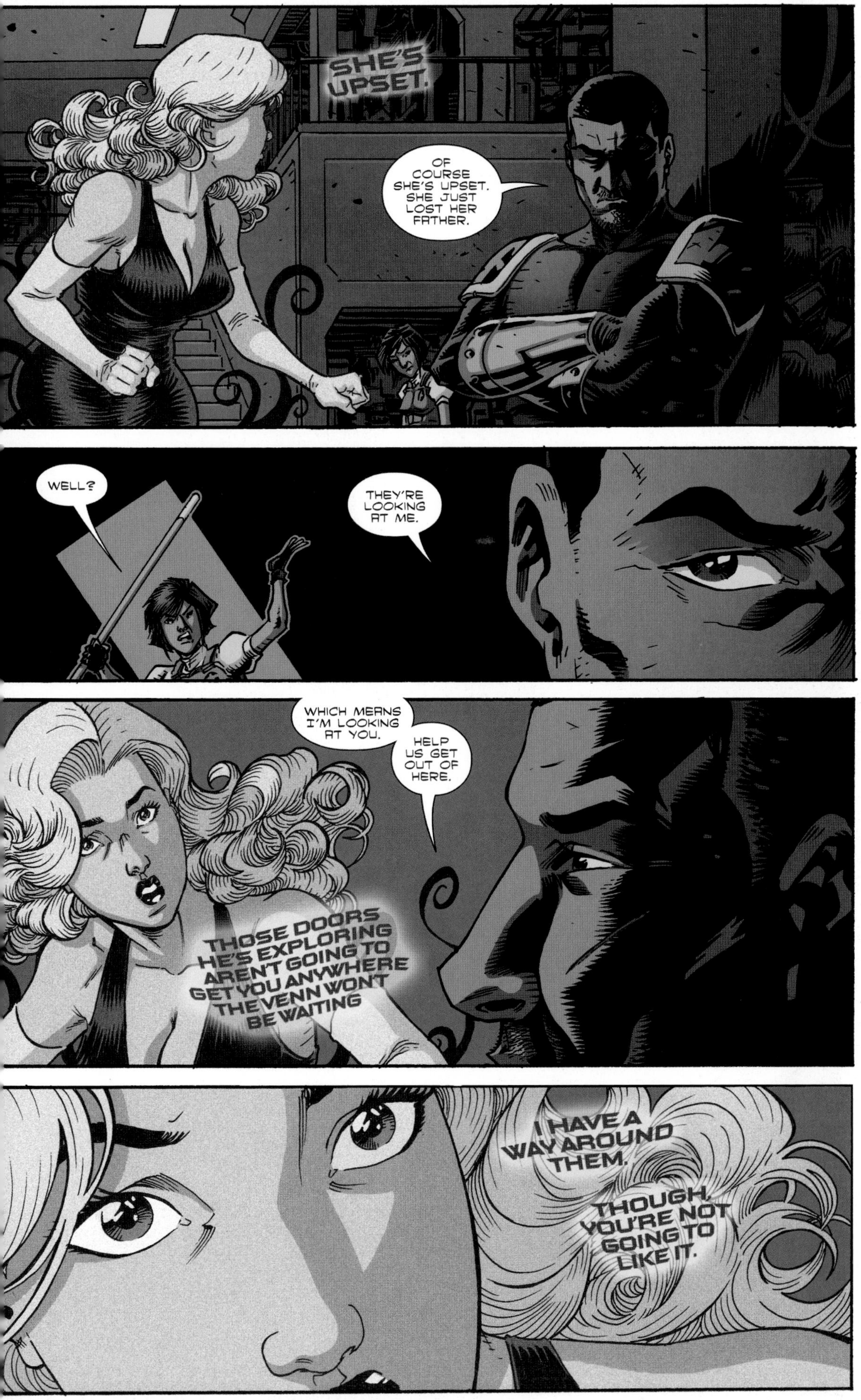
SHE'S UPSET.
OF COURSE SHE'S UPSET. SHE JUST LOST HER FATHER.
WELL?
THEY'RE LOOKING AT ME.
WHICH MEANS I'M LOOKING AT YOU.
HELP US GET OUT OF HERE.
THOSE DOORS HE'S EXPLORING AREN'T GOING TO GET YOU ANYWHERE THE VENN WON'T BE WAITING
I HAVE A WAY AROUND THEM.
THOUGH, YOU'RE NOT GOING TO LIKE IT.

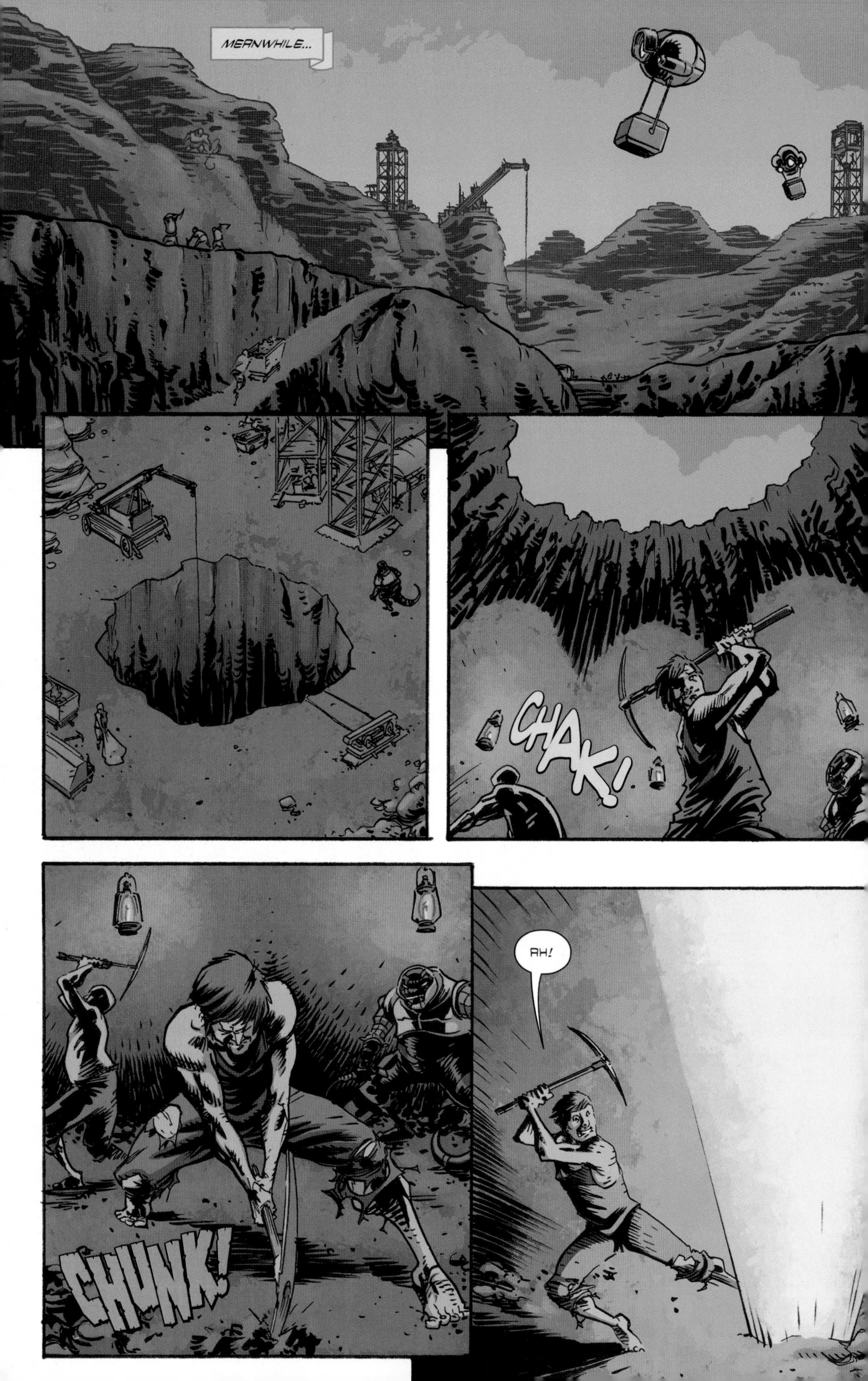
MEANWHILE...
CHAK!
CHUNK!
AH!

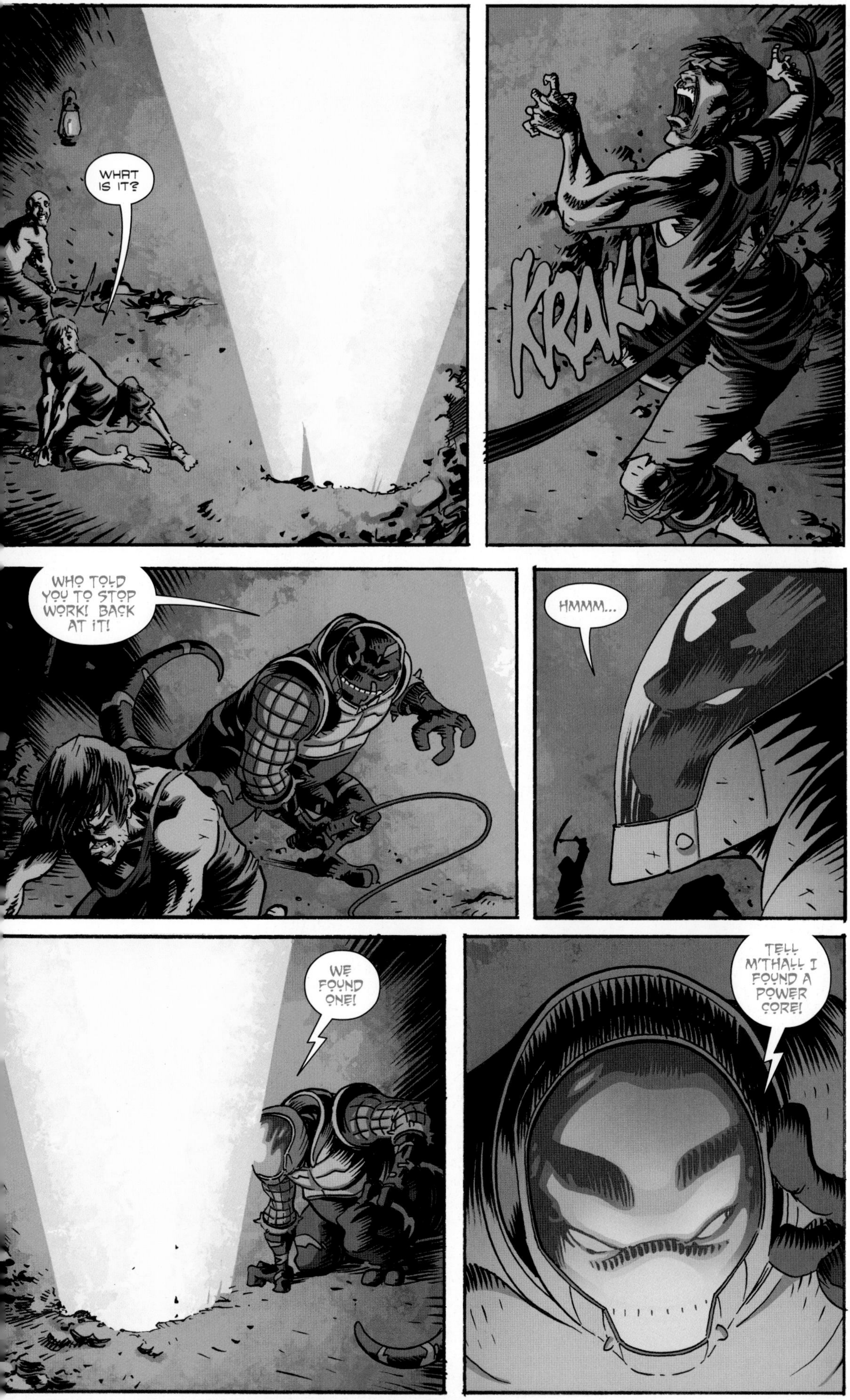
WHAT IS IT?
KRAK!
WHO TOLD YOU TO STOP WORK! BACK AT IT!
HMMM...
WE FOUND ONE!
TELL M'THALL I FOUND A POWER CORE!

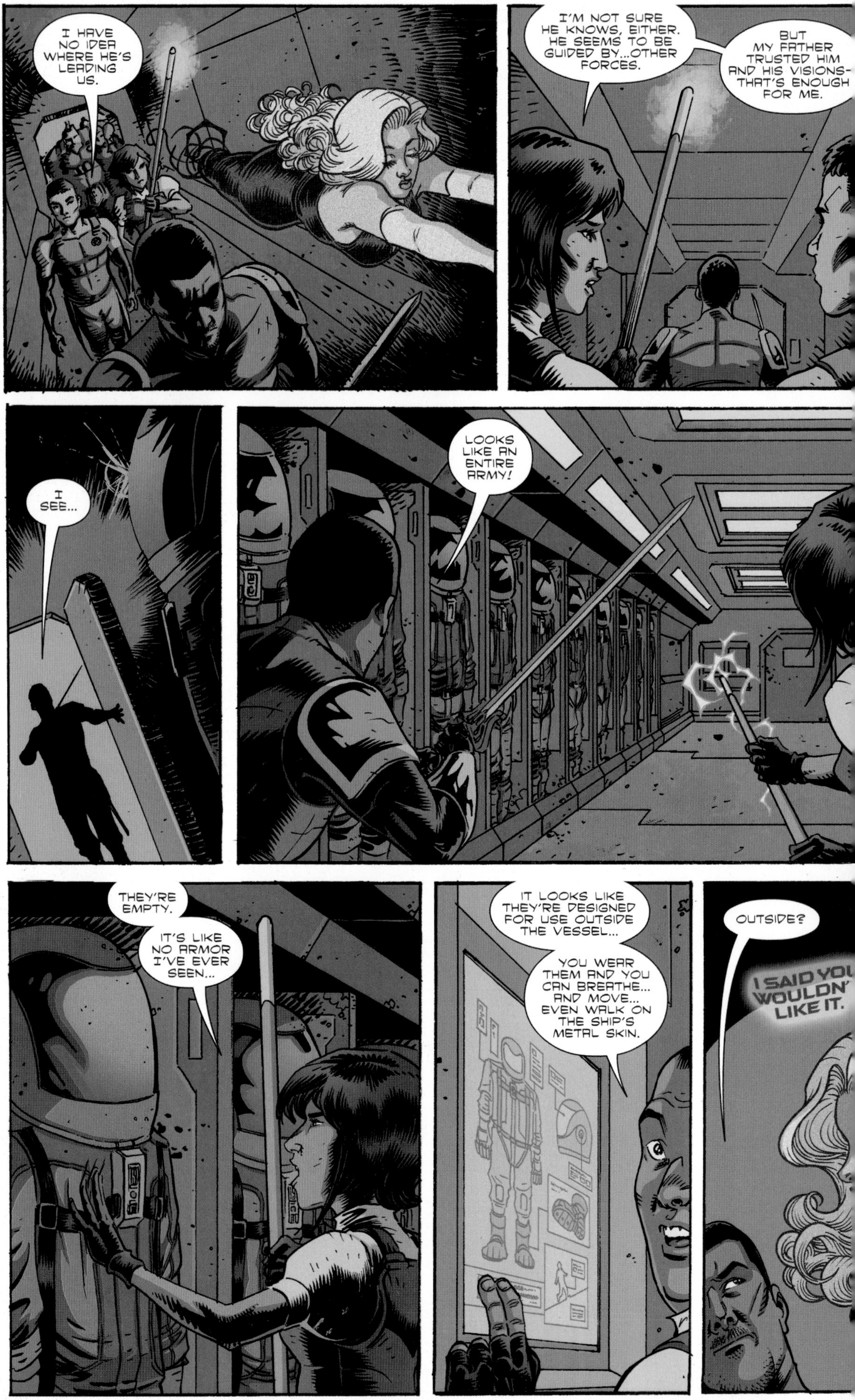
I HAVE NO IDEA WHERE HE'S LEADING US.
I'M NOT SURE HE KNOWS, EITHER. HE SEEMS TO BE GUIDED BY...OTHER FORCES.
BUT MY FATHER TRUSTED HIM AND HIS VISIONS-THAT'S ENOUGH FOR ME.
I SEE...
LOOKS LIKE AN ENTIRE ARMY!
THEY'RE EMPTY.
IT'S LIKE NO ARMOR I'VE EVER SEEN...
IT LOOKS LIKE THEY'RE DESIGNED FOR USE OUTSIDE THE VESSEL...
YOU WEAR THEM AND YOU CAN BREATHE... AND MOVE... EVEN WALK ON THE SHIP'S METAL SKIN.
OUTSIDE?
I SAID YOU WOULDN' LIKE IT.

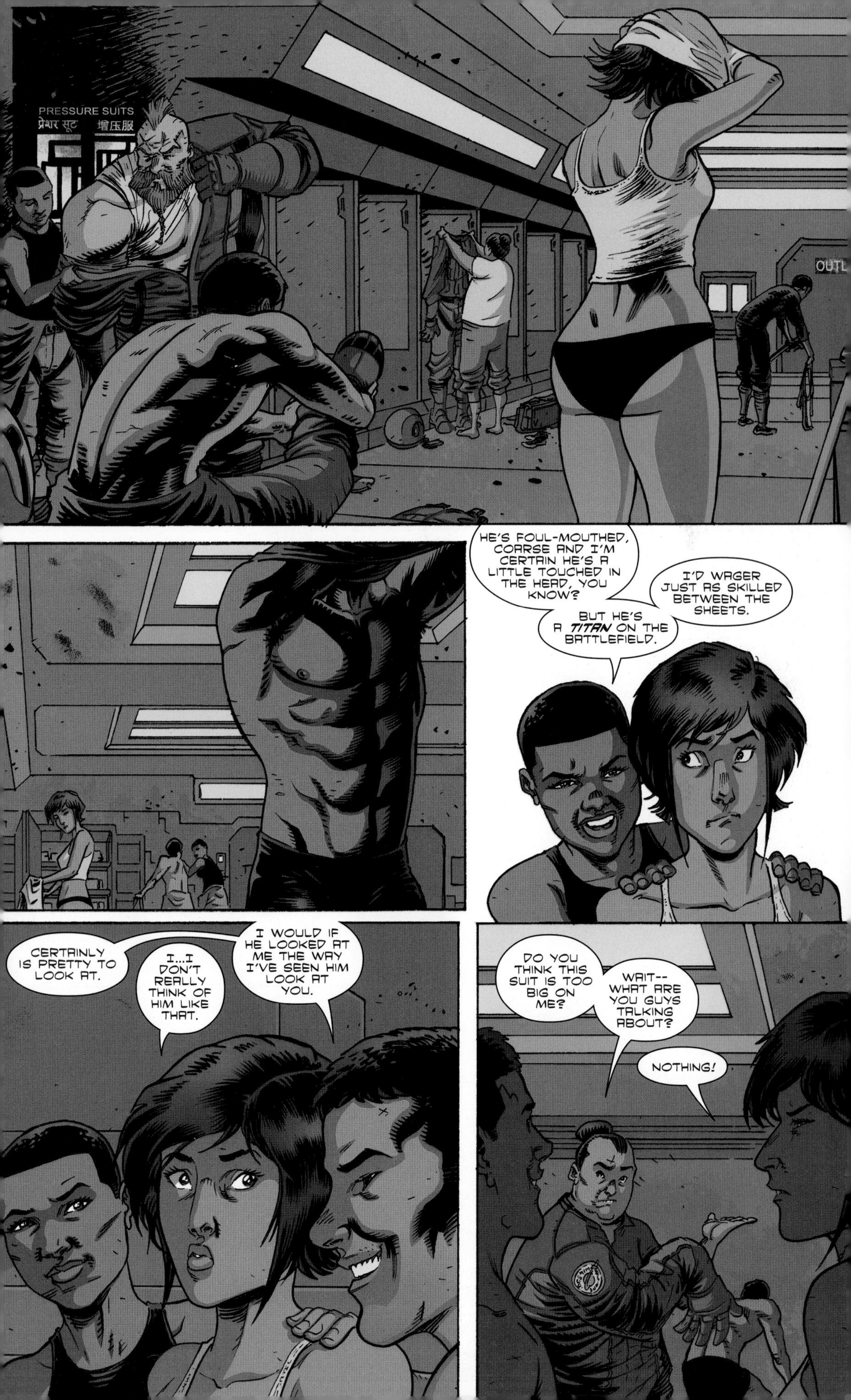
PRESSURE SUITS
प्रेशर सूट 增压服
OUTL
HE'S FOUL-MOUTHED, CORRSE AND I'M CERTAIN HE'S A LITTLE TOUCHED IN THE HEAD, YOU KNOW?
BUT HE'S A *TITAN* ON THE BATTLEFIELD.
I'D WAGER JUST AS SKILLED BETWEEN THE SHEETS.
CERTAINLY IS PRETTY TO LOOK AT.
I...I DON'T REALLY THINK OF HIM LIKE THAT.
I WOULD IF HE LOOKED AT ME THE WAY I'VE SEEN HIM LOOK AT YOU.
DO YOU THINK THIS SUIT IS TOO BIG ON ME?
WAIT-- WHAT ARE YOU GUYS TALKING ABOUT?
NOTHING!

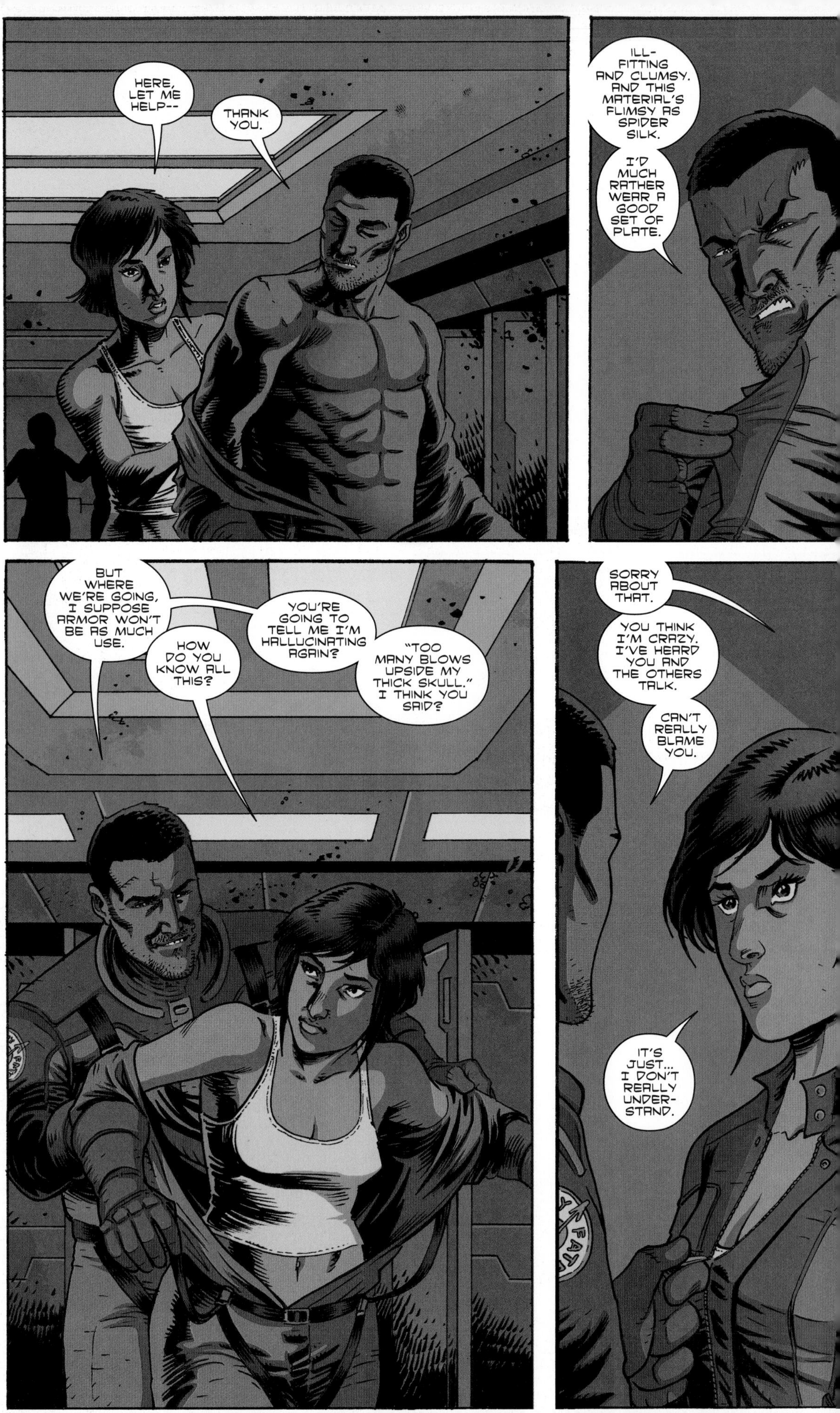
HERE, LET ME HELP--
THANK YOU.
ILL-FITTING AND CLUMSY. AND THIS MATERIAL'S FLIMSY AS SPIDER SILK.
I'D MUCH RATHER WEAR A GOOD SET OF PLATE.
BUT WHERE WE'RE GOING, I SUPPOSE ARMOR WON'T BE AS MUCH USE.
HOW DO YOU KNOW ALL THIS?
YOU'RE GOING TO TELL ME I'M HALLUCINATING AGAIN?
"TOO MANY BLOWS UPSIDE MY THICK SKULL." I THINK YOU SAID?
SORRY ABOUT THAT.
YOU THINK I'M CRAZY. I'VE HEARD YOU AND THE OTHERS TALK.
CAN'T REALLY BLAME YOU.
IT'S JUST... I DON'T REALLY UNDER-STAND.

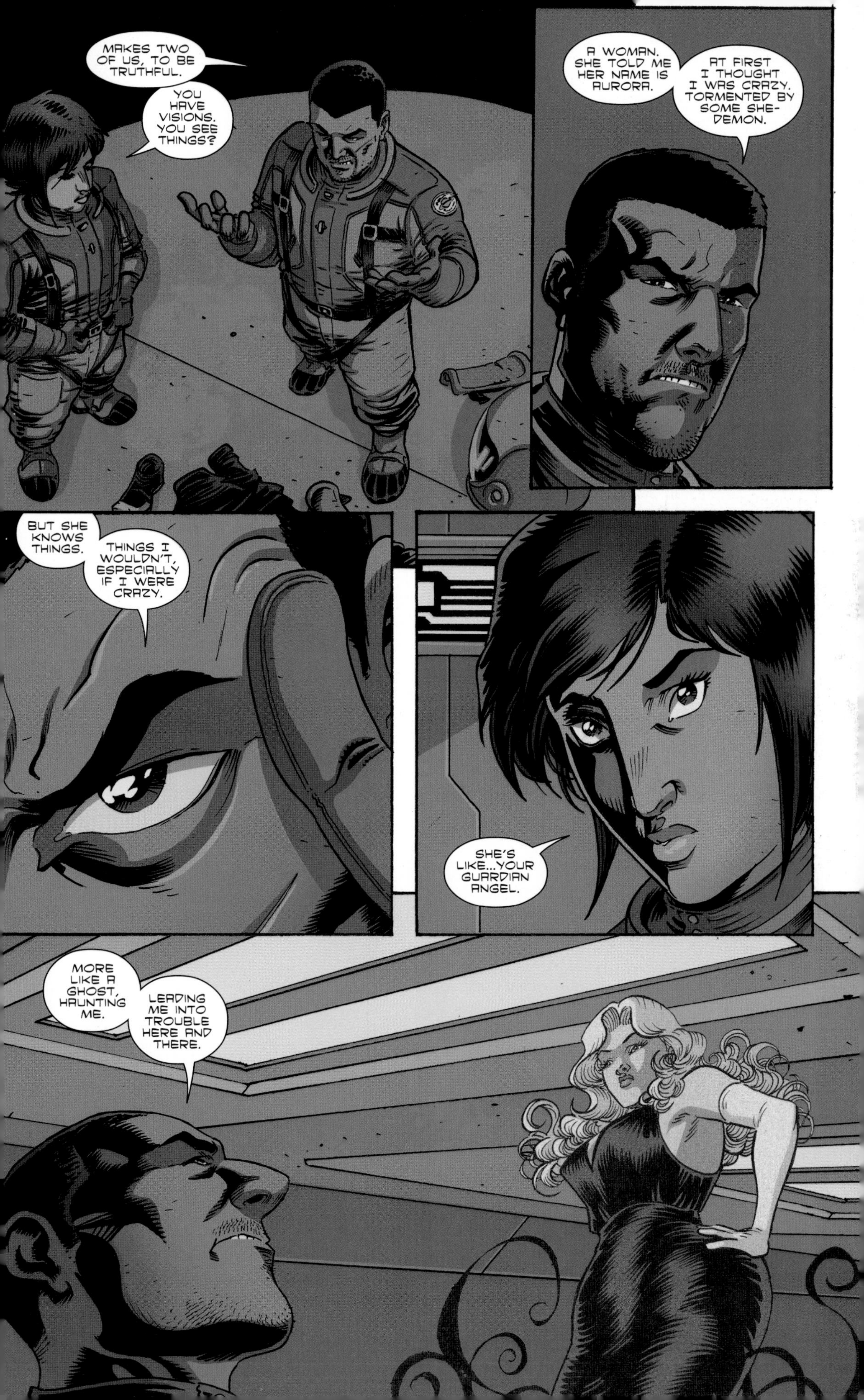
MAKES TWO OF US, TO BE TRUTHFUL.
YOU HAVE VISIONS. YOU SEE THINGS?
A WOMAN. SHE TOLD ME HER NAME IS AURORA.
AT FIRST I THOUGHT I WAS CRAZY. TORMENTED BY SOME SHE-DEMON.
BUT SHE KNOWS THINGS.
THINGS I WOULDN'T, ESPECIALLY IF I WERE CRAZY.
SHE'S LIKE...YOUR GUARDIAN ANGEL.
MORE LIKE A GHOST, HAUNTING ME.
LEADING ME INTO TROUBLE HERE AND THERE.

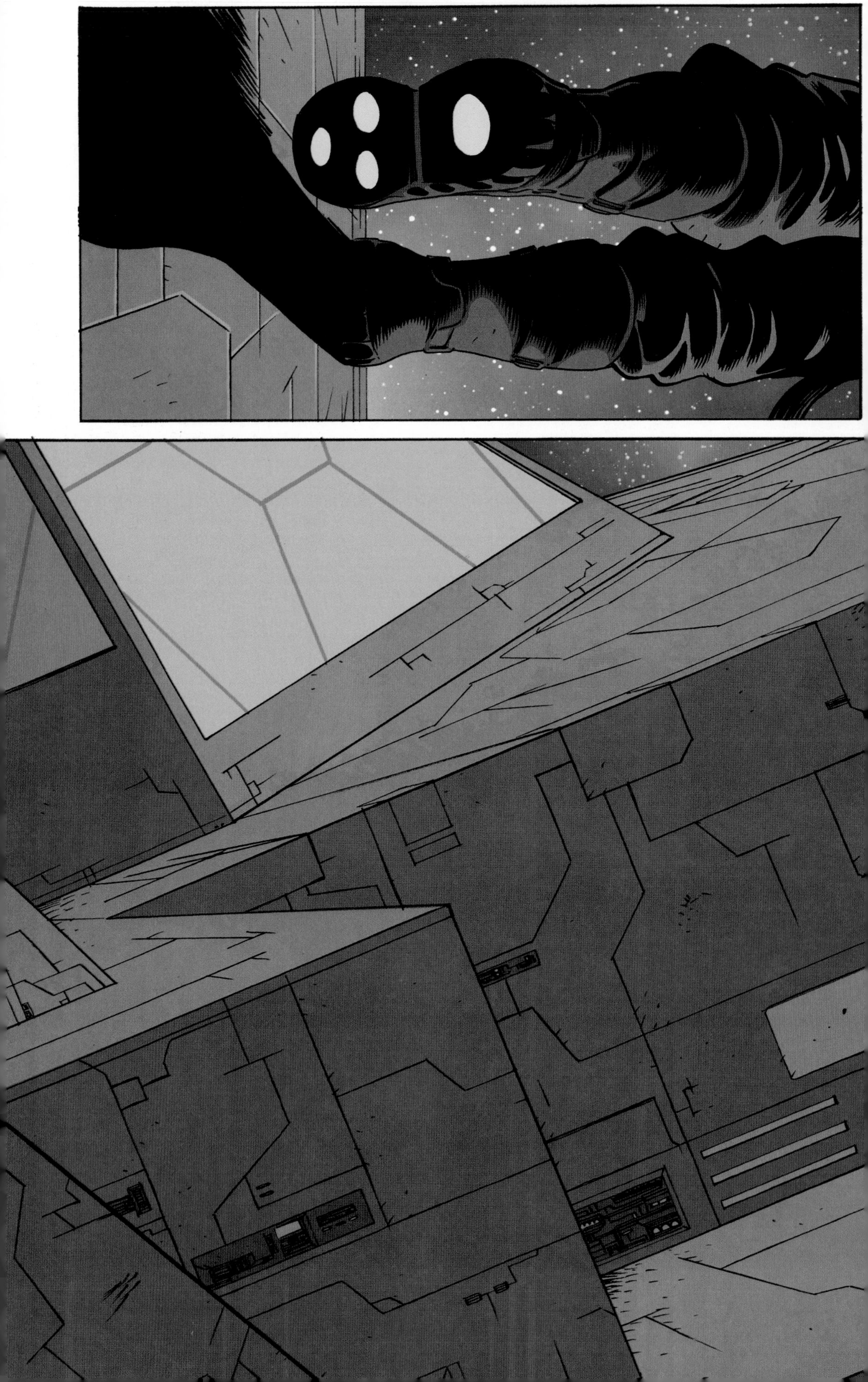

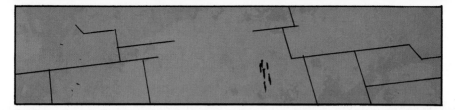

DO WE KNOW HOW MUCH FURTHER IT IS, REYN?

THERE SHOULD BE A WAY BACK IN...

...JUST AHEAD.

THAT'S AN INACTIVE EXHAUST PORT. YOU'LL BE ABLE TO GET BACK ABOARD THROUGH THERE.

THE VENN DON'T KNOW ABOUT IT, AND IT SHOULD EXIT SOMEWHERE IN THE BARRENS.

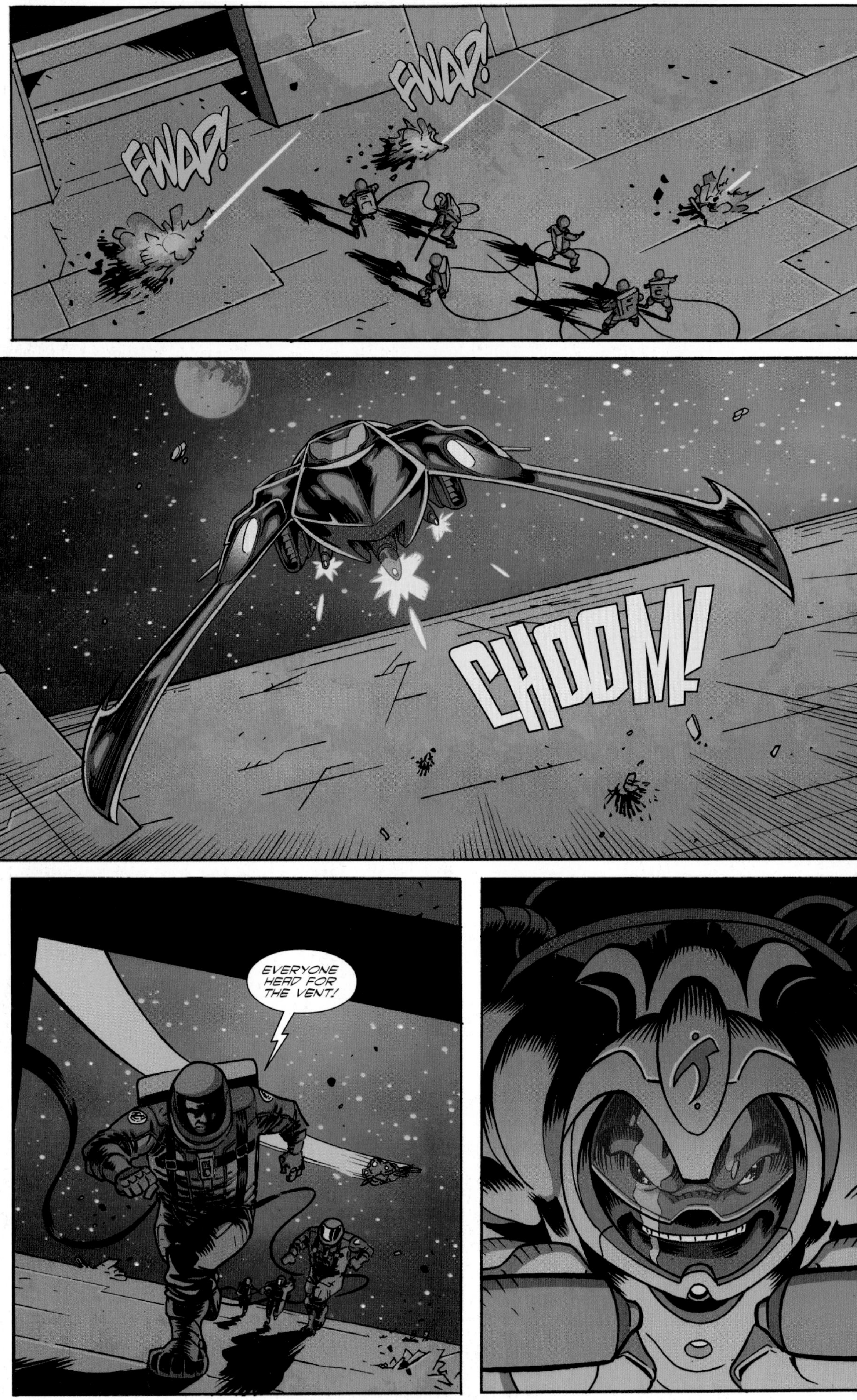
FWAP!
FWAP!
CHOOM!
EVERYONE HEAD FOR THE VENT!

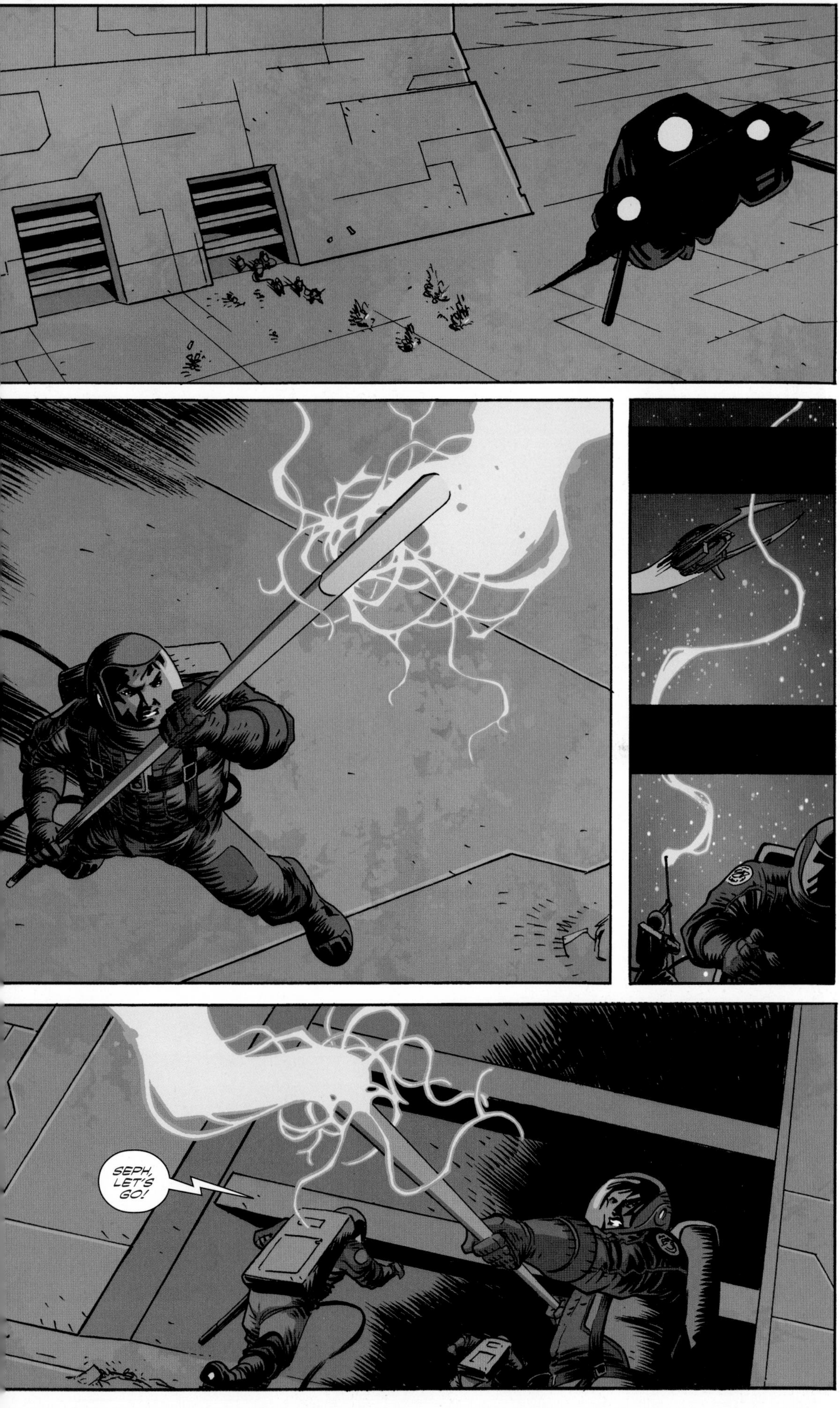
SEPH, LET'S GO!

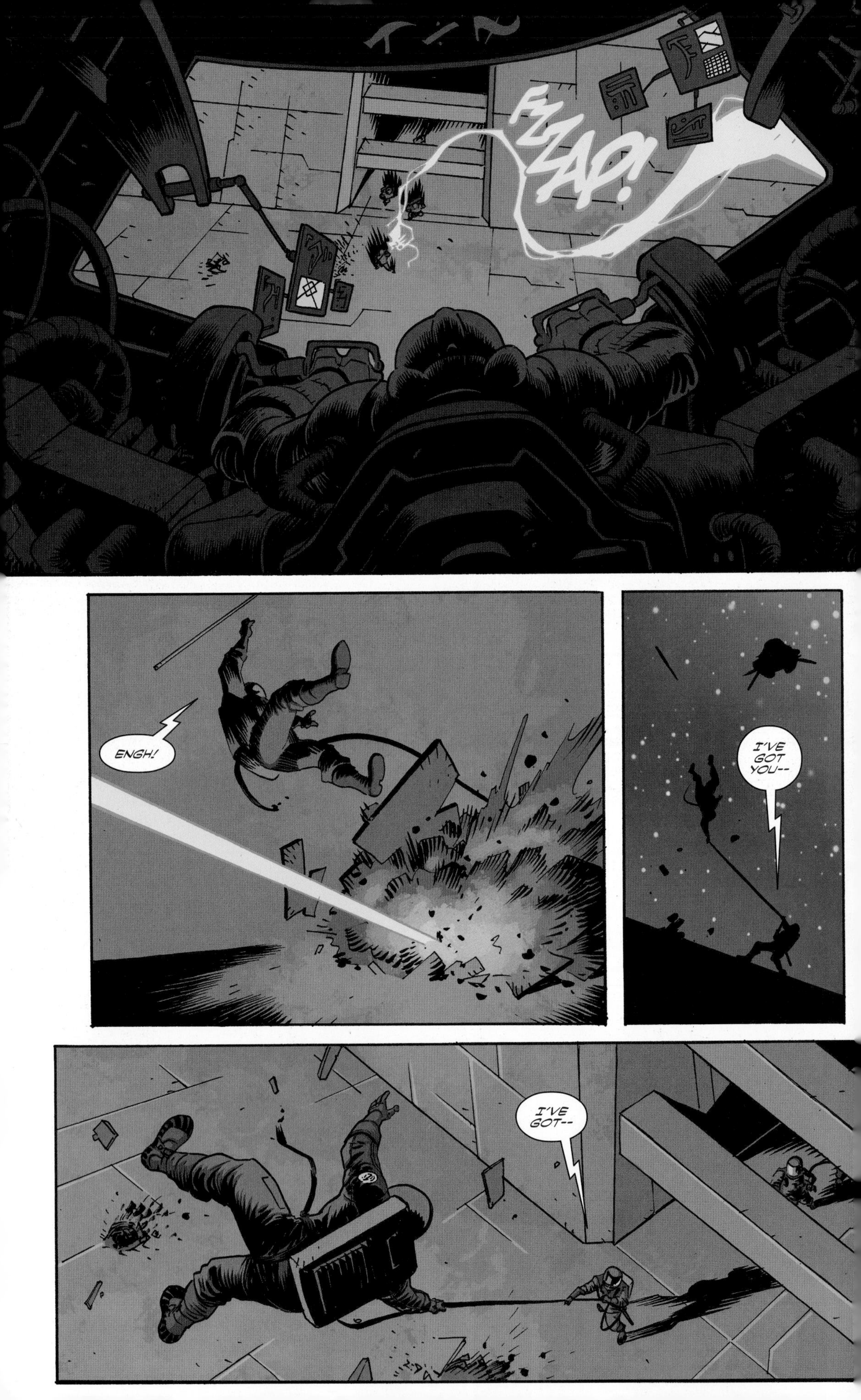
FZZZAP!
ENGH!
I'VE GOT YOU--
I'VE GOT--

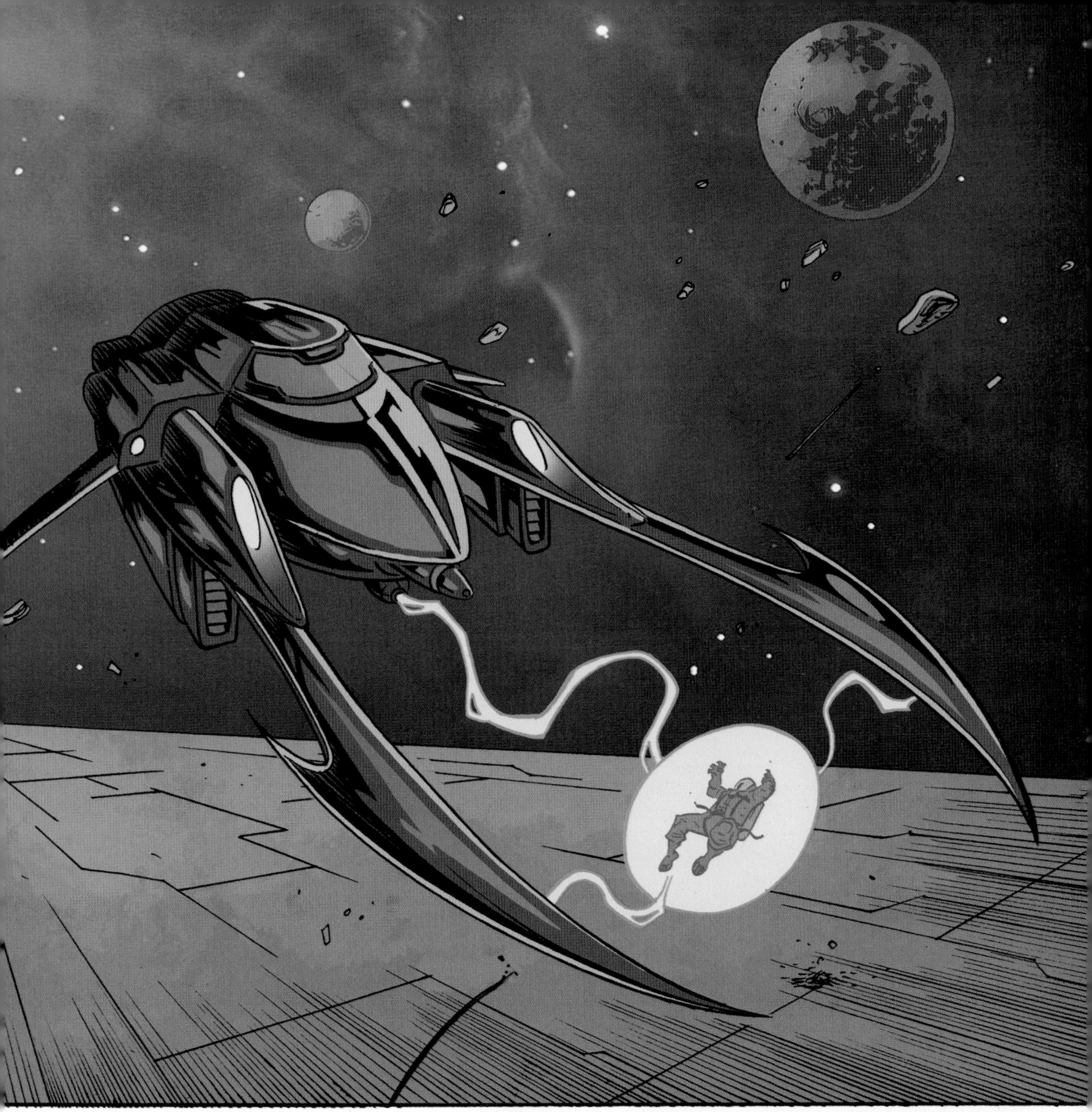

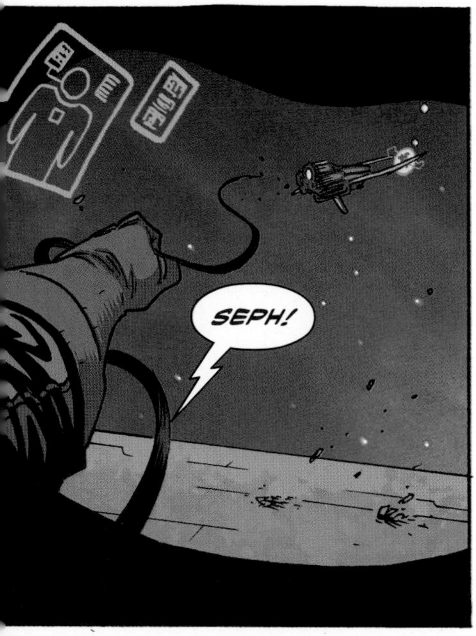
SEPH!

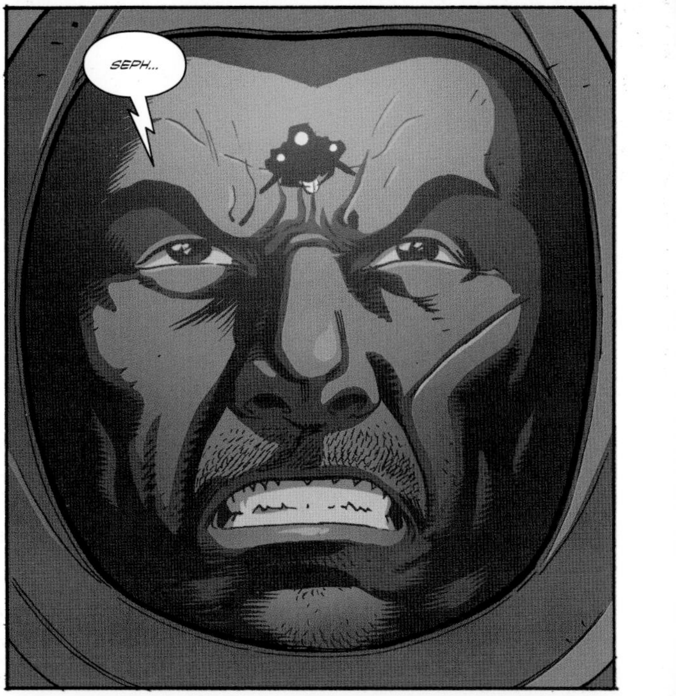
SEPH...

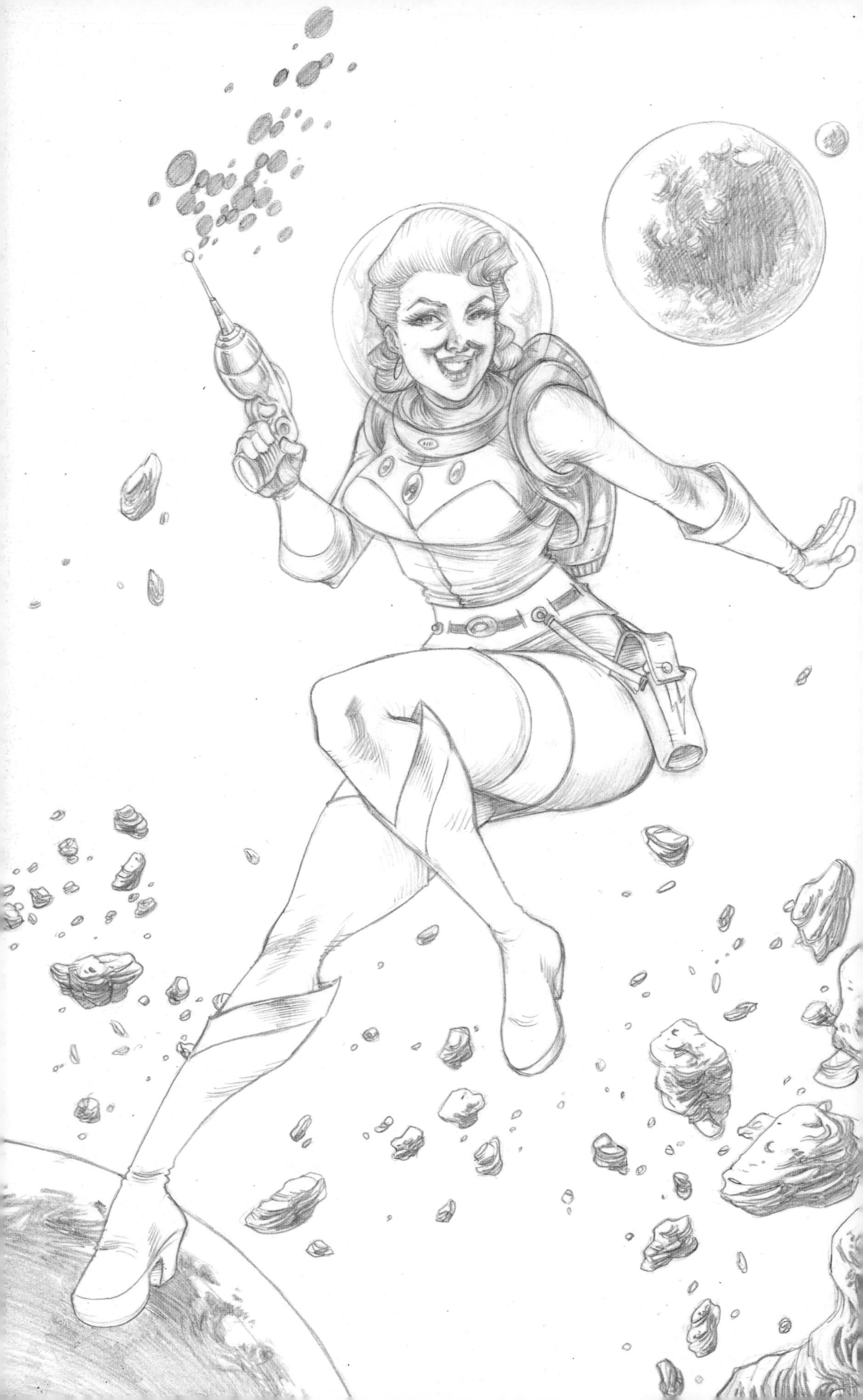

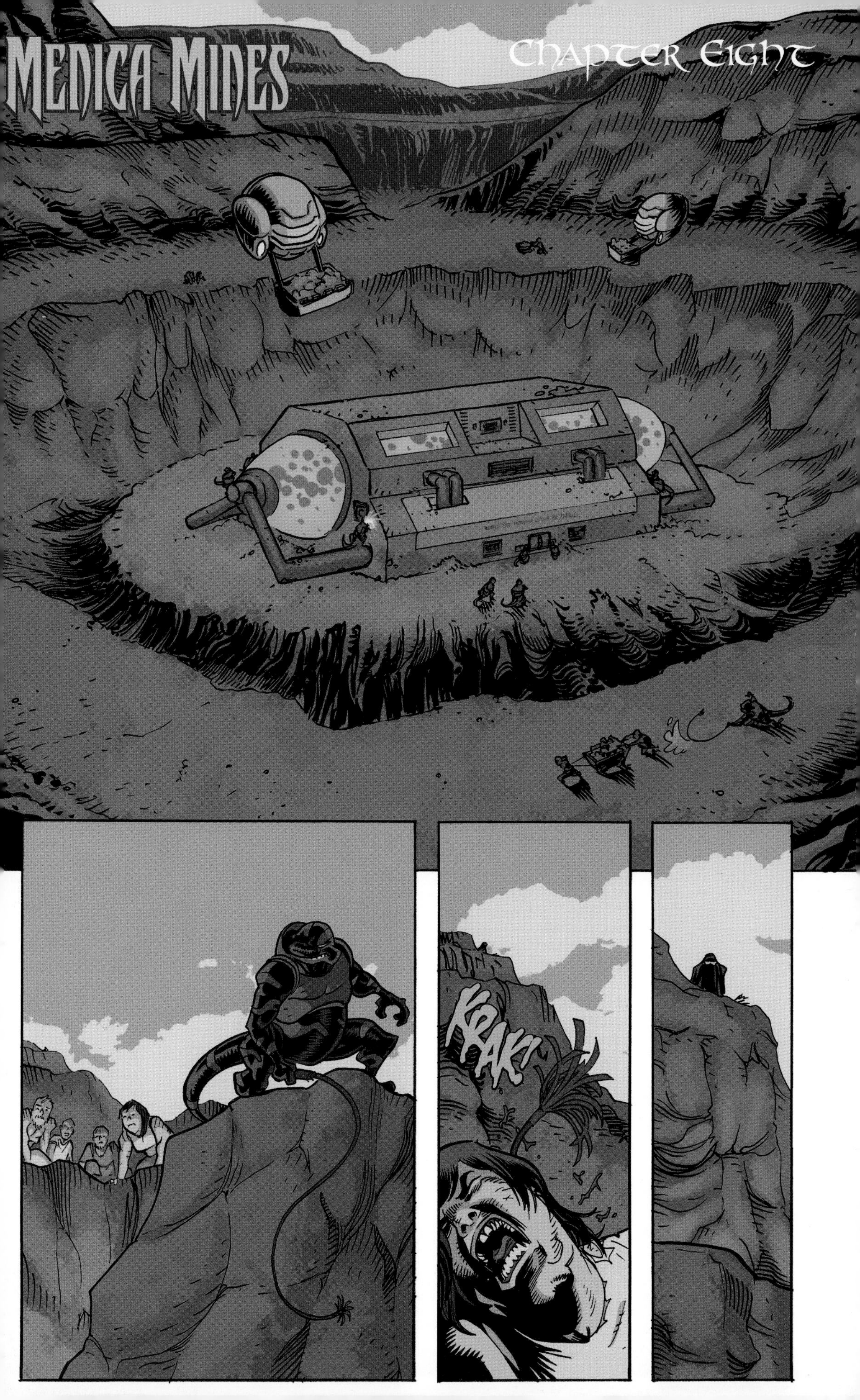
MENICA MINES
CHAPTER EIGHT
KRAK!

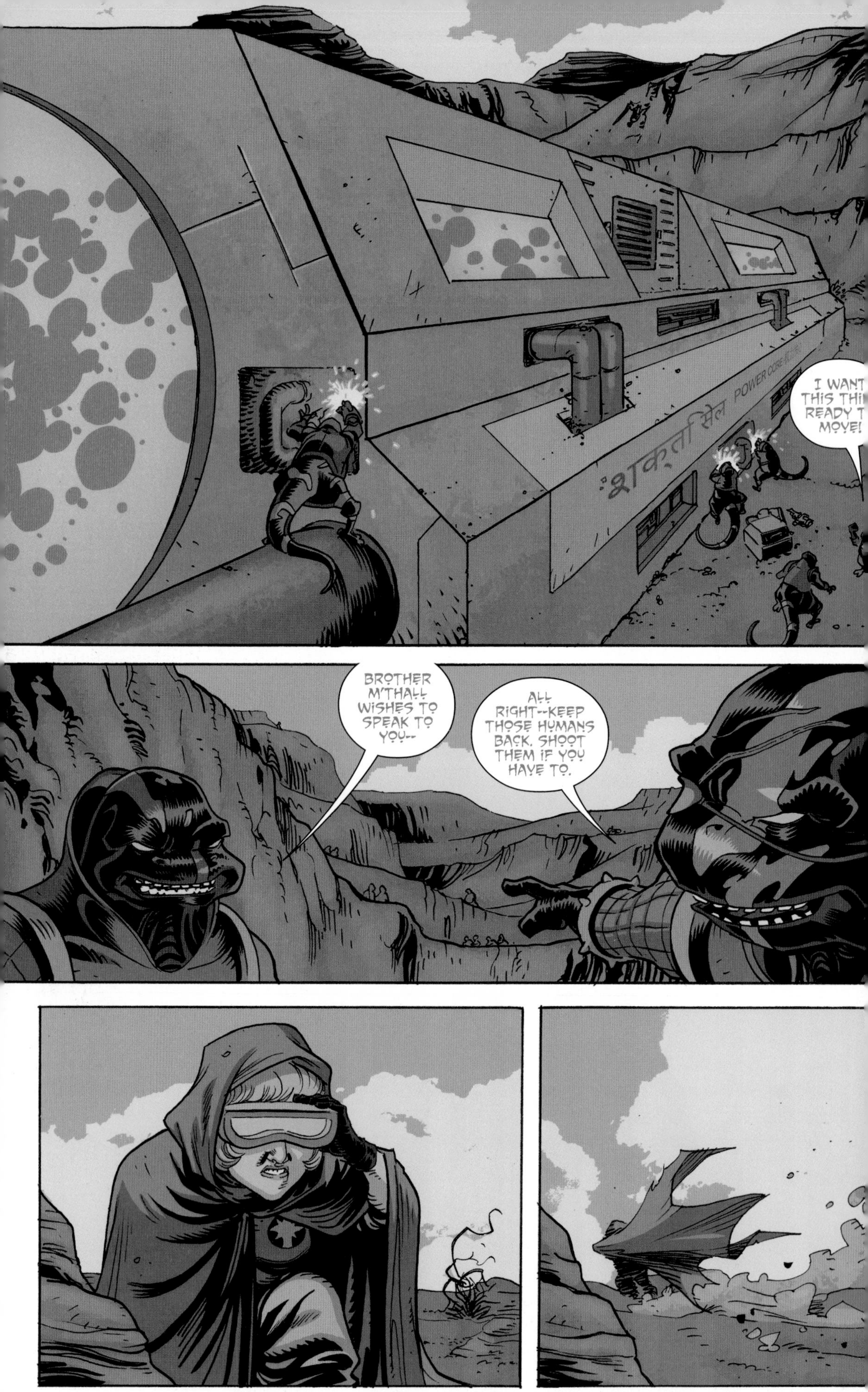
POWER CORE
I WANT THIS THI READY T MOVE!
BROTHER M'THALL WISHES TO SPEAK TO YOU--
ALL RIGHT--KEEP THOSE HUMANS BACK. SHOOT THEM IF YOU HAVE TO.

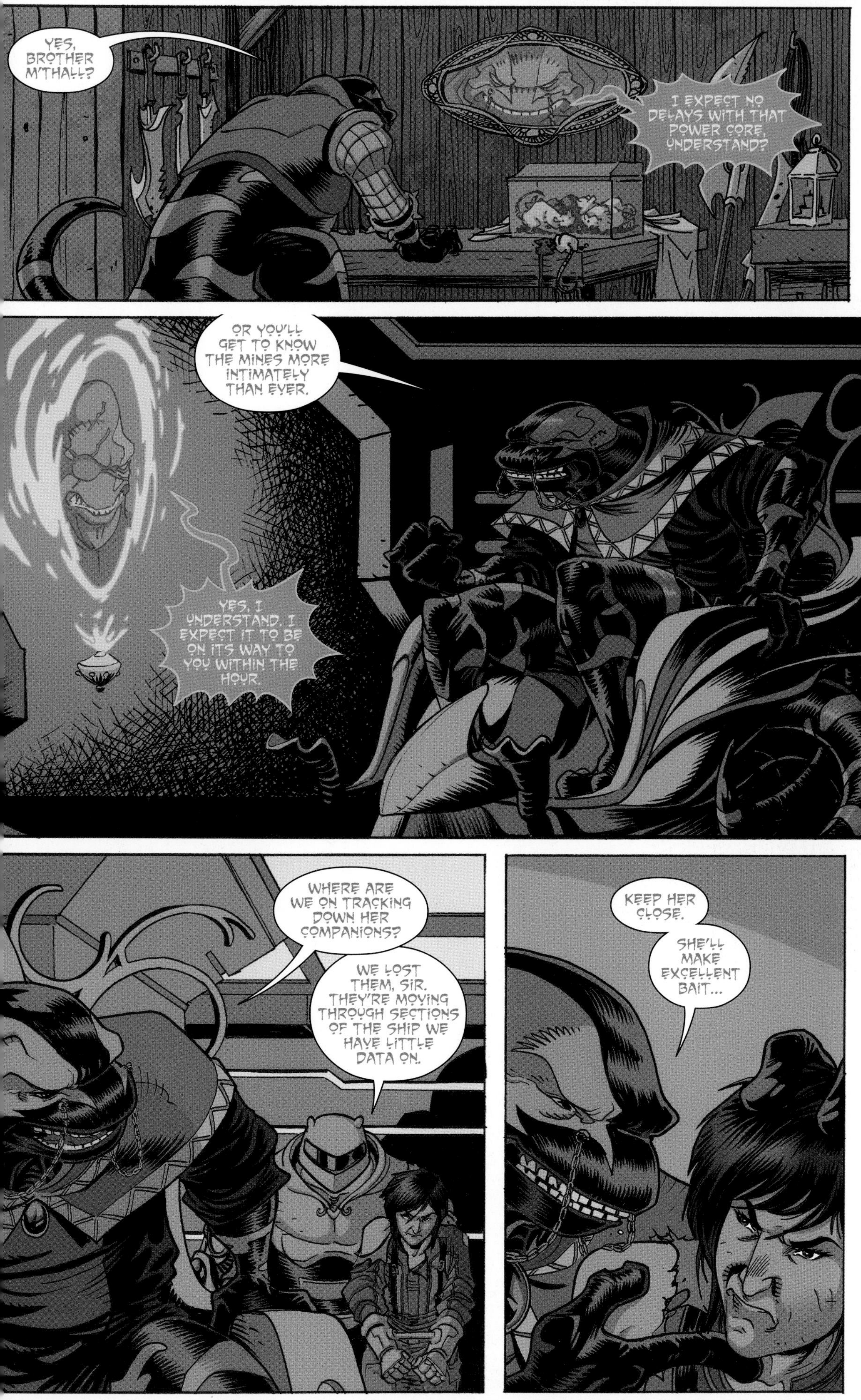
YES, BROTHER M'THALL?
I EXPECT NO DELAYS WITH THAT POWER CORE, UNDERSTAND?
OR YOU'LL GET TO KNOW THE MINES MORE INTIMATELY THAN EVER.
YES, I UNDERSTAND. I EXPECT IT TO BE ON ITS WAY TO YOU WITHIN THE HOUR.
WHERE ARE WE ON TRACKING DOWN HER COMPANIONS?
WE LOST THEM, SIR. THEY'RE MOVING THROUGH SECTIONS OF THE SHIP WE HAVE LITTLE DATA ON.
KEEP HER CLOSE.
SHE'LL MAKE EXCELLENT BAIT...

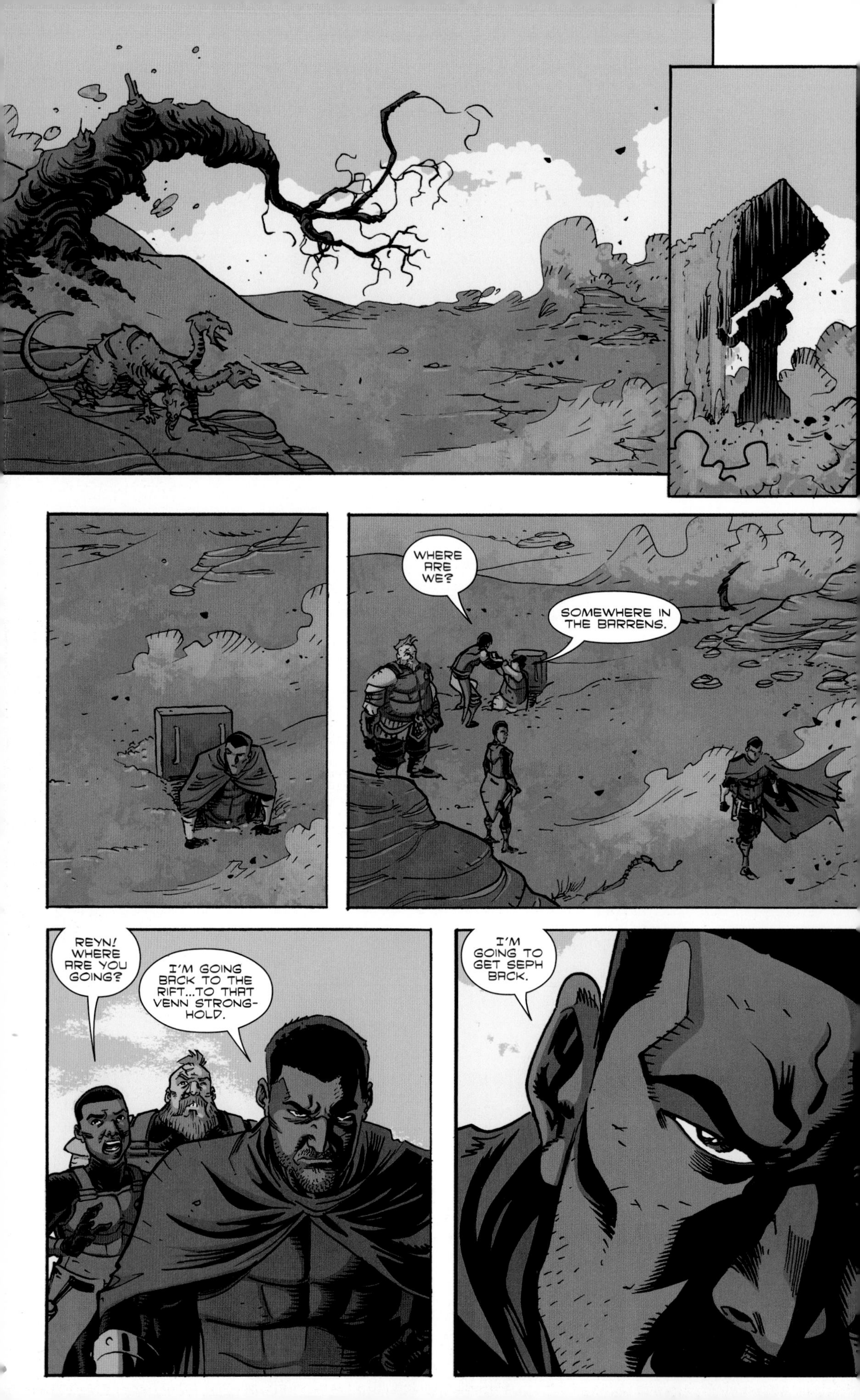
WHERE ARE WE?
SOMEWHERE IN THE BARRENS.
REYN! WHERE ARE YOU GOING?
I'M GOING BACK TO THE RIFT...TO THAT VENN STRONG-HOLD.
I'M GOING TO GET SEPH BACK.

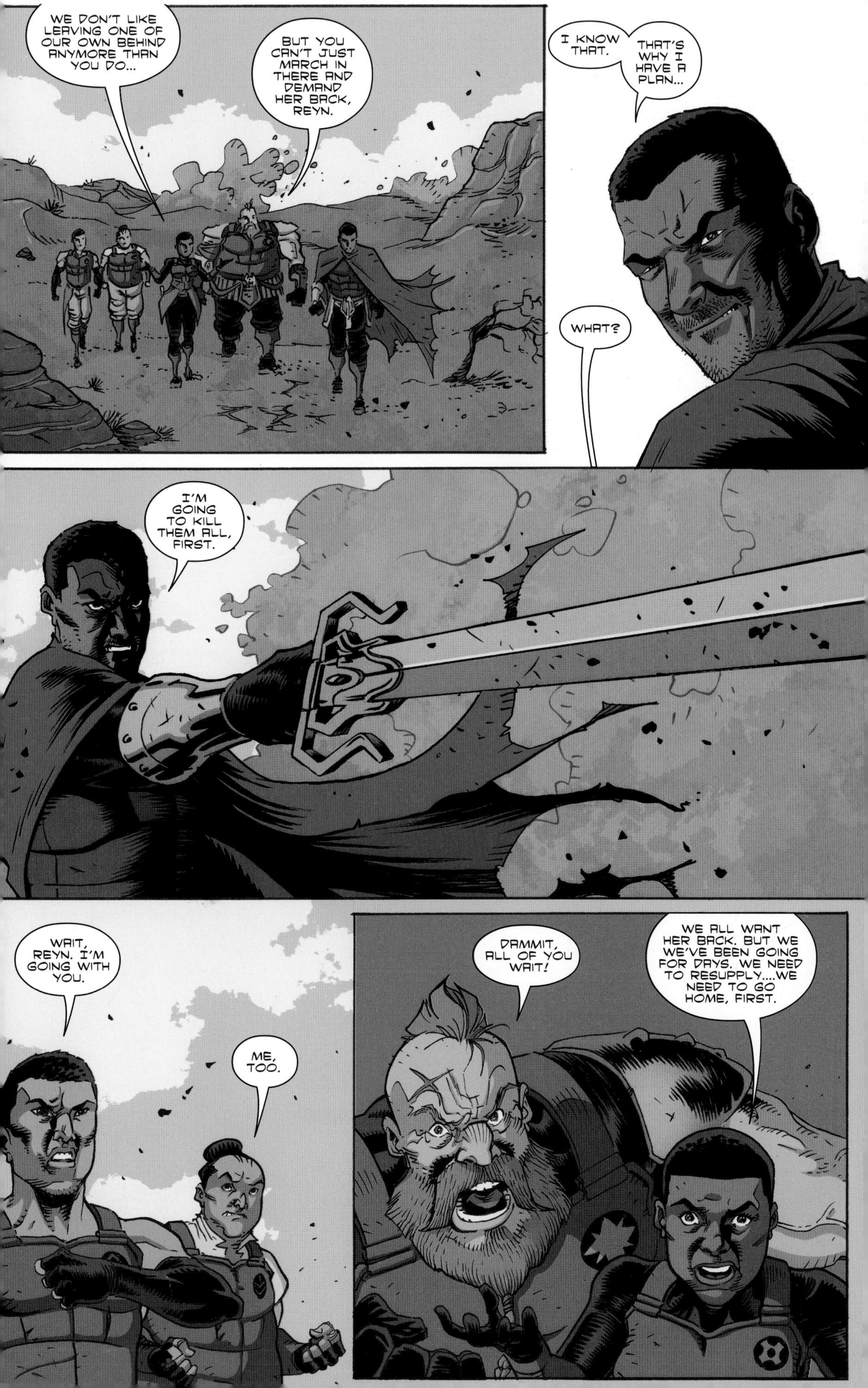
WE DON'T LIKE LEAVING ONE OF OUR OWN BEHIND ANYMORE THAN YOU DO...
BUT YOU CAN'T JUST MARCH IN THERE AND DEMAND HER BACK, REYN.
I KNOW THAT.
THAT'S WHY I HAVE A PLAN...
WHAT?
I'M GOING TO KILL THEM ALL, FIRST.
WAIT, REYN. I'M GOING WITH YOU.
ME, TOO.
DAMMIT, ALL OF YOU WAIT!
WE ALL WANT HER BACK. BUT WE WE'VE BEEN GOING FOR DAYS. WE NEED TO RESUPPLY....WE NEED TO GO HOME, FIRST.

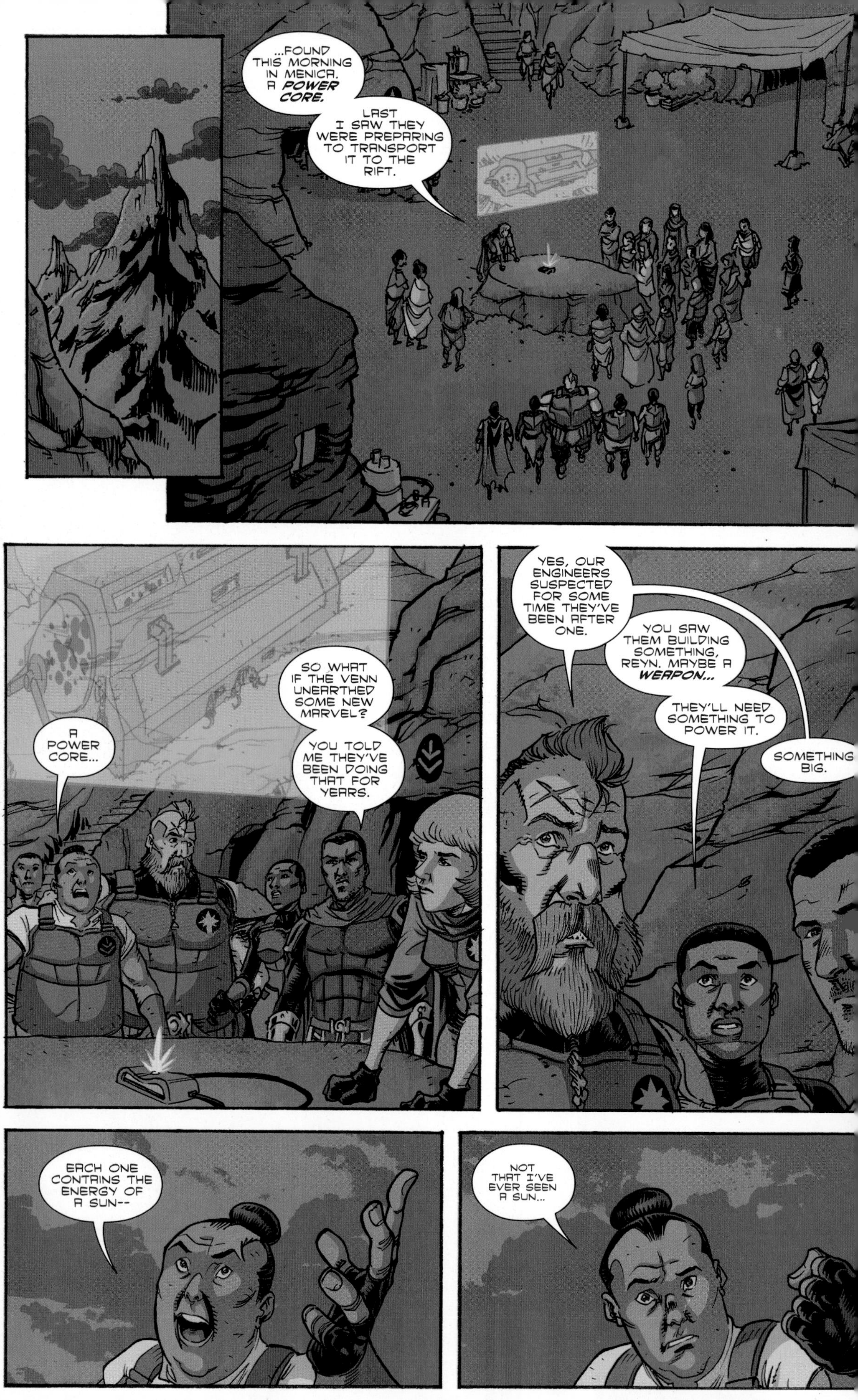
...FOUND THIS MORNING IN MENICA. A POWER CORE.
LAST I SAW THEY WERE PREPARING TO TRANSPORT IT TO THE RIFT.
A POWER CORE...
SO WHAT IF THE VENN UNEARTHED SOME NEW MARVEL?
YOU TOLD ME THEY'VE BEEN DOING THAT FOR YEARS.
YES, OUR ENGINEERS SUSPECTED FOR SOME TIME THEY'VE BEEN AFTER ONE.
YOU SAW THEM BUILDING SOMETHING, REYN. MAYBE A WEAPON...
THEY'LL NEED SOMETHING TO POWER IT.
SOMETHING BIG.
EACH ONE CONTAINS THE ENERGY OF A SUN--
NOT THAT I'VE EVER SEEN A SUN...

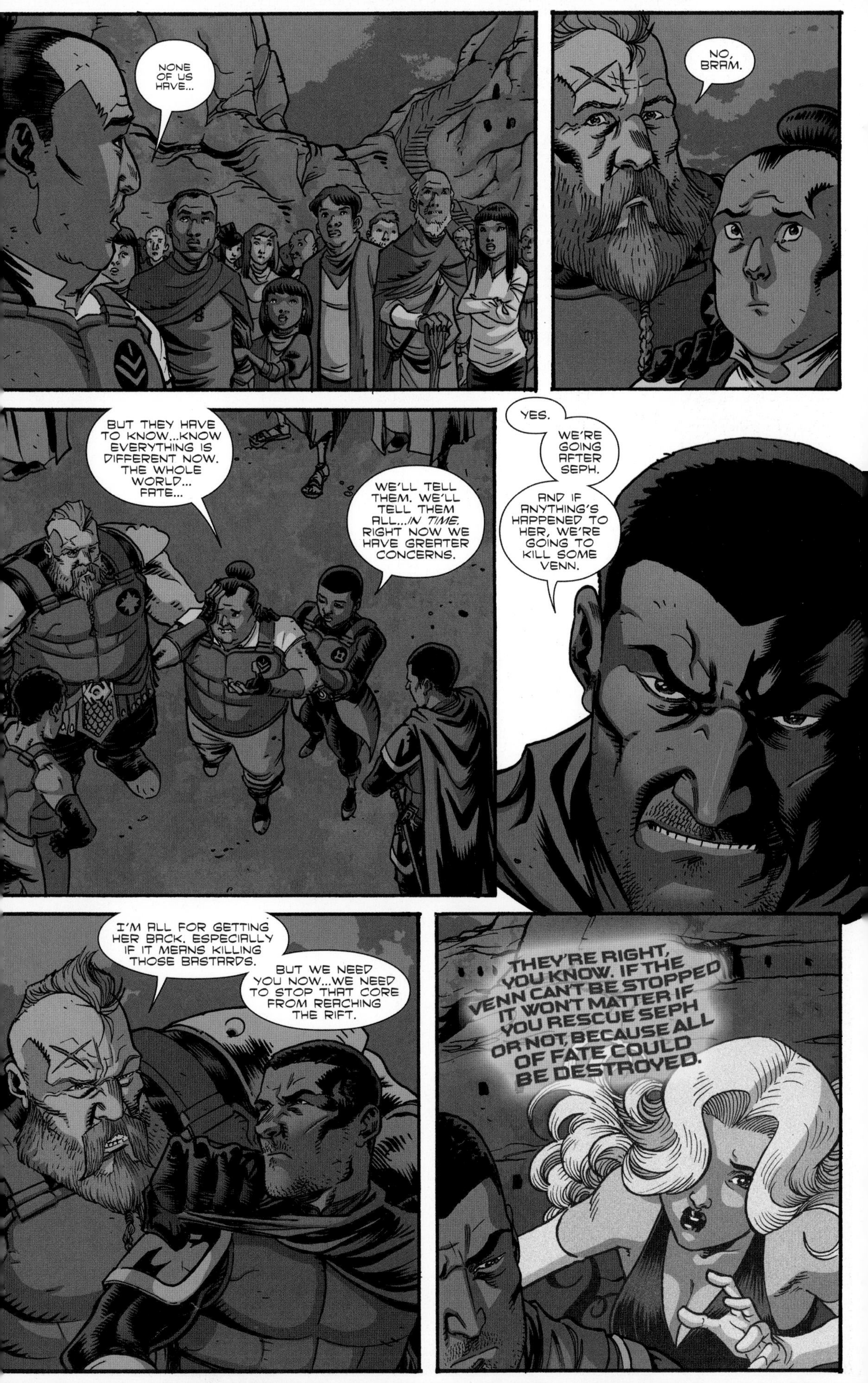
NONE OF US HAVE...
NO, BRAM.
BUT THEY HAVE TO KNOW...KNOW EVERYTHING IS DIFFERENT NOW. THE WHOLE WORLD... FATE...
WE'LL TELL THEM. WE'LL TELL THEM ALL...*IN TIME.* RIGHT NOW WE HAVE GREATER CONCERNS.
YES.
WE'RE GOING AFTER SEPH.
AND IF ANYTHING'S HAPPENED TO HER, WE'RE GOING TO KILL SOME VENN.
I'M ALL FOR GETTING HER BACK. ESPECIALLY IF IT MEANS KILLING THOSE BASTARDS.
BUT WE NEED YOU NOW...WE NEED TO STOP THAT CORE FROM REACHING THE RIFT.
THEY'RE RIGHT, YOU KNOW. IF THE VENN CAN'T BE STOPPED IT WON'T MATTER IF YOU RESCUE SEPH OR NOT, BECAUSE ALL OF FATE COULD BE DESTROYED.

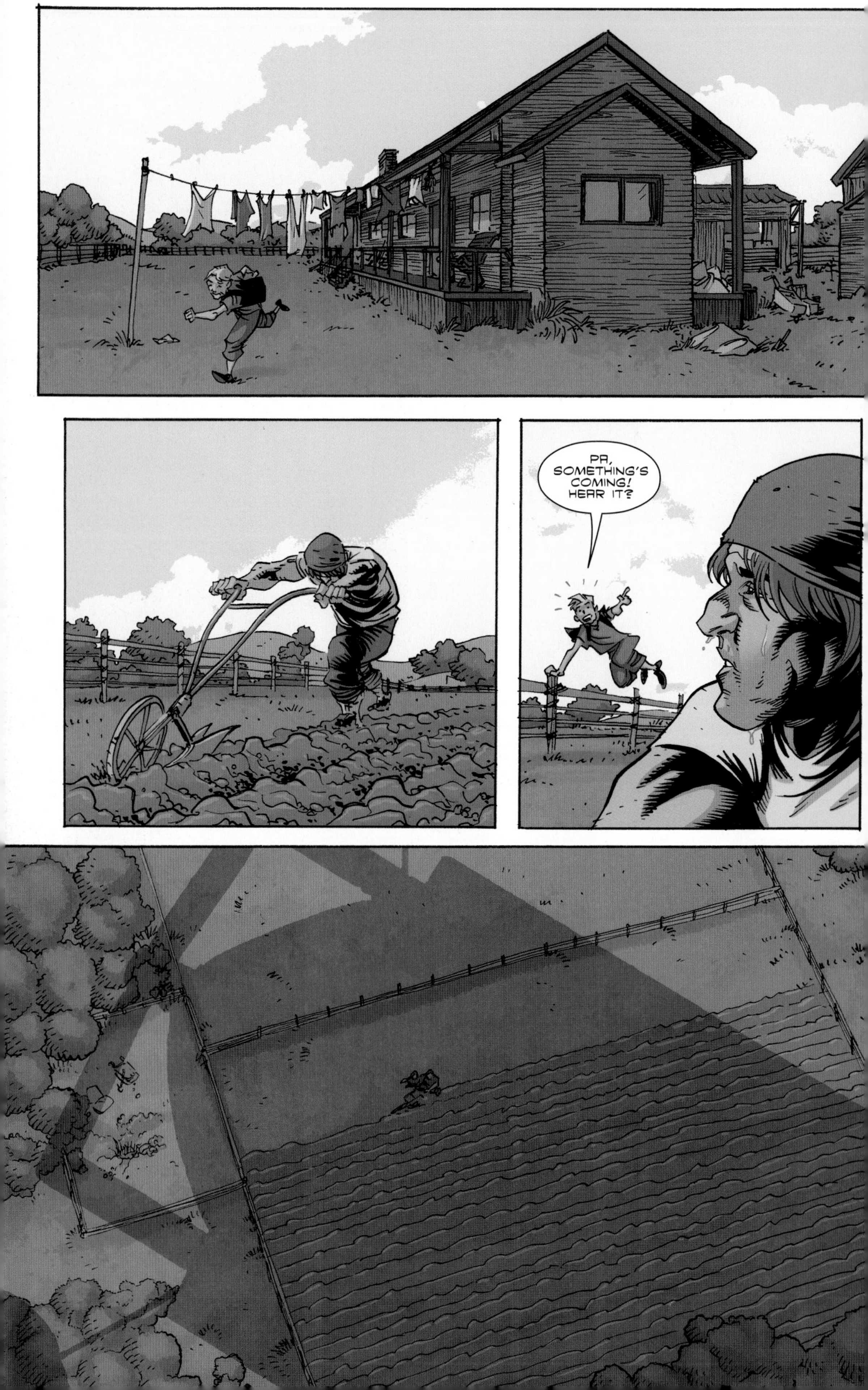
PA, SOMETHING'S COMING! HEAR IT?

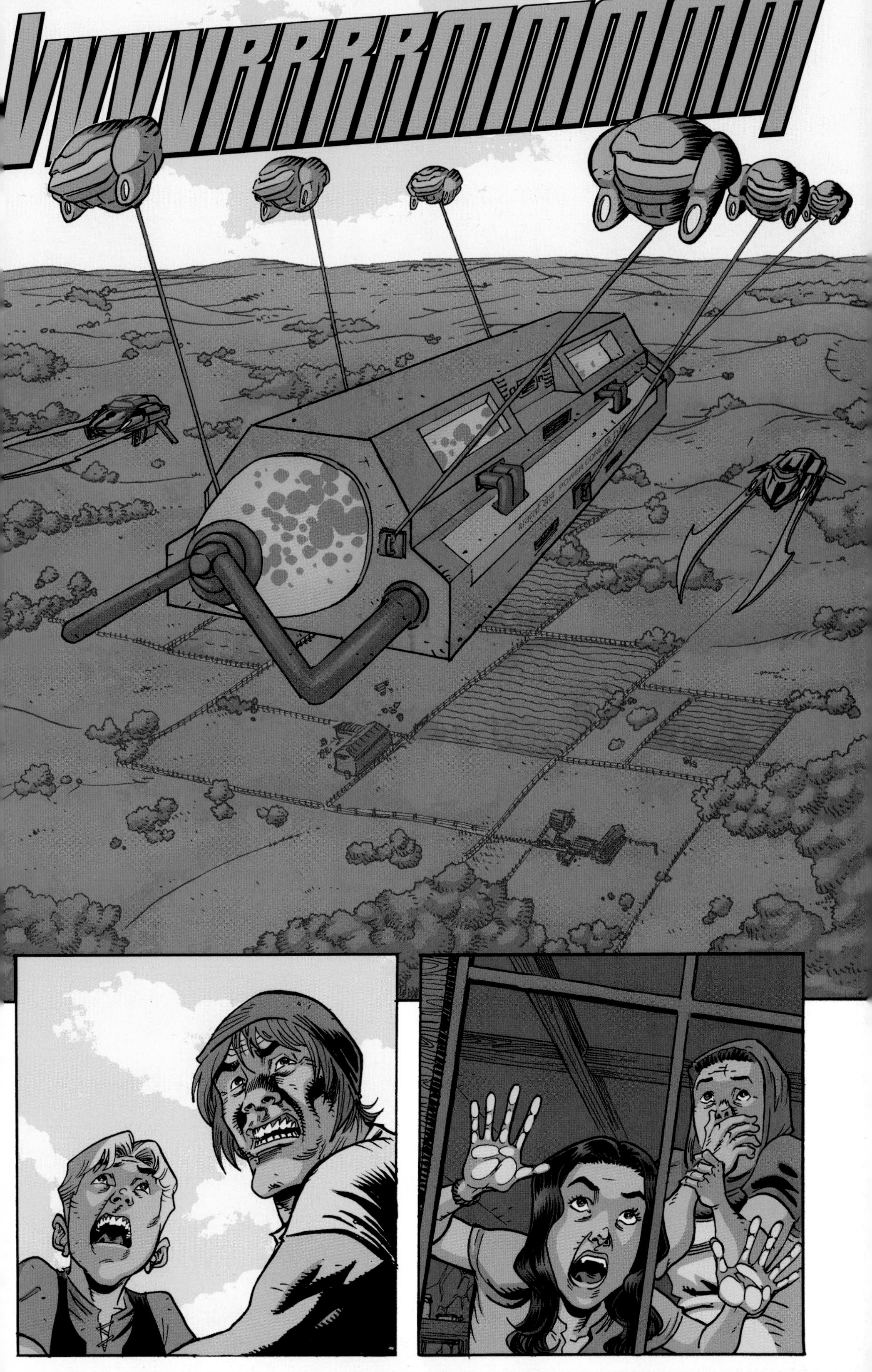
VVVVRRRRMMMMM
POWER CORE

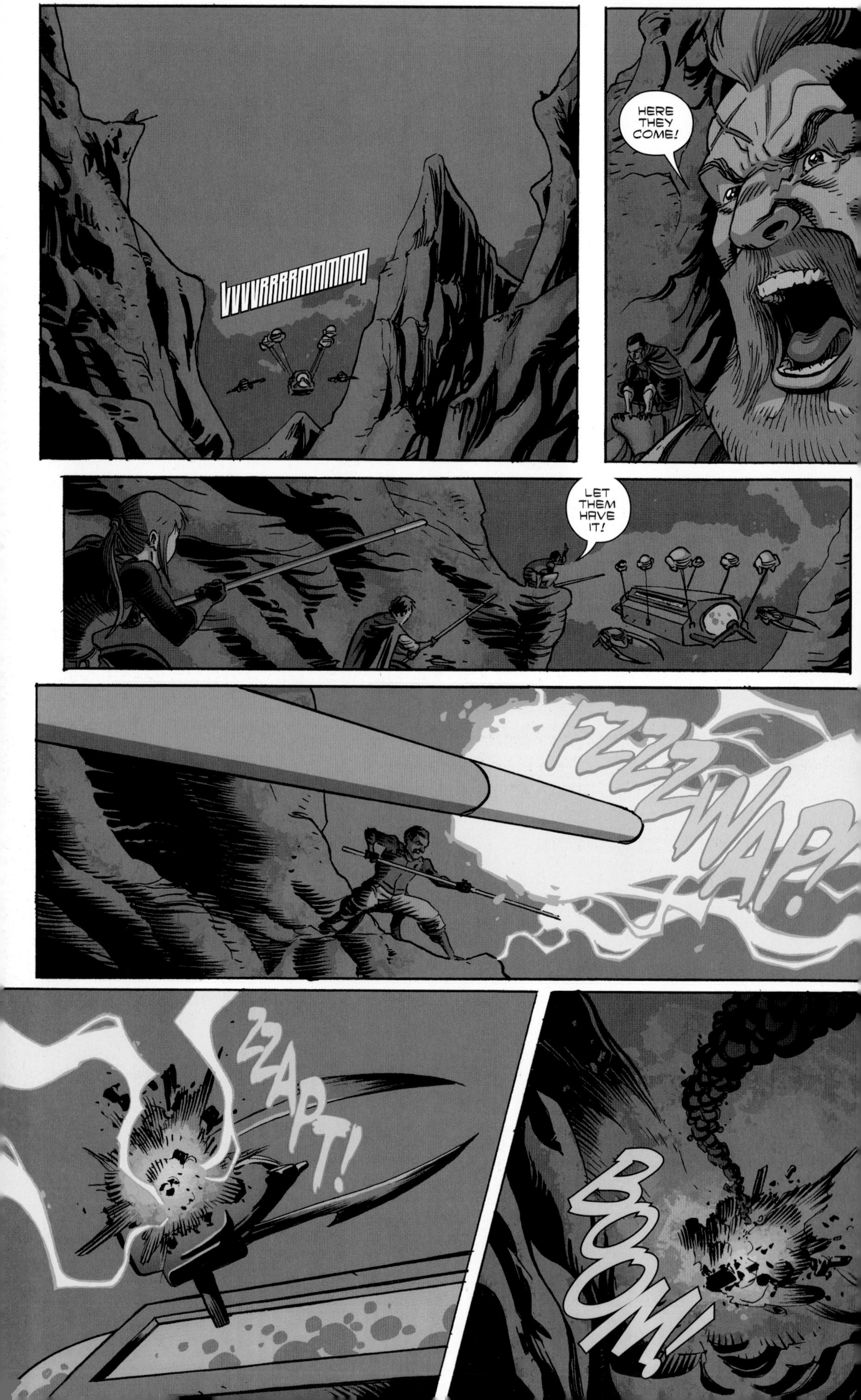
VVVVRRRRMMMMMM
HERE THEY COME!
LET THEM HAVE IT!
FZZZWAP!!
ZZAPT!
BOOOM!

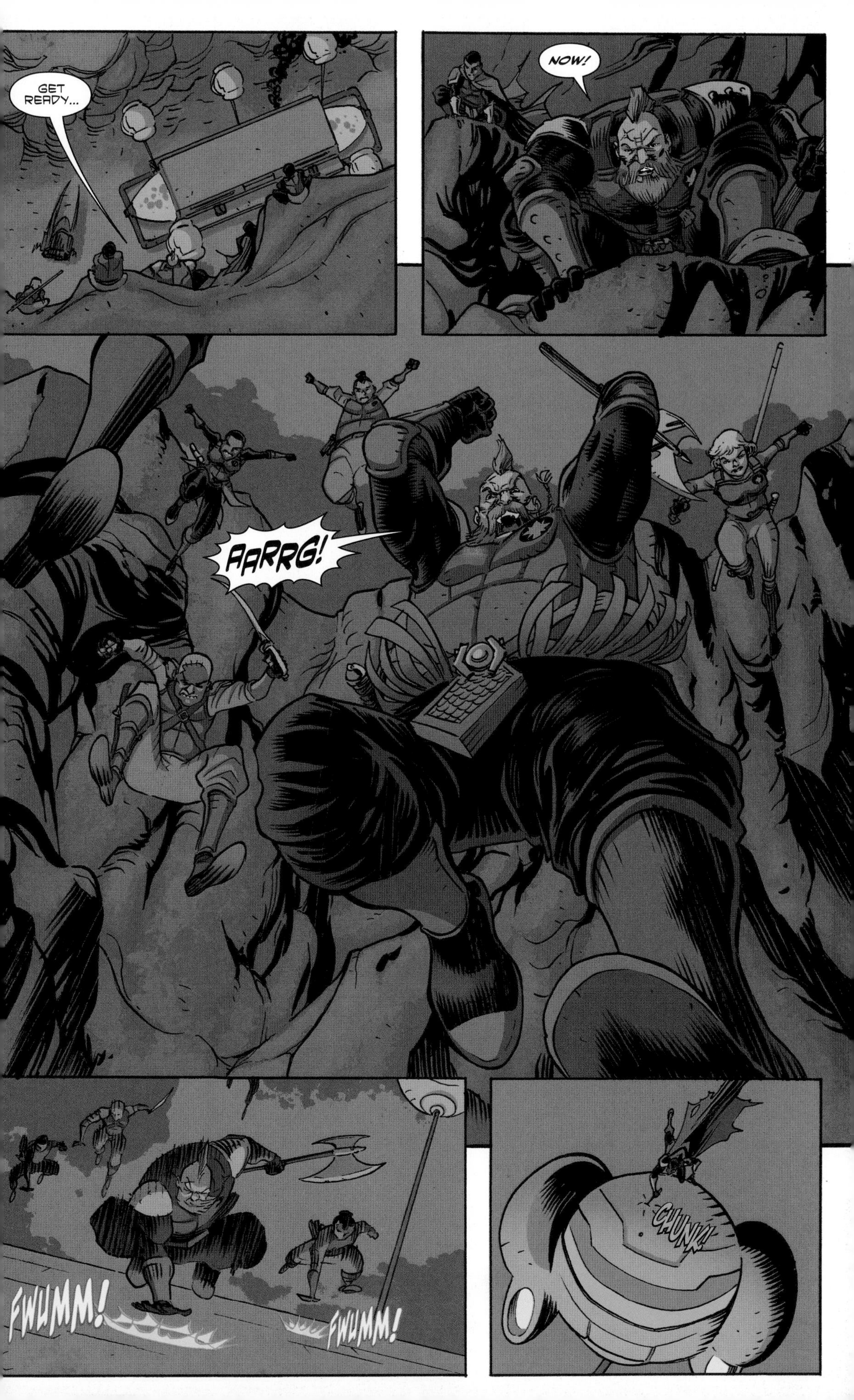
GET READY...
NOW!
AARRG!
FWUMM!
FWUMM!
CHUNK!

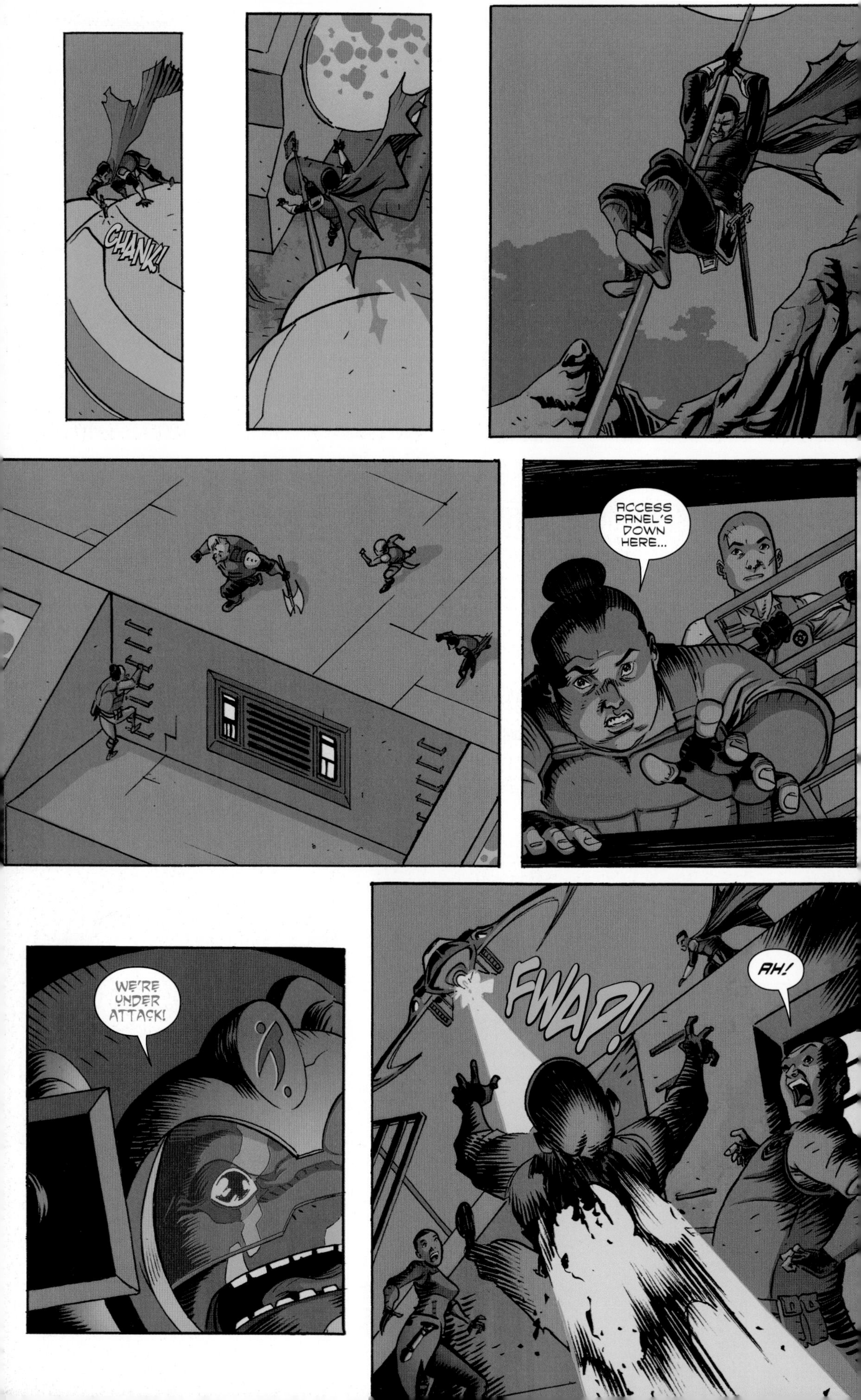

CHANK!
ACCESS PANEL'S DOWN HERE...
WE'RE UNDER ATTACK!
FWAP!
AH!

YOU IDIOT! DON'T OPEN FIRE OR YOU'LL DAMAGE THE CELL!

I'D MAKE THIS FAST...

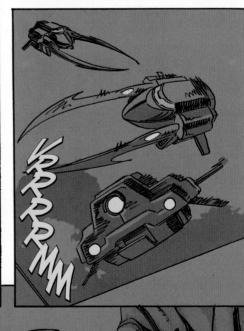

VRRRRMM

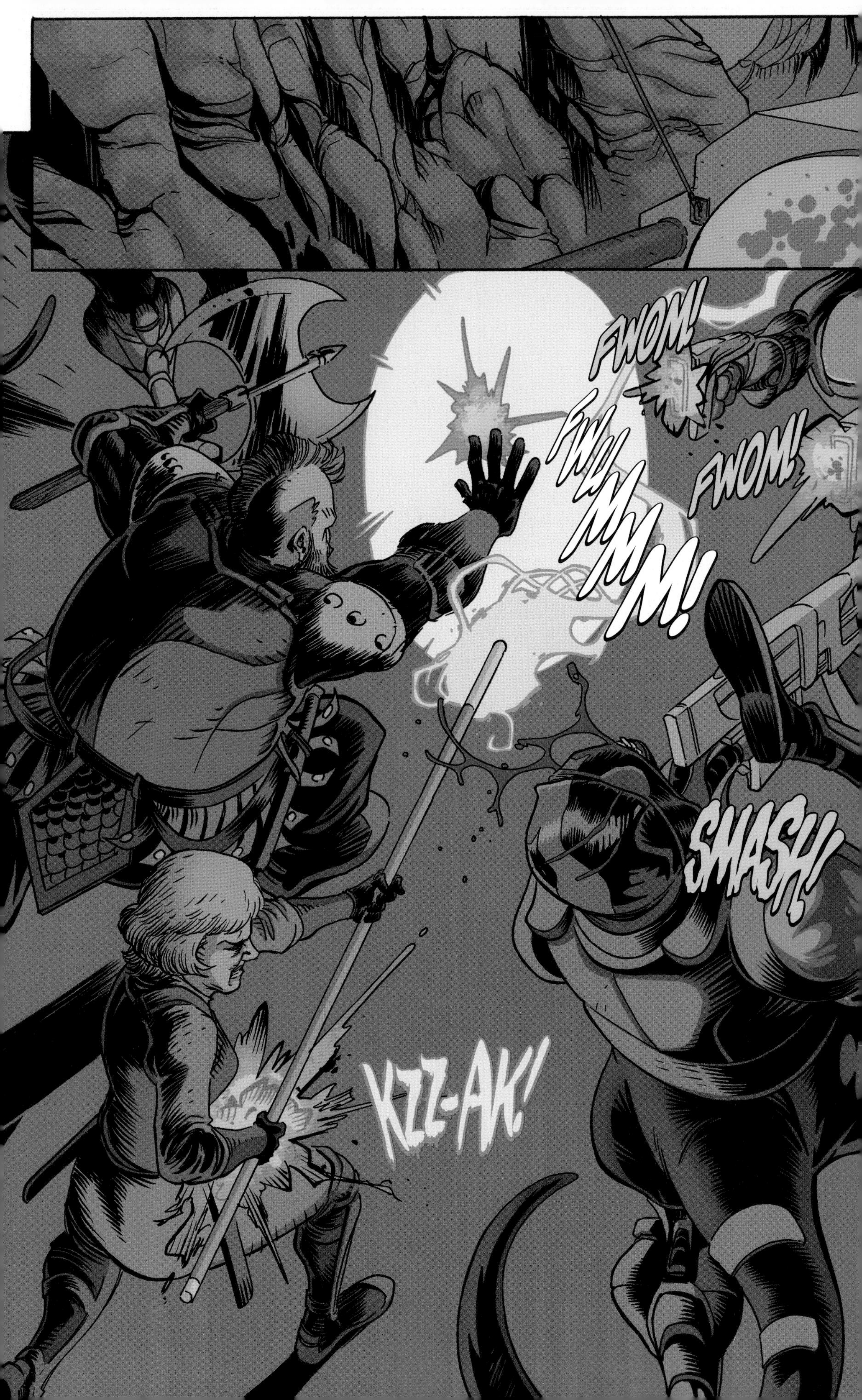
FWOM!
FWUMMMM!
FWOM!
SMASH!
KZZ-AK!

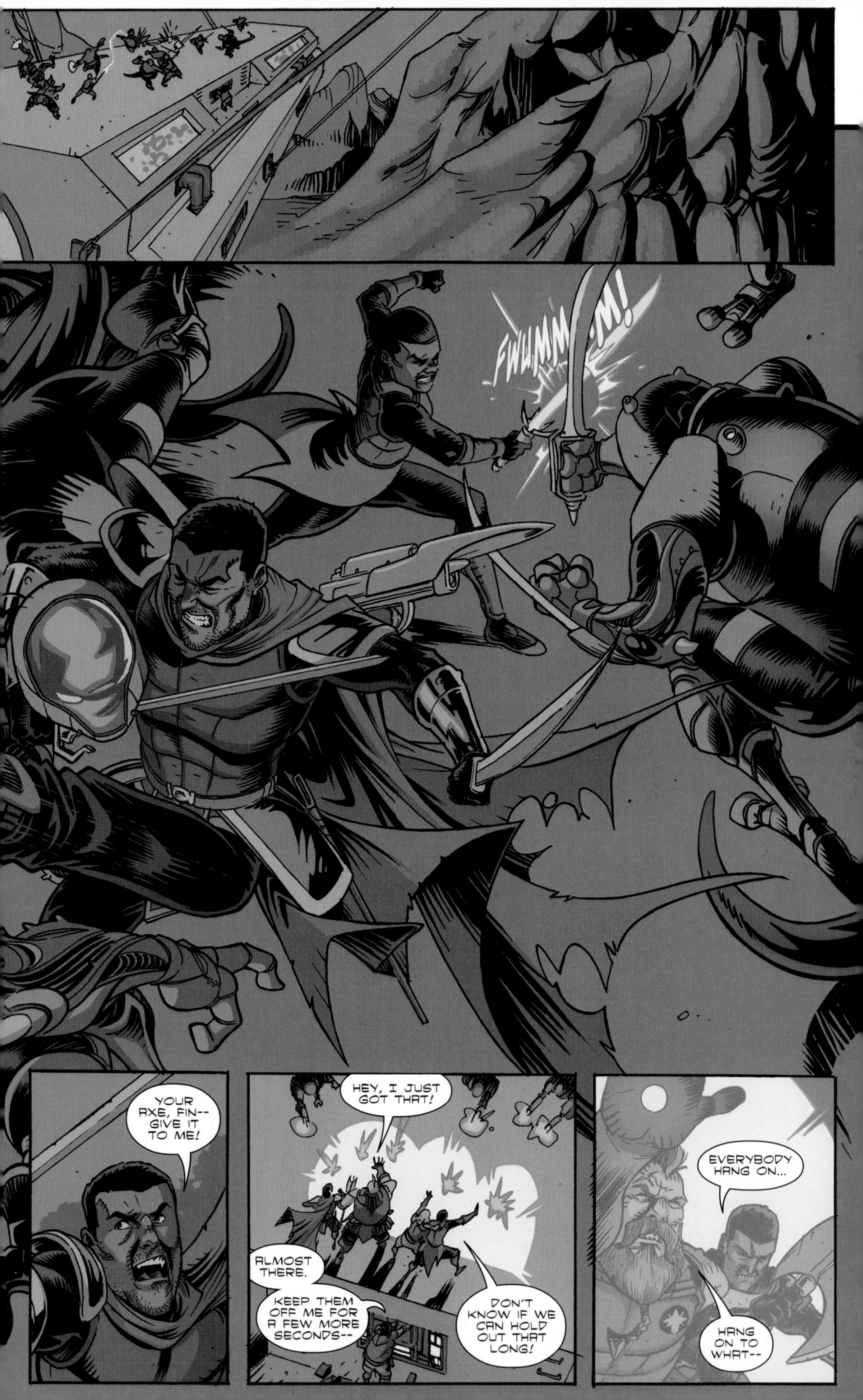
FWUMM-M!
YOUR AXE, FIN-- GIVE IT TO ME!
HEY, I JUST GOT THAT!
ALMOST THERE.
KEEP THEM OFF ME FOR A FEW MORE SECONDS--
DON'T KNOW IF WE CAN HOLD OUT THAT LONG!
EVERYBODY HANG ON...
HANG ON TO WHAT--

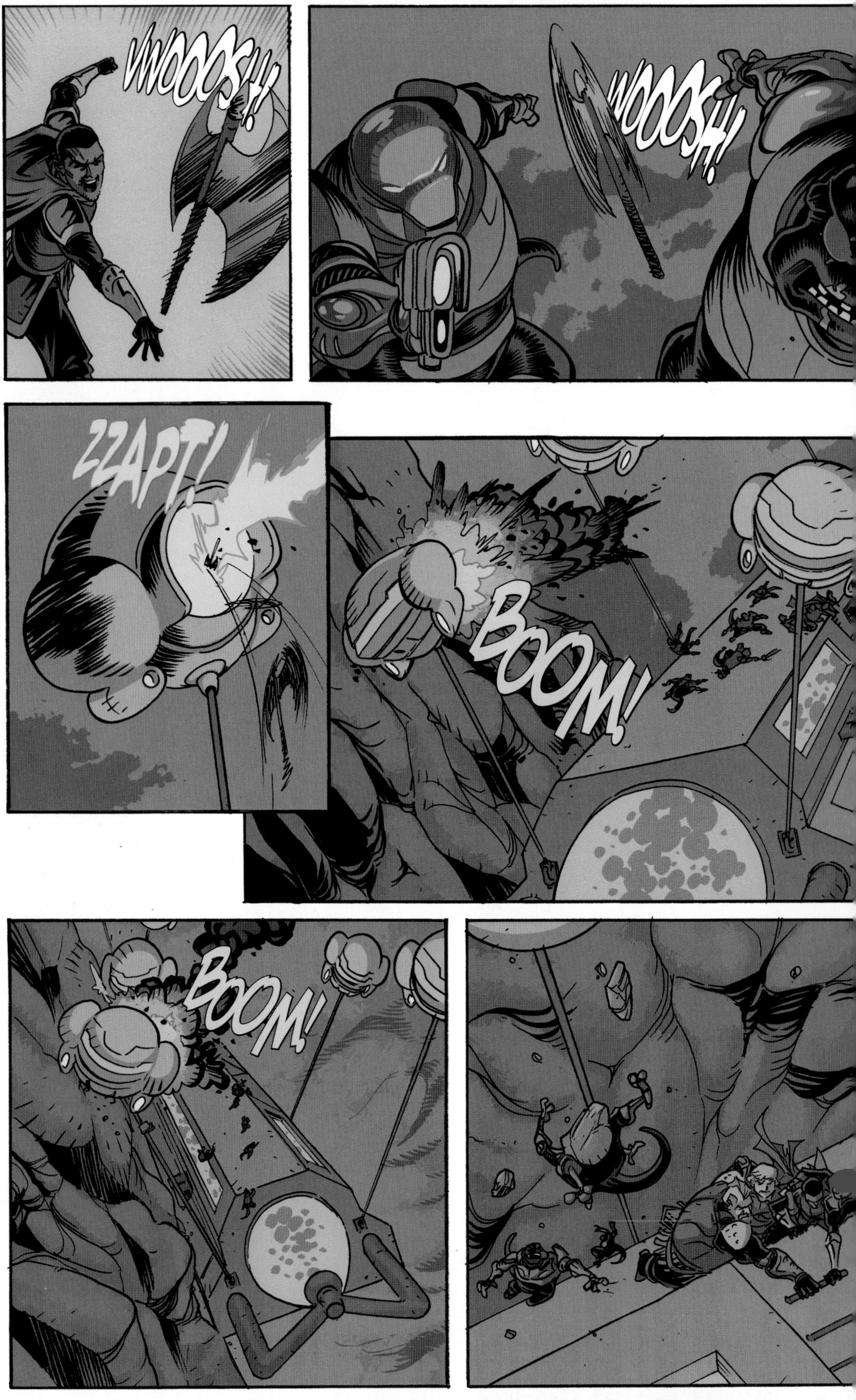
VWOOOSH!
WOOOSH!
ZZAPT!
BOOM!
BOOM!

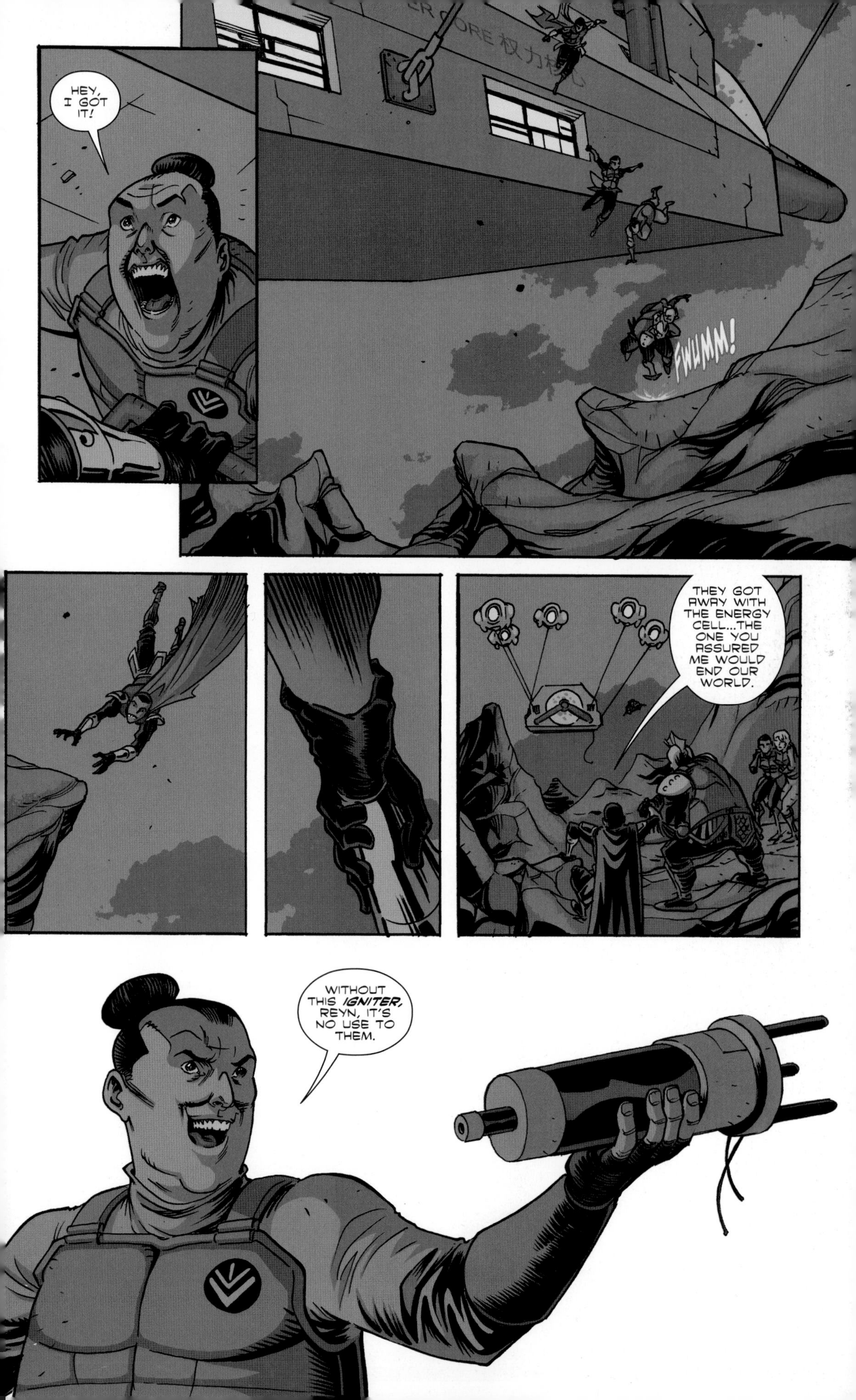

HEY, I GOT IT!
FWUMM!
THEY GOT AWAY WITH THE ENERGY CELL...THE ONE YOU ASSURED ME WOULD END OUR WORLD.
WITHOUT THIS *IGNITER,* REYN, IT'S NO USE TO THEM.

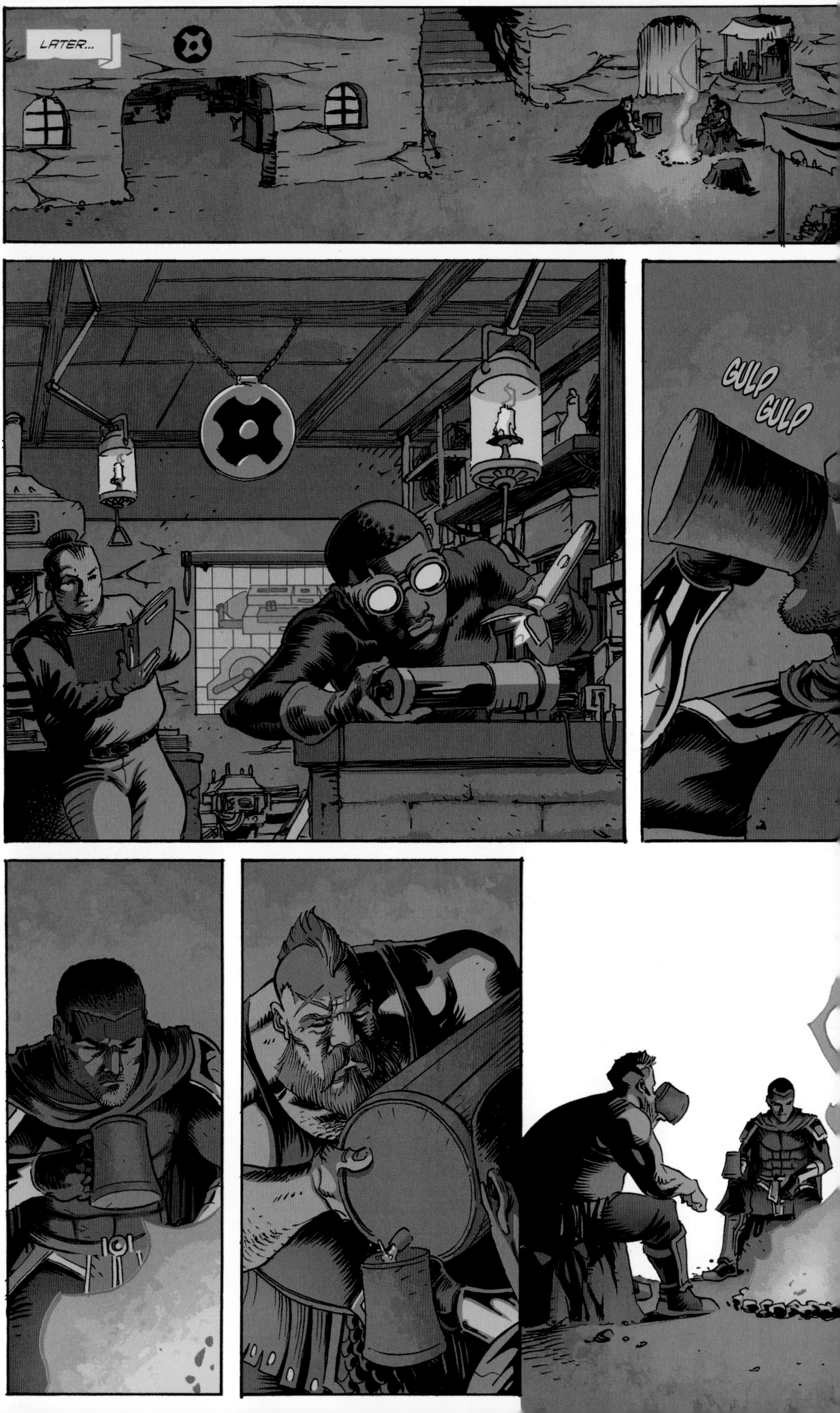
LATER...
GULP
GULP

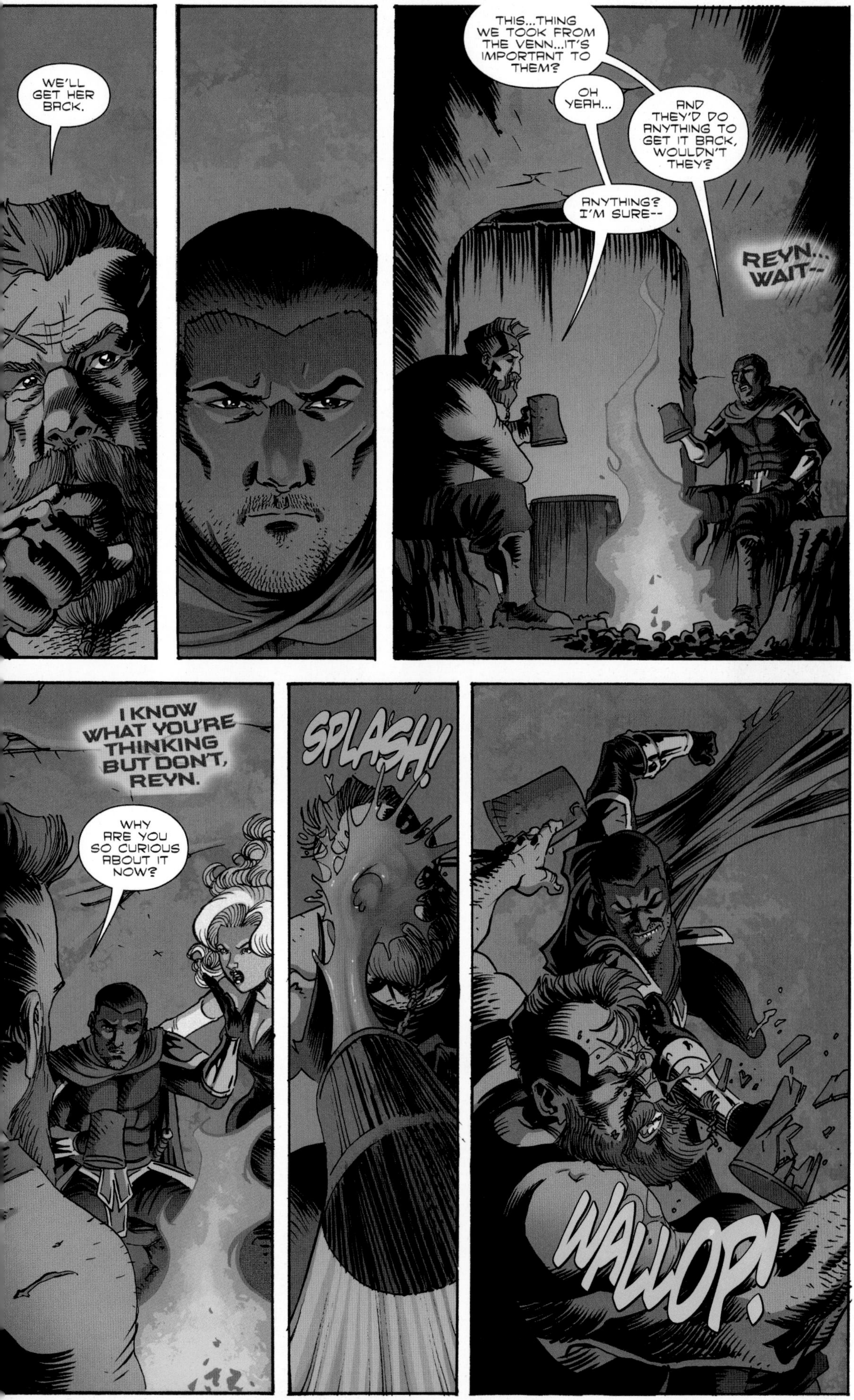
WE'LL GET HER BACK.
THIS...THING WE TOOK FROM THE VENN...IT'S IMPORTANT TO THEM?
OH YEAH...
AND THEY'D DO ANYTHING TO GET IT BACK, WOULDN'T THEY?
ANYTHING? I'M SURE--
REYN... WAIT--
I KNOW WHAT YOU'RE THINKING BUT DON'T, REYN.
WHY ARE YOU SO CURIOUS ABOUT IT NOW?
SPLASH!
WALLOP!

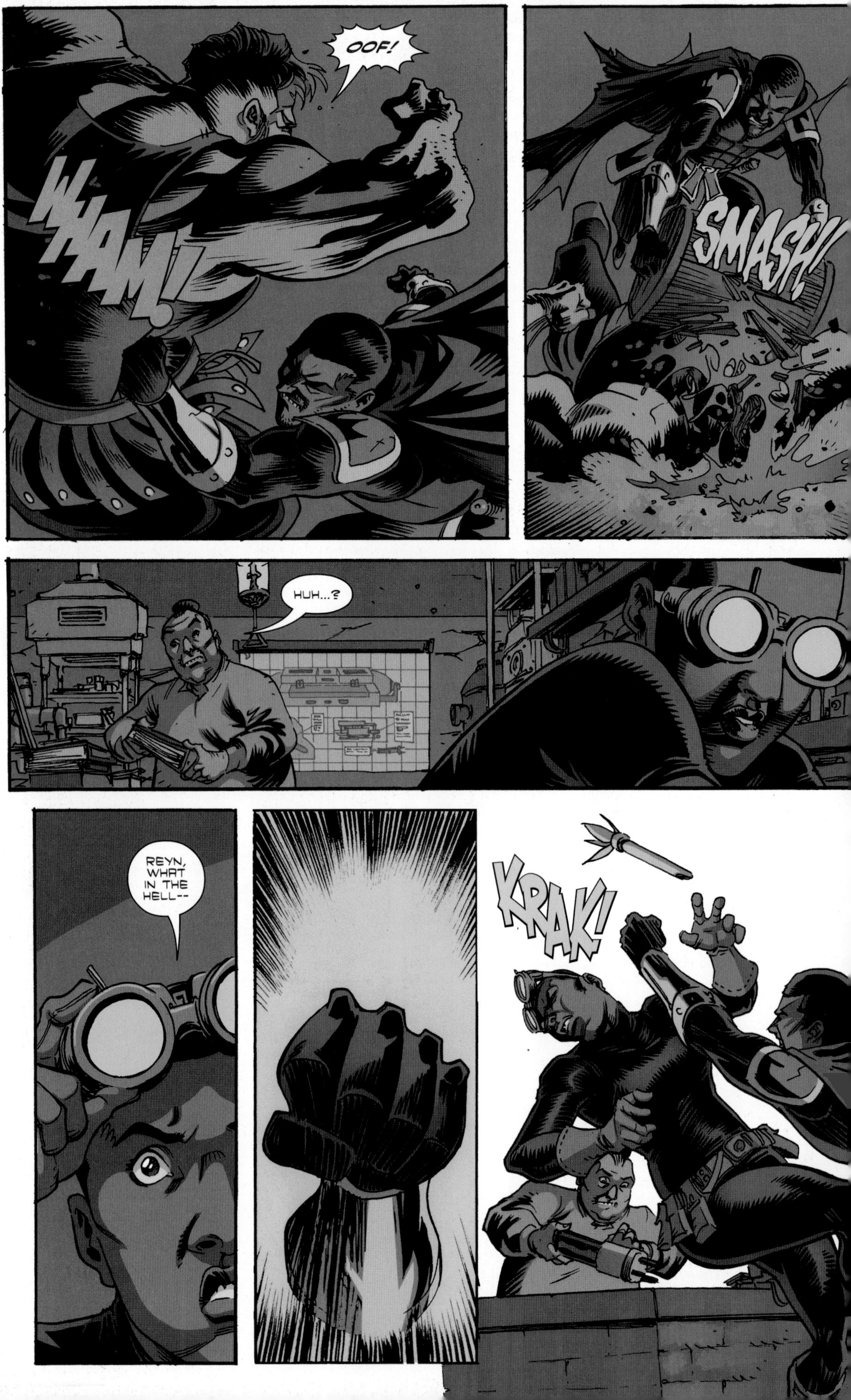
OOF!
WHAM!
SMASH!
HUH...?
REYN, WHAT IN THE HELL--
KRAK!

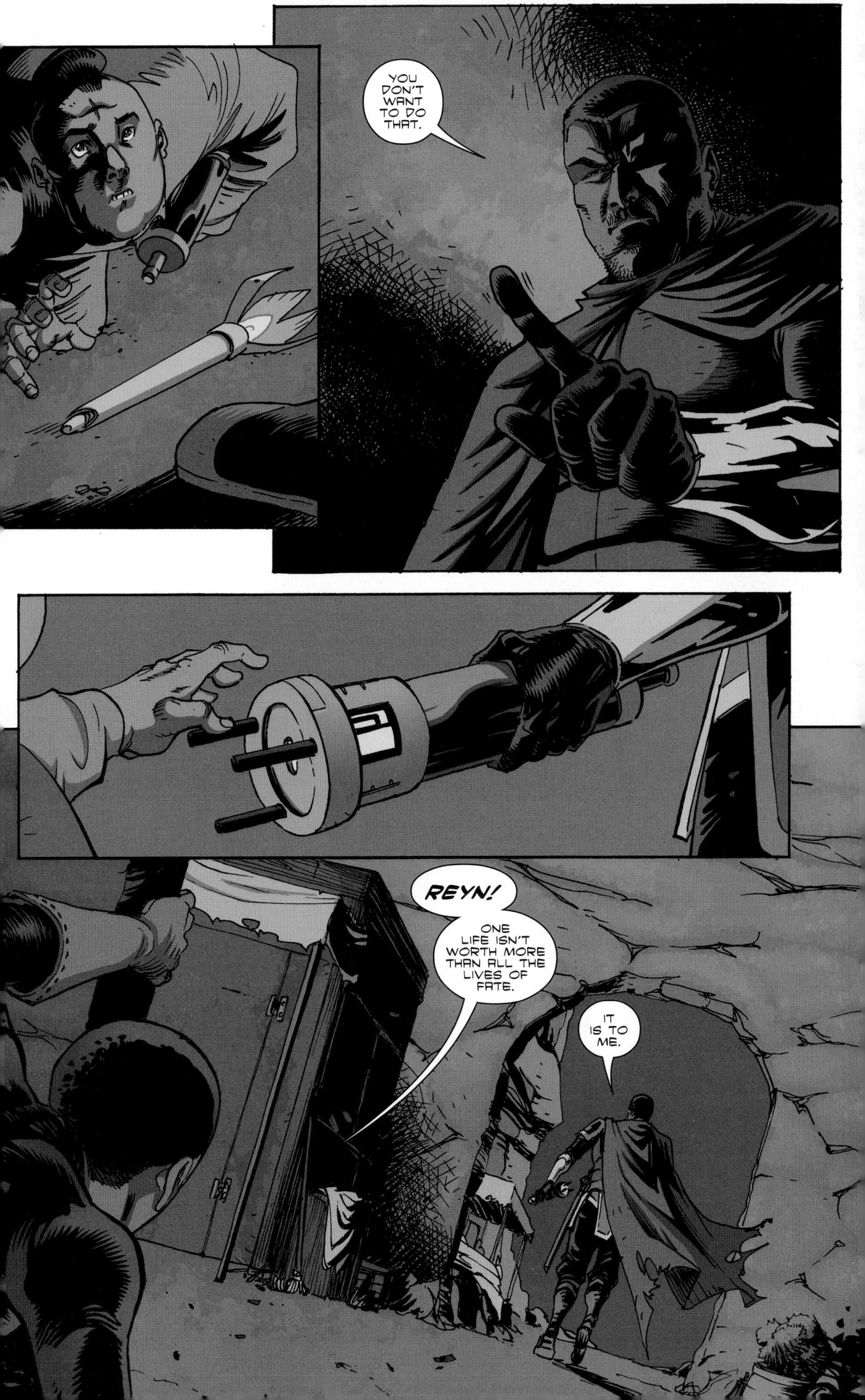
YOU DON'T WANT TO DO THAT.
REYN!
ONE LIFE ISN'T WORTH MORE THAN ALL THE LIVES OF FATE.
IT IS TO ME.

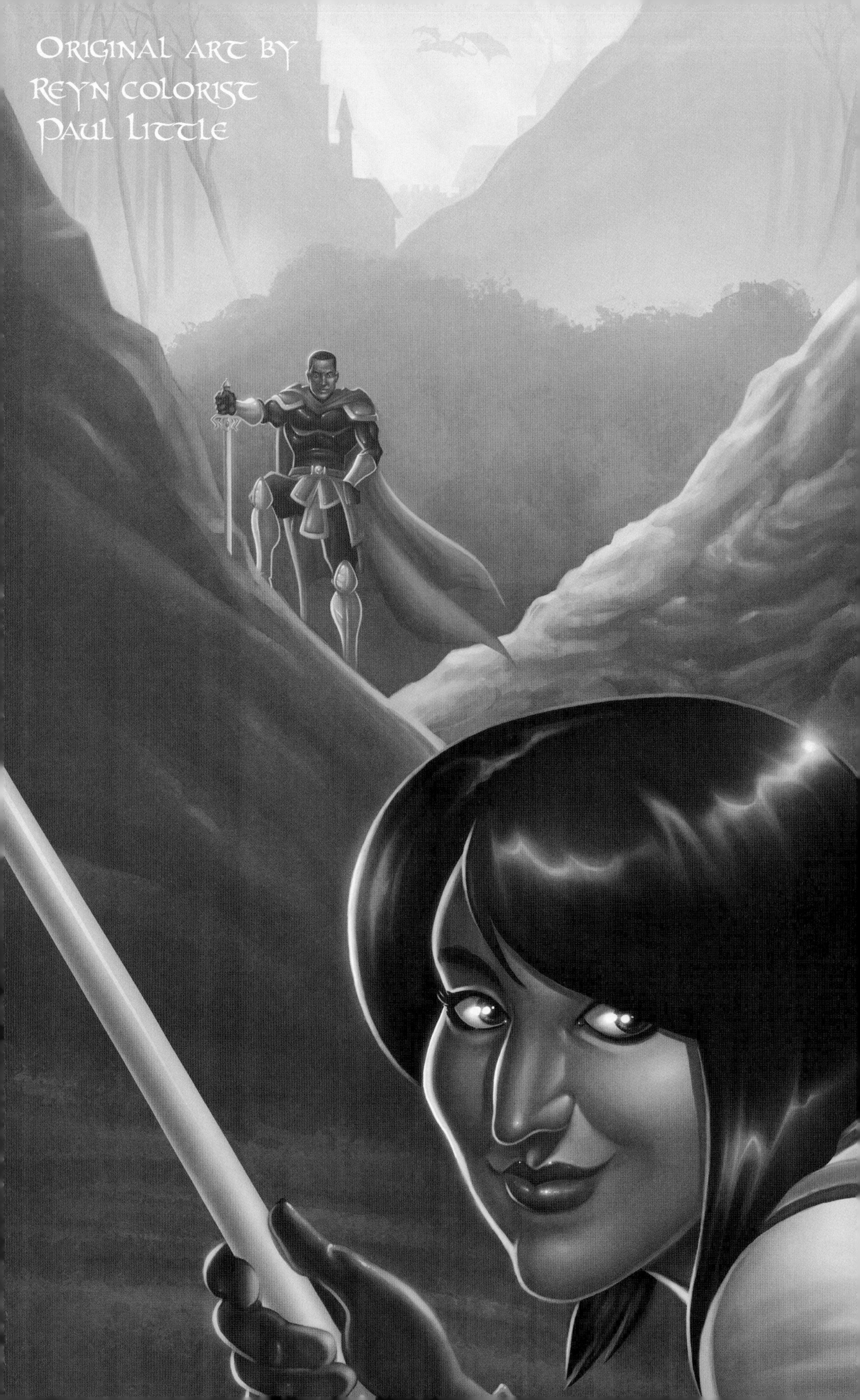
Original art by
Reyn colorist
Paul Little

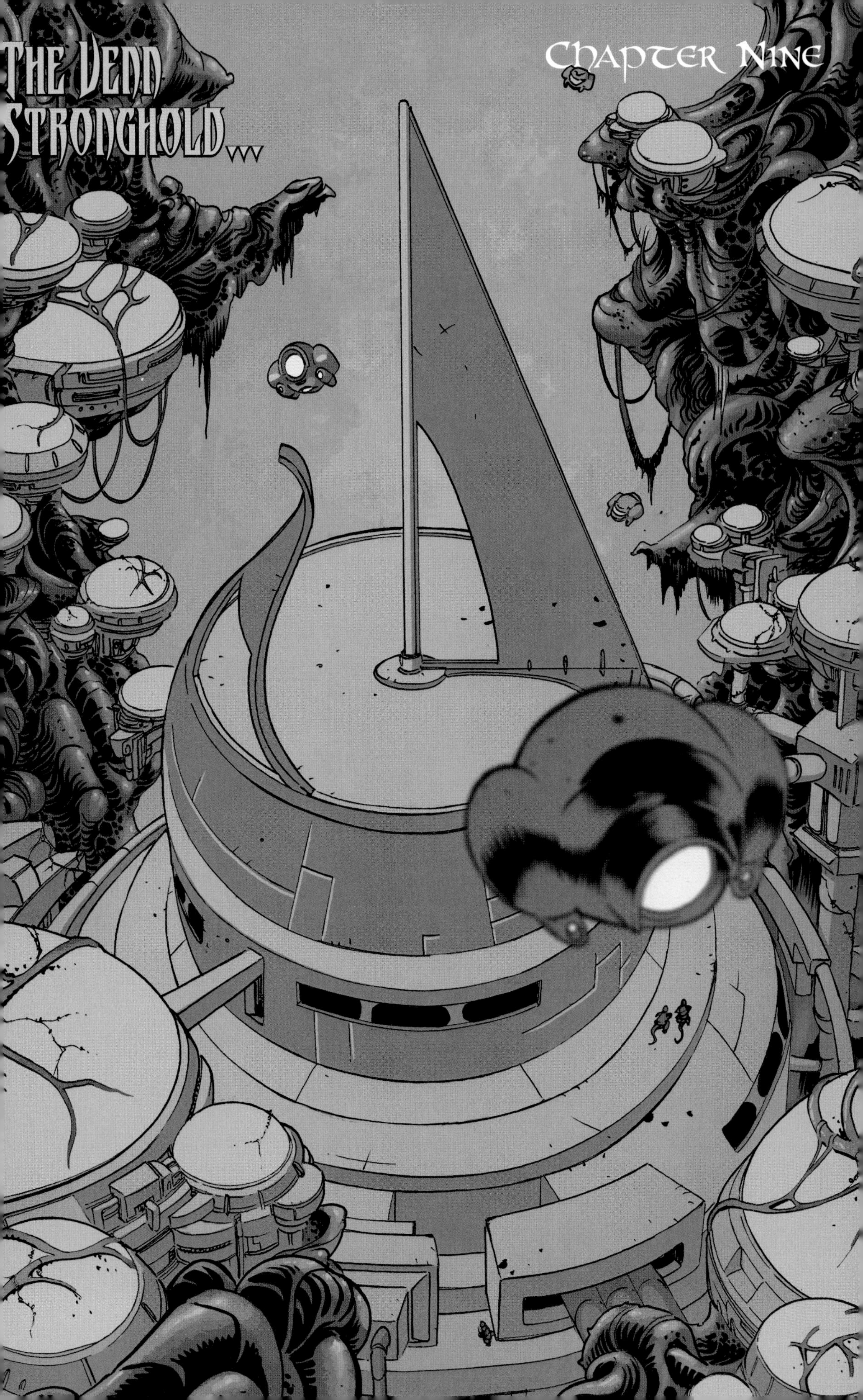
THE VENN STRONGHOLD...
CHAPTER NINE

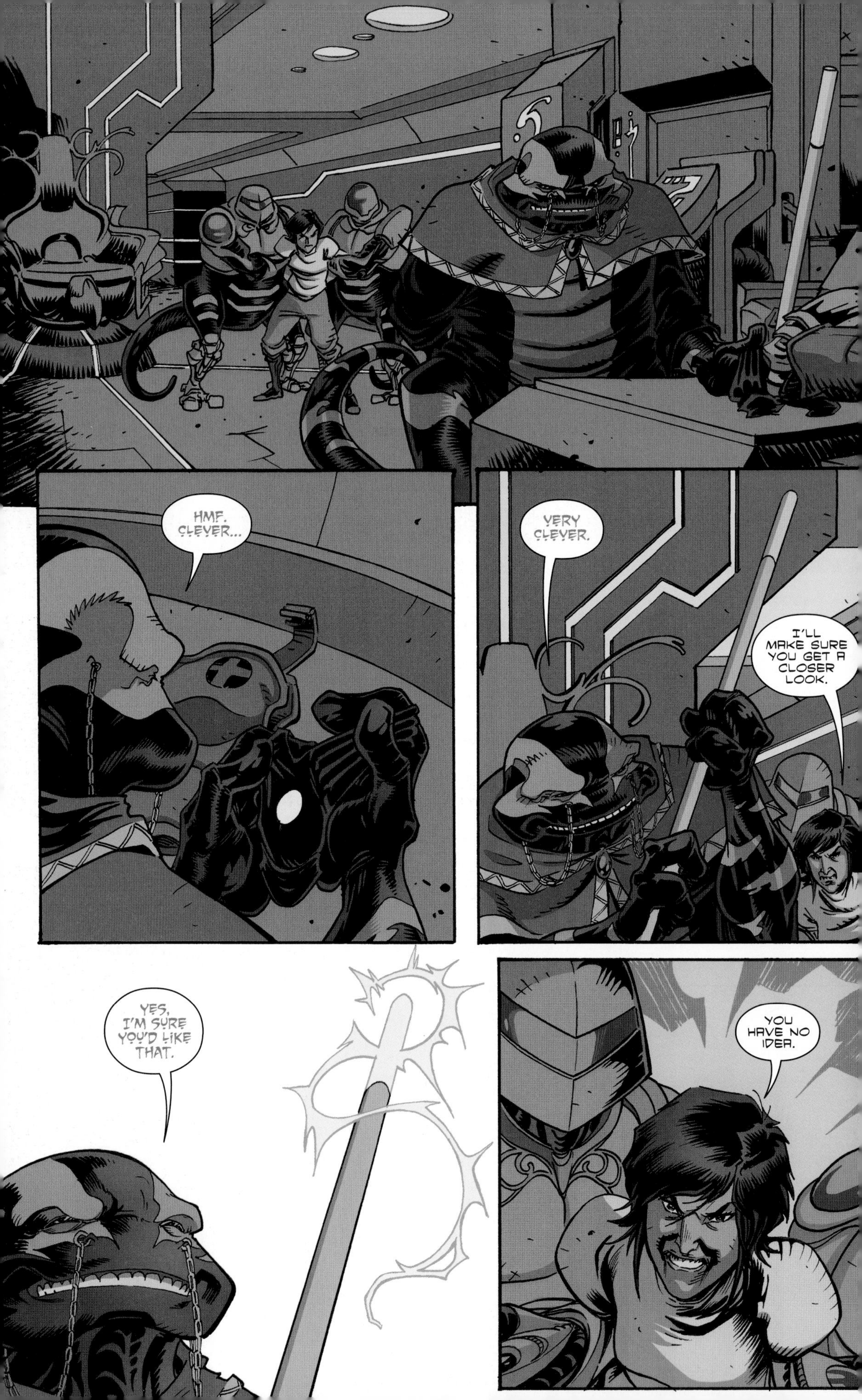
HMF. CLEVER...
VERY CLEVER.
I'LL MAKE SURE YOU GET A CLOSER LOOK.
YES, I'M SURE YOU'D LIKE THAT.
YOU HAVE NO IDEA.

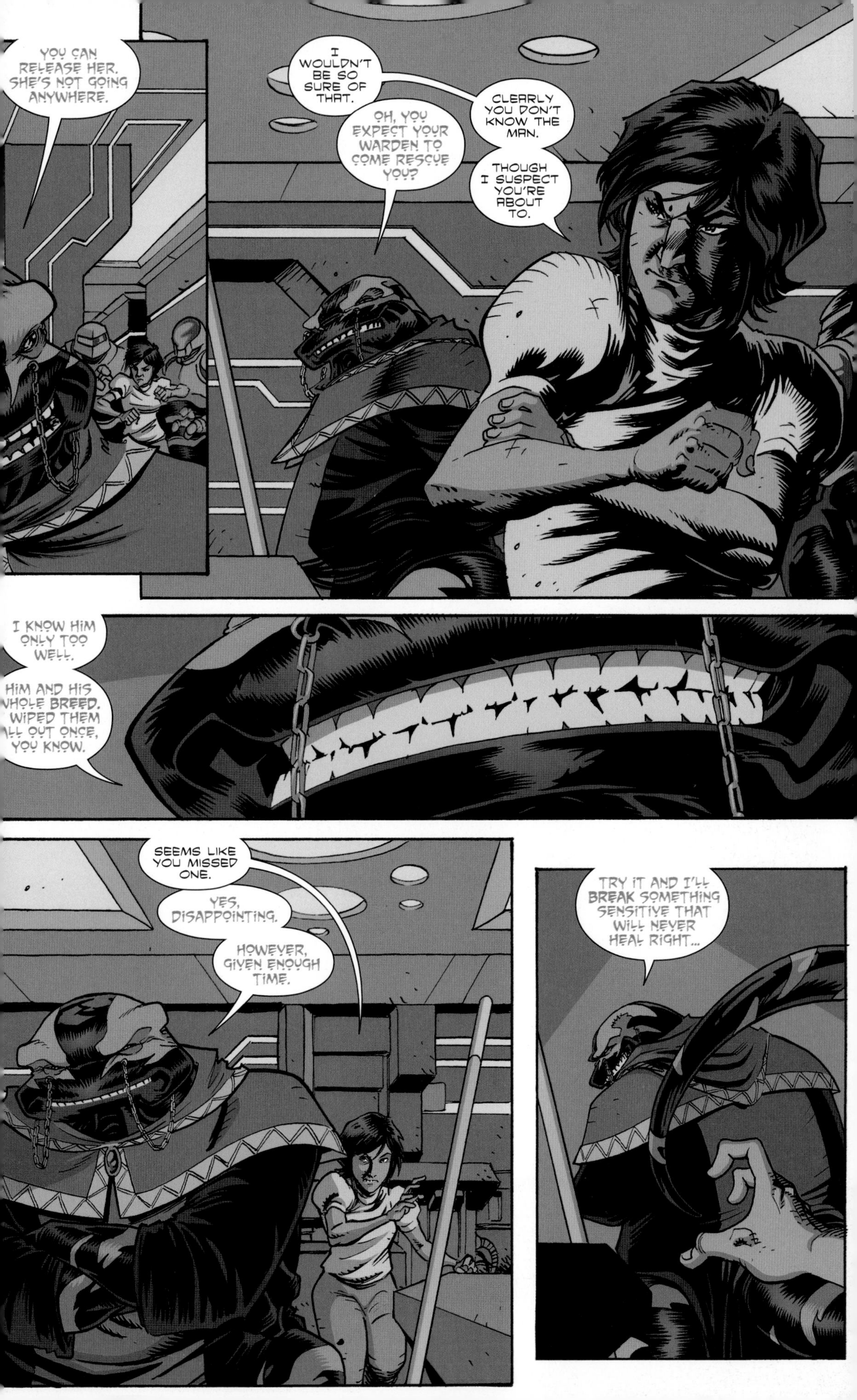
YOU CAN RELEASE HER. SHE'S NOT GOING ANYWHERE.
I WOULDN'T BE SO SURE OF THAT.
OH, YOU EXPECT YOUR WARDEN TO COME RESCUE YOU?
CLEARLY YOU DON'T KNOW THE MAN.
THOUGH I SUSPECT YOU'RE ABOUT TO.
I KNOW HIM ONLY TOO WELL.
HIM AND HIS WHOLE BREED. WIPED THEM ALL OUT ONCE, YOU KNOW.
SEEMS LIKE YOU MISSED ONE.
YES, DISAPPOINTING.
HOWEVER, GIVEN ENOUGH TIME.
TRY IT AND I'LL BREAK SOMETHING SENSITIVE THAT WILL NEVER HEAL RIGHT...

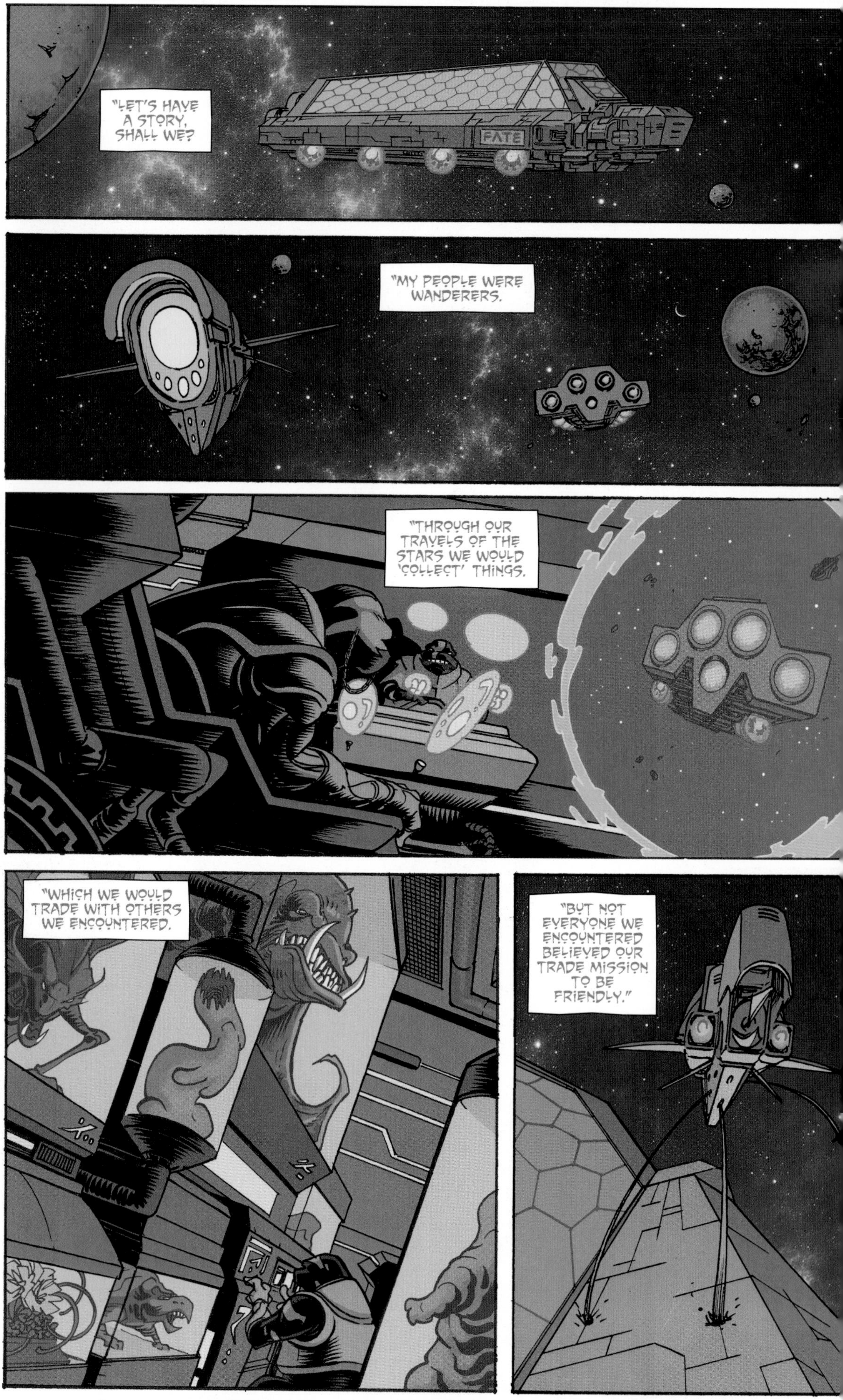
"LET'S HAVE A STORY, SHALL WE?
FATE
"MY PEOPLE WERE WANDERERS.
"THROUGH OUR TRAVELS OF THE STARS WE WOULD 'COLLECT' THINGS.
"WHICH WE WOULD TRADE WITH OTHERS WE ENCOUNTERED.
"BUT NOT EVERYONE WE ENCOUNTERED BELIEVED OUR TRADE MISSION TO BE FRIENDLY."

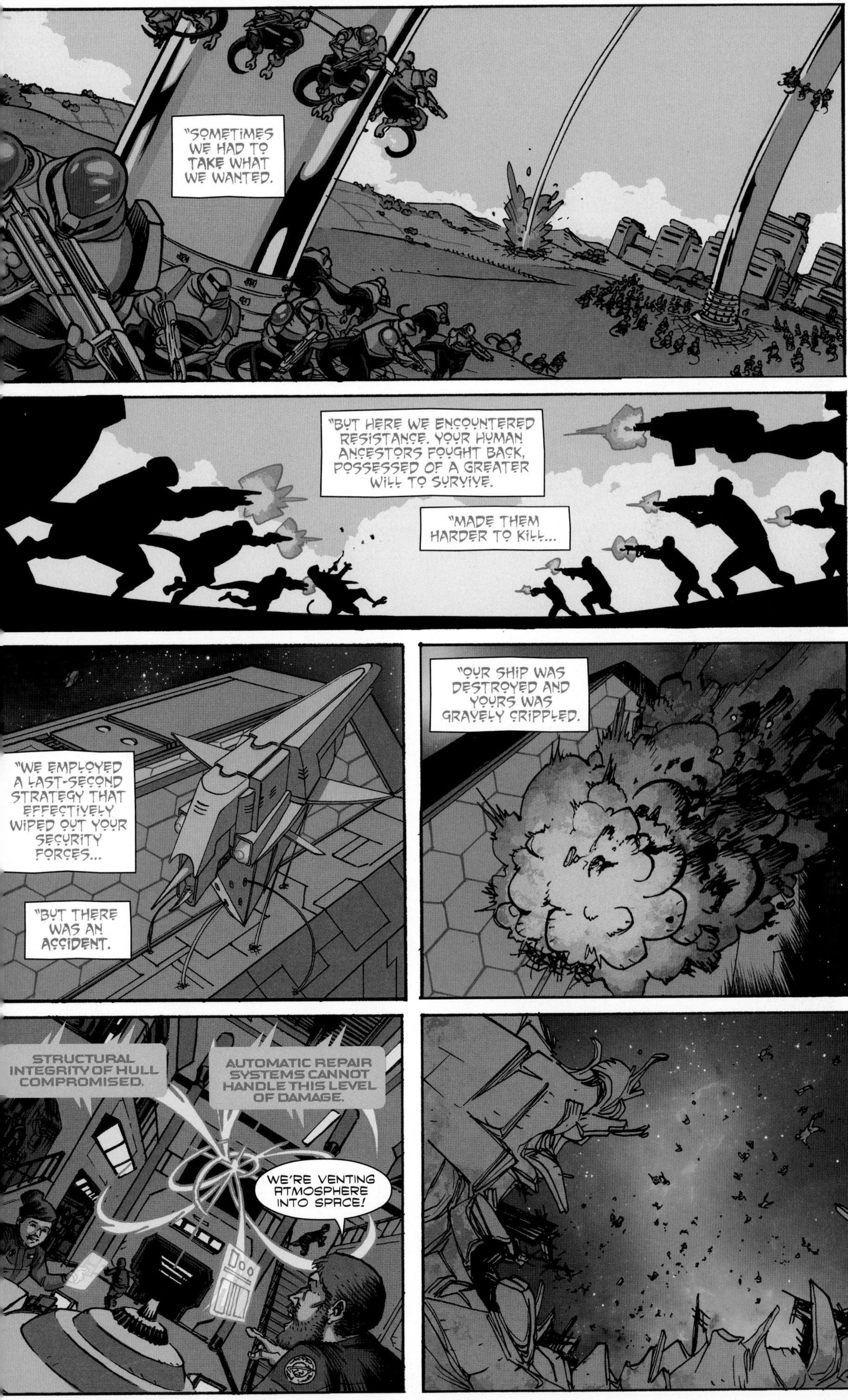
"SOMETIMES WE HAD TO TAKE WHAT WE WANTED.
"BUT HERE WE ENCOUNTERED RESISTANCE. YOUR HUMAN ANCESTORS FOUGHT BACK, POSSESSED OF A GREATER WILL TO SURVIVE.
"MADE THEM HARDER TO KILL...
"WE EMPLOYED A LAST-SECOND STRATEGY THAT EFFECTIVELY WIPED OUT YOUR SECURITY FORCES...
"BUT THERE WAS AN ACCIDENT.
"OUR SHIP WAS DESTROYED AND YOURS WAS GRAVELY CRIPPLED.
STRUCTURAL INTEGRITY OF HULL COMPROMISED.
AUTOMATIC REPAIR SYSTEMS CANNOT HANDLE THIS LEVEL OF DAMAGE.
WE'RE VENTING ATMOSPHERE INTO SPACE!

"YOUR SHIP'S SYSTEMS WERE SEVERELY DAMAGED..."

"THE CLIMATE SHIFTED DRAMATICALLY, AND YOUR WORLD BECAME A FROZEN HELL."

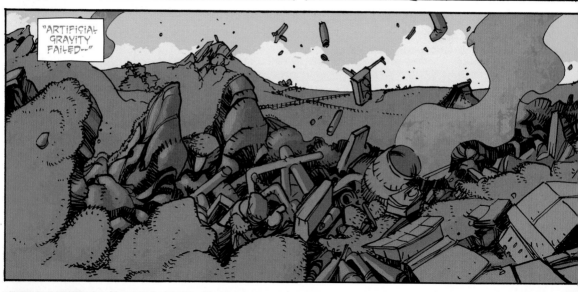

"ARTIFICIAL GRAVITY FAILED--"

ENVIRONMENTAL CONTROLS: OFFLINE.

LIFE SUPPORT: OFFLINE.

GRAVITY COMPENSATORS: OFFLINE.

RECOMMEND BRIDGE CREW REPORT TO EMERGENCY HIBERNATION PODS WHILE AUTOMATIC SYSTEMS ATTEMPT TO ENGAGE.

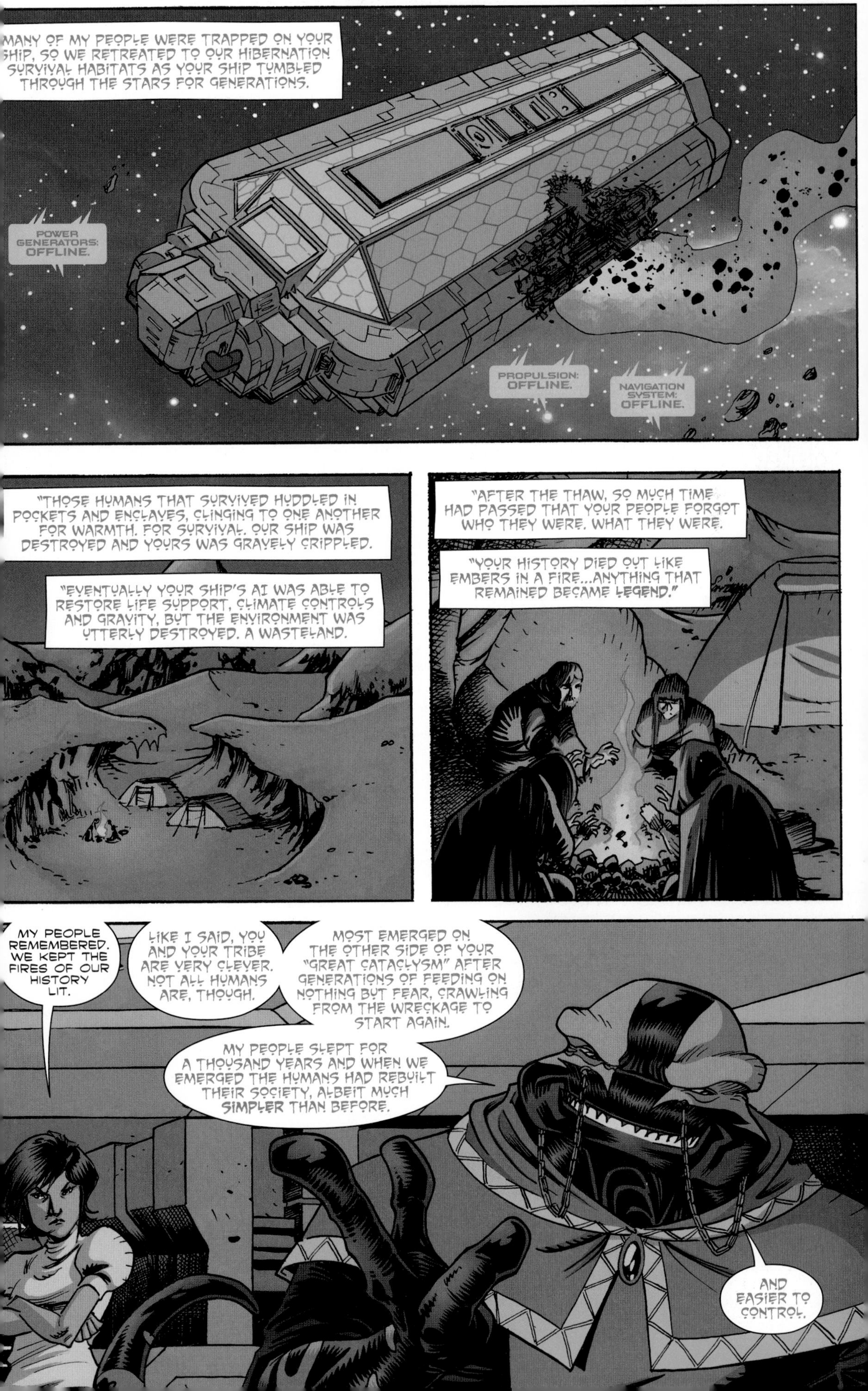
MANY OF MY PEOPLE WERE TRAPPED ON YOUR SHIP, SO WE RETREATED TO OUR HIBERNATION SURVIVAL HABITATS AS YOUR SHIP TUMBLED THROUGH THE STARS FOR GENERATIONS.
POWER GENERATORS: OFFLINE.
PROPULSION: OFFLINE.
NAVIGATION SYSTEM: OFFLINE.
"THOSE HUMANS THAT SURVIVED HUDDLED IN POCKETS AND ENCLAVES, CLINGING TO ONE ANOTHER FOR WARMTH. FOR SURVIVAL. OUR SHIP WAS DESTROYED AND YOURS WAS GRAVELY CRIPPLED.
"EVENTUALLY YOUR SHIP'S AI WAS ABLE TO RESTORE LIFE SUPPORT, CLIMATE CONTROLS AND GRAVITY, BUT THE ENVIRONMENT WAS UTTERLY DESTROYED. A WASTELAND.
"AFTER THE THAW, SO MUCH TIME HAD PASSED THAT YOUR PEOPLE FORGOT WHO THEY WERE. WHAT THEY WERE.
"YOUR HISTORY DIED OUT LIKE EMBERS IN A FIRE...ANYTHING THAT REMAINED BECAME LEGEND."
MY PEOPLE REMEMBERED. WE KEPT THE FIRES OF OUR HISTORY LIT.
LIKE I SAID, YOU AND YOUR TRIBE ARE VERY CLEVER. NOT ALL HUMANS ARE, THOUGH.
MOST EMERGED ON THE OTHER SIDE OF YOUR "GREAT CATACLYSM" AFTER GENERATIONS OF FEEDING ON NOTHING BUT FEAR, CRAWLING FROM THE WRECKAGE TO START AGAIN.
MY PEOPLE SLEPT FOR A THOUSAND YEARS AND WHEN WE EMERGED THE HUMANS HAD REBUILT THEIR SOCIETY, ALBEIT MUCH SIMPLER THAN BEFORE.
AND EASIER TO CONTROL.

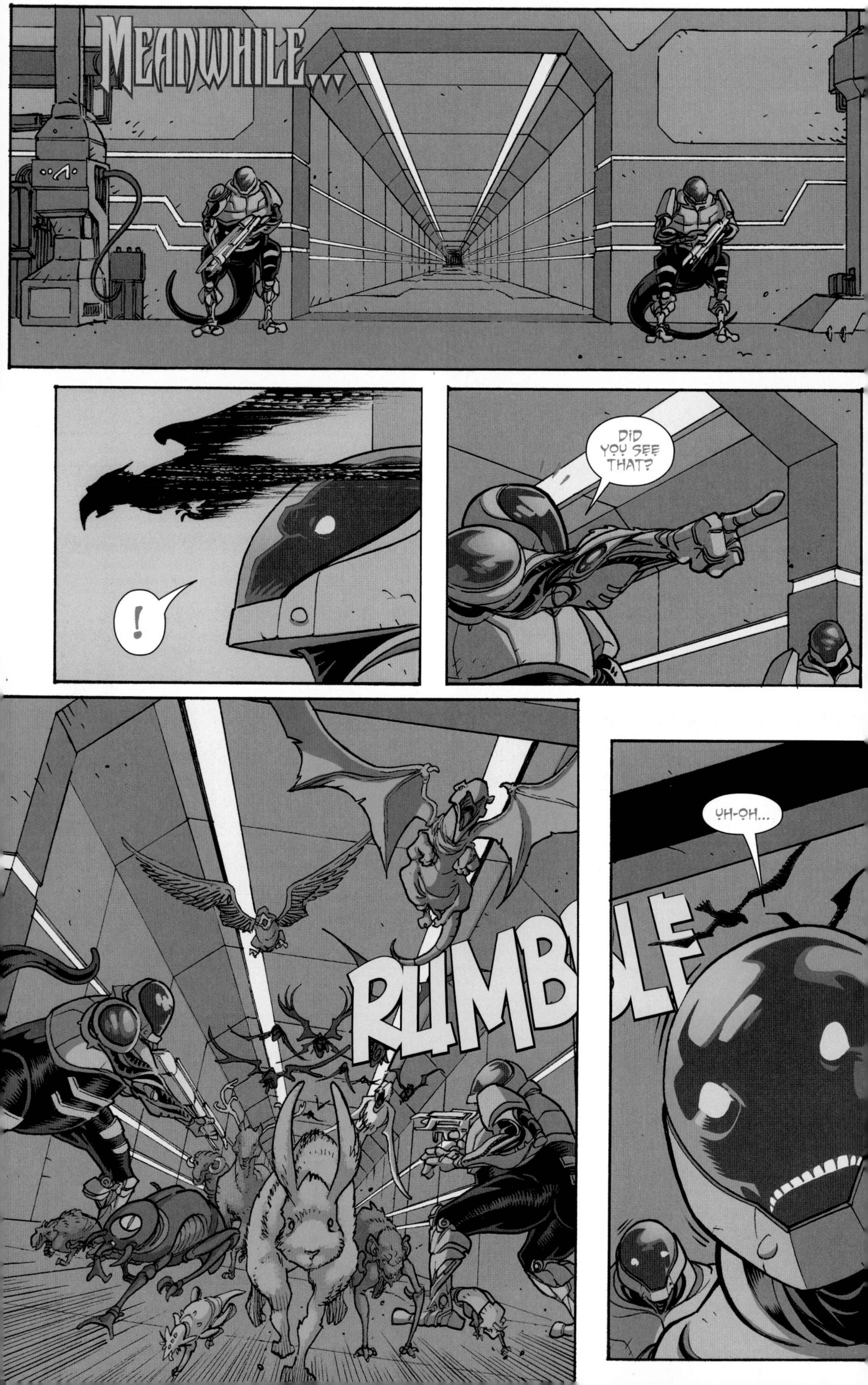
MEANWHILE...
!
DID YOU SEE THAT?
RUMBLE
UH-OH...

SMASH!

STOMP!

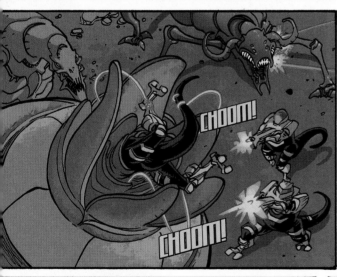

CHOOM!

CHOOM!

WHAT IS IT!?

SIR, WE'VE GOT MULTIPLE BREACHES IN THE STASIS CHAMBERS.

THERE ARE CREATURES LOOSE EVERYWHERE!

AAIGH!

HE'S HERE.

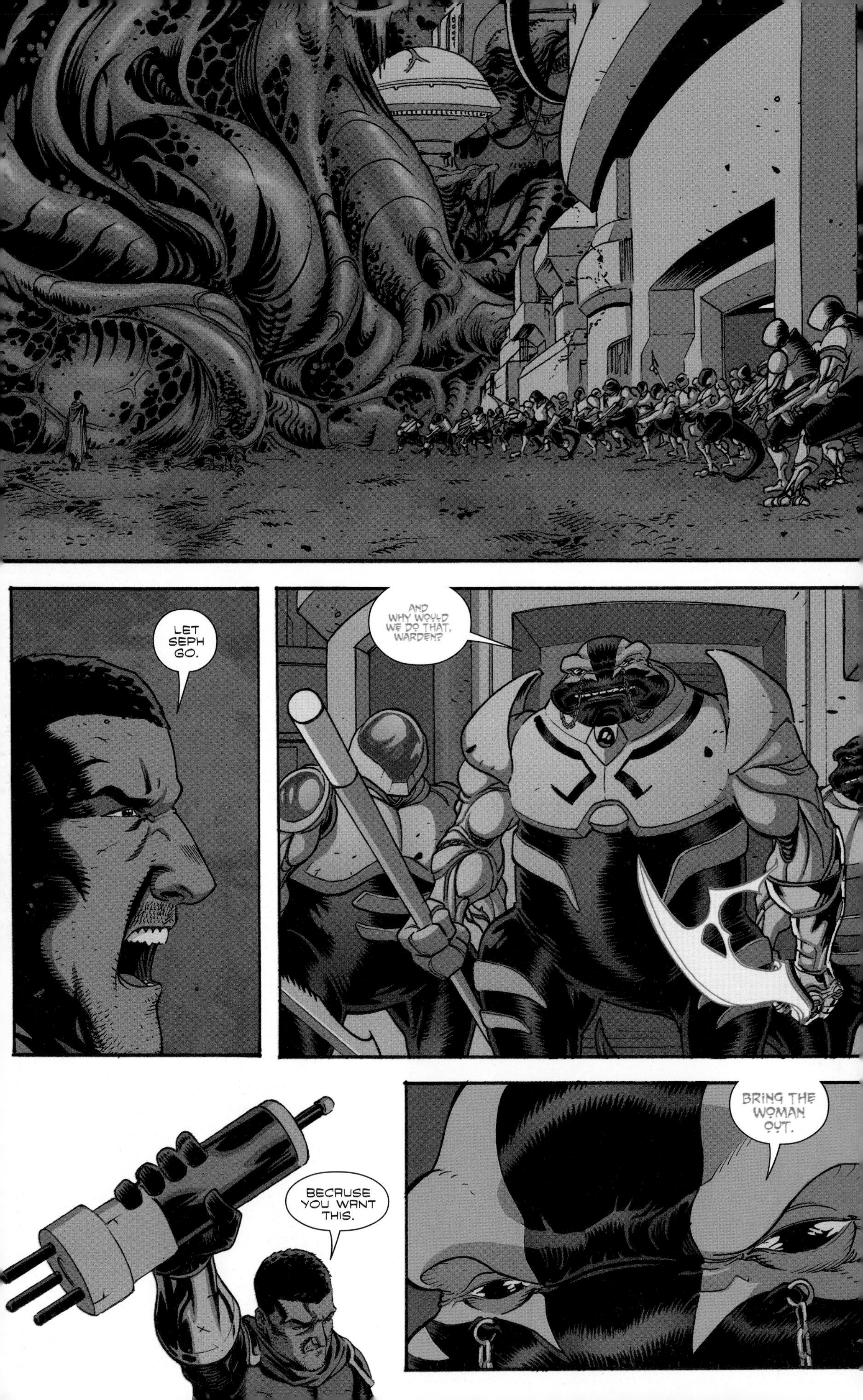
LET SEPH GO.
AND WHY WOULD WE DO THAT, WARDEN?
BECAUSE YOU WANT THIS.
BRING THE WOMAN OUT.

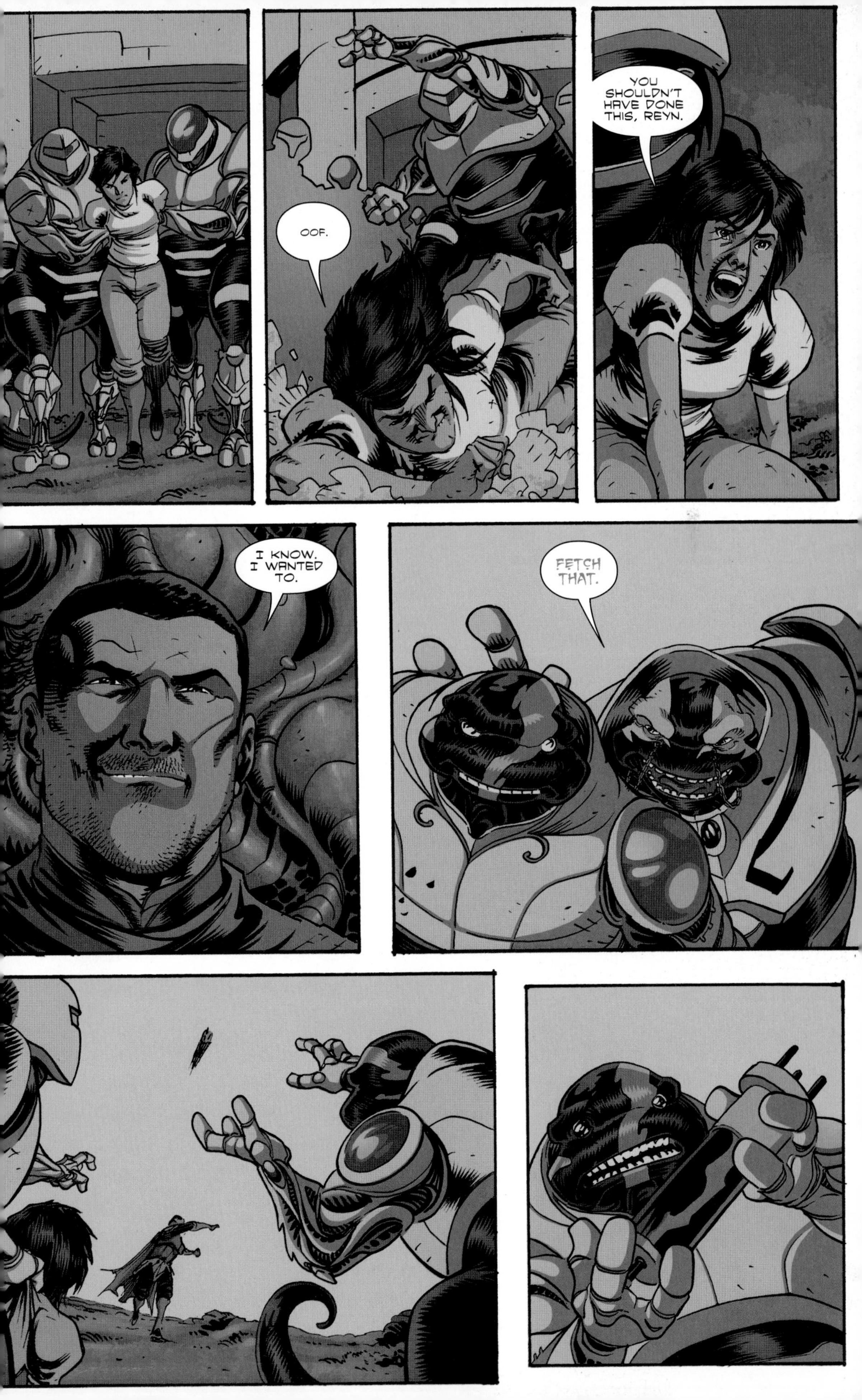
OOF.
YOU SHOULDN'T HAVE DONE THIS, REYN.
I KNOW. I WANTED TO.
FETCH THAT.

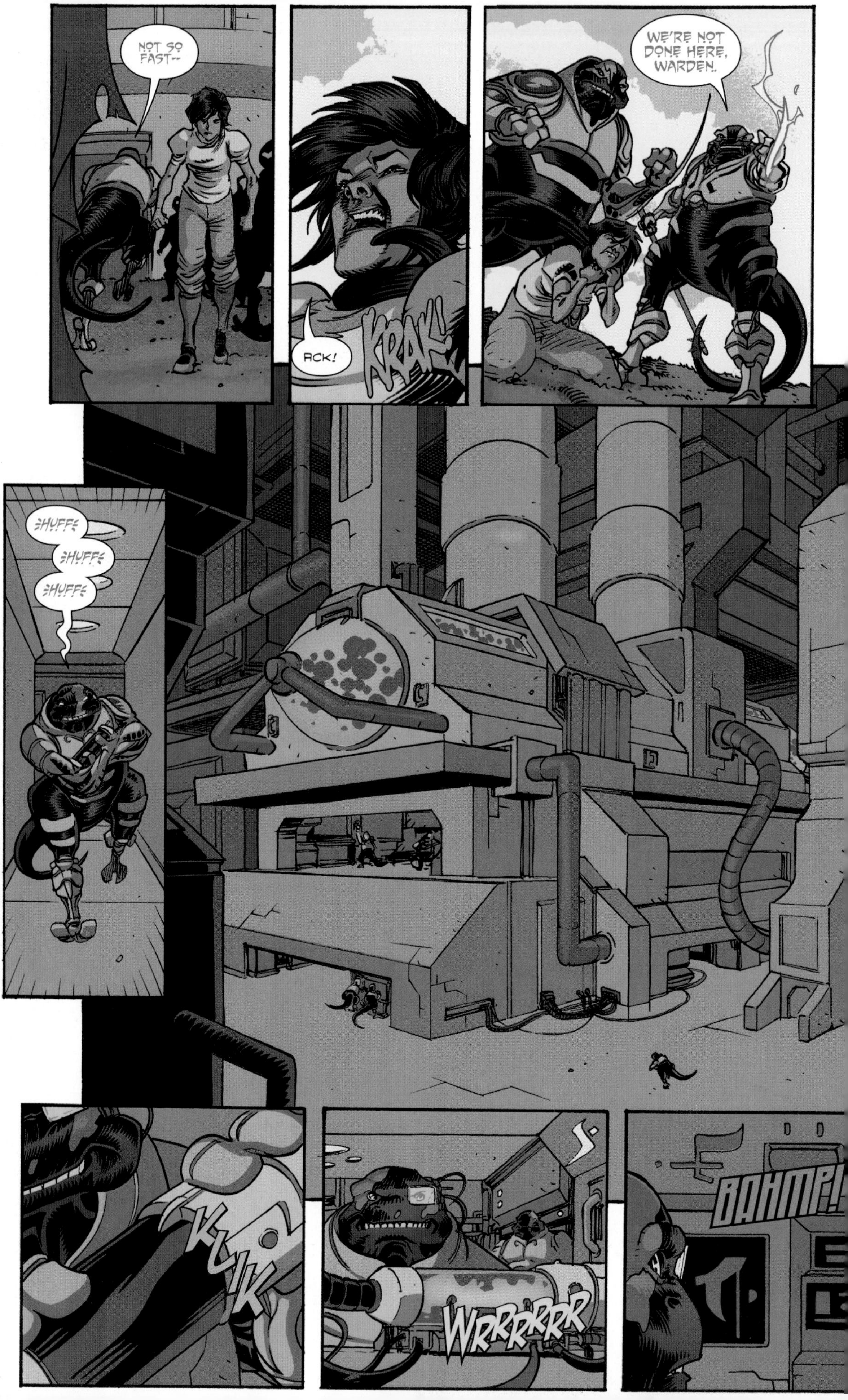
NOT SO FAST--
ACK!
KRAK!
WE'RE NOT DONE HERE, WARDEN.
HUFF
HUFF
HUFF
KLIK
WRRRRRR
BAHMP!

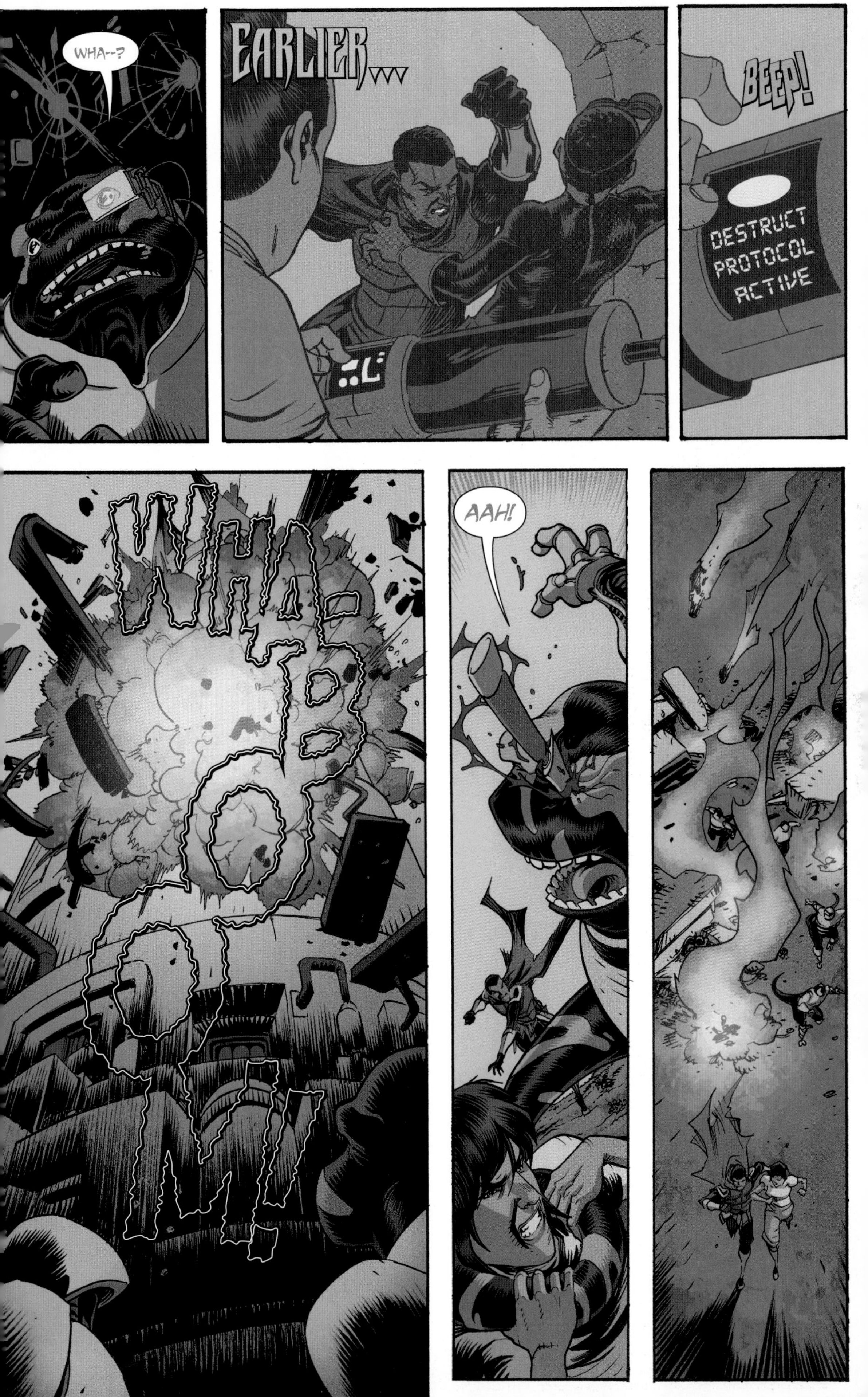
WHA--?
EARLIER...
BEEP!
DESTRUCT PROTOCOL ACTIVE
WHADOOM!
AAH!

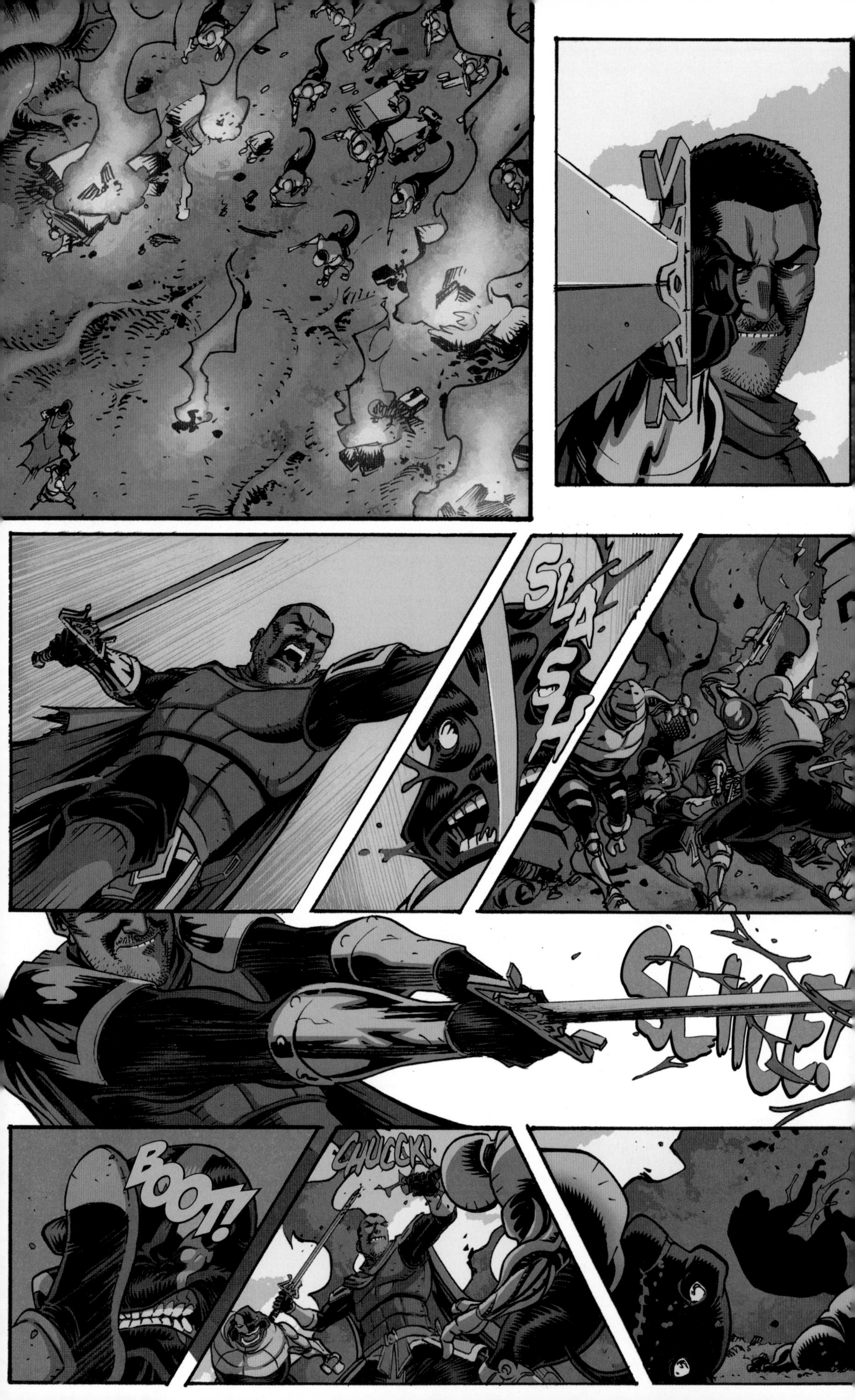
SLASH
SLICE!
BOOT!
CHUCCK!

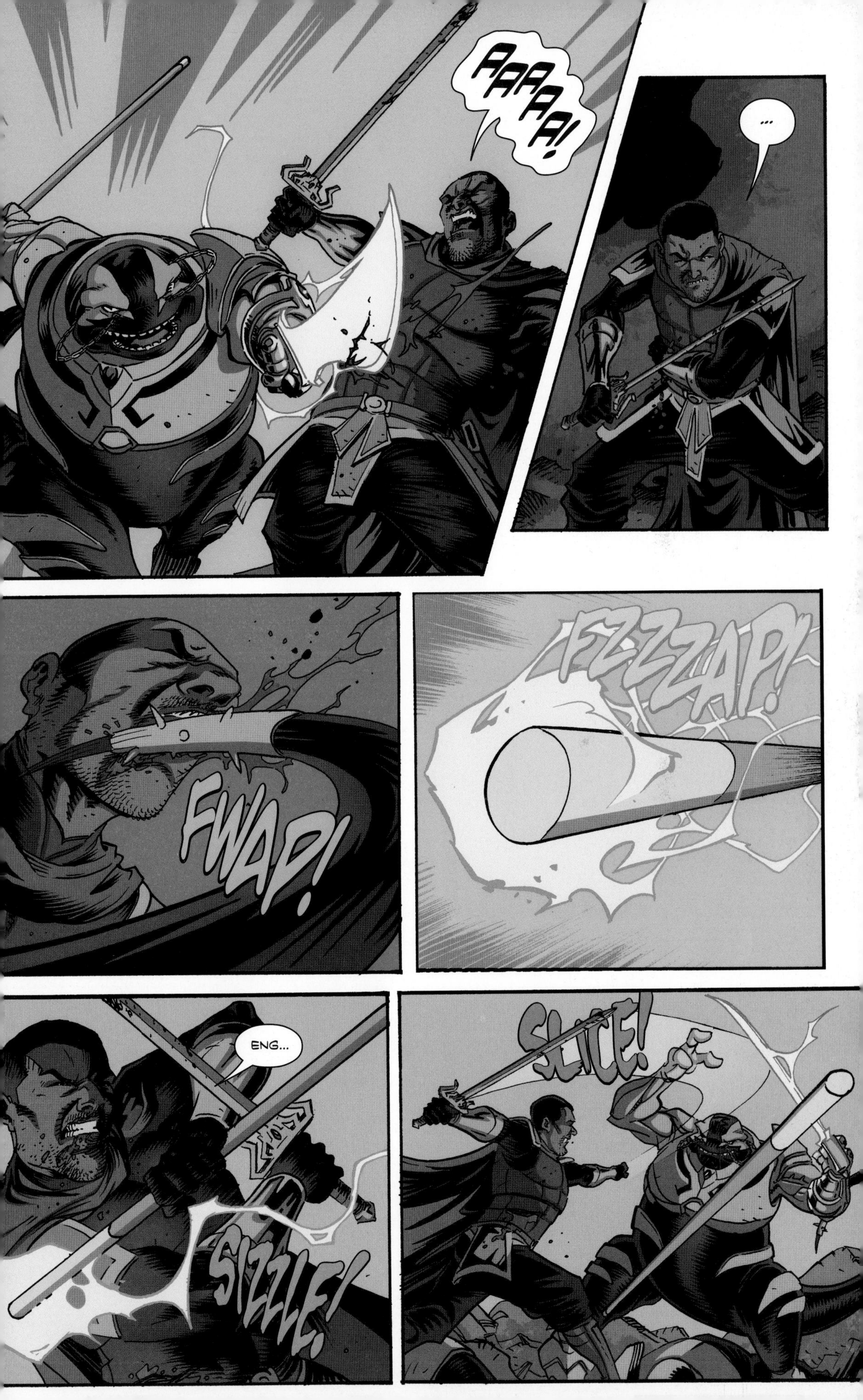
AAAAA!
...
FWAP!
FZZZAP!
ENG...
SIZZLE!
SLICE!

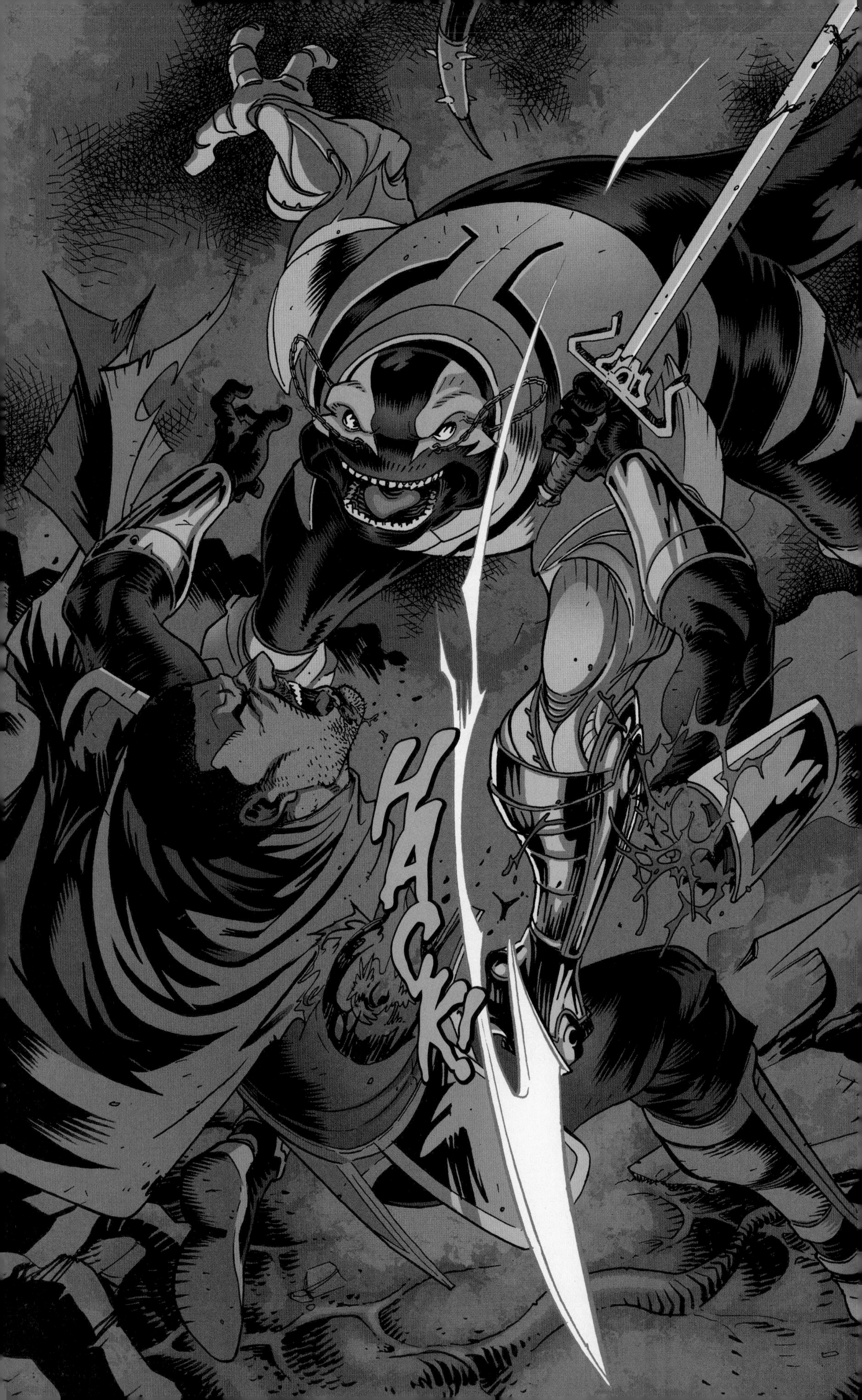
HACK!

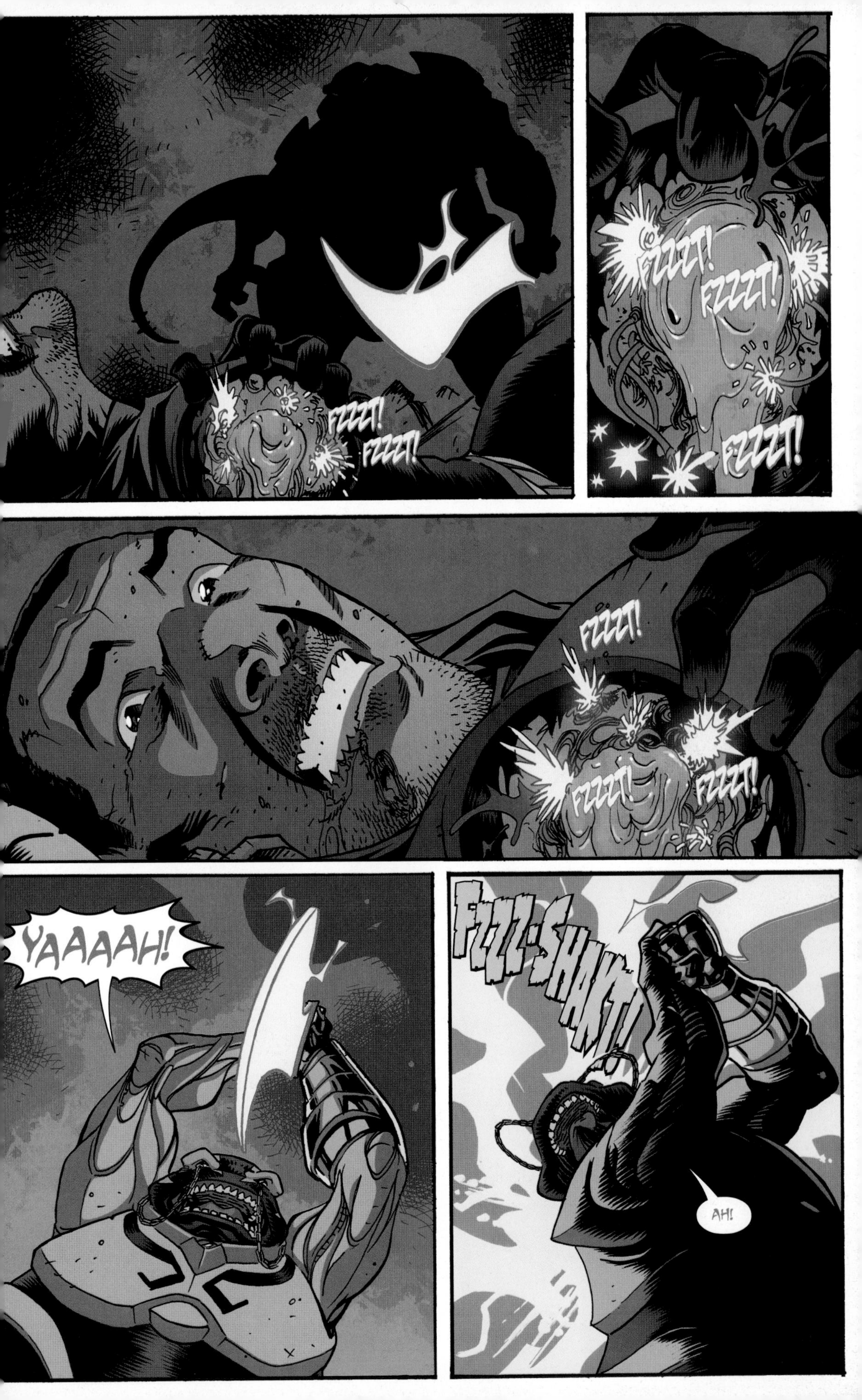
FZZZT!
FZZZT!
FZZZT!
FZZZT!
FZZZT!
FZZZT!
FZZZT!
FZZZT!
YAAAAH!
FZZZ-SHAKT!
AH!

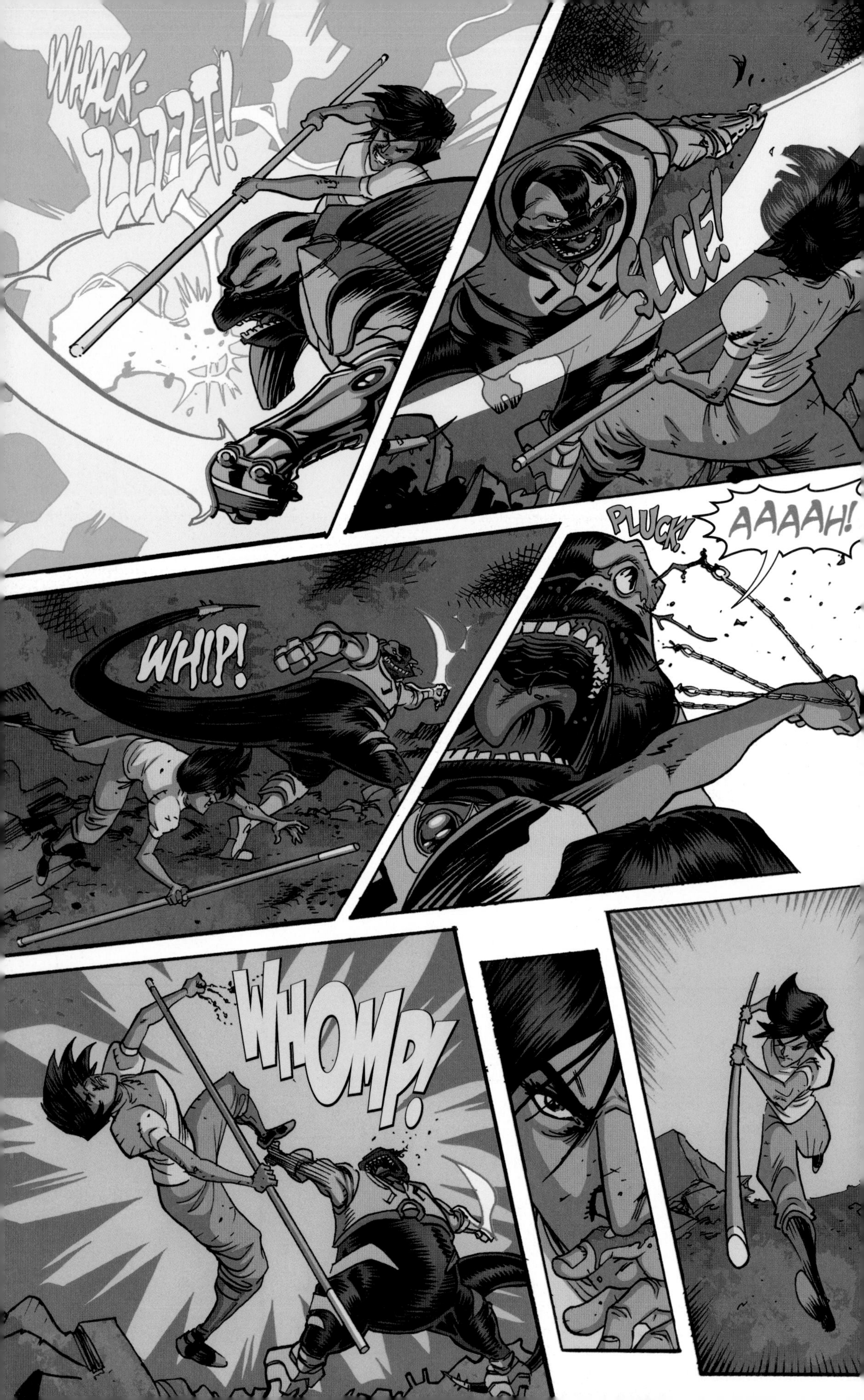
WHACK-
ZZZZZT!
SLICE!
WHIP!
PLUCK!
AAAAH!
WHOMP!

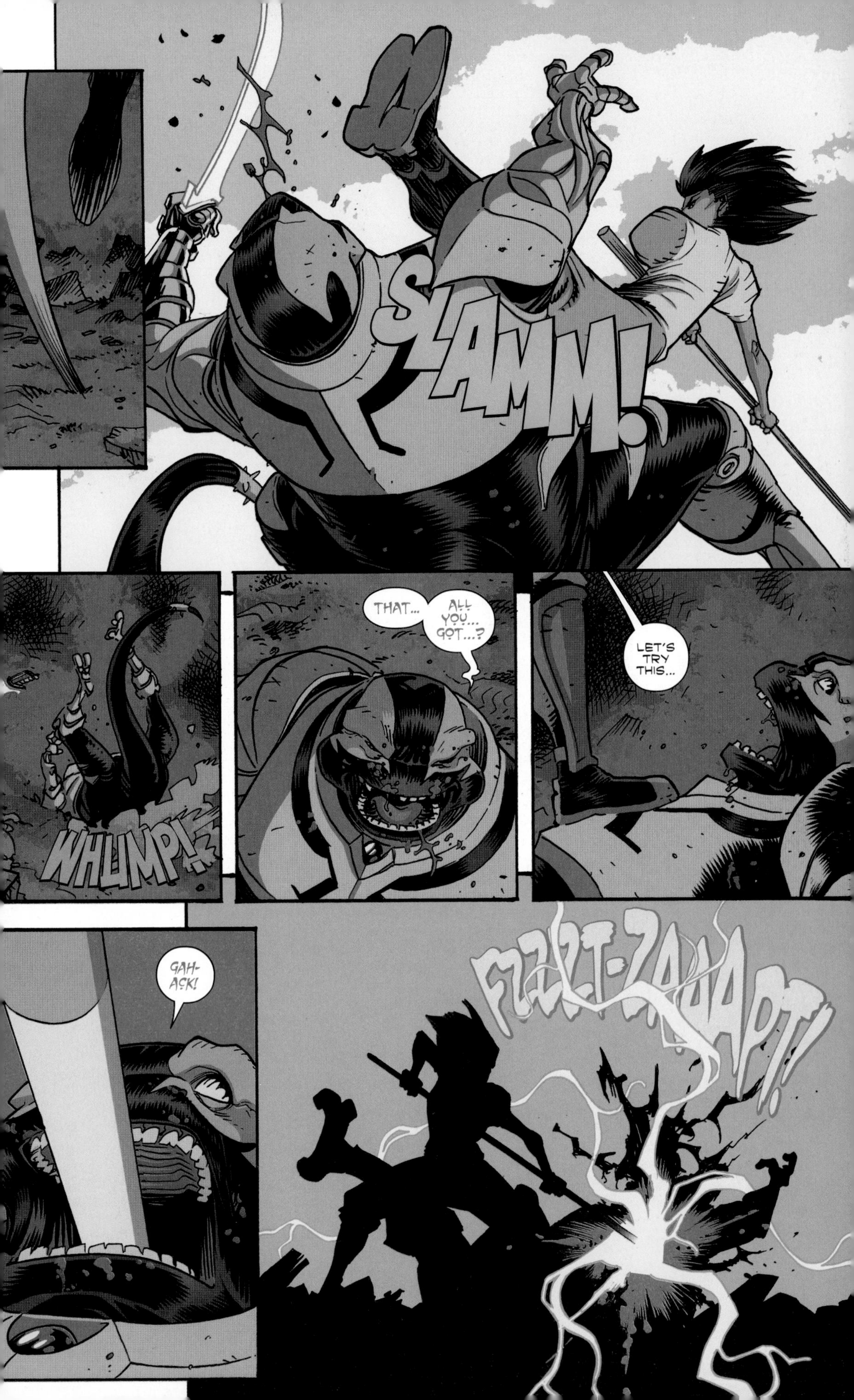
SLAMM!
WHUMP!
THAT...
ALL YOU... GOT...?
LET'S TRY THIS...
GAH-ACK!
FZZZZT-ZAAAP!!

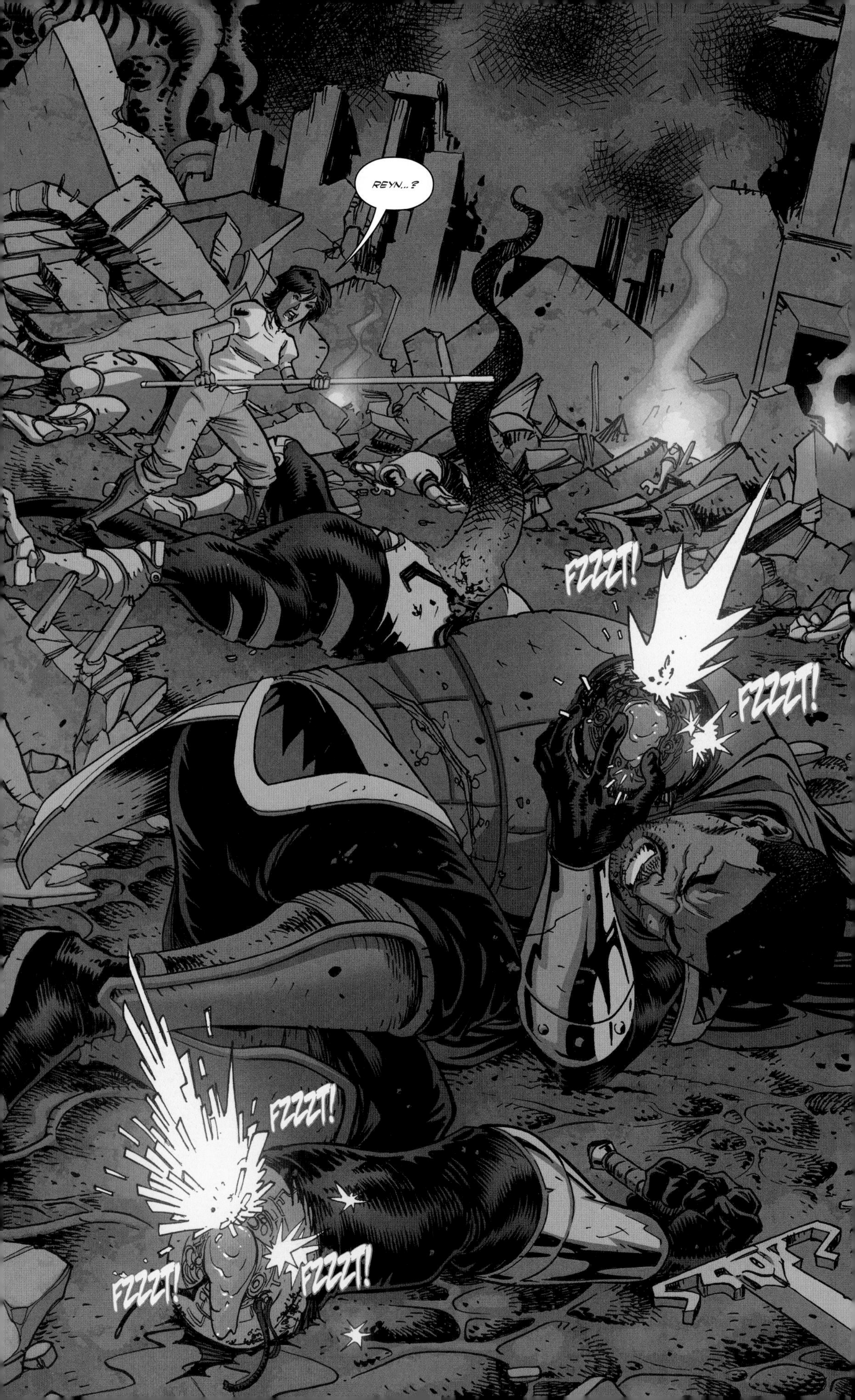
REYN...?
FZZZT!
FZZZT!
FZZZT!
FZZZT!
FZZZT!

Chapter Ten

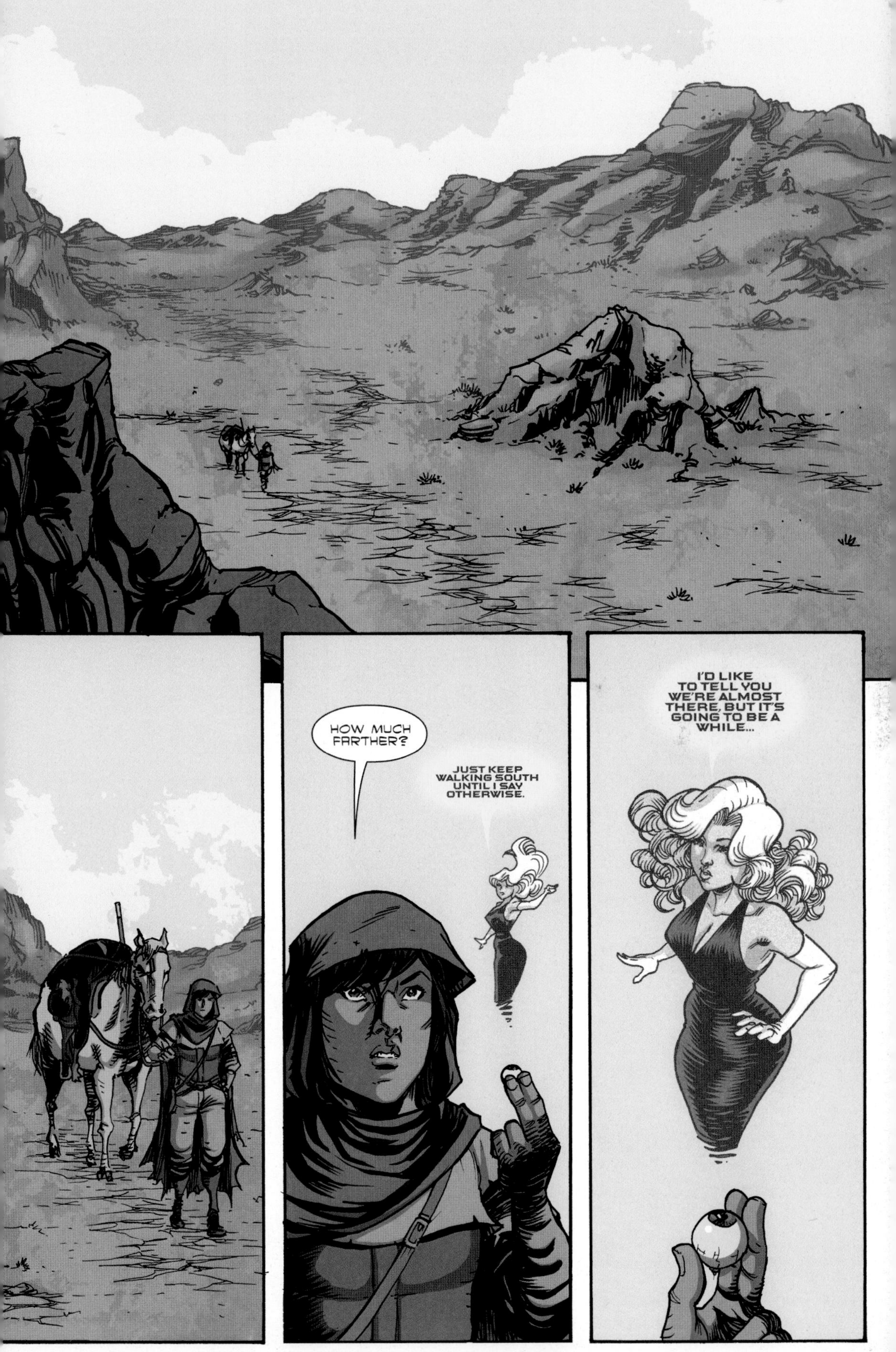
HOW MUCH FARTHER?
JUST KEEP WALKING SOUTH UNTIL I SAY OTHERWISE.
I'D LIKE TO TELL YOU WE'RE ALMOST THERE, BUT IT'S GOING TO BE A WHILE...

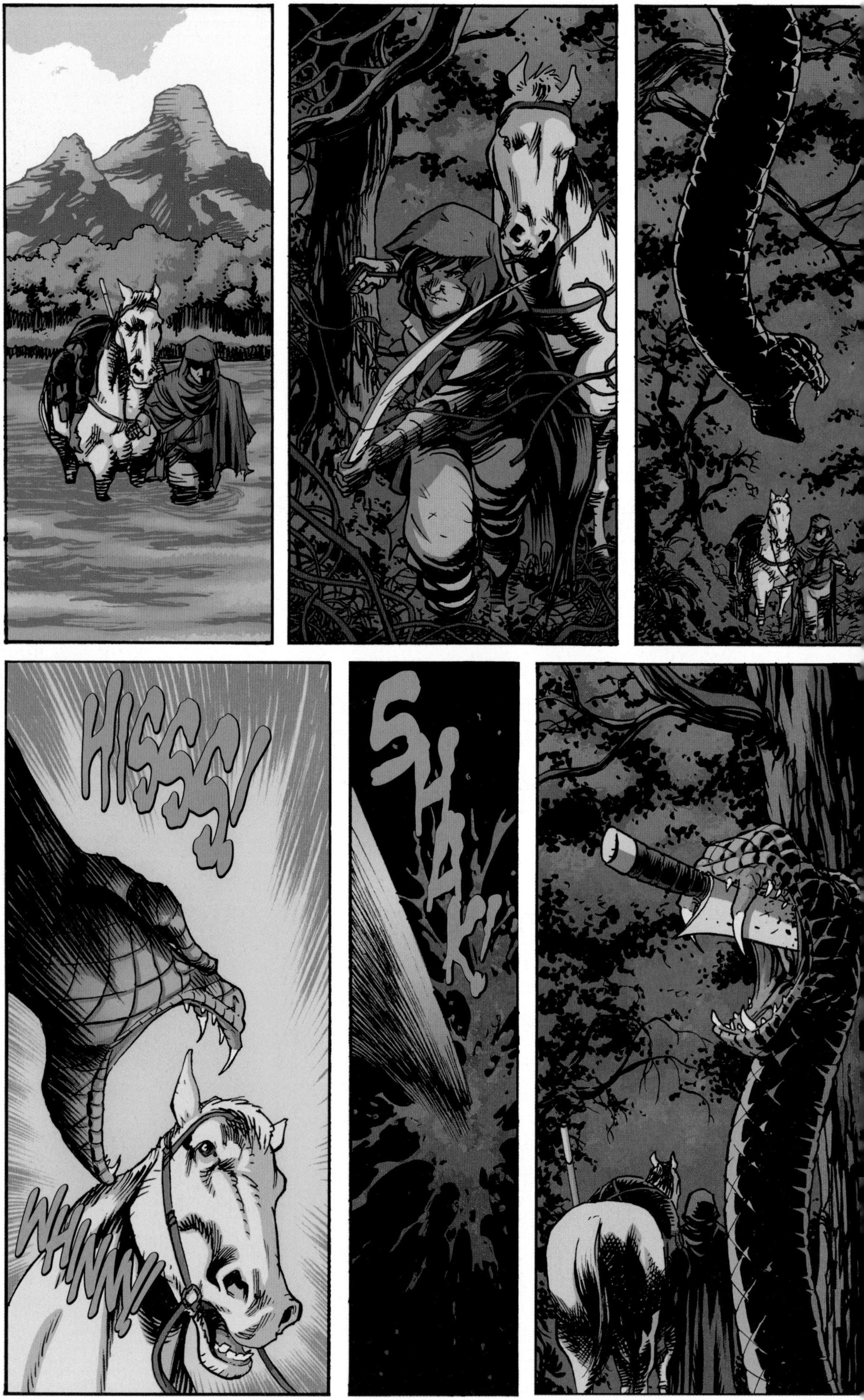
HISSS!
WHINNN!
SHAK!

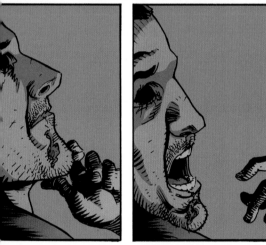

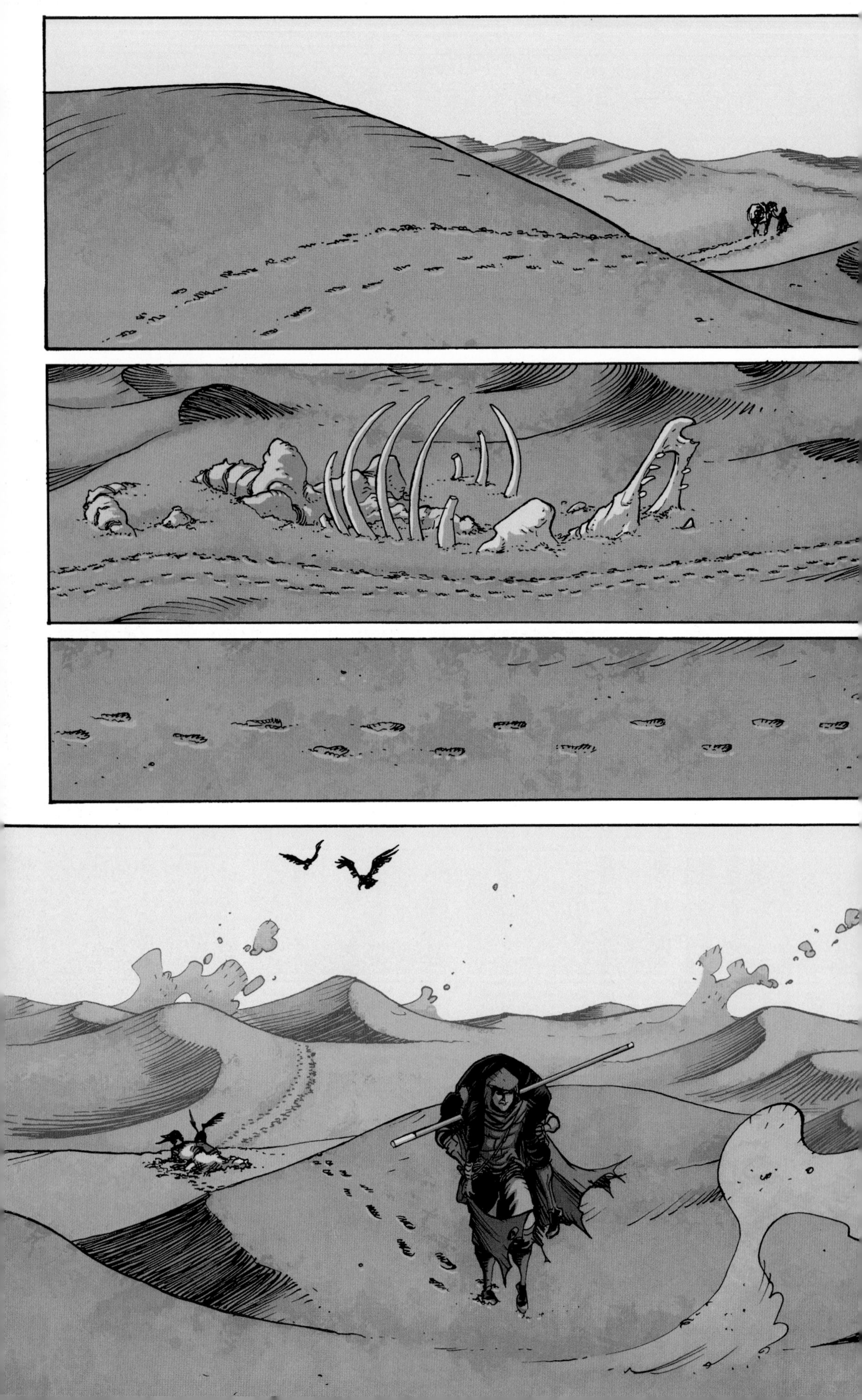

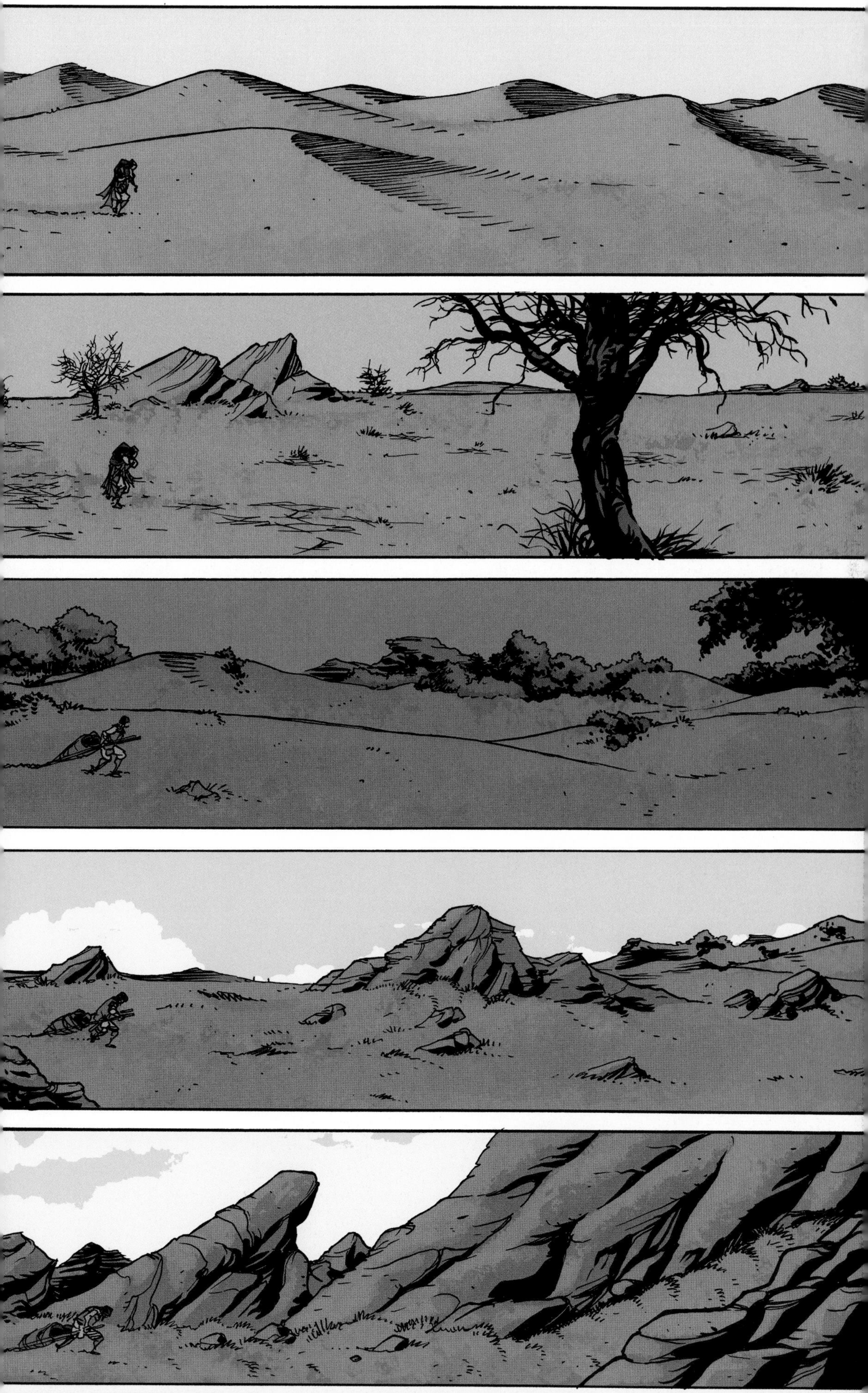

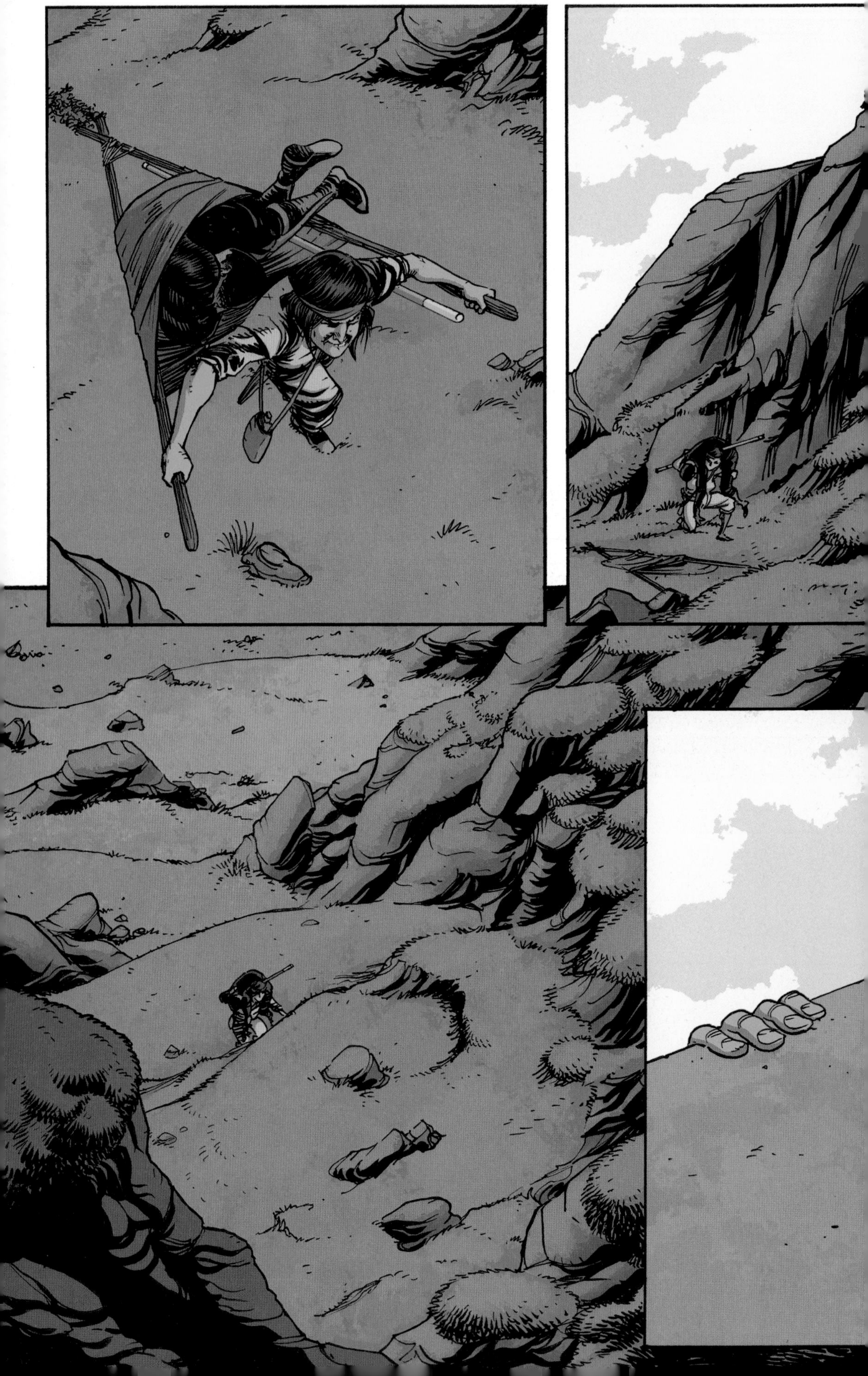

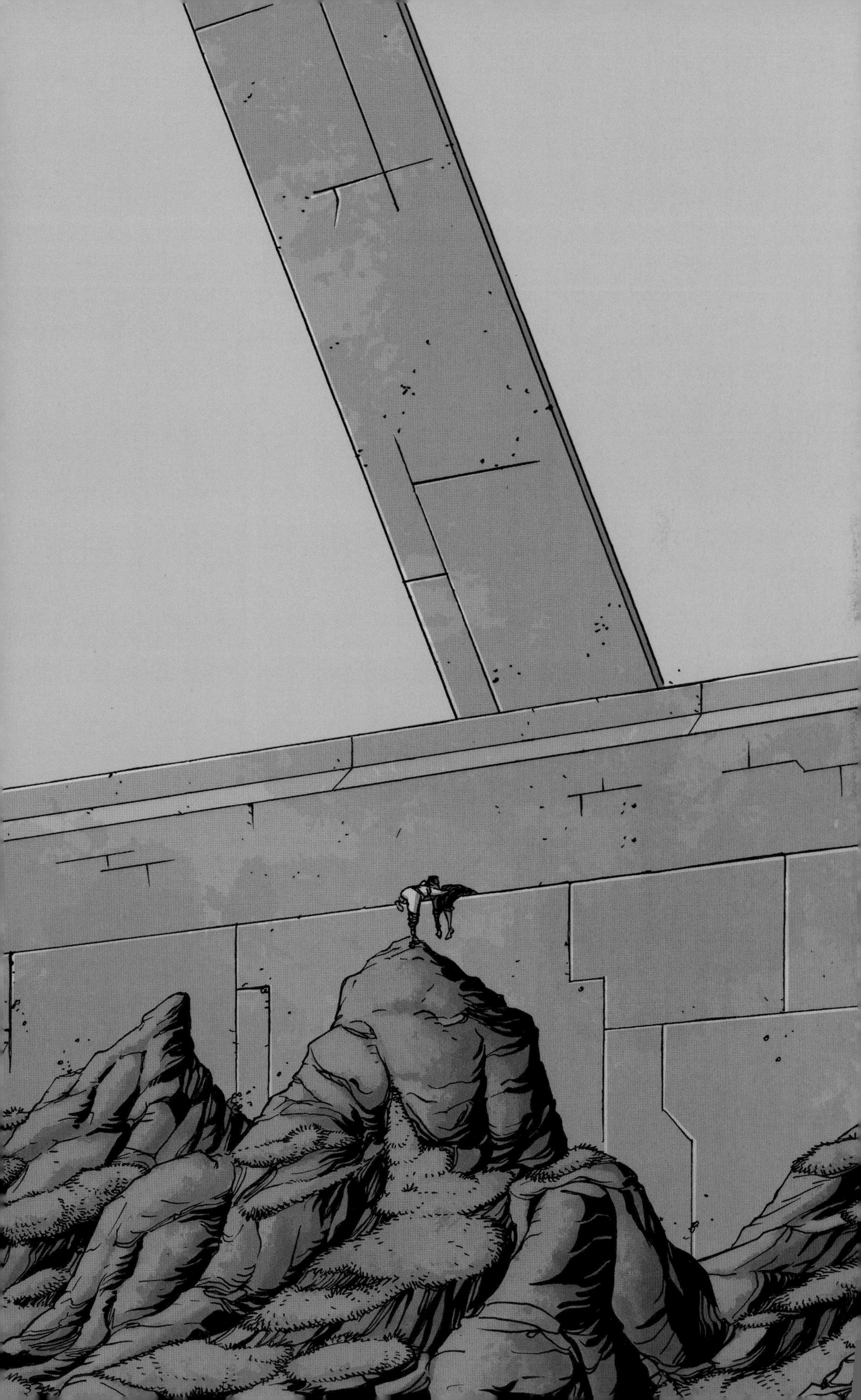

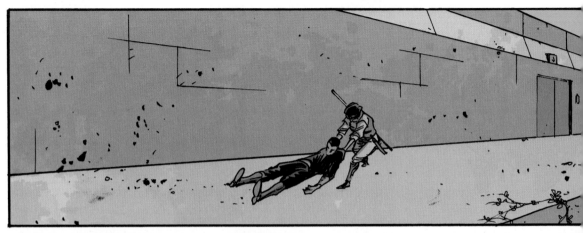

PLACE REVN'S EYE NEAR THE SCANNER.

SCANNING...

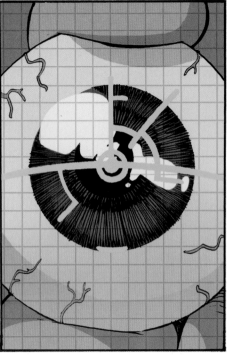

WHOOSH!

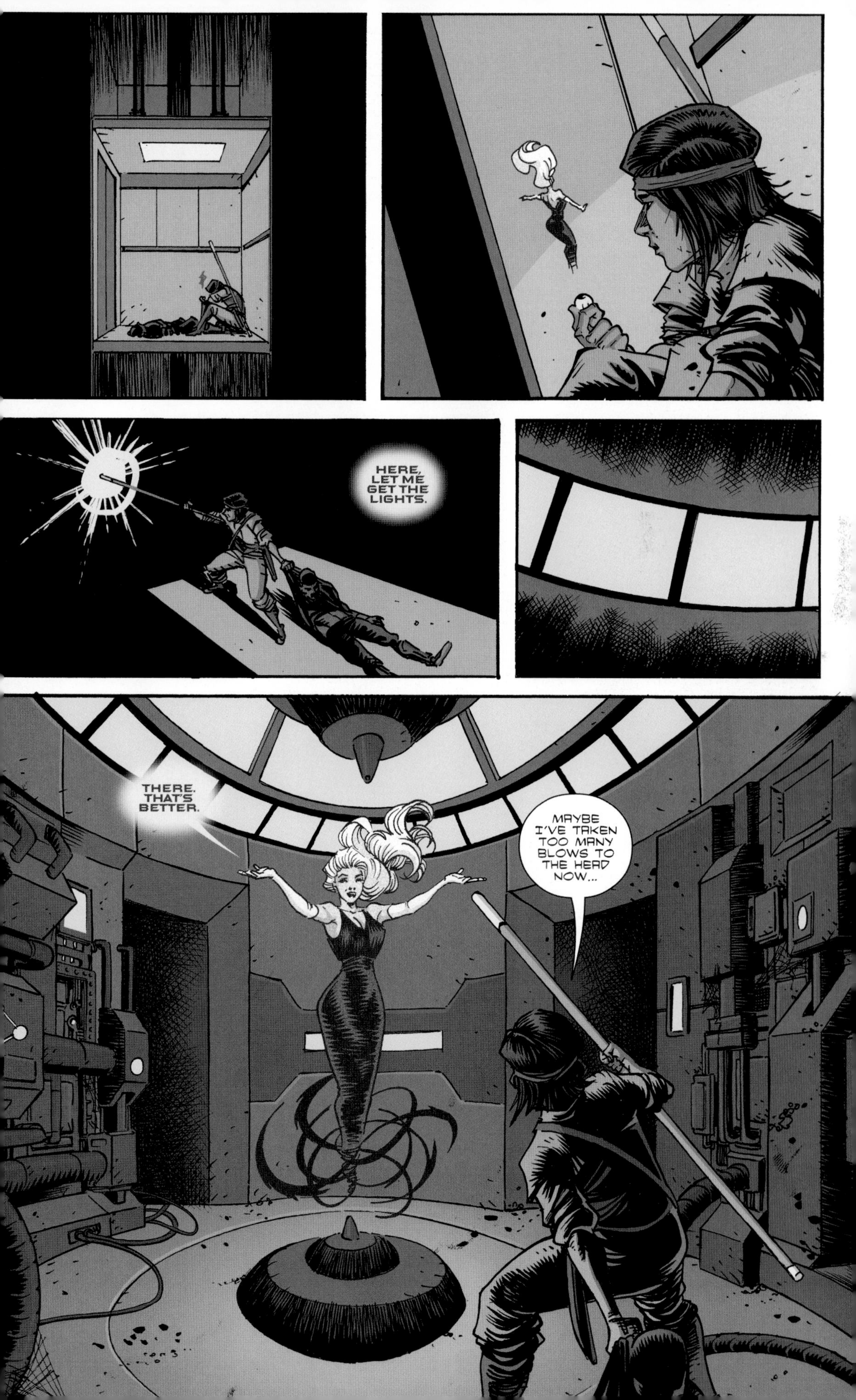
HERE, LET ME GET THE LIGHTS.
THERE. THAT'S BETTER.
MAYBE I'VE TAKEN TOO MANY BLOWS TO THE HEAD NOW...

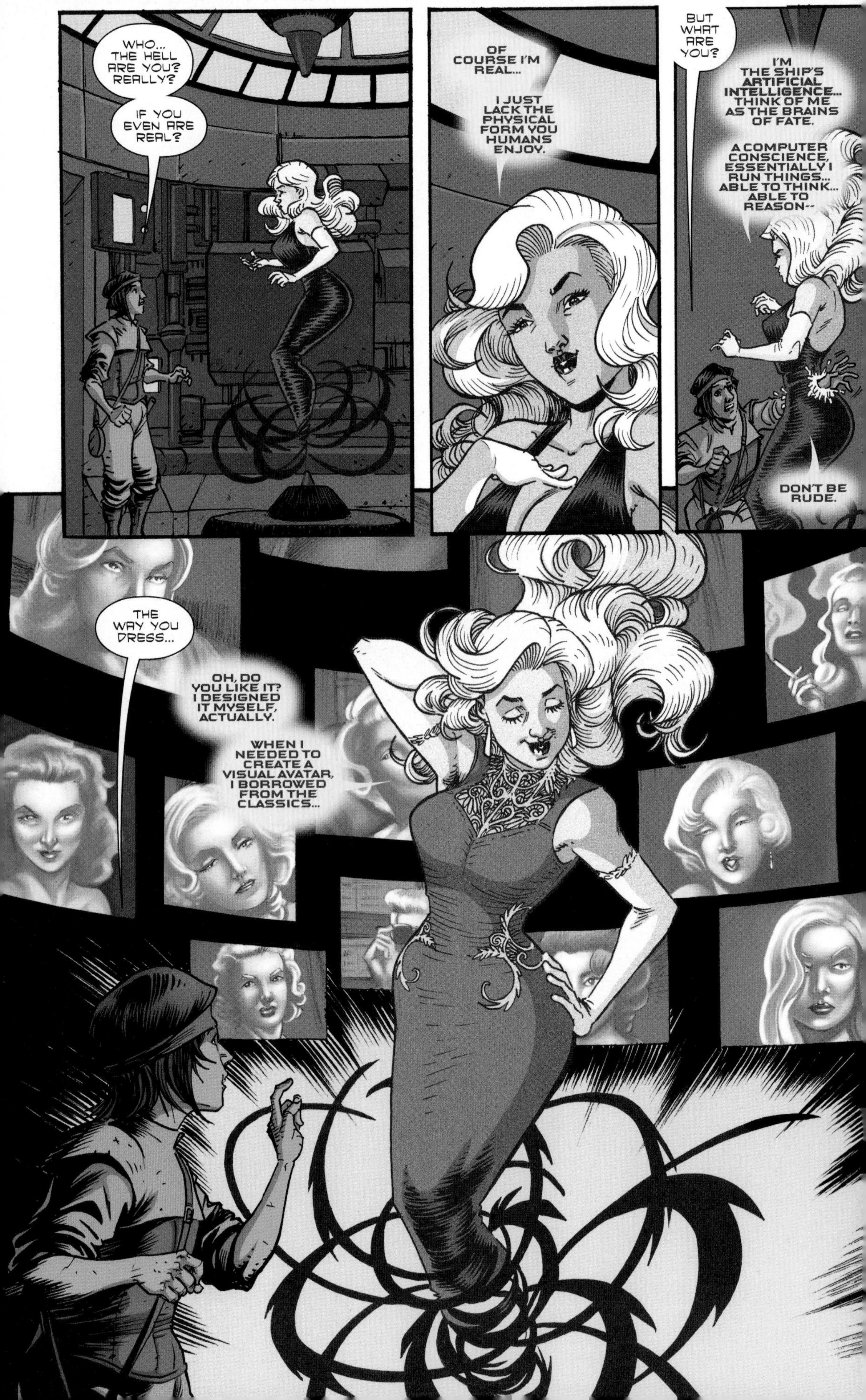

WHO... THE HELL ARE YOU? REALLY?
IF YOU EVEN ARE REAL?
OF COURSE I'M REAL...
I JUST LACK THE PHYSICAL FORM YOU HUMANS ENJOY.
BUT WHAT ARE YOU?
I'M THE SHIP'S ARTIFICIAL INTELLIGENCE... THINK OF ME AS THE BRAINS OF FATE.
A COMPUTER CONSCIENCE, ESSENTIALLY I RUN THINGS... ABLE TO THINK... ABLE TO REASON--
DON'T BE RUDE.
THE WAY YOU DRESS...
OH, DO YOU LIKE IT? I DESIGNED IT MYSELF, ACTUALLY.
WHEN I NEEDED TO CREATE A VISUAL AVATAR, I BORROWED FROM THE CLASSICS...

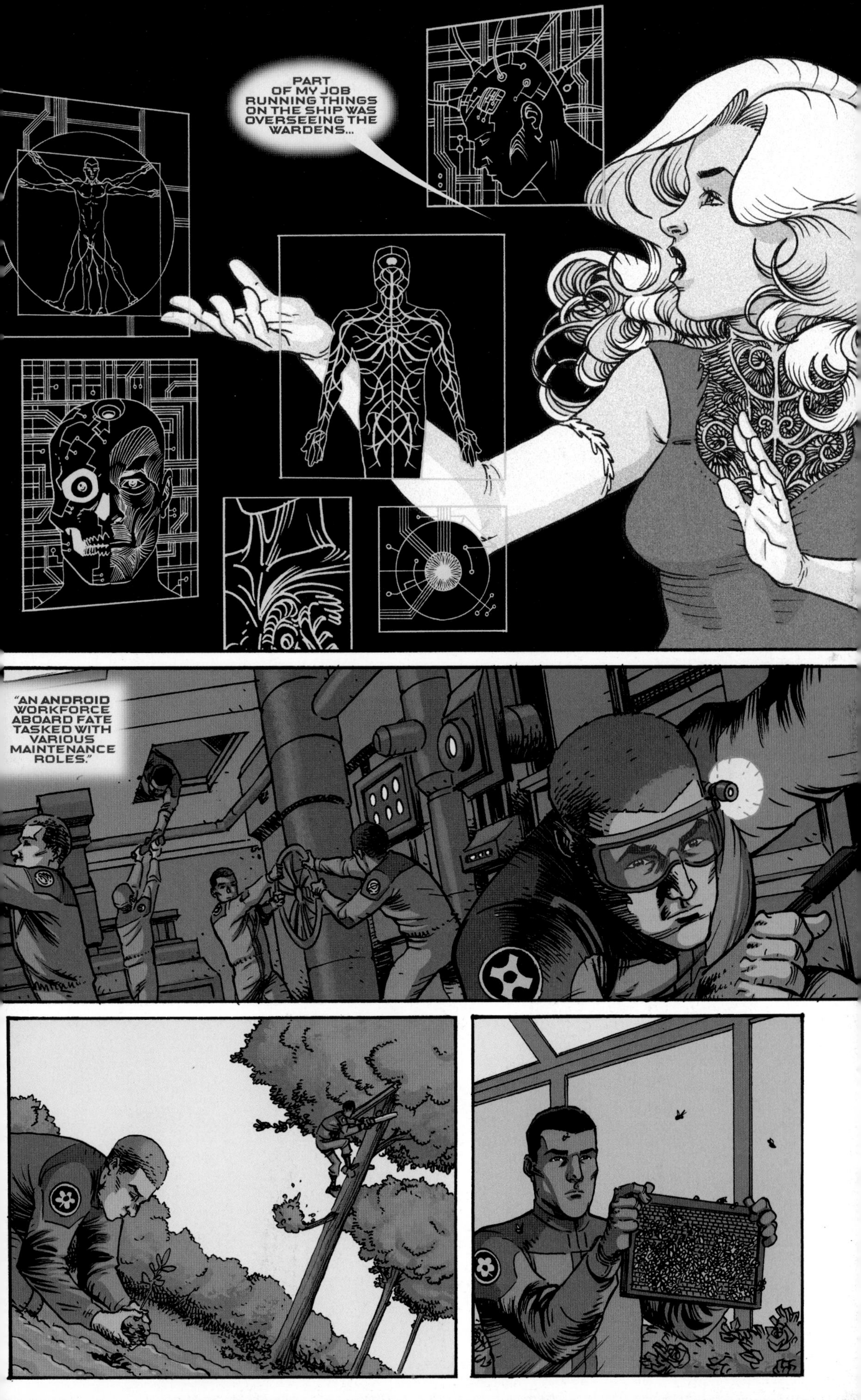
PART OF MY JOB RUNNING THINGS ON THE SHIP WAS OVERSEEING THE WARDENS...
"AN ANDROID WORKFORCE ABOARD FATE TASKED WITH VARIOUS MAINTENANCE ROLES."

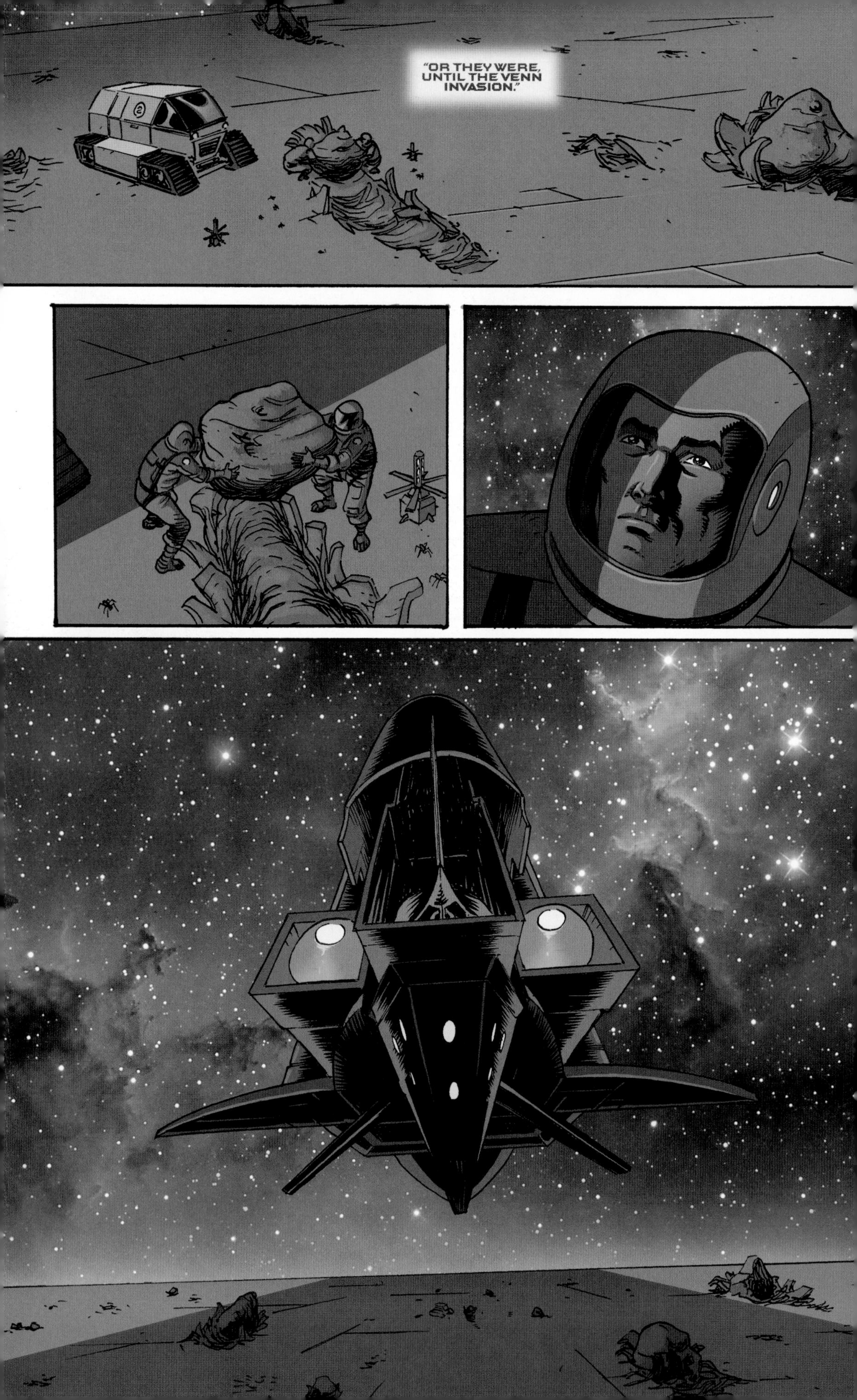
"OR THEY WERE, UNTIL THE VENN INVASION."

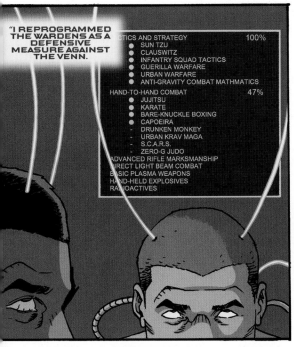

"I REPROGRAMMED THE WARDENS AS A DEFENSIVE MEASURE AGAINST THE VENN.

TACTICS AND STRATEGY		100%
● SUN TZU		
● CLAUSWITZ		
● INFANTRY SQUAD TACTICS		
● GUERILLA WARFARE		
● URBAN WARFARE		
● ANTI-GRAVITY COMBAT MATHMATICS		
HAND-TO-HAND COMBAT		47%
● JUJITSU		
● KARATE		
● BARE-KNUCKLE BOXING		
● CAPOEIRA		
- DRUNKEN MONKEY		
- URBAN KRAV MAGA		
- S.C.A.R.S.		
- ZERO-G JUDO		
ADVANCED RIFLE MARKSMANSHIP		
DIRECT LIGHT BEAM COMBAT		
BASIC PLASMA WEAPONS		
HAND-HELD EXPLOSIVES		
RADIOACTIVES		

"A SECURITY FORCE, I ARMED THEM TO REPEL BOARDERS.

"AND THEY WERE VERY NEARLY SUCCESSFUL AT TURNING BACK THE INVADERS...

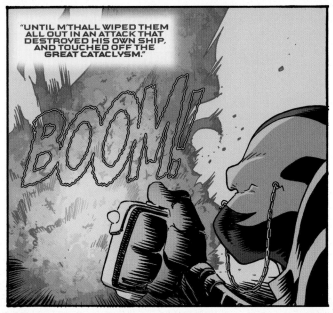

"UNTIL M'THALL WIPED THEM ALL OUT IN AN ATTACK THAT DESTROYED HIS OWN SHIP, AND TOUCHED OFF THE GREAT CATACLYSM."

BOOM!

I JUST CAN'T BELIEVE IT.

THIS WHOLE TIME... HOW CAN REYN NOT BE REAL?

YOU MUST HAVE SUSPECTED...

I MEAN, COME ON...NOBODY GETS THEIR HAIRLINE THAT PERFECT UNLESS IT'S MAN-MADE.

NO, I DIDN'T SUSPECT.

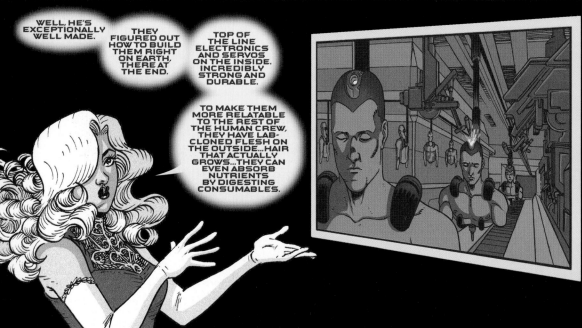

WELL, HE'S EXCEPTIONALLY WELL MADE.

THEY FIGURED OUT HOW TO BUILD THEM RIGHT ON EARTH, THERE AT THE END.

TOP OF THE LINE ELECTRONICS AND SERVOS ON THE INSIDE. INCREDIBLY STRONG AND DURABLE.

TO MAKE THEM MORE RELATABLE TO THE REST OF THE HUMAN CREW, THEY HAVE LAB-CLONED FLESH ON THE OUTSIDE...HAIR THAT ACTUALLY GROWS...THEY CAN EVEN ABSORB NUTRIENTS BY DIGESTING CONSUMABLES.

EVEN HIS...UH...FULLY FUNCTIONAL--

YEAH, I DON'T NEED TO KNOW EVERYTHING.

JUST SAYING...

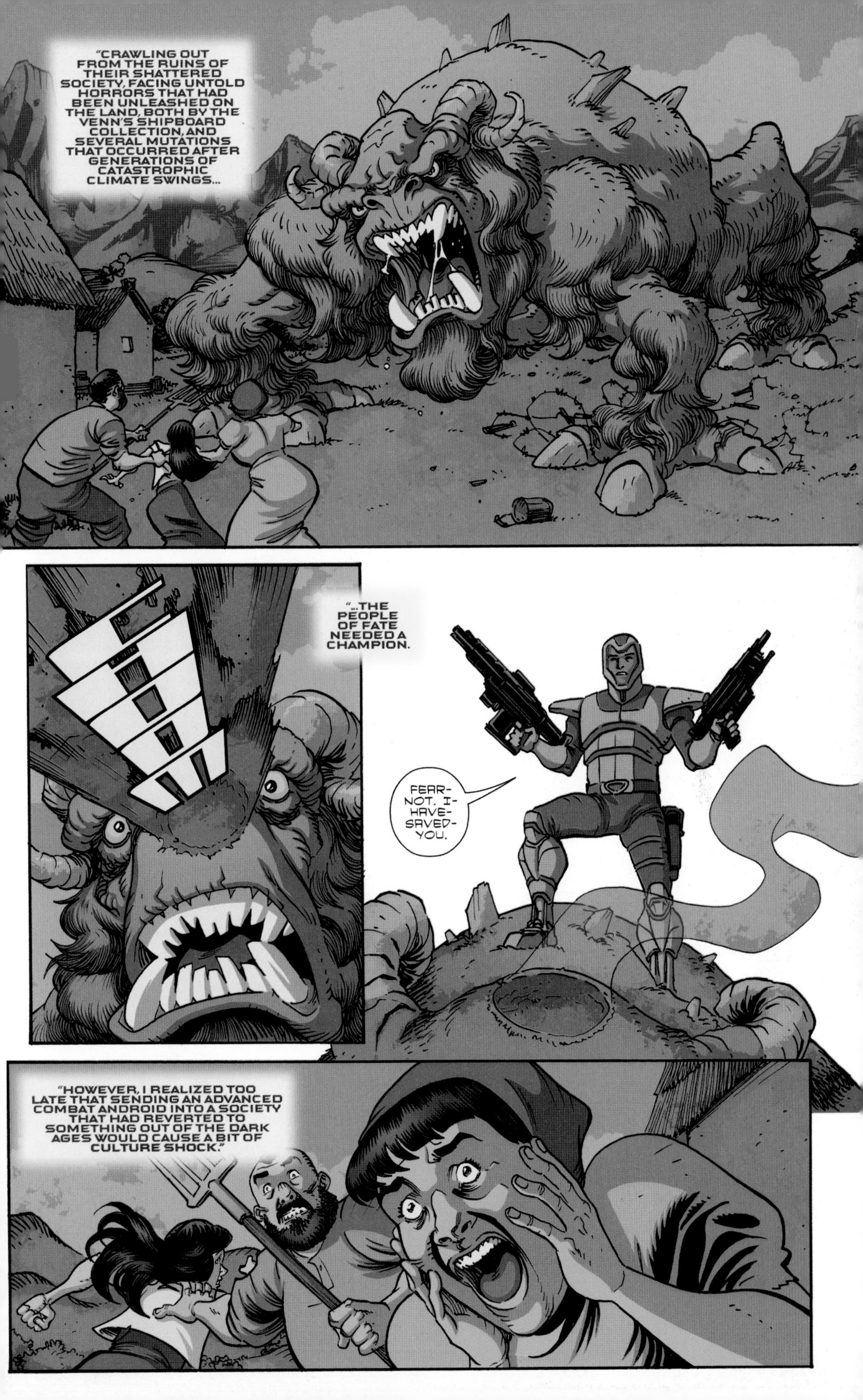
"CRAWLING OUT FROM THE RUINS OF THEIR SHATTERED SOCIETY, FACING UNTOLD HORRORS THAT HAD BEEN UNLEASHED ON THE LAND, BOTH BY THE VENN'S SHIPBOARD COLLECTION, AND SEVERAL MUTATIONS THAT OCCURRED AFTER GENERATIONS OF CATASTROPHIC CLIMATE SWINGS...
"...THE PEOPLE OF FATE NEEDED A CHAMPION.
FEAR-NOT. I-HAVE-SAVED-YOU.
"HOWEVER, I REALIZED TOO LATE THAT SENDING AN ADVANCED COMBAT ANDROID INTO A SOCIETY THAT HAD REVERTED TO SOMETHING OUT OF THE DARK AGES WOULD CAUSE A BIT OF CULTURE SHOCK."

"SO I ADJUSTED REVN'S PROGRAMMING TO ADAPT HIM TO THIS NEW... WELL, OLD WORLD MENTALITY."

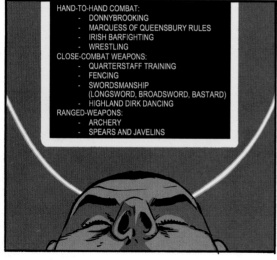

HAND-TO-HAND COMBAT:
- DONNYBROOKING
- MARQUESS OF QUEENSBURY RULES
- IRISH BARFIGHTING
- WRESTLING

CLOSE-COMBAT WEAPONS:
- QUARTERSTAFF TRAINING
- FENCING
- SWORDSMANSHIP (LONGSWORD, BROADSWORD, BASTARD)
- HIGHLAND DIRK DANCING

RANGED-WEAPONS:
- ARCHERY
- SPEARS AND JAVELINS

"TRADED HIS PULSE RIFLE FOR A SWORD."

FEAR-NOT. I-HAVE-SAVED-YOU.

"STILL, AS ADVANCED AS HE WAS, HE KIND OF LACKED... PERSONALITY."

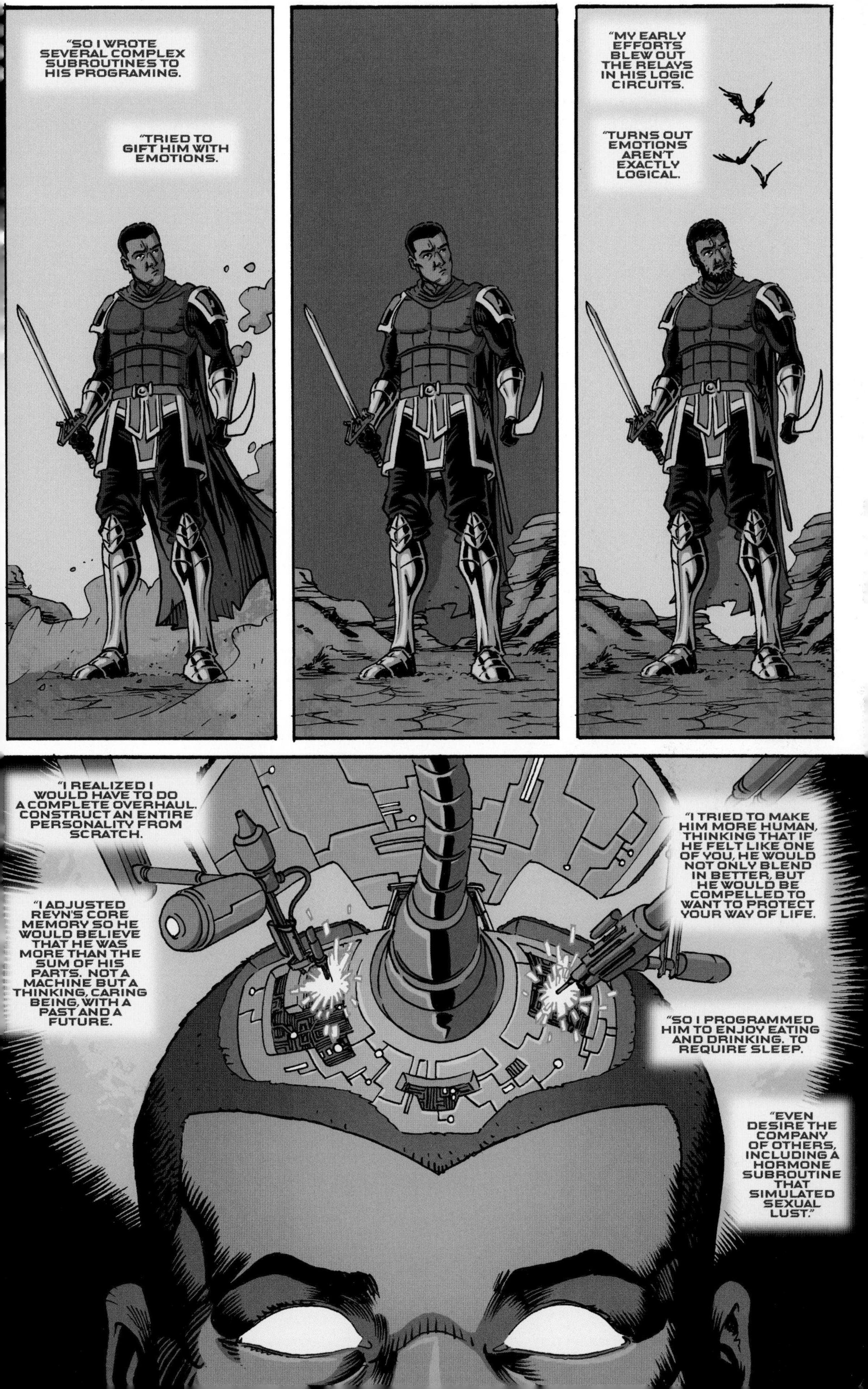
"SO I WROTE SEVERAL COMPLEX SUBROUTINES TO HIS PROGRAMING.
"TRIED TO GIFT HIM WITH EMOTIONS.
"MY EARLY EFFORTS BLEW OUT THE RELAYS IN HIS LOGIC CIRCUITS.
"TURNS OUT EMOTIONS AREN'T EXACTLY LOGICAL.
"I REALIZED I WOULD HAVE TO DO A COMPLETE OVERHAUL. CONSTRUCT AN ENTIRE PERSONALITY FROM SCRATCH.
"I ADJUSTED REYN'S CORE MEMORY SO HE WOULD BELIEVE THAT HE WAS MORE THAN THE SUM OF HIS PARTS. NOT A MACHINE BUT A THINKING, CARING BEING, WITH A PAST AND A FUTURE.
"I TRIED TO MAKE HIM MORE HUMAN, THINKING THAT IF HE FELT LIKE ONE OF YOU, HE WOULD NOT ONLY BLEND IN BETTER, BUT HE WOULD BE COMPELLED TO WANT TO PROTECT YOUR WAY OF LIFE.
"SO I PROGRAMMED HIM TO ENJOY EATING AND DRINKING. TO REQUIRE SLEEP.
"EVEN DESIRE THE COMPANY OF OTHERS, INCLUDING A HORMONE SUBROUTINE THAT SIMULATED SEXUAL LUST."

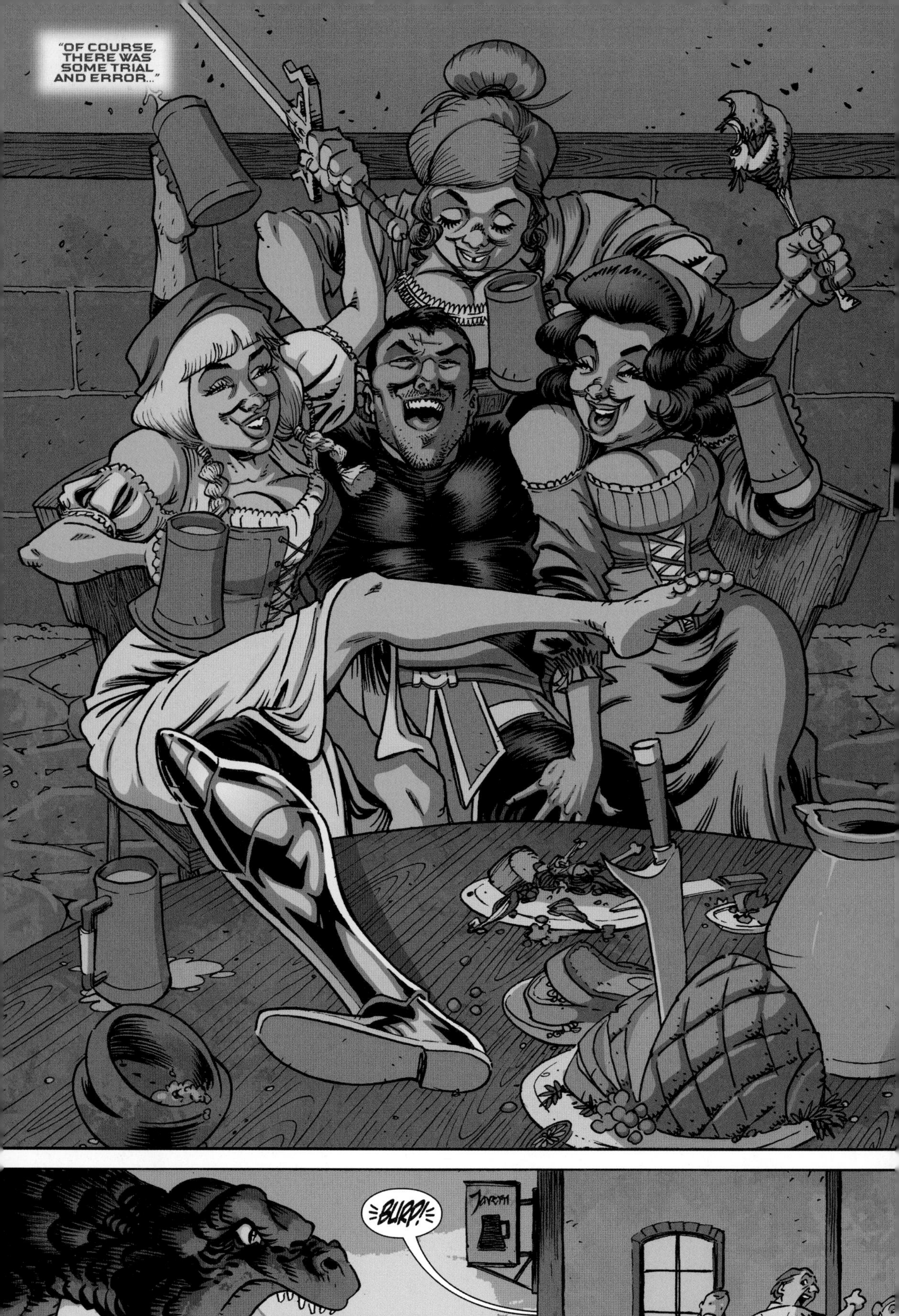
"OF COURSE, THERE WAS SOME TRIAL AND ERROR..."

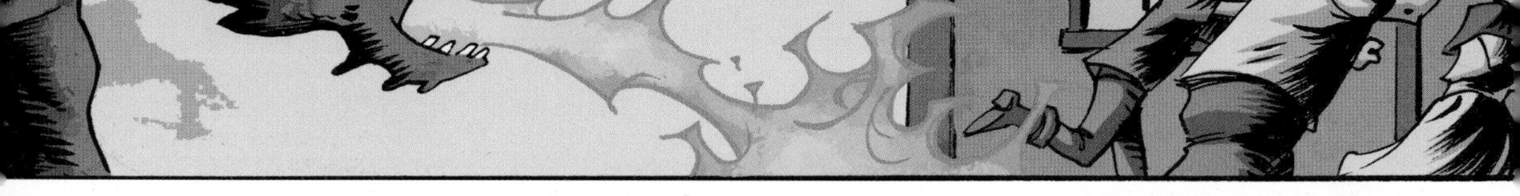
BURP!
Tavern

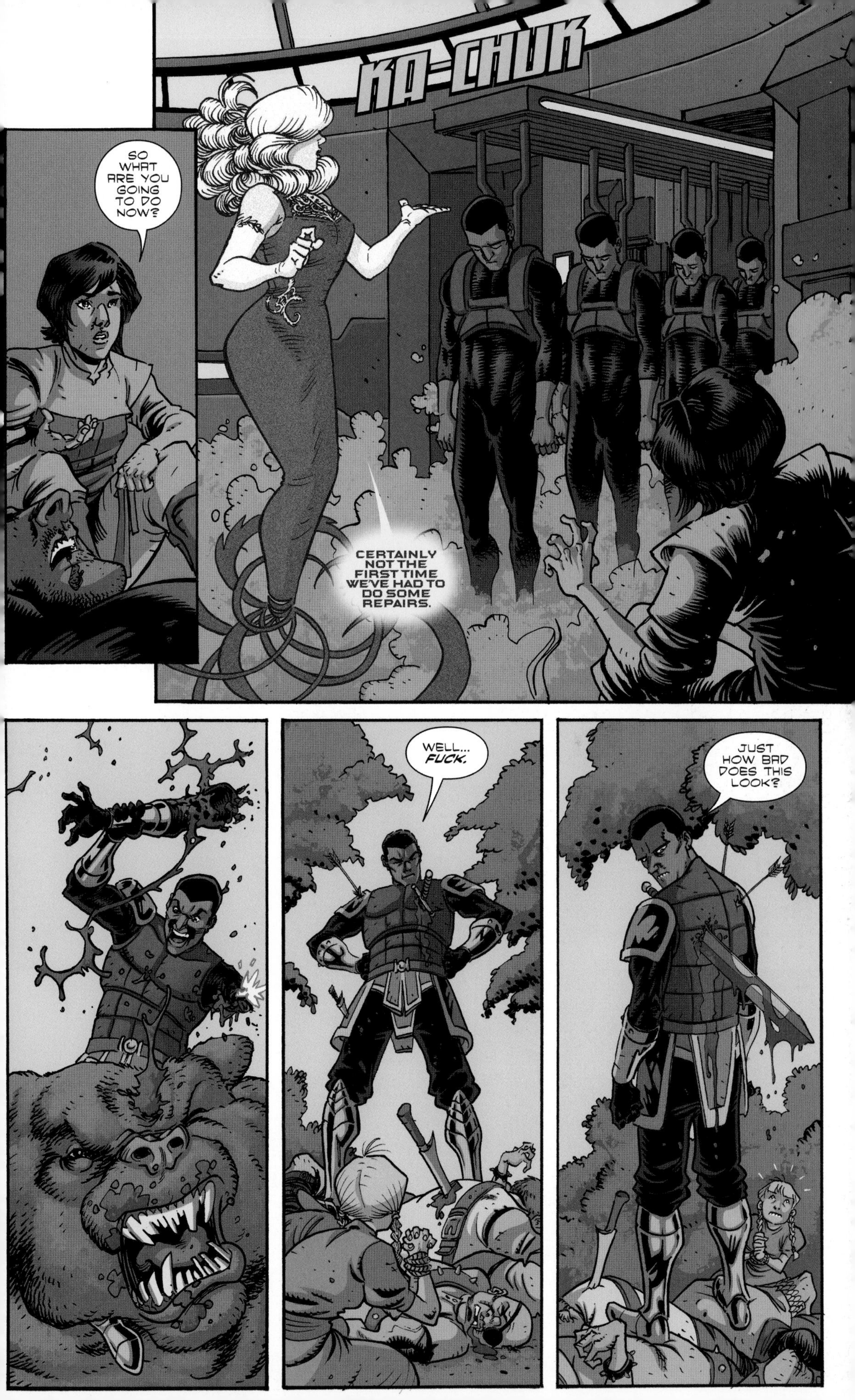
KA-CHUK
SO WHAT ARE YOU GOING TO DO NOW?
CERTAINLY NOT THE FIRST TIME WE'VE HAD TO DO SOME REPAIRS.
WELL... *FUCK.*
JUST HOW BAD DOES THIS LOOK?

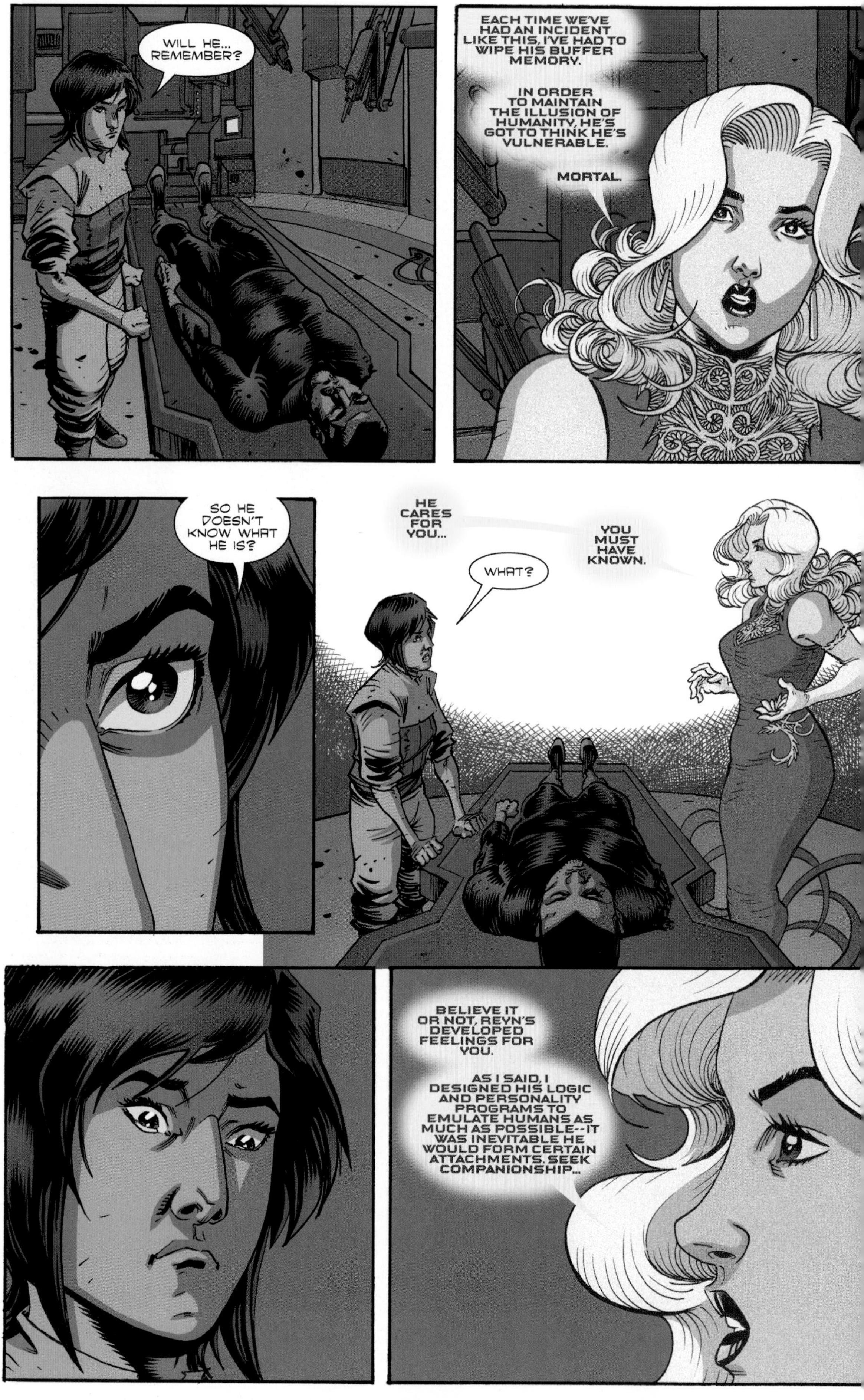

WILL HE... REMEMBER?
EACH TIME WE'VE HAD AN INCIDENT LIKE THIS, I'VE HAD TO WIPE HIS BUFFER MEMORY.
IN ORDER TO MAINTAIN THE ILLUSION OF HUMANITY, HE'S GOT TO THINK HE'S VULNERABLE.
MORTAL.
SO HE DOESN'T KNOW WHAT HE IS?
HE CARES FOR YOU...
YOU MUST HAVE KNOWN.
WHAT?
BELIEVE IT OR NOT, REYN'S DEVELOPED FEELINGS FOR YOU.
AS I SAID, I DESIGNED HIS LOGIC AND PERSONALITY PROGRAMS TO EMULATE HUMANS AS MUCH AS POSSIBLE--IT WAS INEVITABLE HE WOULD FORM CERTAIN ATTACHMENTS. SEEK COMPANIONSHIP...

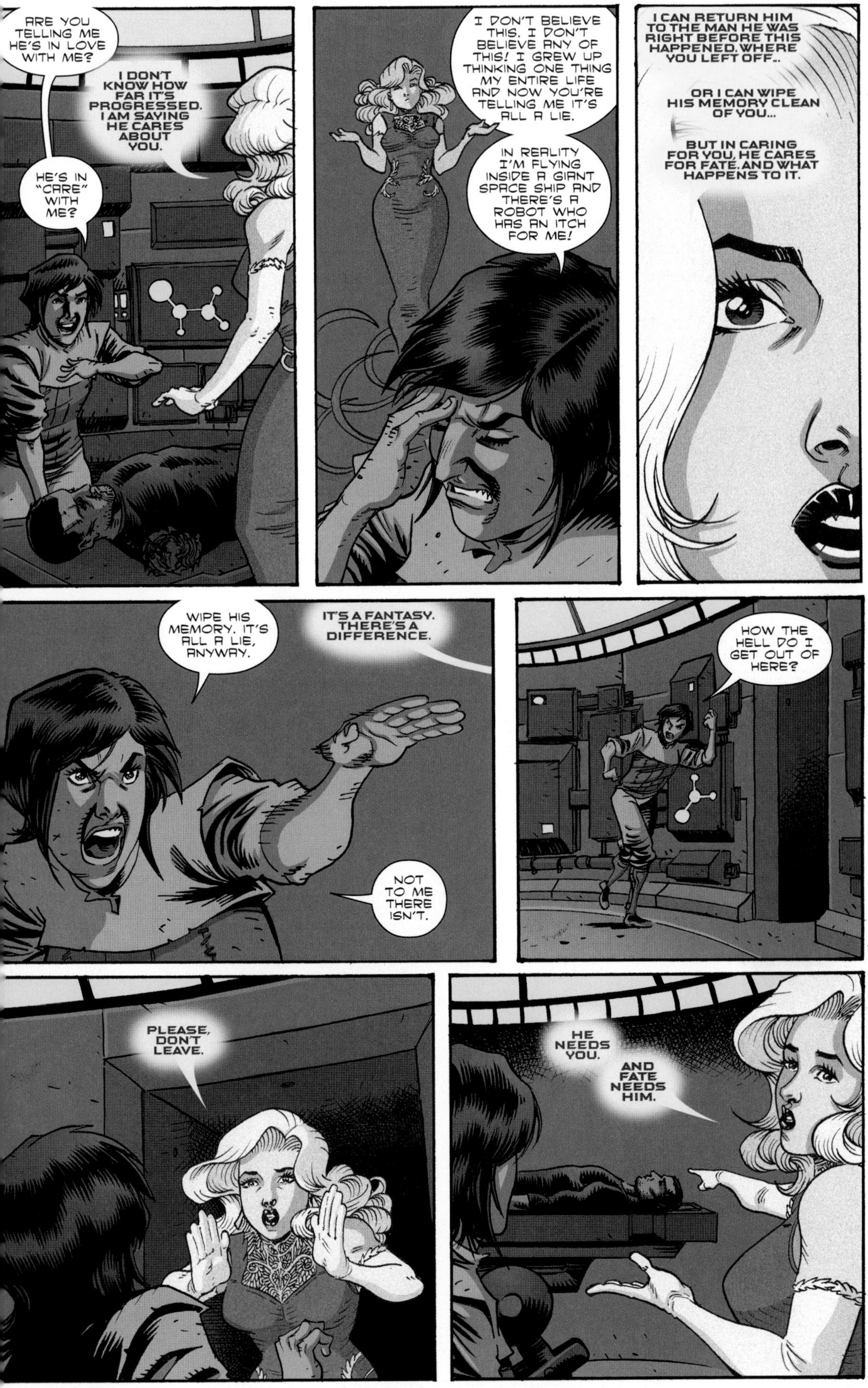
ARE YOU TELLING ME HE'S IN LOVE WITH ME?
I DON'T KNOW HOW FAR IT'S PROGRESSED. I AM SAYING HE CARES ABOUT YOU.
HE'S IN "CARE" WITH ME?
I DON'T BELIEVE THIS. I DON'T BELIEVE ANY OF THIS! I GREW UP THINKING ONE THING MY ENTIRE LIFE AND NOW YOU'RE TELLING ME IT'S ALL A LIE.
IN REALITY I'M FLYING INSIDE A GIANT SPACE SHIP AND THERE'S A ROBOT WHO HAS AN ITCH FOR ME!
I CAN RETURN HIM TO THE MAN HE WAS RIGHT BEFORE THIS HAPPENED, WHERE YOU LEFT OFF...
OR I CAN WIPE HIS MEMORY CLEAN OF YOU...
BUT IN CARING FOR YOU, HE CARES FOR FATE, AND WHAT HAPPENS TO IT.
WIPE HIS MEMORY. IT'S ALL A LIE, ANYWAY.
IT'S A FANTASY. THERE'S A DIFFERENCE.
NOT TO ME THERE ISN'T.
HOW THE HELL DO I GET OUT OF HERE?
PLEASE, DON'T LEAVE.
HE NEEDS YOU.
AND FATE NEEDS HIM.

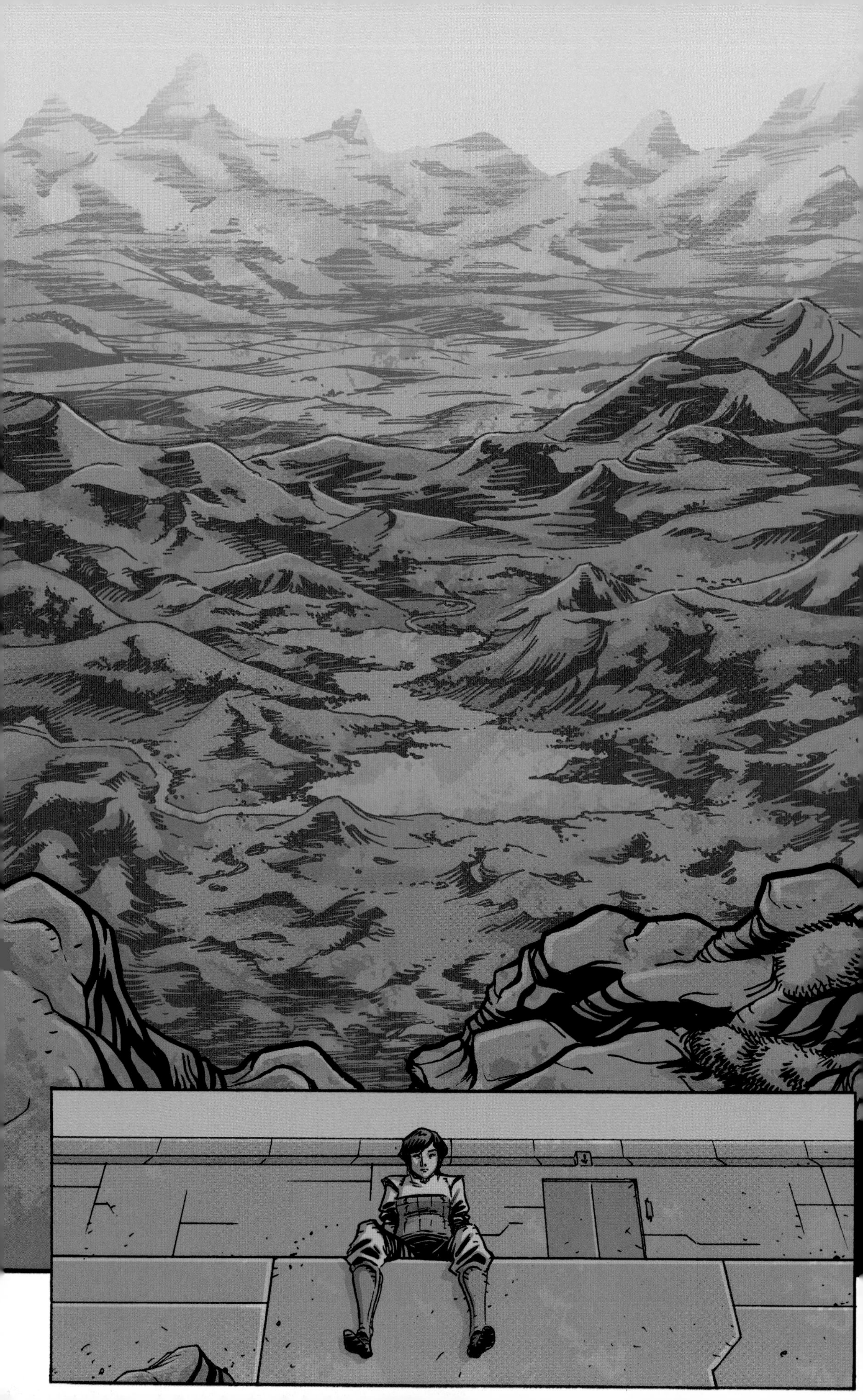

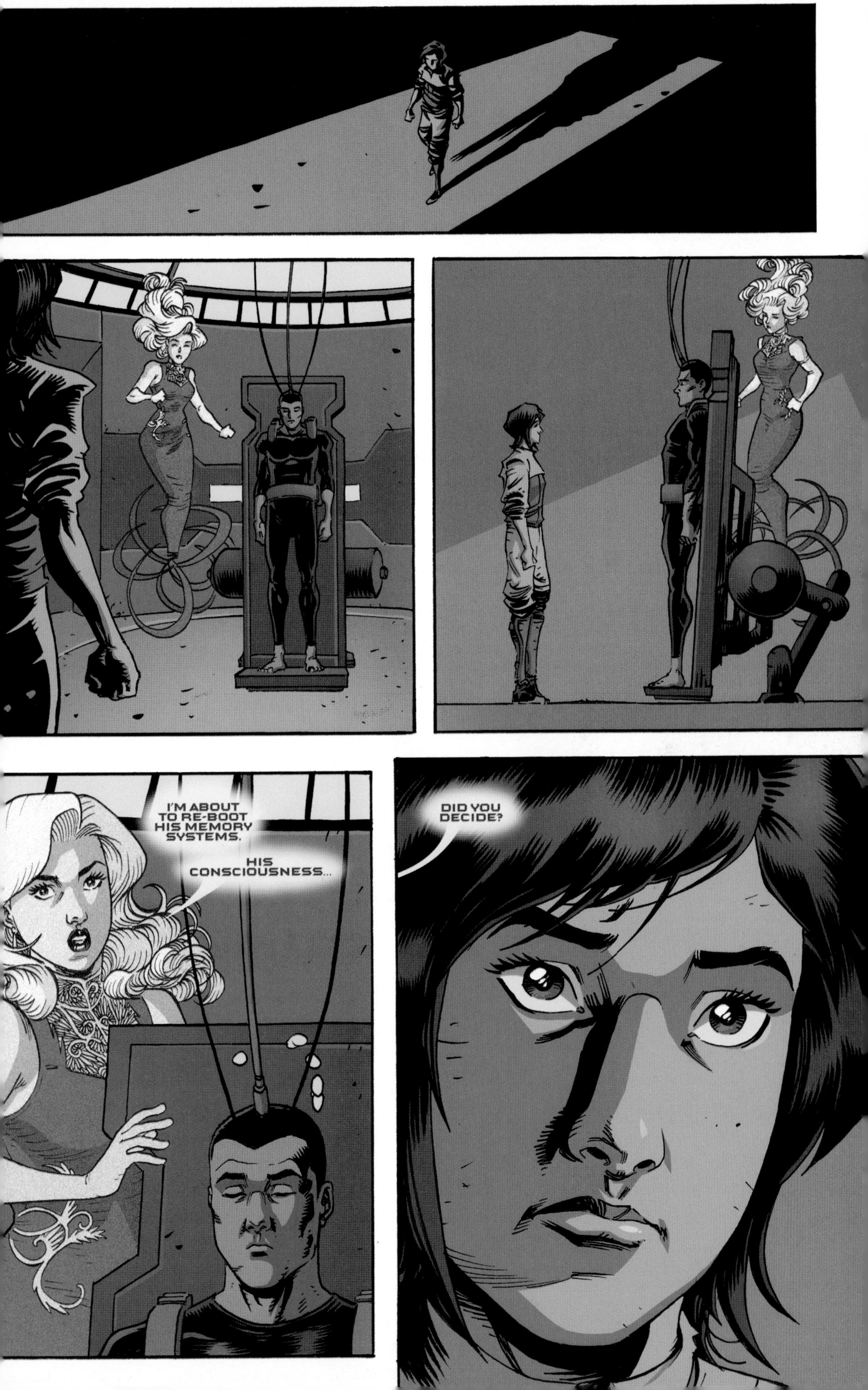
I'M ABOUT TO RE-BOOT HIS MEMORY SYSTEMS.
HIS CONSCIOUSNESS...
DID YOU DECIDE?

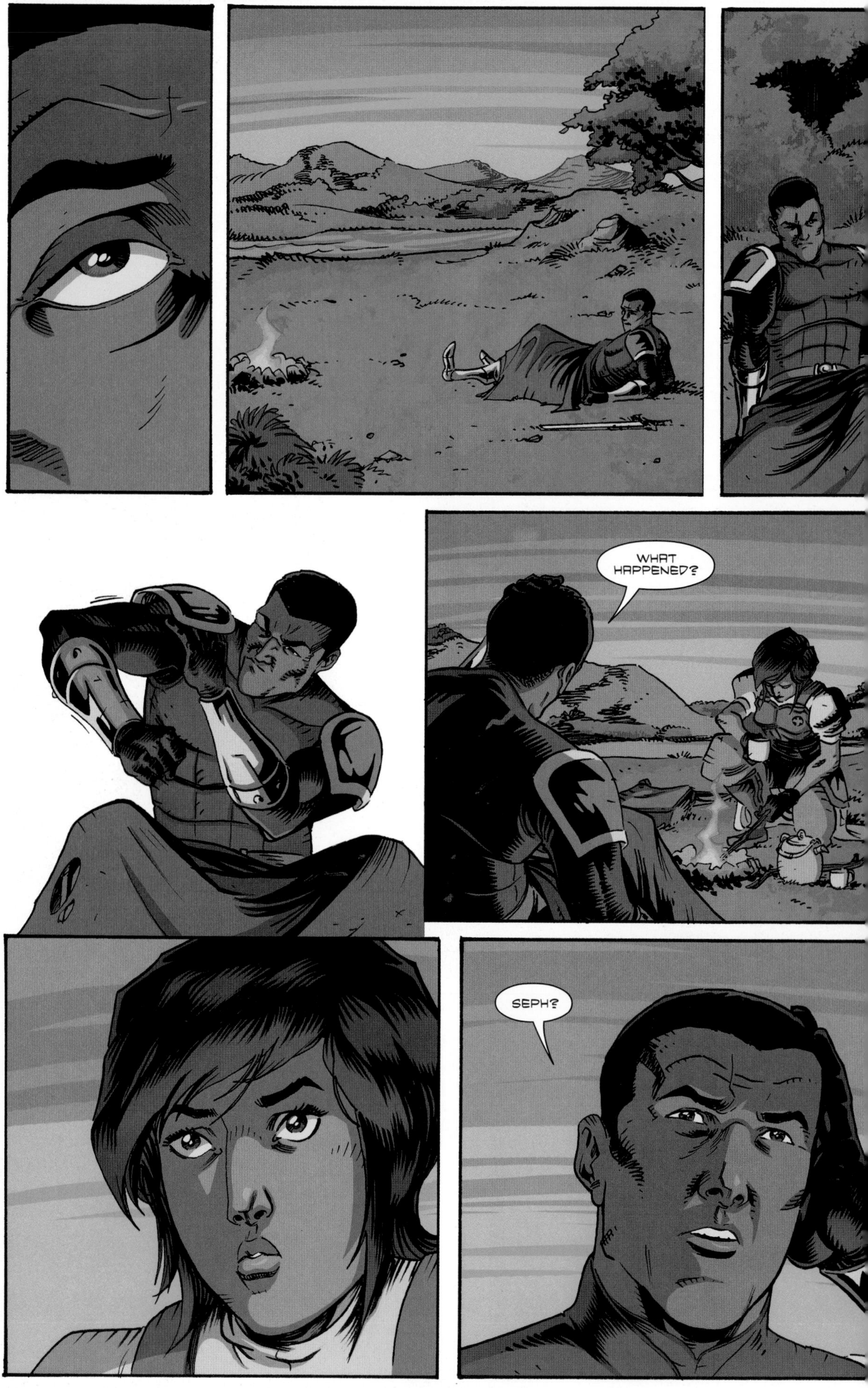
WHAT HAPPENED?
SEPH?

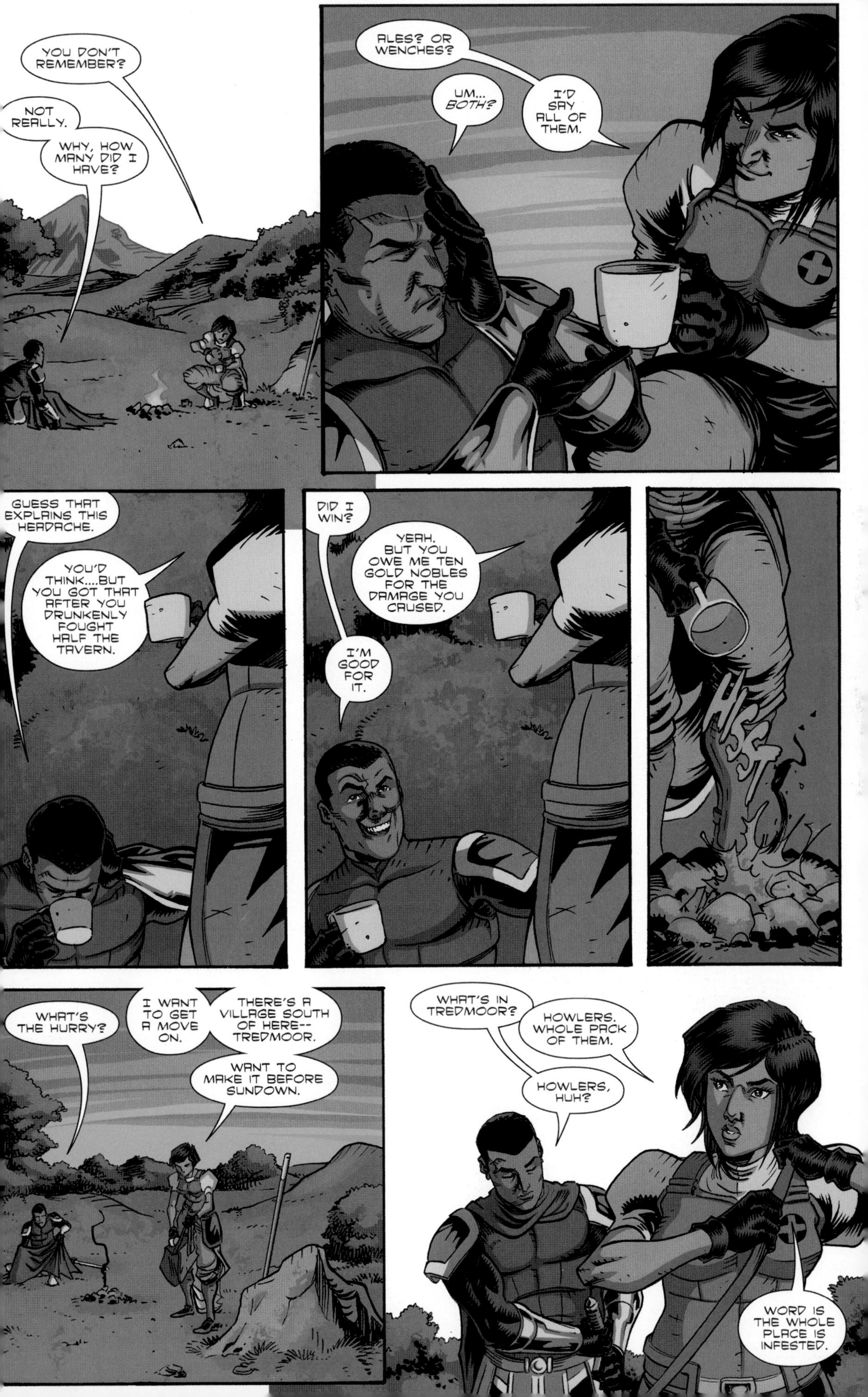
YOU DON'T REMEMBER?
NOT REALLY.
WHY, HOW MANY DID I HAVE?
ALES? OR WENCHES?
UM... *BOTH?*
I'D SAY ALL OF THEM.
GUESS THAT EXPLAINS THIS HEADACHE.
YOU'D THINK....BUT YOU GOT THAT AFTER YOU DRUNKENLY FOUGHT HALF THE TAVERN.
DID I WIN?
YEAH. BUT YOU OWE ME TEN GOLD NOBLES FOR THE DAMAGE YOU CAUSED.
I'M GOOD FOR IT.
HISS
WHAT'S THE HURRY?
I WANT TO GET A MOVE ON.
THERE'S A VILLAGE SOUTH OF HERE-- TREDMOOR.
WANT TO MAKE IT BEFORE SUNDOWN.
WHAT'S IN TREDMOOR?
HOWLERS. WHOLE PACK OF THEM.
HOWLERS, HUH?
WORD IS THE WHOLE PLACE IS INFESTED.

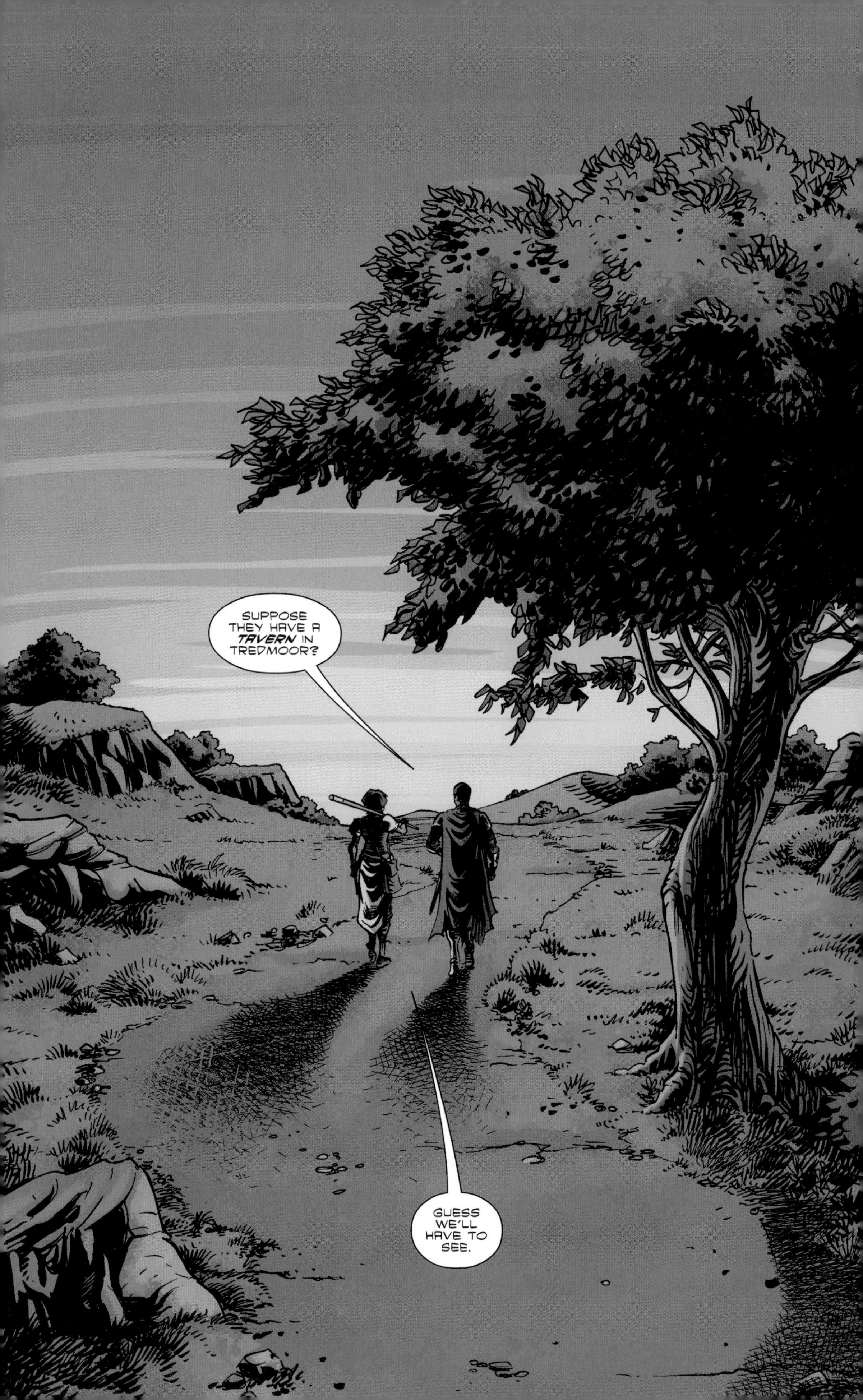
SUPPOSE THEY HAVE A *TAVERN* IN TREDMOOR?
GUESS WE'LL HAVE TO SEE.

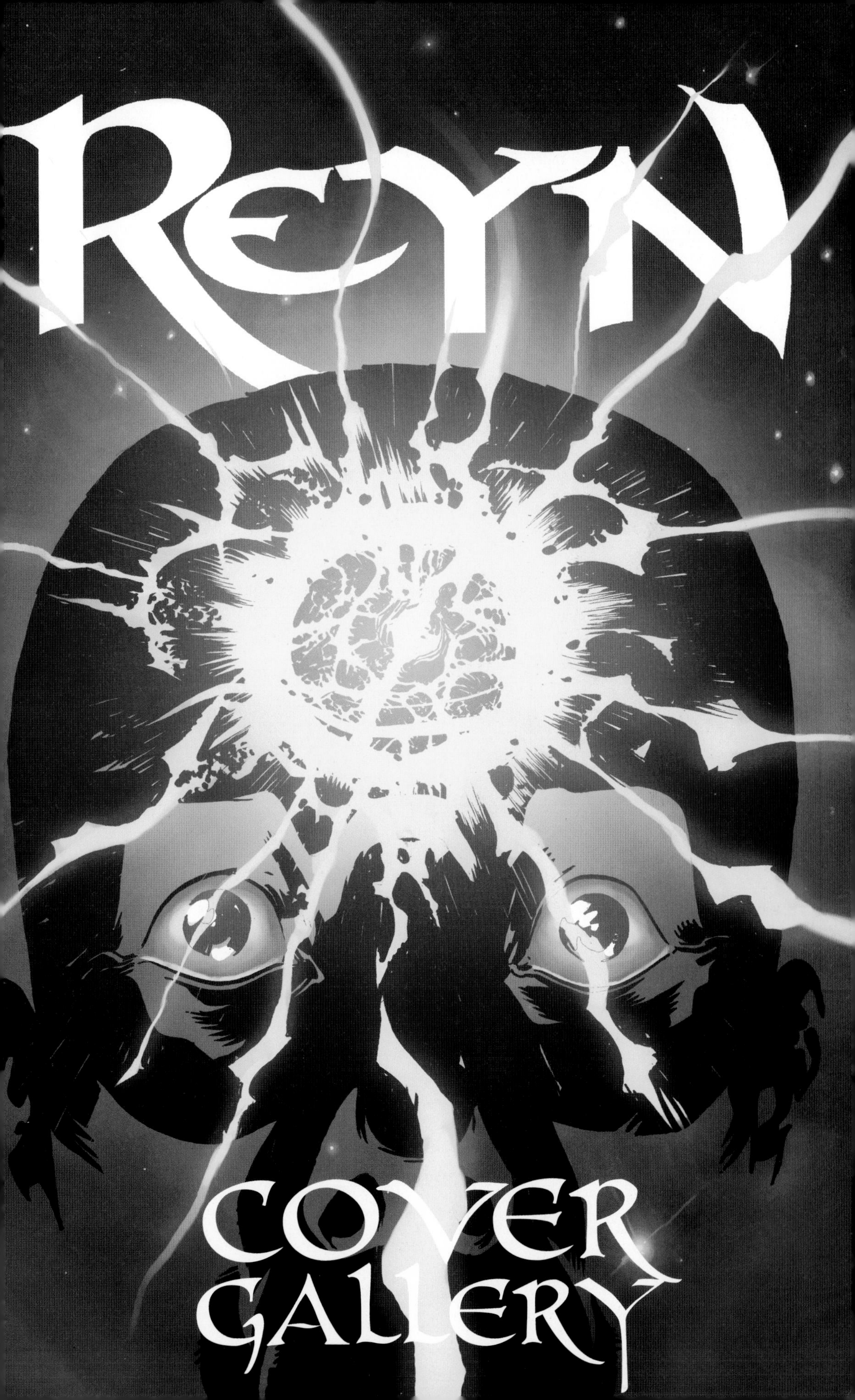
REYN
COVER
GALLERY

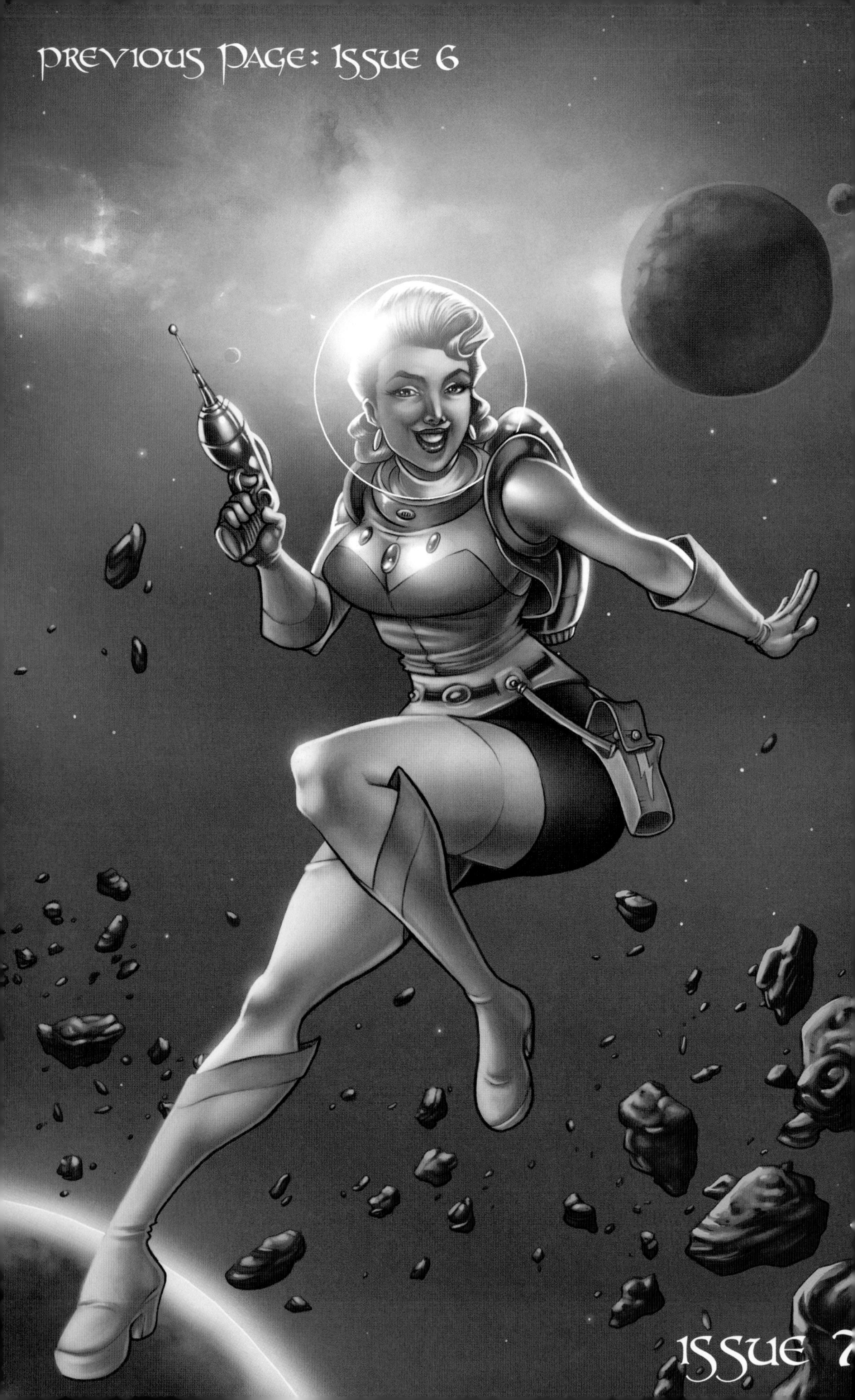

PREVIOUS PAGE: ISSUE 6

ISSUE 7

SSUE 8

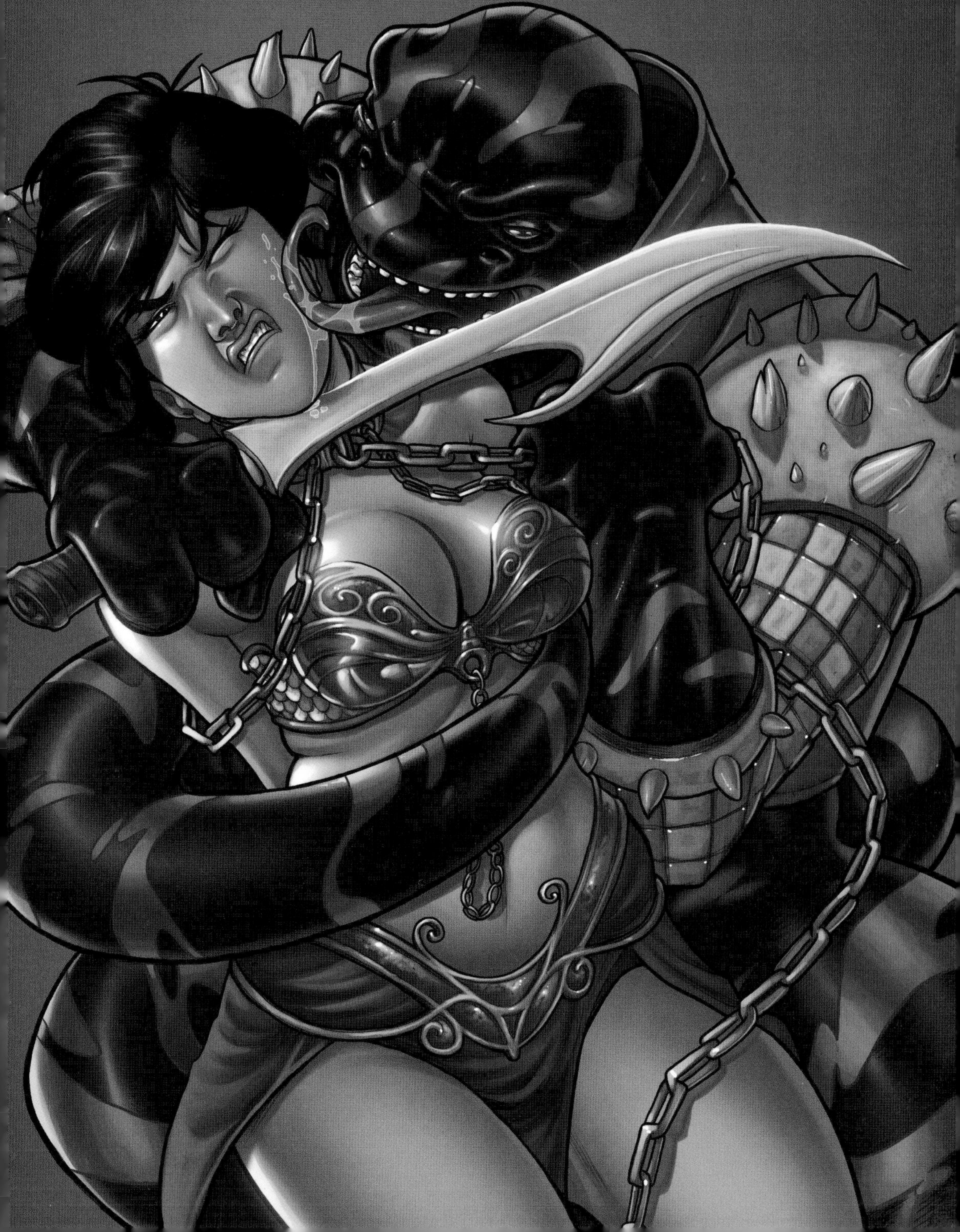

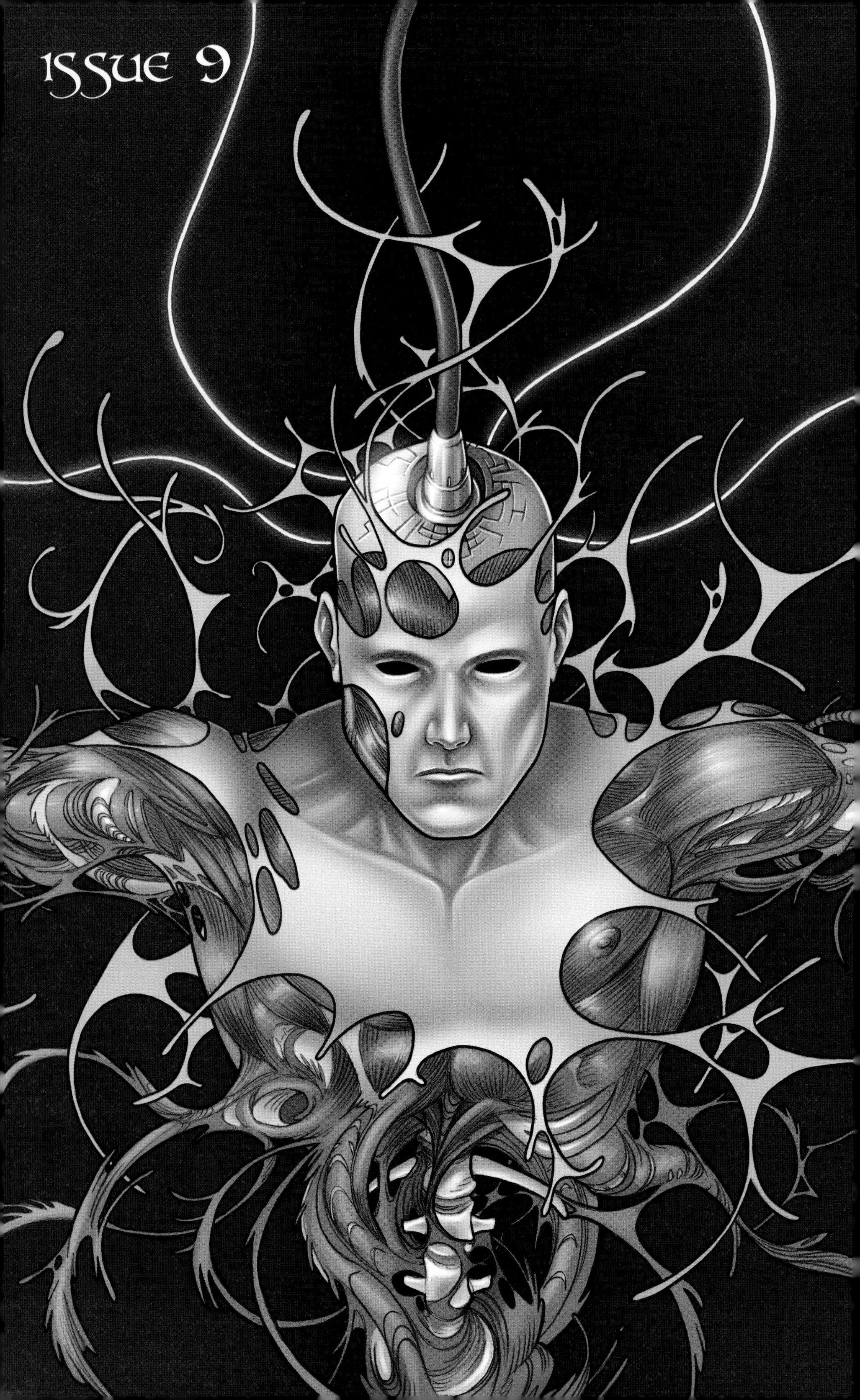
ISSUE 9

SSUE 10

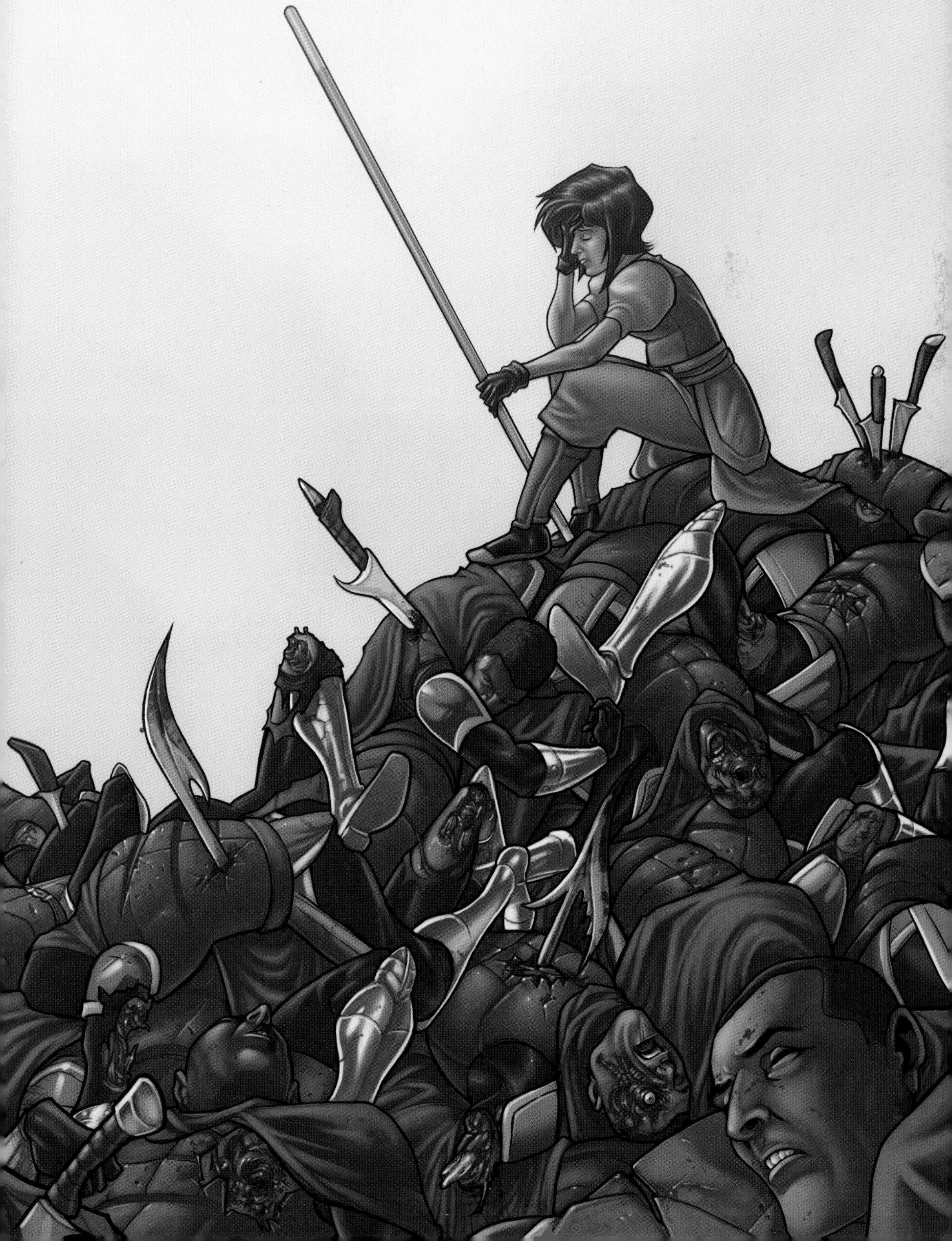

Unused Cover

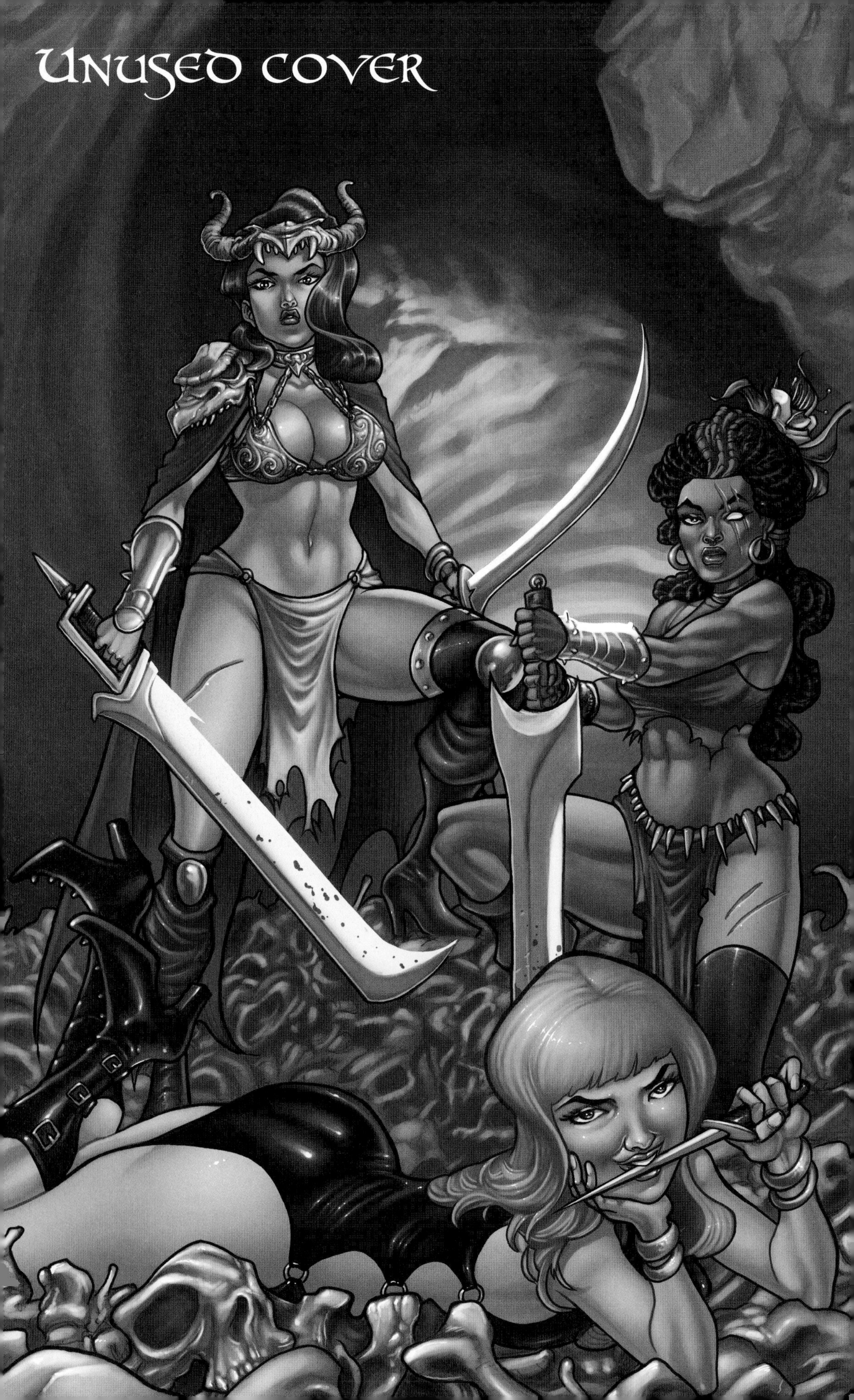

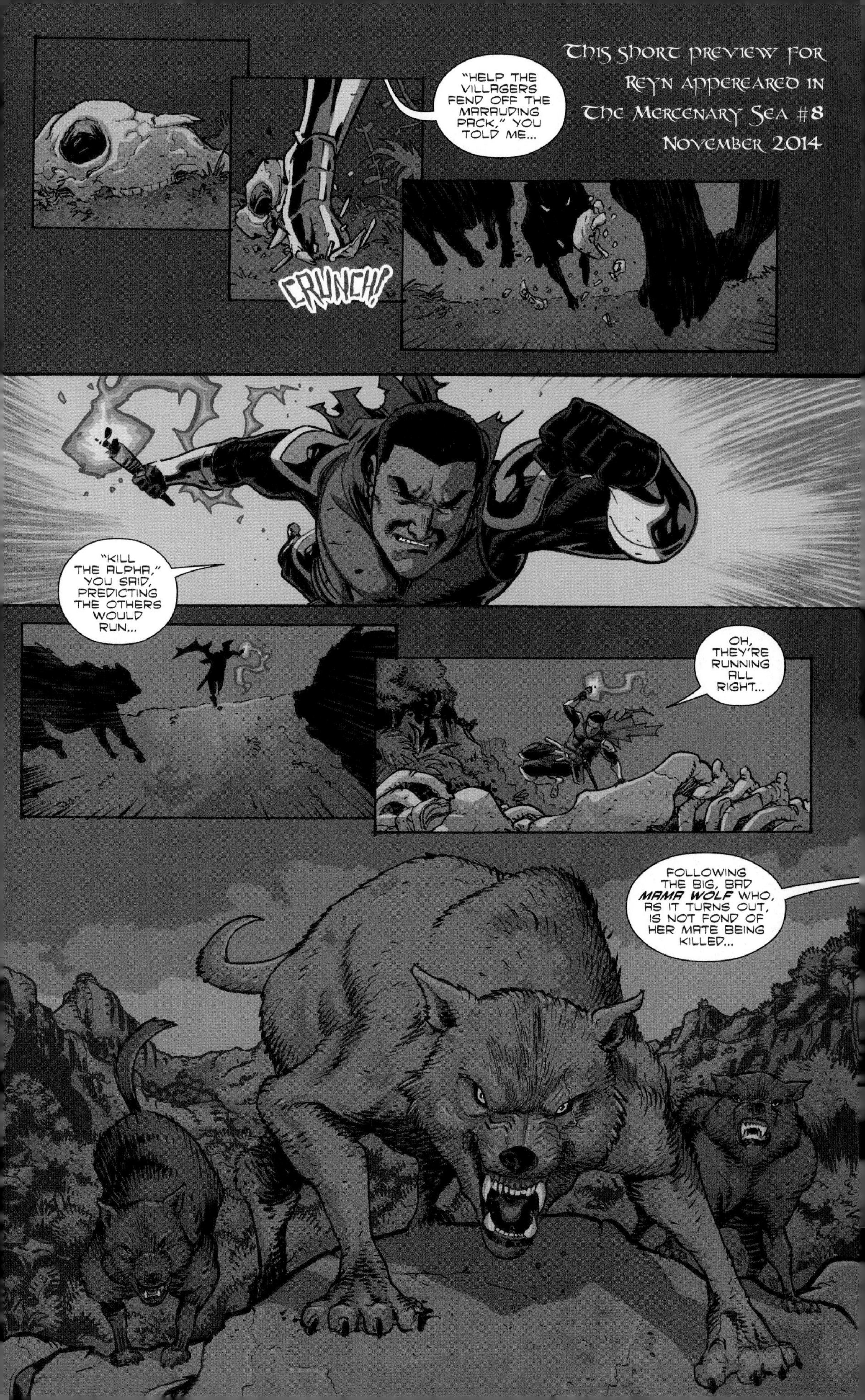
This short preview for
Reyn appereared in
The Mercenary Sea #8
November 2014
"HELP THE VILLAGERS FEND OFF THE MARAUDING PACK," YOU TOLD ME...
CRUNCH!
"KILL THE ALPHA," YOU SAID, PREDICTING THE OTHERS WOULD RUN...
OH, THEY'RE RUNNING ALL RIGHT...
FOLLOWING THE BIG, BAD MAMA WOLF WHO, AS IT TURNS OUT, IS NOT FOND OF HER MATE BEING KILLED...

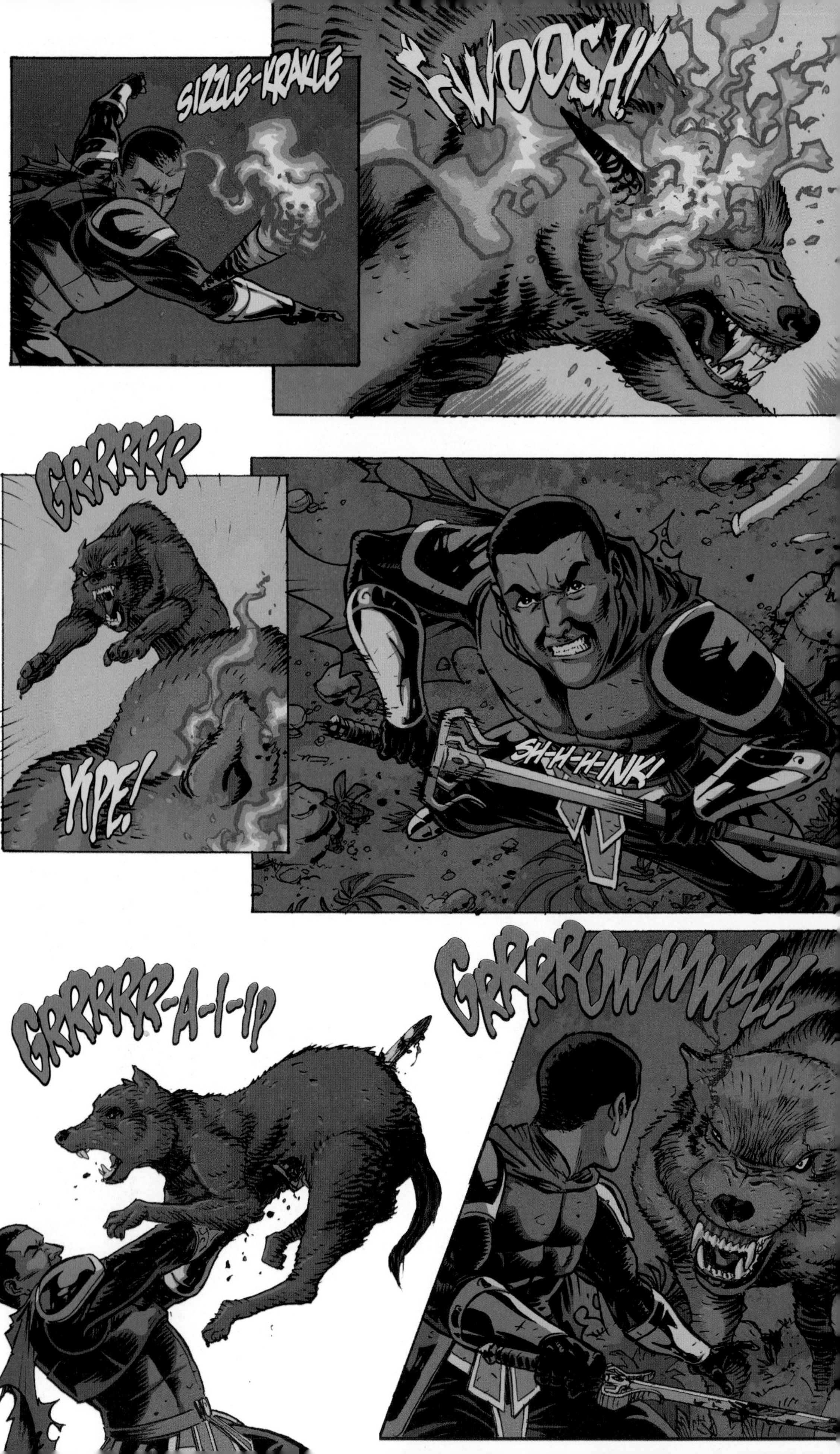

SIZZLE-KRAKLE
WOOSH!
GRRRRR
YIPE!
SH-H-H-INK!
GRRRRR-A-I-IP
GRRROWWWLL

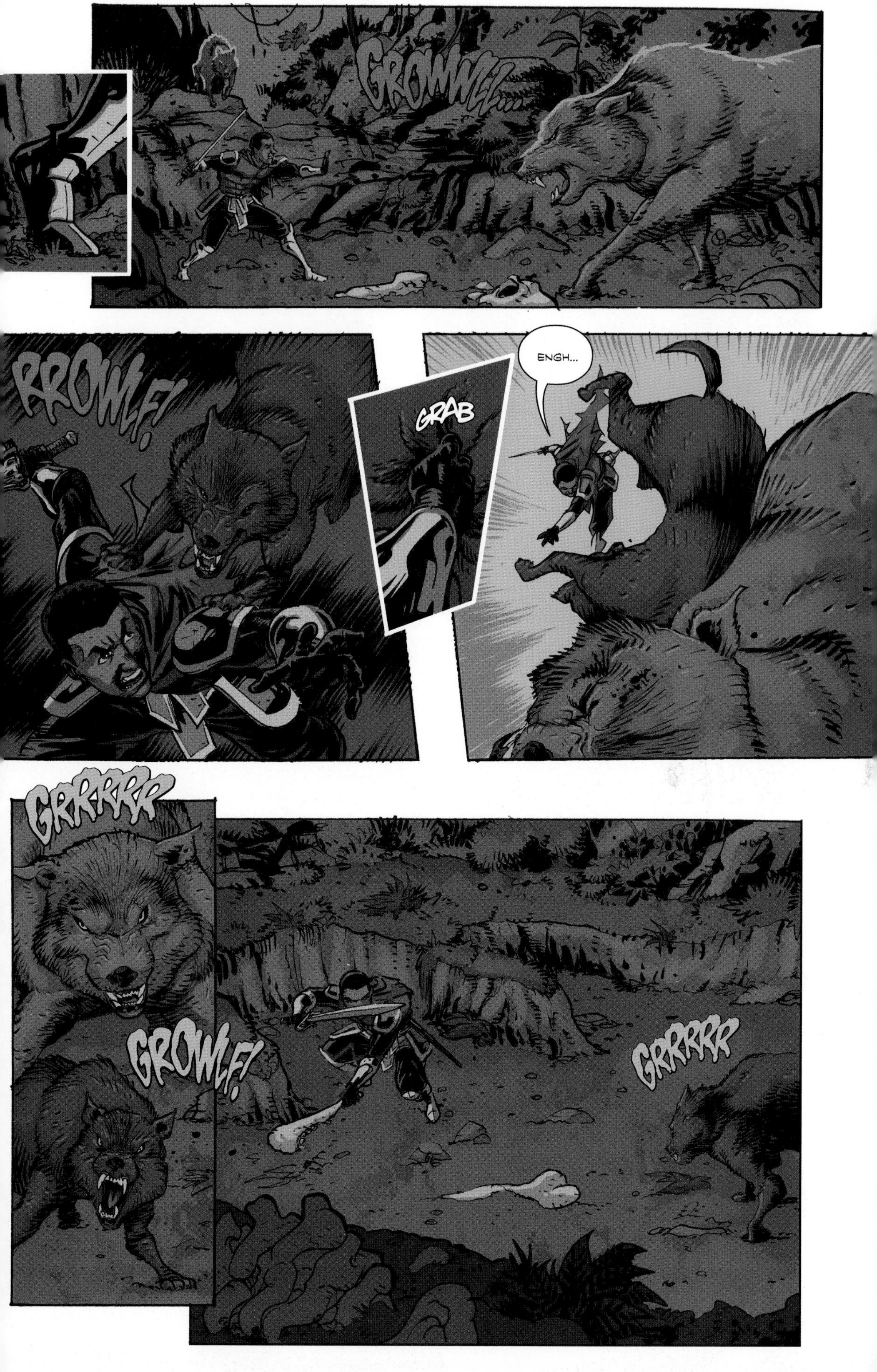
GROWWL...
RROWLF!
GRAB
ENGH...
GRRRRR
GROWLF!
GRRRRR

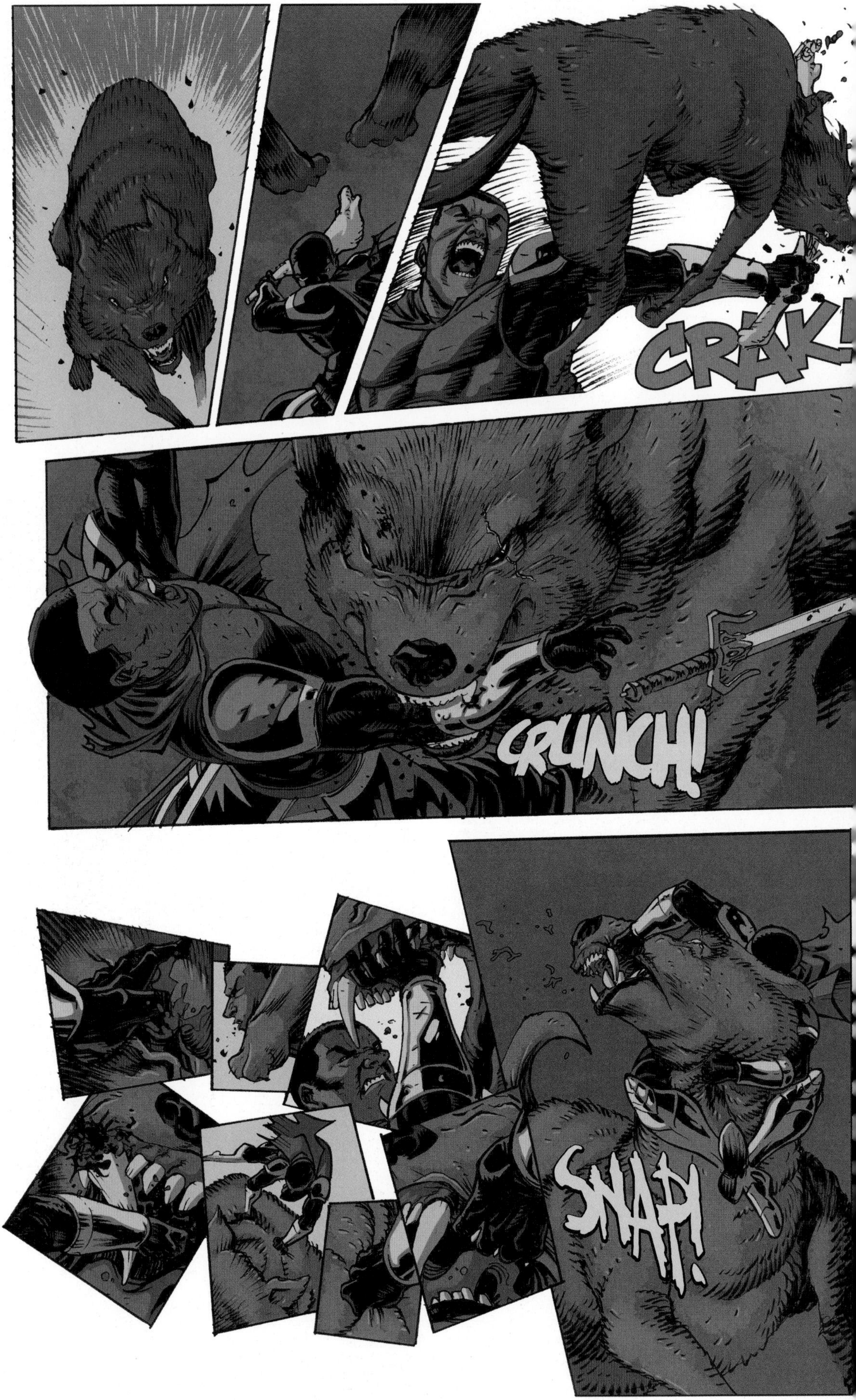
CRAK!
CRUNCH!
SNAP!

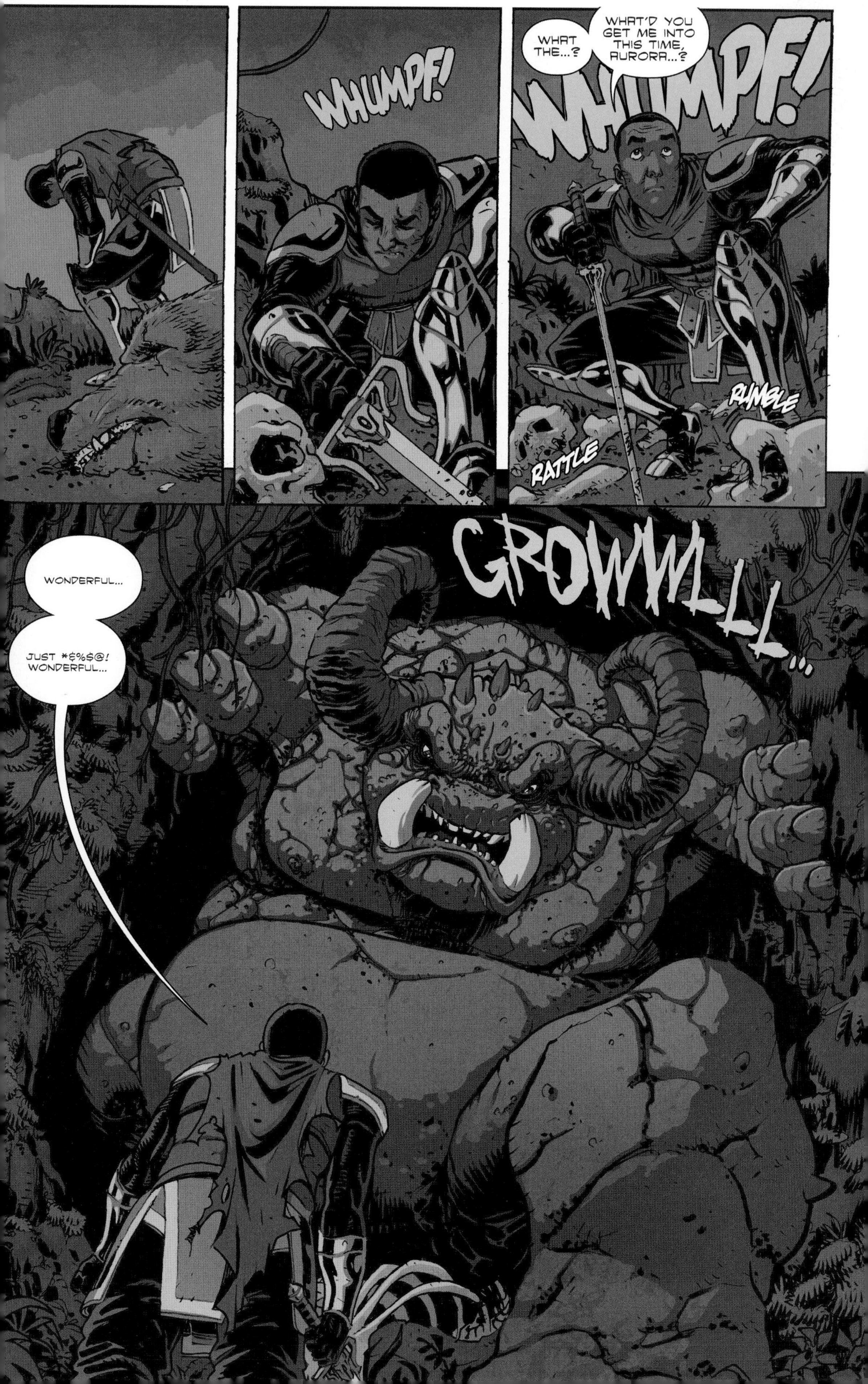
WHUMPF!
WHAT THE...?
WHAT'D YOU GET ME INTO THIS TIME, AURORA...?
WHUMPF!
RUMBLE
RATTLE
GROWWLLL...
WONDERFUL...
JUST *&%$@! WONDERFUL...

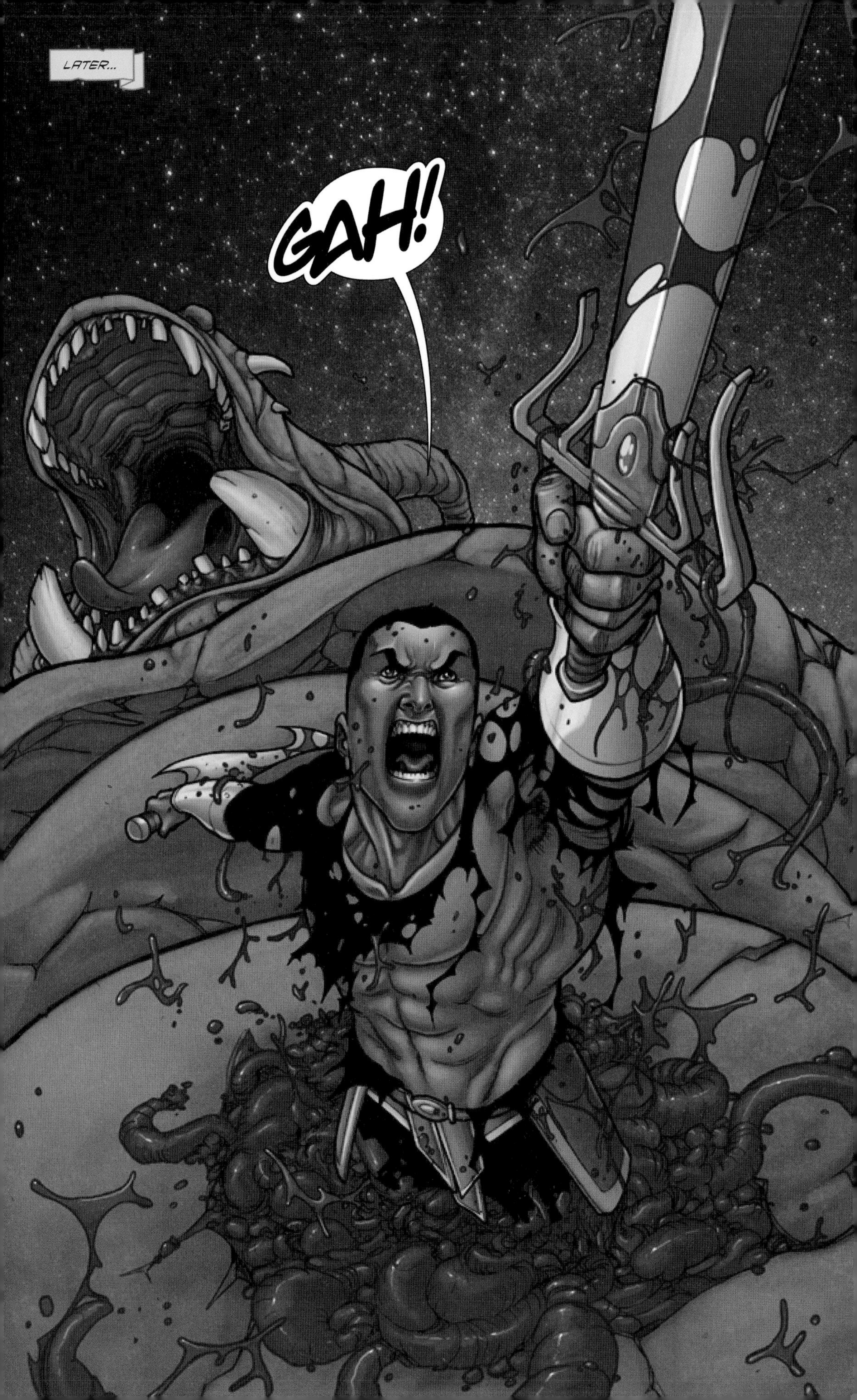
LATER...
GAH!

Concept Designs

Venn Mothership Concept

Warden Concept

Spacesuit Concept

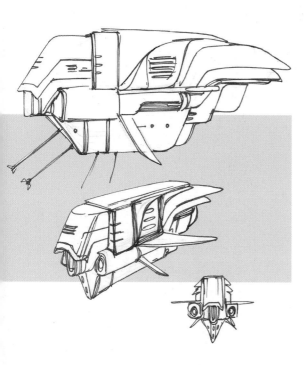

INTERIOR PROCESS

Panel 1

A family - not the one from the first issue, but similar, is terrorized by some giant mutated monstrosity that was unleashed on Fate - your call on how it looks. They are simple fold.

Aurora: Crawling out of the ruins of their shattered society, facing untold horrors that had been unleashed on the land, both by the Venn's shipboard collection, and several mutations that occurred after generations of catastrophic climate swings..

Panel 2 That monstrosity has a giant sizzling and smoking hole blown right though it killing it and stunning the common folk, who look off panel at their savior.

Aurora: ...the people of Fate needed a champion.

Panel 3

Now they see their savior - it's Reyn, but he's wearing a space uniform, a belt and equipment harness packed with all sorts of high-tech gear, ammo, weapons, and grenades, holding a pulse rifle that just blasted that beastie. He should have a rather slack look on his face - not much personality, as he robotically says-

Reyn: Fear-not. I-have-saved-you.

Panel 4

Cut pack to those simple folk who are absolutely HORRIFIED at this warrior from the future. He looks almost as terrifying to them as that beast he dispatched. One of them even runs off for the hills, screaming.

Aurora: However, I realized too late that sending an advanced combat android into a society that had reverted to something out of the Dark Ages would cause a bit of a culture shock.

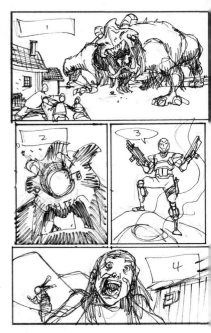

ROUGH LAYOUT

PENCILS

INKS

"CRAWLING OUT FROM THE RUINS OF THEIR SHATTERED SOCIETY, FACING UNTOLD HORRORS THAT HAD BEEN UNLEASHED ON THE LAND, BOTH BY THE VENN'S SHIPBOARD COLLECTION, AND SEVERAL MUTATIONS THAT OCCURRED AFTER GENERATIONS OF CATASTROPHIC CLIMATE SWINGS...

"...THE PEOPLE OF FATE NEEDED A CHAMPION.

FEAR NOT. I HAVE SAVED YOU.

"HOWEVER, I REALIZED TOO LATE THAT SENDING AN ADVANCED COMBAT ANDROID INTO A SOCIETY THAT HAD REVERTED TO SOMETHING OUT OF THE DARK AGES WOULD CAUSE A BIT OF CULTURE SHOCK."

COVER PROCESS

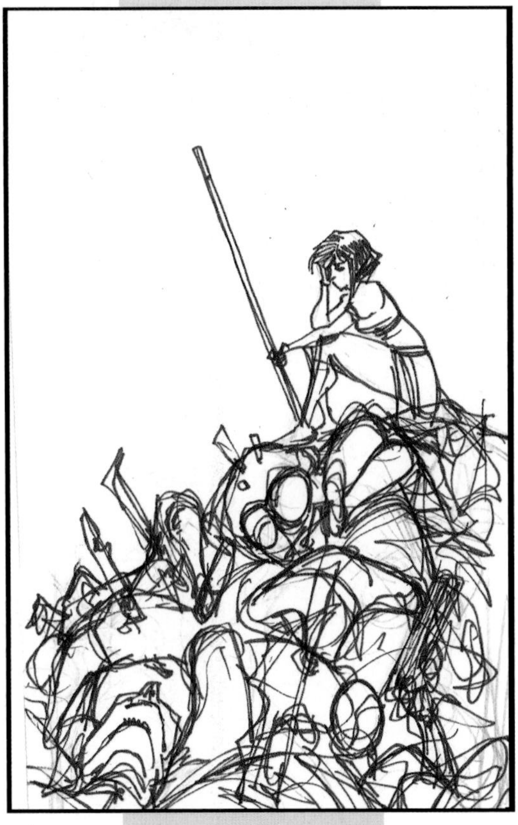

Rough Layout

Pencils

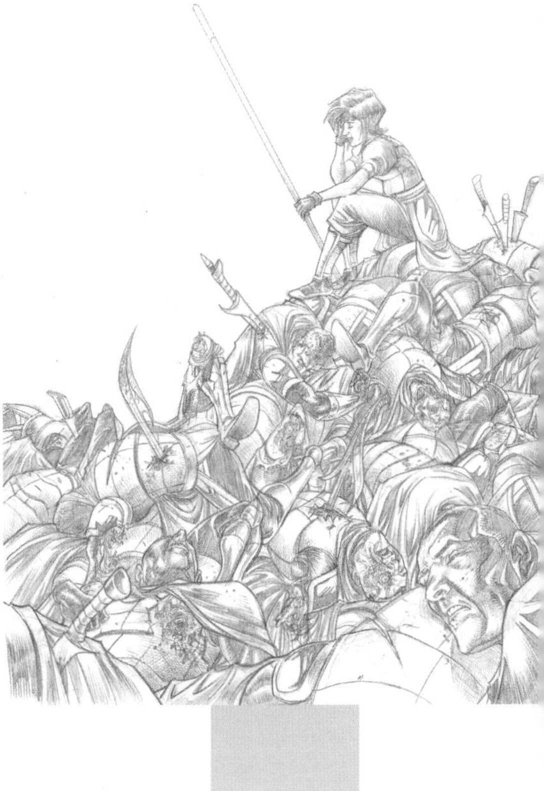

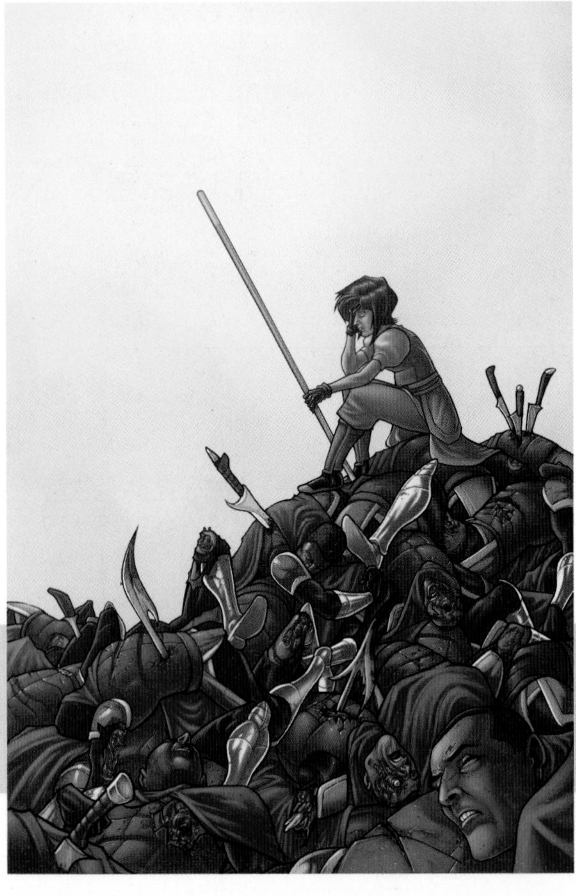

Colors